See M

By Janelle Harris

Copyright © 2016 Janelle Harris

Editing and Proofreading: Jenny Sims @editing4indies

Cover design: Najla Qamber @najlaquamberdesigns.com

Also by Janelle Harris
No Kiss Goodbye

By Janelle Harris writing as Brooke Harris
Rules of Harte
Change of Harte
Queen of Harte's

For Laura

Rest in peace, my beautiful niece.
I miss you every single day.

Chapter One

EMMA

Fourteen Years Ago

'Miss, Miss. You can't sit there.'

I look up at the man rushing towards me, shouting. He's wearing a yellow, high-visibility vest. An old-school walkie-talkie hangs off his belt, crashing against his hip as he hurries. *He must work here at the train station,* I think. Maybe he's a conductor or something.

I look back down at the loose rubble between the train tracks and continue to swing my legs from side to side over the edge of the platform.

'Are you bloody crazy?' he says, reaching me and tapping me on the shoulder. 'Get up, will you?'

I tilt my head to one side and take in his face. He's in his mid-fifties, I guess. His thin-on-top grey hair and the tired lines around his eyes emphasise his worried expression. He needn't be concerned. I'm not going to jump under a train on his watch. I've thought about it, I won't lie. More so in the last few days than I ever have before. But I don't have the balls for it. Thinking about it is all I ever do. Besides, I don't need to jump. I'm already dead inside. The guilt has eaten me alive.

'Please, Miss. There's a train due in less than five minutes. You'll lose your legs. And that's if you get lucky and the train doesn't pull you under completely. Will you, for the love of God, stand up?'

I press the palms of my hands on the ground by my sides and slide my arse back along the cold concrete beneath me. The backs of my calves scrap against the edge of the platform as my body drags my legs to stretch out straight in front of me. I keep shuffling backwards until my toes are behind the yellow line. The train won't touch me now.

Other commuters have started to stare. That's just normal, I know. They're curious. I would be too in their shoes.

The middle-age man stays beside me. I really wish he'd leave, but I know he won't. It's obvious he still doesn't trust that I won't dive in front of the train as soon as it arrives. *He's giving me far too much credit.*

'I won't jump,' I finally say.

He reaches his hand out to me, and I surprise myself as I take it. He pulls, and my legs automatically scramble to stand up.

'There we go.' He smiles. 'That's much better. Where are you headed?'

'Eh … Greystones,' I say, sputtering the first town that comes to mind.

'Ah, okay. You need to be on the other side of the tracks then. This side heads back into the city.'

I force a redundant smile.

'Are you in a hurry?' he asks.

I shrug. 'Nah, not really.'

I'm not going to Greystones. I don't know where I'm going. Or even if I'm going anywhere. But I do know where I'm *not* going. *Home.*

'It's just ... I'm on my break in a few minutes, and it gets fierce bloody lonely in that little shack.' He points towards a small, porta cabin with STAFF painted in handwritten letters on the door. 'I've decent tea in my flask, if you fancy a sip. I'd be glad for the company.'

I want to tell him that he's wasting his time on me; that he won't talk my troubles away. I've done something terrible, and no amount of talking can help. But, hell, maybe this is his good deed of the day. Maybe his days are as empty as mine are, and he really would enjoy some company. *Who am I to deny him that?*

'Okay.' I nod.

'I'm Danny,' he says, extending his hand as his smile reflects the friendliness in his voice.

'Emma,' I reply, shaking his hand.

'Pleased to meet you, Emma. I've a feeling we are going to be good friends.'

This stranger is even crazier than I am, I decide, looking him up and down.

'C'mon, love. That tea won't drink itself. And your train will be here soon.'

Present Day

The text message comes from a number I don't recognise. A friend or relative of Danny's, perhaps. Maybe someone has taken it upon themselves to text everyone in his contacts. I'm glad; otherwise, I may never have known.

**Just to let you know Danny passed away yesterday
Funeral service @ St. Michael's on Saturday 5th**

Call for directions if needed

No flowers please, donations if desired to hope.com

I half fill the kettle and flick it on. I'm not sure I even want coffee now, but I feel like my hands need to do something. I haven't seen Danny in weeks. I haven't been getting the train as often as I used to because I'm trying to drive to work more. Morning traffic is a bitch and almost constantly lands me late for work, but my driving test is looming, and I need the practice. I concentrate and try to remember the last time I was at the train station; the last time I spoke to Danny. It must have been at least three months ago. Not long after my wedding. He didn't look sick then. *Why the hell didn't he tell me?*

Chapter Two

EMMA

I barely notice David has appeared in the kitchen behind me. I jump when he places his hand on my shoulder, and I spill some instant coffee grains on the countertop.

'Oops. Sorry. Didn't mean to startle you,' he apologises.

I try to smile, but tears are swelling in the corners of my eyes. I know David will guess something is wrong before I even say a word.

He takes the open coffee jar out of my hand before I drop it and rests it on the countertop beside me.

'Okay. What is it? You look like you've seen a ghost.'

I shake my head; unable to hold my tears back, I pass him my phone.

'Oh, Emma,' he says as his light blue eyes flick from side to side reading the text. 'Danny? The old guy from the train station?'

I nod and drag the sleeve of my blouse under my nose as I sniffle.

'You really had a soft spot for him, didn't you?'

'He was lonely,' I explain.

'I know. I know.' David's voice is softer than usual, and he actually looks upset too. 'Did you know he was sick?'

I shake my head. 'I haven't seen him in a while.' I snort, choking on my words.

'What age was he?'

I shrug my shoulders, disgusted with myself. 'I dunno. In his sixties, I think. I don't even know his last name. All these years,

11

I never thought to ask. He was just Danny from the train station – you know.'

'Oh, Emma. I'm sorry. I know you liked him.' David cups my face in his palms and strokes his thumbs over my cheeks. 'Are you going to go to the funeral?'

I pull away and reach for the jar of coffee again. My hands are restless and shaking. I need a distraction. I spoon some coffee into the two mugs waiting on the countertop. 'Funeral?' I repeat; the word tastes vulgar in my mouth.

I can feel David's eyes on me, but I purposely stare at the tiles lining the wall. One is crooked, and it's bugged me since we moved into this house almost a year ago. I stare until my vision goes a little blurry and I begin to sway on the spot.

'Okay, okay,' David says, taking a step backwards to give me some breathing space. 'Well, if you decide to go, I'll go too.'

'What about work?' I say, lifting the kettle shakily and pouring some water into each cup.

David shrugs. 'It's a Saturday, Emma. I'm just missing some overtime hours. It's okay. Don't worry.'

'You just started there.' I put the kettle down before I burn myself. 'It'll seem weird if you take time off to go to a funeral …' I raise my hands and add some sarcastic air quotes '… of the man your wife knows from the train station.'

David snorts. 'Well, I won't sell it quite like that, Emma. But Danny mattered to you, so his funeral is important to me. Anyway, my new boss seems nice. She'll understand. She's not much older than we are actually. And she grew up around here. She lives on the other side of the city now, but she used to take the train into town most days when she was younger. Maybe she even knows Danny too.' David clears his throat with an uncomfortable cough. 'Knew. I guess I mean knew. Sorry, sweetheart. I'm sure Amber will be okay with me taking a couple of hours off. Don't worry.'

I stir each cup of coffee and pass David one. 'Thanks,' I mumble. 'I really don't want to go alone.'

Chapter Three

EMMA

We park our car a comfortable distance between the church and the gates of the adjoining graveyard. David suggests it's polite to save room nearer the church for those close to Danny. Not being family, or even close enough friends, we don't want to intrude. And I know David doesn't want to hang around after the service to make small talk with people we don't know. I understand. It's easier to make a subtle exit if we keep our distance.

The church is smaller inside than I anticipated. And it's warm. The heat caresses my face as we make our way up the narrow side aisle. The warmth should be a pleasant contrast to the vicious November wind that pinched at my skin moments before, but despite the radiator blasting out heat beside me, the atmosphere inside the church is even icier than the winter air was. Ten, maybe fifteen, people maximum sit scattered in the pews, and that's including David and me in the numbers. They're Danny's colleagues, principally, I realise. I recognise most of their faces from the train station. I don't see a wife or kids. In fact, I don't see any family at all.

David and I take a seat in one of the middle rows and bow our heads. I check my watch. *Maybe I got the time wrong.* But as the minutes pass, it doesn't take a genius to realise more people won't be coming.

I look up to the sound of coughing and see that the priest is standing at the edge of our pew.

'Would you like to come sit up in the front?' he asks.

I shake my head. Some of the other people in the church stare our way. The collar of my blouse suddenly becomes uncomfortably tight. The priest must assume David and I are the chief mourners. Possibly because we are the only people present under fifty. We look about the right age to be Danny's kids. Danny often told me he'd be proud to have a daughter like me. I liked when he said that.

The priest subtly passes David a sheet of folded paper. David's nose and cheeks turn a very unflattering pinkish-red as he shifts in his seat.

'It's the reading.' The priest smiles.

I lean forward, and I'm about to explain that there's been a mix-up. At the very least, I want to elucidate that we're not family. But the priest catches my eye and nods before I have a chance to speak.

'Please,' he says, lowering his voice to a dull whisper. 'There's no one else to do it.'

David passes me the paper, and I unfold it to find a handwritten paragraph scribbled in blue ink. I force a smile and sit up straight. The priest leans across David to place his hand on mine. He smiles. He doesn't say the words thank you, but he doesn't have to. I understand.

I glance around once more at the dried-eyed, composed handful of people in the other pews. No one is wearing black except for me. Some are even in their work clothes. Their coats are clearly marked *Irish Rail and Transport.* They're here on their lunch break, I guess. It's good of them to come, but I know after they leave the funeral, they'll go back to work, and their day will continue as normal. I drag my eyes to the front pews. The empty seats and the little piece of paper I hold in my hand

15

punctuate the absence of family. The already broken fragments of my heart shatter even more. No one comes into this world alone. Danny was someone's son, once upon a time. He had parents. Siblings, maybe. A family. But no family now.

'I knew Danny was lonely,' I whisper, choking back tears. 'I just never knew how lonely.'

David shakes his head, but he doesn't say a word.

We all stand as the mass begins. I don't think anyone notices the girl who arrives late. Heads don't turn, and David doesn't see her either, but I do. She closes the side door gently behind her, so it doesn't bang and slides into the nearest pew. She's wearing a dark top with the hood pulled over her head. I squint, trying to make out her face, but she's at an odd angle to me, and the material of her hood flops so far forward, it hides her features, and I wonder if she can see out beneath it.

She's slim, tallish, and she's dressed completely inappropriately for a funeral. Blue jeans ripped at the knees, and a pair of faded, pink Converse make up the rest of her outfit. She spends the duration of the mass twirling the strings of her hood around her finger. Her hands are young. She sports beautifully manicured nails, and from what I can tell, she has clear ivory skin. I guess she's in her early thirties, like me. She leaves the church before everyone else.

I search for her in the graveyard, but she's not here. There are so few of us present I couldn't have just missed her. She didn't come, and her absence makes me even sadder than I already am. I can't stop thinking about her. I wonder if she was another friend of Danny's from the station. Another commuter Danny had gotten to know over the years. I hope so. I like to think Danny had lots of friends who he chatted with and had tea with on the days I wasn't there.

We've barely sat back into the car when David is on his phone. I get it; I know he's busy. It's great, really. Lots of overtime makes saving for the deposit on our own place much easier. Our wedding five months ago had run quite a bit over budget, so we had to dip into our house-buying fund. David's new job was a godsend and couldn't have come at a better time. But I feel like we never have a conversation anymore. When he's not physically in the office, he's stuck to his laptop or on the phone, but I can't complain. I was delighted when they headhunted him, and I encouraged him endlessly. He had warned me about the demands of the new role before he even interviewed.

'Can't expect a big boy salary without putting in big boy hours,' he had joked.

I had laughed and said, 'I'll just have to occupy myself with *big* bottles of wine.'

But the reality of long hours hasn't been funny in practice, and I try not to dwell on it. I'm already in a terrible mood. Thinking about how much I resent David's overzealous work ethic will only drag me lower. David's six-day workweek is taking its toll on him and our marriage. I can't remember the last Saturday David didn't put in overtime. The money is great, and I know he's pushing himself hard to buy us our dream home, but what good is a beautiful house if I have to spend all my time alone in it?

I weave in and out of city traffic, frustrated that we've moved less than five miles in the last twenty minutes or so. David is staring out the window with his phone stuck to his ear, and I'm decidedly bored. My mind drifts to the bottle of Pinot Gorgio chilling in the fridge at home, and I sigh. David had suggested we get the train; we'd have been home in half the time if we had, but I wanted to drive. I didn't want to go near the station. Not today, of all days.

I tilt my wrist towards me, still gripping the steering wheel, and glance at my watch. It's coming up on four o'clock. I hope David will say it's too late to head into the office now. Maybe we could spend our first Saturday night together in months. My belly rumbles, and I realise I've forgotten to eat today.

David finally hangs up as we break away from the heavy traffic.

'We'll be home in ten minutes,' I say as if my husband doesn't drive this road every day to and from the office. 'I was thinking we could get a takeaway. How does Chinese sound? We keep saying we should try that new place on the corner. I've heard great things about it.'

David adjusts his seat belt, slacking it enough so he can turn his whole body towards me.

My shoulders grow heavy, and the only thing stopping me from slouching over completely are my arms stretched out, gripping the wheel. I know what he's going to say.

'Oh, c'mon, David. Not tonight. Please.'

'I'm sorry, baby.' He sighs. 'That was Amber calling.'

I roll my eyes.

'Chinese does sound great, though. You should still get some.'

'It's not the same when I have to eat it on my own.'

'I know, I know. Sorry.'

'So how late do you think you'll be? I'll wait up; there's a new series starting on Netflix.'

'Erm …' David shakes his head. 'It's a whole weekend thing, Emma.'

'What?'

'The client is flying in from Boston. We're meeting four of the top guys from their head office at the airport.'

'You're their chauffeur now too,' I snarl.

'There are six companies in Dublin alone pitching for their business. We need to do something to stand out. We'll take in all the tourist attractions and stuff with them. Butter them up while we're out and about and then pitch them for the big bucks first thing on Monday morning.'

'So you have to work all weekend? Will you be late every night?'

'Actually, we're heading straight from the airport to Kilkenny. Tonight. I'll be staying over. I'm so sorry, baby. I know the timing sucks.'

'Oh, come on. I can handle late nights, but no weekends now either. Jesus, David. This is ridiculous. No job is worth this.'

'I know. I know. But this is a once-off, Emma. I promise. These guys are big players. It could potentially be worth a fortune.'

'No amount of money is worth this. I never see you anymore. I miss you.'

'I miss you too. But this weekend could mean a huge bonus.' I shrug as we turn on our road.

'It could be enough to put the deposit down on that cottage you like.' David tries a toothy grin. 'As soon as we buy our own house, all these crazy hours will stop, Emma, and it will all be so worth it. We just have to stick it out for a little longer. We can do this, baby, can't we?'

I shake my head, but I'm smiling. David can read me like the map of my soul is imprinted inside his head. He always knows exactly what to say to soothe me. I'd love to buy our own place, and that cottage we viewed last week blew my mind. Cosy without being too small. The perfect size, especially if we want to start a family soon. I was hoping to talk to David about it this weekend. I guess I'll have to wait for another opportunity to tell him I want a baby.

'So will you be okay on your own?' David asks as if I'm a child who needs babysitting.

'I'll be fine.' I sulk, defiant.

David hops out of the passenger side door and is dashing into the house before the car even comes to a complete stop in our driveway.

Chapter Four

EMMA

I flick through all the channels on the television haphazardly. I'm not really planning to watch anything. The half-empty bottle of wine on the coffee table calls to me, and I pour another glass. Dinner consisted of two bars of chocolate and a bowl of popcorn washed down with the first half of the bottle of wine. Restless, I turn off the television. I sit in near darkness with just the streetlights shining through the drawn curtain. A pain chatters in my temples like one of those little clockwork monkeys clanging his tiny brass cymbals over and over. Ironic, as it's the silence of the house that's really getting to me. And I wonder if this is how every evening felt for Danny; coming home to an empty house after a long day at work. He must have been even lonelier than I ever realised. Maybe he just couldn't take it anymore. He jumped. Or at least that's what everyone at the graveyard today said. Whispers and mumbles carried in the air. Gossip outweighed grief. Colleagues dotted around Danny's open grave with upturned noses, judging a man after his death.

I replay the day in my mind. *I'll miss him.*

I reach for the bottle of wine and pull a face, disgusted to find I've drank it all. I make my way towards the kitchen, in the dark, in search of another bottle. I flick on the light and reach for the cheap stuff on the wine rack above the fridge. My phone vibrates in my jeans pocket, making me jump, and I drop the bottle. It smashes against the floor tiles with a loud bang, sending wine halfway up my legs and all over the cupboards. I ignore my ringing phone and bend down to pick up the shards of glass. A jagged edge nicks my finger, and bright red blood trickles past my knuckle. I lean my back against the nearest cupboard and slide all the way to the ground. The puddle of wine beneath me soaks into my jeans, but I ignore the wetness. I tuck my knees into my chest. I rock from side to side, and I cry.

Loud, angry sobs echo around the kitchen. My finger stings as I watch the blood with fascination. And I remember. I remember all the times I hurt myself. All the times I was desperate to feel physical pain. I needed it to hurt so bad that the pain of my bleeding flesh drowned out the pain of my bleeding mind. When I cut deep enough, the sting would hurt more than the guilt.

I wasn't crazy or stupid; I knew where to cut. My thighs and my tummy yield quite a lot of blood without getting too close to an artery. I didn't want to kill myself. Well, not usually. I just wanted to forget the terrible thing I'd done, but I couldn't. Not even now. Not even fourteen years later.

Most of the scars have faded now. They just look like stretch marks across my thighs. And David has stopped checking my body for new scars when he thinks I'm asleep. He stopped a few years ago. He stopped after I took it too far. When I scared him. When I scared myself.

It was a Saturday afternoon. I'd spent twenty minutes, sitting alone on the bathroom floor, fishing the blade out of an old razor with a pair of tweezers, and then, when I finally freed it from the plastic, I just sat staring at it for ages. I almost chickened out. But I'd replayed the conversation I had with my best friend on the phone moments before. Kim was angry, and she was crying. She said if I didn't tell David, she would. She said she couldn't lie to him anymore. She was taking the decision out of my hands, and it wasn't fair. I had to take back control, and bleeding was the only way I knew how.

I didn't feel the pain. I didn't feel anything. I was numb. The blade slid across my wrist like a hot knife through butter. The blood was dark at first, like a fine red wine. It didn't fade to bright red until it began dripping onto the bathroom floor.

I didn't pass out or feel faint like you see in the movies. But I did feel sick. I threw up a couple of times. I dropped the blade and stood up from crouching over the toilet bowl, my legs shaking. I took a moment to catch my breath. But my chest tightened, and it was hard to suck in air as guilt smacked me across my face, hurting far more than the blade. This was different from the guilt I usually felt. I wasn't pining over the past—I was regretting the present moment. This was guilt for something I was doing right now. Something I could control; something I could stop. I had to stop.

I caught the gaping edges of my skin and pulled them back together. I grabbed a towel off the edge of the bath and wound it tightly around my wrist. I scooped the bloodied blade off the floor and wrapped it in some toilet paper before throwing it into the bin. I ran to the train station. Danny didn't usually work on Saturdays, but he was there. Thank God, he was there. We even had tea, as usual, as we waited for the ambulance. Surreal, I know, but Danny was calm and as understanding as ever. I began to breathe again, and the fog that usually invades my head when I get like that cleared. Danny's words could always clear the fog.

But Danny is gone now. Maybe the fog will come back.

23

I close my eyes and try to shake off the thoughts of the past. I suck my bleeding finger, making a face at the taste of blood in my mouth. When I open my eyes again, I stare at the broken wine bottle on the floor. The pieces are sharp like blades. You could do some fatal damage with one of the larger pieces. I sigh and shake my head, knowing that I won't go there. I'm confident I'll never get to a place that dark again. And it's all because of Danny. I owe him my life. That's why I can't understand how he could take his. It just doesn't make any sense to me. Why would he counsel me, pull me back from the darkest corners of my own mind, only to hurt himself? He was lonely. Depressed even. But I can't believe he was suicidal. Danny wasn't a hypocrite.

The national newspapers are carrying the story. I'm trying to avoid reading any, but my Facebook newsfeed was riddled with links to articles this morning. It seems the press are diluting the drama; simply running the story as a tragic accident. *RAILWAY WORKER SLIPS*, one headline read. A fall? *Yeah, right.* Danny knew every inch of the platform inside out. He was forever warning people of the dangers of the tracks. He'd never be careless or complacent. He'd never fall. *And he'd never, ever fucking jump.* That just leaves one other scenario. *He was pushed.*

I roll my eyes and laugh out loud at my own ridiculousness. It's funny the crazy theories your mind will conjure when you're desperate for an alternative to the truth. I sigh and accept all I know for certain is that I will miss him.

My phone vibrates again, and I slide it out of my pocket, finally becoming aware of how damp my jeans are. A text message waits for me. I smile as I think of my husband. He's been gone for hours now. He must be at the hotel. *Lucky bastard.* I wish my job came with such lavish perks. We get excited when a cake comes into the staffroom at the school. Or when a parent drops in a bottle of wine and a thank-you note for helping out with an extracurricular activity. David and my careers are poles apart. A bit like our personalities. But they do say opposites attract, so it must be true. We've been together almost fifteen years.

I read the words on the screen. It's not a message from David. I'm disappointed.

Girls nite out 2nite.

U so better come.

See u @9

Kim must be psychic, I smirk to myself. Or David has text her. My smile grows, knowing it's the latter. But my cheesy grin is quickly wiped as I overthink it. I'm not sure if David is feeling guilty and thinks distracting me with dancing and booze will get him off the hook, or if he's actually afraid to leave me on my own after today. *Christ, am I that predictable?*

I glance at my watch. It's almost eight p.m., and I just want to sleep. I glance up at the wine rack, and its emptiness stares back at me like a teasing metaphor for how I feel. I'm a mess. The thought of grabbing a shower and actually putting on makeup makes me feel even more exhausted, but I want another couple of glasses of wine before I doze off. A night out with the girls is my answer.

Twenty minutes later, I'm washed, dressed, and somewhat sober. I haven't been out with the girls in months. Maybe even a year. Paying off stuff for the wedding nearly killed David and me, and things are even tighter now since we're saving for a house. Our social lives are practically non-existent. Maybe I need this opportunity to unwind. Maybe this. Will. Be. Good.

Chapter Five

EMMA

Kim arrives at half eight and marches up my driveway carrying a large, luminous green sports bag.

'The front door's on the latch,' I shout out the open, upstairs window while trying not to poke myself in the eye with my mascara wand.

Seconds later, Kim barges in my bedroom door and throws the contents of the green bag onto my bed. Tiny dresses and backless tops litter the duvet like a rainbow. Kim spreads them out and takes a step back to admire her handiwork then scrunches her nose as she looks me up and down.

'You're not wearing that, are you?'

'Yes, Kim, I'm wearing this.'

I glance in the mirror. I like my grey skinny jeans and dusty pink blouse. Teamed up with a pair of five-inch heels, I feel pretty. David is right. I do need a girls' night out, and I snigger to myself as I realise his cunning plan has worked. He's off the hook.

'Oh, c'mon. I want to try that new place on Sweeny Avenue.' Kim folds her arms across her chest and pouts. 'It's super posh, you know.'

'Okay, sounds great. But I'm still not changing my clothes.'

'Gah. But I brought you loads of dresses. I don't want to look like a hooker on my own.'

I snort. 'You don't look like a hooker,' I lie. 'You look great.'

'Okay fine, but at least, let me curl your hair.'

I nod. 'Deal.'

At five to nine, the honking horn outside the house startles us. We laugh at ourselves and each other. We throw some makeup into our handbags, grab our coats, and hurry downstairs. I lock up quickly, remembering to set the alarm, and hop into the waiting taxi.

Kim gives the directions while I mess around with my phone, trying to take a selfie.

'Ugh, God, these are terrible,' I moan. 'I can't use any of these.'

'For Facebook, is it?'

'Nah.' I shrug. 'I want to send them to David. I'm going to tell him I've sexy lingerie on underneath and he's missing out.'

Kim's eyes widen. 'Do you?'

'What? Do I have frilly knickers on? No, of course not, but he won't know that. Anyway, this is the third weekend in a row he's abandoned me for work crap. The least he deserves is a little teasing.'

A wicked laugh gargles in the back of Kim's throat. It's contagious and makes me giggle too.

'Here,' she says, taking my phone. 'Let me take one. Selfies always come out crap. This will be better.'

Kim snaps several shots and forwards the one I approve of most to David. She captions it with something silly about him missing all the action.

'There.' She winks, handing my phone back to me. 'Serves him right.'

After some more girly giggling, the conversation moves to more serious topics, such as work, babies, and sex. After a couple of glasses of wine, Kim is guaranteed to bring shagging up at some point. Kim gets cranky when she's not getting any, and she's been single for three months now. *It's going to be a long night.*

'You wouldn't understand, Emma. You have sex on tap. And David's hot, so it's even better.'

I try to hide the sting of rejection from Kim's words. Kim's right. David and I should be going at it like a pair of rabbits. Everyone says that's what newlyweds do. But that's only true for newlyweds who actually spend time together. I can't really remember the last time David and I were intimate. Three or four weeks ago, maybe. And even at that, it was just a quickie on a Saturday morning before Amber text him, and he had to dash into the office. These days, the closest we get to each other all day is the routine kiss he gives me in the morning before he runs out the front door.

I change the subject to cocktails and sexy bartenders, two of Kim's other favourite topics, and breathe a sigh of relief when she begins to ramble off a list of her favourite drinks.

We split the cost of the taxi, thank the driver, and fumble out the car door. I can barely walk in my ridiculous heels, but I'm like an elegant swan gliding across a pond compared with Kim's duck waddling in her huge, over-the-knee boots. But the boots prove a distinct advantage as Kim tosses the bouncer a salacious grin. He steps aside and allows us to skip the queue and make our way inside.

It's overcrowded and stinks of sweaty bodies. The bar is hiding at the extreme back and can only be reached by navigating our way through a sea of drunk teenagers. I quickly remember why I haven't been inside a club in nearly ten years.

It takes us at least an hour to find our friends, but our mission isn't helped by the constant distraction of needing to buy more alcohol. The wine is reasonable, and the cocktails are potent, so it doesn't take Kim or me long to channel our inner teenager and get our grove on out on the dancefloor.

We finally find Liz and Ruth hiding in the corner. I can't decide if I'm more relieved that our search is over or that they've been keeping seats for us. Content that I'm not abandoning Kim and leaving her alone, I excuse myself and make my way back across the dancefloor towards the toilets.

'I'm going to the loo,' I splutter to anyone who happens to step out in front of me along the way.

Some people look horrified, others tell me to get lost, and some even give me a high five. It's only when I finally make it into the cubicle after pulling instead of pushing on the door for at least three attempts that I realise how very drunk I am. This was not how I wanted today to end. *I'm sorry, Danny.* My chest pinches, and I know Danny would be so disappointed if he could see me now. I dread tomorrow already. I've told Danny more than once how distressed the low of a hangover after the buzz of being drunk makes me feel.

Chapter Six

EMMA

I sit on the toilet and check my phone again. David still hasn't text me back. I hope Kim sent him the right picture and not my selfie with three chins. I haven't heard from David at all since he left hours ago. It's grating on my nerves that he won't take thirty seconds to let me know he's arrived at the hotel safely. It's not like him. He's usually in touch so regularly while he's away that we often stay up half the night texting like a pair of lovesick teenagers. *I guess he's just too busy today.*

The cubicle door rattles and shakes as someone pounds their fist against the other side.

'Emma. Is that you? Are you in there?'

'Kim?' I mumble, looking up from staring at my knickers around my ankles.

'Yeah. Jesus, missus,' Kim growls. 'Where have you been? You've been in the loo forever.'

'Coming … coming …'

I wobble on the seat as I pee. The alcohol coursing through my veins messes with my dexterity, and I make zipping my jeans back up seem as complicated as rocket science. I finally open the door and stumble out.

'Liz and Ruth are totally pissed off, by the way. They think you've been ignoring them all night,' Kim moans.

I toss my head to one side and throw my handbag over my shoulder as I make my way to the sink. I splash water everywhere, much to the disgust of everyone else.

'What? No, I haven't.' I snort.

Kim's face sours before she looks at the ground. 'Umm, Emma. They have a point. You've been in here nearly an hour. I was getting worried. I barely know Liz, so I can only make small talk without you for so long, you know.'

I blush. Kim must have asked Liz along to cheer me up, and I didn't even notice or care. I look in the mirror. *Christ.* I'm unsightly. Mascara is smudged around my eyes and runs down my cheeks like a really tiny rally car with mucky tyres has run a full circuit on my face. My cheeks are red and puffy, and my foundation sits too heavy in the lines around my nose and eyes.

'I can't believe he's gone, Kim,' I say, gagging on some snot.

Kim raises a confused eyebrow. 'David?'

I shake my head, but the movement makes me unstable, and I fall over, cracking my back off the sink ledge on the way down.

Everyone stares and Kim's cheeks flush as she shakes her head. 'You okay?' she whispers, stretching her arm out for me to take her hand.

I stay in the position I've landed in on the ground and laugh and cry at the same time. 'I just can't believe it, you know?'

'Emma, get up.'

My shoulders round and slouch towards my knees.

'Okay, seriously, Emma. This is embarrassing. And I'm pretty sure you're sitting in a puddle of piss.'

I reach my arm up and grab the sink overhang behind me. I scramble to stand. I'm not embarrassed, but I should be. I would be if I wasn't too drunk to see straight. David would freak if he saw me like this. He worries when I drink myself stupid.

'Danny's dead, Kim. He's dead.'

'I know. I know. But getting yourself worked up over it isn't going to change anything. It's just the drink, you know. I think you've had enough. Maybe we should go. The DJ is on the last set anyway. It'll be easier to get a taxi if we leave now.'

'They say he jumped.'

'Yeah, Emma. I heard. Crazy.'

'Jumped. Fucking jumped. Who does that?'

'A lot of people feel they've no other option. He wasn't right in the head. Poor man,' Kim says as she drapes her arm over my shoulder and leads me towards the door. 'C'mon. I'll stay at your place with you tonight, yeah?'

I nod and walk. 'He was good to me, Kim. So good to me.'

Kim turns her head towards me and kisses my forehead. 'I know.'

'I don't think he jumped.' I throw my arms out to each side.

'Okay. Okay.'

Kim leads me back into the busy body of the club. She has one arm draped over my shoulder. She kept the other arm free and stretched out in front like an arrow navigating our way through the throngs of people in front and all around us. People are dancing on the dancefloor. People are drinking at the bar, and couples are kissing the face off each other in the booths and in the corners. And I want to be somewhere else. *I shouldn't have come out.*

I stop walking as we near Ruth and Liz's table. 'He didn't jump, Kim. He didn't fucking jump. He wouldn't.' I take a deep breath and exhale like my lungs have just vomited. 'He. Was. Pushed.'

'Oh, Emma, come on.' Kim groans, her wilting patience obvious in her tone. 'That's just the drink talking. You're being silly now.'

'Kim. You don't understand. But *I do*. I know the truth.'

Kim unwraps her arm from around my shoulder and grabs my hand in hers, charging ahead of me to drag me to the table. She presses on my shoulder and forces me to sit. There's a glass of water waiting on the table in front of me.

'Drink this,' Kim barks.

My friends gather up their coats and their handbags. Kim drapes my coat over my shoulders and passes me my bag, but she takes it back again almost instantly.

'I'll hang on to this,' she says, linking her arm around mine and helping me up. 'Let's go, Emma. It's time to go home.'

Despite leaving the club an hour before closing, we still end up having to wait for ages on the side of the street for a taxi. It's painfully cold, and I quickly stuff my arms into my coat and pull it so tight around me my ribs protest. Liz and Ruth pop into the chipper and come back with a greasy takeaway for us all. I wolf my chips down, and Kim passes me half her burger.

'I skipped dinner,' I explain, noticing the look of disgust on all their faces.

'Skipped dinner all week?' Ruth jokes.

'Here,' Kim says, laughing as she passes me my handbag. 'Your phone is beeping like crazy in there. It must be David.'

I gulp down the last mouthful of burger and rummage in my bag for my phone. A taxi finally pulls up, and Kim has to actually grab me by the sleeve of my jacket to get my attention.

'C'mon. You can sext your hubby from the backseat,' Kim teases.

Kim, Liz, and Ruth chat as we make our way out of the city. Their giddy voices are way too loud for the confined space of the car, and it all just resonates as a noisy blur in my head. Maybe they try to involve me in the conversation, I don't know. Their words just wash over me. I can't take my eyes off my phone screen. My notifications are buzzing wildly. I scroll through five or six recent text messages. Reading the same ones over and over. Trying to make sense of them.

The taxi pulls into a large estate on the outskirts of the city and comes to a stop. Lauren and Ruth lean from the backseat into the front and take turns giving Kim a hug.

'Great night, Kim,' Liz gushes. 'Thanks for asking me along.'

'Totally was a great night,' Ruth adds. 'We have to do it more often.'

'See you at work on Monday, Emma,' Liz says, and I'm vaguely aware of her arms around my neck.

I'm about to say good night when I'm distracted by another incoming text.

'Okay then,' Liz snorts. 'Don't say good night. Whatever.'

'She just drank too much, as usual. Ignore her,' Ruth groans.

'Girls, seriously. Can we be a bit more sensitive? Please?' I can hear the strain in Kim's voice as she tries to protect me.

'No, actually, we can't be. We only came out tonight because you said Emma needed cheering up. But sure, she spent the whole night on her bloody phone. I could have stayed in and watched *Game of Thrones*. I missed this week's episode, and I want to know what the hell happened,' Liz barks, and I look up to find her glaring at me red faced.

'I know you lost your friend from the train station, Emma,' Liz continues. 'But seriously, how well did you even know the old guy? You're kind of overreacting. It's a bit weird, to be honest.'

'Okay, girls. Good night, then,' Kim says, extra breezy.

Her efforts are sweet, but she needn't bother. I suppose I am a bit weird. Ruth and Liz don't know about what I did years ago. They don't know how much Danny helped me. So I can understand them thinking our relationship is unusual. I would too in their shoes. To them, Danny was just the chatty old guy down at the station. To me, he was like a father.

Ruth and Liz leave some money with Kim to split the cost of the taxi and hop out. The driver pulls back onto the main road before they even make it inside the house.

Kim spins around in the front seat awkwardly and faces me. 'So are you going to tell me what's wrong? You haven't said a word since we got into the taxi. Has David said something to upset you? You've been glued to your phone, and I can hear it beeping every two seconds. Are you two having a row or something?'

I shake my head. I wish we were having a fight. That I could understand.

'Look.' I pass Kim my phone. 'It's the photo we sent David earlier.'

'Yeah ... and ...'

'Someone has sent it back to me.'

'Okay?'

'From a number I don't recognise.'

Kim pulls the phone closer to her face. 'That's weird. Did David send the picture on to someone?'

I shrug. 'There's more. Read what it says below the picture.'

'Not missing much. Not a great photo.' Kim reads out loud.
'Cheeky bastard. Who is this?'

'I don't know.'

'If this is David's idea of a joke, it's really not funny,' Kim complains. 'What's he playing at?'

'David wouldn't send me something like that. He wouldn't say these things.'

Kim's eyes widen. 'There's more?'

'Yeah. Read all the messages in my inbox.'

Kim falls silent. Her eyes move back and forth across the screen as she reads the cryptic texts I've been receiving from the same number for the last half an hour. It started with my picture being sent back to me and escalated into this stranger asking me how well I know my husband.

'I don't know whether to reply or not,' I mumble, breaking the silence.

'Do,' Kim says, passing me back my phone. 'Text back and tell this asshole to piss off.'

'But I don't know who it is.'

'It's obviously someone David knows. How else would they get the picture?'

I shake my head. 'I told you. David wouldn't show my photo to someone else. Especially not people from work. Maybe we sent it to the wrong number. Some weirdo out there is just having a laugh. I'm going to ignore it.'

'Take the next left,' Kim says, pointing as she directs the taxi driver into my estate before turning her attention back to me. 'Yeah, okay. I think you're right, Emma,' she continues. 'It's probably just a freak with too much time on their hands. Jesus, good thing it wasn't a naked photo. We could have given some old fella a heart attack.'

I cringe. 'Ugh, God. Could you imagine? Yuck.'

'Third house on the right,' Kim tells the driver, tapping her finger against the window.

My phone vibrates in my hand as it rings, and I yelp. Kim can't hold back a throaty laugh.

'David?' she asks, catching her breath between snorty giggles.

'No. It's another number I don't know.'

Kim groans. 'Here,' she says, unbuckling her seat belt and turning around in the passenger's seat to face me completely. 'Gimme it?'

Kim stretches her arm out to me and opens her hand. I pass her my phone. She turns it off and hands it back to me. 'There. All better. Now, no one can bother you.'

I smile at the simplicity of Kim's solution.

'C'mon,' Kim says, spinning back around. 'We're home.'

We pay the driver and hurry into the house out of the cold. I don't tell Kim about the final message I received. The one I deleted straight away. The photo of David and Amber out to dinner with their arms wrapped around each other.

Chapter Seven

DAVID

I wake to a ferocious banging noise pounding against my skull from the inside out. *What the hell did I drink last night?* The banging continues. I rub my eyes, and it takes me longer than it should to realise someone is knocking on my hotel bedroom door. I throw back the duvet and hop out of bed. I'm a little taken aback to discover I'm naked. I always sleep in boxers when I'm away from home. I toss the sheets around the bed, looking for my underwear and pants, and I find them on the far side of the bed.

The banging on the door stops. But the banging inside my head doesn't. *Christ! This is the worst headache I've ever had.* I rummage around some more, trying to find my shirt. I'm desperate to climb back into bed and close my eyes, but we're supposed to be taking the guys from Boston to see Kilkenny Castle this morning. And I have a vague memory of Amber saying something about us all meeting for breakfast downstairs before we head out for the day. The thought of food right now makes me want to throw my guts up, but I know breakfast wasn't just a polite platitude. It's expected. This is not how I should be spending my morning. I really wanted to be there for Emma this weekend because I know Danny's death is hitting her harder than she's letting on. Maybe Emma's right; no job is worth this much sacrifice. I decide to take a few euro out of our savings account to buy her something nice. I'll stop by the shops on my way home tomorrow. Roses and some jewellery would be good.

Moments later, I find my shirt tangled in a ball under the bedside table. There's no chance I'll get another day out of it, but I shake it out anyway. Lacy, black silk knickers fly out one of the sleeves. My jaw drops, and I hold my breath. It must have been up my sleeve all day yesterday. I hope no one noticed. *God, how embarrassing.* I pick up the lacy culprit and drop it almost immediately. It's not one of Emma's. She hardly every wears frilly stuff, and when she does, they're never that skimpy. Who the hell owns them? And more importantly, how did they get inside my shirt?

I close my eyes and replay last night. My brain physically hurts as I sieve through my hazy thoughts. I remember dinner. I sat between Amber and one of the guys from Boston. We talked mostly about work. Some of the Boston guys spoke about their families. I think I mentioned I was married. Amber didn't reveal anything personal. She never does. I get the impression she has demons in that closet, so I never push her to talk about any of it.

I remember moving to the resident's bar. I constantly had a gin and tonic in my hand. Every time I drained one, it was replaced with another. I don't even know who was giving them to me, maybe Amber. She must have been charging them to the company. I should have asked. I've no idea how many I had. Ten, at least. And that's before I lost count. *Christ*, no wonder my head feels this bad.

I grab a quick shower, brush my teeth, and gag as the taste of minty toothpaste makes my stomach churn. I pull some clean clothes out of my bag and get dressed. Waking up naked is still unsettling me as I cast my eyes back to the lacy knickers

I've discarded on the ground. *I'd never do anything to hurt Emma*, I think. I'm not sure if I'm telling or asking myself.

I check my watch; it's almost nine a.m., so I'll be a few minutes late for breakfast. I should text Amber. I glance around the hotel room, searching for my phone, and my hand flies of its own accord to slap my forehead as I remember losing it last night. Somewhere between the restaurant and the bar. *Dammit.* Emma will kill me. It's new. I spent half a week's wages on it, and I insisted that I didn't need insurance. I'll check with reception later. Hopefully, someone has handed it in.

I remember some middle-age man in the bar loaned me his phone last night to call Emma, but she didn't answer. I think I tried her again later from Amber's phone. Maybe I sent her a text. I'd better find an old payphone today and give her a call. I'll be in the bad books otherwise. I hope she had a good night with the girls last night and had a few drinks. Enough drinks that she won't have been concentrating on her phone. Danny's death is affecting her badly, and the rumours about suicide are really hurting her. She's suffering so much right now, and I really don't want her to worry that I'm ignoring her. I hope today doesn't drag on. I could have a word with Amber and try to escape early. It would be a nice surprise for Emma if I could make it home tonight. I'm sure the rest of the team could handle tomorrow without me.

Chapter Eight

EMMA

I roll my tongue past my teeth and poke it out between my lips. My throat is parched. It edges on painful, like I've stayed up all night licking the carpet and my tongue is covered in fluff. I open my mouth wide and sigh as I toss and turn, but I close my lips again quickly as my rancid morning breath stings my eyes. I try not to think about how thirsty I am. I don't want to go downstairs to get some water. Once I get up, I'll never be able to go back to sleep, and I'm too exhausted to face the day just yet. I open my eyes. My bedroom is dark, and I guess it's still early. I've had a restless night so far tonight; too many dreams pinched my brain. I roll over and wrap my arm around my husband.

'Thanks, doll. But you're not my usual type.' Kim laughs.

I rub my eyes and remember last night. The club, my friends, the drink. And I remember that David isn't here.

'Sorry. Sorry. My bad.' I blush. 'Go back to sleep.'

I've no memory of Kim and me going to bed last night. I don't remember suggesting we share my bed, but I must have at some point. The ache in my temples reminds me that we polished off a bottle of wine between us downstairs in the kitchen after we got home. Kim was reluctant to open it. I cringe, realising she only drank a couple of glasses to prevent me from polishing the bottle off solo.

'Coffee?' Kim asks, throwing back the duvet to swing her legs out of bed.

I glance towards the window. The curtains are drawn, and not even a hint of light peeks through the material.

'Ugh, what time is it?' I croak, rubbing my eyes.

'Almost eight.'

'Oh, c'mon, Kim. It's Sunday. Why are you getting up so early?'

'Early to bed, early to rise,' Kim chants as she makes her way towards the bedroom door.

'Early to bed?' I echo. 'It must have been after three a.m. before we went to sleep.'

'Actually, it was closer to four.' Kim laughs. 'I couldn't get you to stop talking … or drinking.' Her laughter dies. 'Anyway, coffee, yeah? I'll make it.'

I nod sheepishly. 'I hate morning people, you know?'

''Really? I never noticed,' Kim jokes, poking fun at our years of living together while we were in college. 'You'll take a spoon of sugar in your coffee, then?'

I stick out my tongue. 'Ugh. No. Are you trying to poison me?'

'Okay, then, two it is. You need something to sweeten you up a bit.' Kim giggles as she disappears behind the door, and I hear her bouncing down the stairs.

I flop onto my belly and reach for my phone waiting under my pillow. I prop myself up on my elbows and unlock it. The light from my screen illuminates half the room. I stare at the screen, and a sting of disappointment hits me as the light goes out. I flick my finger up and down, scrolling to sync. Nothing happens. No messages, calls, or emails. David still hasn't bothered to get in touch. I close my eyes and allow my forehead to flop onto the pillow. On the bright side, there are no more messages from that random number from last night either. I deleted all the texts last night, on Kim's advice, and I'm glad now. I don't need a reminder of that crap this morning. I guess it really was just some bored stranger. *Weirdo.*

I dial David's number, but it rings out. I try him a few more times, but there's still no answer. I don't bother to leave a voicemail. Flustered, I slide my phone back under the pillow. For a moment, I think about popping down to the train station for a cup of tea and a rant with Danny once Kim goes home. But then, I remember.

I wipe my eyes before tears begin to fall. My legs flop over the side of the bed, and my bare feet hit the timber floorboard with a dull slap. I stand up, grab my dressing gown from the end of the bed, and slip my arms into the sleeves. The house is cold, and I need to turn on the heat. I follow Kim downstairs. I pause outside the kitchen door, hearing voices and laughing. It takes me a couple of seconds to realise that Kim has her phone on loudspeaker, and she is flirting shamelessly with a man on the other end of the line.

I make my way to the kitchen table, tossing Kim a look that tells her I want all the juicy gossip as soon as she hangs up. Kim picks her phone up off the countertop as soon as she sees me and turns off the loud speaker. She tilts her head to one side and brings her shoulder up to meet her ear, sandwiching her phone between as she continues to potter about my kitchen. I offer to help her cook breakfast, but she dismisses my suggestion with a wave of her hand. I'm relieved. My head is throbbing, and all I want to do is sit.

Kim places a cup of steaming coffee and a plate of scrambled eggs in front of me. And despite the majority of her attention going toward whoever is on the phone, she manages to toss me a smile. She fetches another cup of coffee and a second plate of eggs and sets them on the opposite side of the table. She sits, eats, and talks. I'm not hungry, but I nibble so I don't offend Kim and all her hard work.

Finally, when we're both finished eating and the coffee has cooled enough to drink, Kim hangs up. She places her phone face down on the table, and for the first time since she sat down, she makes eye contact with me.

'He's such a chatterbox.' Kim giggles and shakes her head.

'He?'

'Yeah, Andy. The guy from last night?'

'There was a guy last night?'

Kim's eyes narrow, and she pulls her head towards her chest until she has three chins. 'Yes. You liked him. You said he was hot.'

I shake my head and take a sip of my coffee.

'Andy Taylor. Thirty-five. The cop. Jesus, Emma. You spent twenty minutes last night teasing me about guys in uniform.'

'Really?'

Kim's whole face scrunches, and I know she's frustrated. 'Seriously? Were you really that wasted that you don't remember? You told him you didn't think he was a real cop. You said you'd bet he was a stripper.'

'Oh. God.' My eyes widen. 'I didn't.'

'Umm. Yes. You did. It was hilarious. I can't believe you don't remember.'

I rest my coffee cup back on the table and stare into the black, tar-like liquid. 'Sorry, Kim. I guess I must have had more to drink last night than I thought. But he definitely seems interested. I mean, if he's calling you the next day. That's good. If you like him.'

'Actually,' Kim says, her voice adopting a suddenly serious tone. 'He was calling to check if you were okay.'

'Me?' I squeak, tapping my chest with my fingertips.

'He was concerned about those weird text messages you were getting last night.'

'You told him?' My hands cover my mouth.

'Yeah. I was texting him for a while last night after we got home. I had to explain why I didn't invite him back to my place.'

'And I was your excuse.' I drag my hands down my chest and cross my arms.

'Well, actually, yeah.' Kim tosses her head to one side. 'If I wasn't minding your drunk ass last night, I'd have screwed his brains out. He was seriously hot, Emma. Even you thought so.'

'Oh, great - thanks, blame me.' I shrug. 'Anyway, what did you tell him?'

'Dunno. Just the usual stuff. My name, job, hobbies, blah, blah.'

'I mean about the stalker, Kim. What did you say about that weirdo?'

'Oh, right, yeah.' Kim blushes. 'Just that some stranger was sending you weird shit.'

I roll my eyes. 'You do see the irony here, Kim?'

'Huh?'

'You told one stranger about another stranger. Don't you think that makes us sound stupid?'

Kim laughs. 'Nah. Andy's a cop. He's probably used to hearing crazy shit like that all the time.'

I shake my head and sit up straight. 'Or he says he's a cop. You just met this guy. He could *be* the bloody stalker, for all we know.'

'Oh, seriously, Emma.' Kim snorts. 'And where exactly did he get your phone number?'

'I dunno.' I shrug. 'From your phone?'

'Really?' Kim stands up and clears the plates from the table, clattering them against each other as she tosses them into the sink. 'So you're saying Andy managed to get his hands on my phone without me noticing, found your number, and then spent half the night texting you all while he was talking to me? And I just didn't see any of this happen. Face it, Emma. It's one of David's workmates acting like an asshole. They were probably drunk and thought it was funny. And I don't blame you for being annoyed. I would be too.'

I stand up and bring the coffee cups over to the sink. 'Just leave all this, Kim. I'll wash up later.'

Kim sways, and her stiff upper body softens. 'I'm sorry. I didn't mean to bite your head off. It's just … I like this Andy guy. I'm sorry if you didn't want me to tell anyone about the weird texts. I wasn't thinking. I just got caught up in the heat of the moment. He asked me questions about the taxi ride home. You know, like people do. He was just making conversation, and I needed something to say, and it all just came out. I really am sorry if I've overstepped a line.'

'It's okay.' I sigh. 'It's just those messages freaked me out a little. I want to forget about them now. Okay?'

'Did you delete them?' Kim asks.

'Yeah. All of them. You said I should, remember?'

47

'Yeah, I know. I know.' Kim shakes her head. 'But did you not keep one to show David?' Kim's surprise registers in the contorted lines of her forehead.

I shake my head. 'No. I don't think I'll mention them to him. He's already worried about me. I don't want to stress him out even more.'

'Have you heard from him yet?'

My lips form a flat line, and I try to mask my disappointment. 'Not yet. But he's up to his eyes with this client from the States. I'd say he hasn't had a second to himself. I'm sure he'll get in touch as soon as he can.'

Kim runs her hand through her hair. She's known David as long as I have. She's comfortable enough to call him out when he's being an ass, but she doesn't say anything this time. I think she knows how sensitive I am right now, and she's afraid to add fuel to the fire.

'I'm supposed to meet Andy this afternoon. He suggested the cinema,' Kim explains. 'Will you come along too?'

I laugh out loud. 'And tag along on your first date? Oh. God. I'm sure Andy would love that.'

'No, seriously, it'll be fun.'

'No, seriously, it won't. Kim, I'm fine. Go enjoy your date,' I say. 'And if he's as hot as you say he is, send me a photo, yeah?'

Kim scrunches her nose. 'No. No. I'll cancel. We can go to the cinema some night after work instead. It's okay.'

'It's not okay. Please, Kim. Go have fun. He sounds nice. I mean it. You'll make me feel bad if you cancel.'

Kim leans her back against the sink and looks me up and down. 'Are you sure you'll be okay?'

I smack Kim on the shoulder playfully and wobble my head spasmodically. 'Yes, silly. Of course, I'll be fine. Actually, I have plans for this afternoon too.'

Kim raises a patronising eyebrow, and I know she doesn't believe me.

'Kim,' I say sternly. 'I'm calling around to my parents' house for lunch. And even if I wasn't, I'm a big girl. I am perfectly capable of being left alone for a few hours.'

'You're grieving, Emma. I'm just worried.'

'I know.' I smile. 'And I love you for it, but I really am okay. I'm not a silly seventeen-year-old anymore. I can handle grief now, you know.'

Kim swallows so hard I can actually see her throat flinch. 'Okay. Okay. But promise you'll call me if you need me. And let me know if you get a hold of your hubby.'

I don't tell her that as soon as she leaves, I'm going to text my mother to cancel. I've no intention of getting a shower or even changing out of my pyjamas. I plan to bring a box of paracetamol and a bottle of wine to bed with me.

Chapter Nine

DAVID

My feet hurt as I walk down the busy streets of Kilkenny City. Despite the temperature being close to freezing, the place is thronged with tourists and locals. A group of drunken women staggers up the street in front of me. Their skirts are too short, and their voices are too loud as they chant some made-up mantra about being the World's Best Hen party. Young families are dotted all around, enjoying a winter morning in the city. A man, about my age, wrestles a screaming toddler as he tries to prevent the youngster from dashing into traffic. A woman and a man I'm guessing is her husband or boyfriend scream and shout at each other mid-argument. It's a stereotypical Saturday in the lively city; it's noisy and crowded, and I don't want to be here.

I throw the paper cup in my hand into the first bin I find. I've had my fill of cheap, takeaway coffee. I can't tolerate any more mindless chitchat about accounts and budget projections with the client. I'm cold, tired, and beyond pissed off that everyone around me is enjoying downtime this weekend while I'm working. I can't stop thinking about the knickers I found in my bedroom this morning. My stomach heaves every time the image parades across my mind. Where the hell did they come from? *Do I even want to know?*

Amber is marching about five paces in front of me as we walk back to our hotel. I've noticed she won't stand directly next to me today. She has been icy all morning. She mumbled something incoherent earlier at breakfast, and when I asked her to repeat herself, she glared at me like she wanted to slice my face in half with her eyes. She ignored me the whole time we were taking a boring, guided tour of the castle. I hope I wasn't a drunken asshole last night and maybe said something offensive to piss her off. But I wish she'd just tell me instead of giving me the cold shoulder since the Boston guys are picking up on it. It looks unprofessional, and I know if Amber's sulk costs us their business, I'll be the one who gets the blame.

The hotel comes into view as I round the next street corner, and I can't wait to pack my bags and tell Amber I'm leaving. I just want to get home to my wife.

*

Two hours later, I'm sitting in the front passenger seat of Amber's Audi A4 as we drive back to Dublin. We've been together in the confined space of the car for a strong hour, and besides a quick, pointless discussion on the weather, we haven't conversed.

'I really appreciate the lift, Amber,' I say, unable to take the silence any longer.

Amber nods, and her grip on the steering wheel tightens until her knuckles whiten.

'Umm, you can just let me out when we get into town,' I suggest. 'I'll get the train the rest of the way home. I don't want to drag you all the way over to the far side of the city.'

'I don't mind dropping you home.'

'Honestly, Amber. There's no need. I wouldn't feel right taking you so far out of your way.'

'David. I said it's fine, okay,' Amber snaps.

'Okay, thanks,' I agree reluctantly.

I stare out the window as we whizz down the motorway. I really don't want Amber to chaperone me to the front door like a lost puppy. I'll feel obliged to invite her in, then. With conversation this stilted, it would be a nightmare if she accepted. I know Emma wouldn't appreciate spending her Sunday afternoon entertaining my boss. And without my phone, I can't even text ahead to warn her it might be a possibility. I roll my eyes, disappointed in myself. If I had any balls, I'd insist Amber drop me in town so I could go shopping and pick up jewellery and flowers for Emma. But whatever was pissing Amber off this morning was only made worse when I suggested going home early. The Boston boys overheard and were delighted to give the rest of the tourist sights a miss. They planned to flitter away the rest of the afternoon sampling Guinness in the hotel bar. I got a thumbs-up from the rest of the team, too, who were all relieved to get home early, but Amber's face was puce, and she did a terrible job hiding her irritation. She quickly suggested I travel home with her. It would have been rude to refuse, even though I was certain I was in for a lecture. This damn silent treatment is worse.

'So do you think the Boston boys like us?' I ask, desperate for her to say something. 'They seemed really interested, didn't they?'

Amber's response is a barely noticeable twitch. *This is torture.*

'Do you want to run over the pitch for tomorrow's meeting? I'd be happy to listen. Might help you work the nerves out?' I say.

The car slows, and Amber turns to glare at me. Her eyes are only off the road for a few seconds, but it's long enough to unnerve me.

'The pitch?' She snorts, finally turning her head back to look out the windscreen. 'You think that's my problem. Work stuff. You think I'm nervous about the goddamn fucking pitch.'

'Amber, I don't know. You're just not yourself today.' I run my thumb up and down the edge of my seat belt. 'I know there's a lot resting on winning this business. All our futures depend on it. It's understandable to feel pressure. I do.'

Amber cackles. I've never heard her laugh like that before. It's as ridiculous and forced as a Disney villain, and it pisses me right off. We speed up and weave in and out between motorway traffic. Amber's grip on the steering wheel looks painfully tight. My arms fall rigidly by my sides, and I clutch the edges of the leather seat in my fists.

After a mile or two, Amber swerves to the left without slowing and pulls onto the hard shoulder. The passenger-side wheel rumbles loudly as we roll over cats eyes. The rear of the car skids as it attempts to cope with car's sudden change of direction.

'Jesus Christ, Amber. Stop the car. Stop the fucking car,' I shout.

My body flies forward, and the seat belt compresses my ribs as we come to a sudden, jerky stop. I pant. I sit statue-like for a few seconds. My heart is racing so fiercely I can hear my pulse pounding in my ears. I jump suddenly and reach across Amber to grab the keys out of the ignition.

'What the hell was that?' I growl.

Amber sits thrashing her head from side to side. She's pale. Even her lips are lacking colour. She opens her door, swings her body as if she's about to get out, but she stills again and closes the door.

'I can't do this,' she says, throwing her hands in the air. 'I'm sorry. I just can't.'

'Do what?'

'Keep up this act.'

'Amber, I have no idea what the hell you're talking about. I know you're pissed off with me. You've been in weird humour all day. But you're talking in riddles. You've lost me.'

'Oh, c'mon, David. Don't pretend like you don't feel guilty,' Amber mumbles. 'You've been sucking up to me all day. Trying to be my best friend. Trying to pretend like nothing happened. Oh, David. What have we done?'

The pounding of my heart in my ears turns to ringing, and I'm certain if I could see myself, I'm now as pale as Amber. An image of the knickers I found in my hotel room this morning shoots around my head. Thoughts of the silky black lace smack off my skull, punching me from the inside out. I drag my hand over and back across my jaw, pulling my skin so roughly it stings.

'I don't remember,' I stutter.

Amber throws her head back and snorts. 'Huh, well, that's convenient.'

'No. Honestly.' I undo my seat belt and twist in my seat so I can face her. 'I don't remember much after losing my phone. I had too much to drink, I know. But I don't remember us …' I pause and swallow the bile that's creeping up the back of my throat. 'I don't even remember us kissing or anything like that.'

Ambers folds her arms across her chest and rocks back and forth as much as the limited space behind the steering wheel will allow. 'And I can't forget.'

'Forget what, Amber. Say it?'

'I could lose my job, David. If people find out about this.'

'How?' I sigh, my head sinking into my shoulders as I reluctantly accept what Amber is insinuating.

'Soliciting a junior member of staff. It's very serious.'

'Christ, Amber, you make it sound like I'm a child. I'm a grown man, for fuck's sake.'

'Yes, David. And a married man. Oh, this is bad. So bad.'

Amber drops her head and bangs her forehead against the steering wheel. It looks like it hurts, but I don't try to stop her.

'What happened?' I ask sheepishly. 'I mean when did we, ugh, how did we … oh, God.'

Amber jerks upright, like she's just been Tasered and glares at me glassy-eyed. 'Is that a serious question?' She snarls.

'Yes, actually, it is. I need to know.'

Amber covers her face with her hands and thrashes her whole upper body from side to side. She crashes against the driver's door on her side, but she doesn't come close enough on my side to touch me. I reach my hand out to clasp her shoulder, to try to steady her, but she smacks me away. My touch repulses her; it's written all over her face, like just sitting next to me right now makes her want to vomit. But her distaste pales in comparison to my self-disgust.

Traffic roars past us on the motorway. I close my eyes and listen to the sound of their engines and the whistle of the wind as they pass. Forty-foot trucks carrying heavy loads rumble by. The car rattles as the gust of wind they drag behind them grazes past the driver side in a split second. I keep my eyes firmly shut. My body knows where it is; nestled amongst the familiarity of day-to-day traffic on the motorway, but my mind is somewhere else entirely. Somewhere new. Somewhere scary.

Somewhere I don't want to be. I think of Emma. Her beautiful face. Her amazing body. She's tiny; barely scraping five foot. Even in her skyscraper heels, the tip of her head sits neatly under my chin.

I remember her face as she stood on our front porch yesterday evening waving me off. She was so sad. So sad she looked even smaller than usual. I knew she wanted to ask me to stay. I knew her heart was hurting, and she craved me beside her to make it hurt just a fraction less. But I didn't put her first. I knew how much she needed me, and I still left. Christ, I'm some bastard. *And now this.*

I open my eyes and look at Amber. Her hands still hiding her face. I understand she feels bad, but she can't possibly feel as awful as I do. Or as horrible as Emma will. *What have I done?* I've betrayed the person I love most in the world. Emma's so fragile right now. This could destroy her completely. For the first time in my life, I think I understand the low Emma sometimes feels. The desperation, the self-hatred. The pain. Because I know, it's not possible to hate myself any more than I do right now.

'Tell me what happened,' I say.

Amber ignores me and begins to cry. I catch her hands and pull them roughly away from her face. She refuses to look at me.

'Tell me, Amber. For fuck's sake, tell me.'

'Tell you what, David?' She sniffles, dragging the length of her arm under her nose.

It's disgusting, and my skin crawls at the thoughts of watery snot sitting in the creases along the sleeve of her knitted cardigan.

'Please, Amber?' My aggression from seconds before melts into passive pleading.

'What do you want, David? All the gory details. Or do you just want to hear that we drank so much we lost the ability to control ourselves and gave in to our desires.'

I shake my head. 'I never desired this.'

Angry, tearless sobs shake Amber's body. I don't intend for my words to hurt her, but I have to say it. It's true. I don't desire anyone except my wife.

'Look at us,' I say, pointing at her and then dragging my finger back across the air to point at myself. 'This isn't what desire looks like. We didn't desire this. We're both miserable.'

'So you're saying it's regret?' Amber slurps her words like she drinking soup that's too hot for her mouth.

'Isn't that what we're both saying?'

Amber nods.

'Okay then.' I exhale sharply through my nose.

I don't know why it's a relief to hear her admit she regrets it, but it is.

'What are we going to do?' she says, finally making eye contact with me.

I stroke my chin between my thumb and forefinger as if I'm contemplating something. Formulating a plan. I'm not. The words *oh my God, oh my God* playing on repeat is all that's going through my mind.

'No one can know about this, David,' Amber says, sounding much more together than she was seconds before. 'Seriously. You can keep a secret, can't you?'

I swallow a lump of air too wide for my throat and cough. 'Not from Emma. I can't keep this from Emma.'

'What?' Amber slaps her thighs with her hands, repeatedly. The loud smacks ring in the air. She repeats the process several times before stilling completely and staring out the window.

If possible, she's making me feel even more uncomfortable than I already do.

'You really want to tell your wife what you've done?' she asks, somewhat sedate now.

'I have to.'

'How can you be that selfish?'

I snort. 'How is *not* keeping a horrible secret from Emma selfish?'

'Because you'd only be telling her to ease your guilty conscience.'

'That's not true. I'd be telling her because we don't have secrets. Emma and I know everything about each other. We've been together since we were kids, for God's sake. I could never hide something like this from her. '

'Every couple has secrets, David,' Amber accosts.

'We don't,' I retaliate, bluntly.

Amber tosses her shoulder towards her ear. 'Okay. If you say so.'

'We. Don't.'

'Okay, David. I said I believe you. But I still think you're being selfish. We've already made love. It's done. You can't change that. Neither can I. But you don't have to tell Emma and break her heart. What good will it do?'

'Made love?' I echo. Amber's choice of term leaves a sour taste in my mouth.

'Screwed. Shagged. Banged each other ten ways backwards. Does it matter what we call it? You and I were a pair of horny idiots last night. One night. That's all it was. Let's not let it ruin our lives, okay? No one needs to know. It doesn't need to destroy *your* marriage or *my* career.'

I run my hands through my hair and tug. *Her career*, I think bitterly. I wish that's all I stood to lose. My goddamn job.

'Okay,' I say, nodding. 'Okay.'

'You won't tell Emma?' Amber reiterates.

'I won't tell anyone.'

'Okay. Me too. It's our secret,' Amber says.

Our secret, I repeat silently. *Our dirty little secret.* My fingers fumble and struggle to find the door handle in time to open the door. I lean out and throw up. I wipe my mouth with the back of my hand and close the door again.

Amber ignores my meltdown and sits like a statue staring into space.

'Can I use your phone, please?' I ask, concentrating on pushing the words that try to stick in my throat out and past my lips.

Amber reaches across me and bends down. I jump, like a fucking idiot. Now, I'm the one who can't bear to be touched. She fishes for her handbag that's resting at my feet and lifts it onto her knees to take out her phone.

'Here,' she says, passing her iPhone to me, but keeping her fingers wrapped around it like dangling spiders legs. 'Remember, don't tell her.'

'As if I'm going to tell her over the phone anyway,' I puff out. 'I just want to call. I want to make sure she's okay.'

'Yeah. Of course. Sorry,' Amber narrows and lets go of her phone.

Chapter Ten

EMMA

I rub my eyes, squint, and yawn loudly. I'm surprised to discover darkness has swept the day away, and my bedroom is poorly illuminated by a green-blue hue omitted by my laptop screen. I flittered most of the afternoon away in bed watching DVD boxed sets I've seen a hundred times before. I didn't intend to nap, but I must have dozed off quite some time ago because the DVD is almost halfway through a second loop, and my tummy is rumbling angrily, protesting that I've forced it to endure another day of unintentional fasting.

The duvet is twisted around me uncomfortably, pulling my knees in opposite directions. I flap my arms and kick my legs, shaking myself free. The bottle of wine I brought upstairs is unopened on the bedside table. The paracetamol box is open, but I remember that I only took two. They must have worked because the headache that was tormenting me earlier is gone. My phone rests on David's empty pillow – flashing. I roll over onto my tummy and pick it up. I'm disappointed to discover all that awaits my attention is a friend request on Facebook. I've no missed calls or texts from my husband.

I ignore the Facebook request from some Asian guy I don't know who probably wants to sell me fake Louboutins or a Russian bride. I send David a snarky message asking why he hasn't been in touch and throw my phone back onto his side of the bed as I get up. I wobble a little as my legs object to sustaining the weight of the rest of my body. I pick up the bottle of wine and tuck it under my arm, ready to carry it back downstairs and put it in the fridge. Just as I reach my bedroom door, my phone rings, startling me.

I toss the bottle of wine onto the bed and grab my phone.

'Hello,' I say, without checking the number flashing on the screen.

'Hey, baby.'

'David,' I beam. 'I was worried.'

I sit on the end of the bed and cross my legs; instantly feeling lighter just because I hear his voice.

'I'm so sorry,' David mumbles. 'I lost my phone yesterday. I tried to get in touch last night from another phone, but you weren't picking up.'

'Oh. Right. That was you?' I remember ignoring a call in the taxi last night. 'Sorry, I didn't recognise the number …'

'That's okay. I guessed as much.'

David sounds oddly jumpy. Losing his phone must be really bothering him. I remember our argument about taking out insurance, and I grunt. I won't bring it up now. He sounds like he's already beating himself up a lot. But it's money down the drain that we really can't afford to lose. It's hard to hide my frustration, and I hold the phone away from my ear for a moment. I sigh deeply and roll my eyes before placing the phone back to my ear.

'So,' I say, 'how's your weekend going?'

David exhales. He actually sounds upset or maybe just exhausted. It's worrying.

'The client seems nice,' he says after a long pause.

61

'Well, that's good.' I smile. 'The weekend will be worth it if they give you their business, right?'

I hear David clear his throat. 'How has your weekend been?' he asks, changing the subject. 'Did you get out for a drink with the girls?'

I don't blame him for steering the conversation in a different direction; I don't want to talk about work stuff, either. 'Yeah, we went to some posh place in town that Kim picked. It was nice. Actually, she stayed over last night.'

'Good, good,' David says, followed by another long pause. He's unusually pensive.

'Baby, it's just a phone,' I say, finally.

'Hmm?'

'I can hear how upset you are. Don't let it get to you. It's just a lost phone.'

'It's not the phone.' David sighs. 'Listen, baby …'

My face falls, and I'm glad he can't see me. I know he's going to say something I don't want to hear. Like he's stuck in Kilkenny entertaining the client for the week. Or even worse, he has to take a last-minute trip to Boston.

'Yeah …' I reluctantly encourage him to go on.

'Things have changed a little,' he says, almost whispering. 'I thought I'd make it home tonight. Actually, I thought I would even be early. I wanted to surprise you.'

'But?'

'But something has come up. I don't think I'll be home tonight after all.'

My heart sinks. But I tell myself it's better than him jet setting to the States.

'Okay.' I sigh. 'I'll see you tomorrow after work, then. Yeah?'

'Are you going to work?' he squawks.

'Well, yeah. Monday's usually start that way, don't they?'

'But you've been feeling terrible. How will you face a class of thirty-two five-year-olds?'

I can hear the concern in his voice. It's sweet if not somewhat irritating. Facing my pupils on Monday will be a hell of a lot easier than facing this weekend alone was.

'Work is good, David. It's a distraction. It beats being all by myself with my thoughts.'

Shit! I panic as soon as the words leave my mouth. I shouldn't have said that. He'll worry. I know he worries when I'm alone normally. He's probably freaking out that I'm by myself so soon after Danny's death now. And there's nothing he can do about it. He has to work. I *do* understand. And I *am* okay. Or I'm as okay as any normal person can be at a time like this. I. Am. Normal. For once, I'm totally in control of how I feel. Even if that feeling is awful and crushing my heart. I know I'm grieving, and I accept it. It hurts—of course, it does. But I can cope. In a weird way, I want to feel it. I loved Danny. I miss him. I ache for him, and I want to experience that ache.

I don't want to hurt myself. Not this time. I don't need to drown out the emotional pain with a physical pain like I've done before. I am coping. I. Am. Okay.

'Okay, baby. If you're sure you're ready for work?' David's gritty voice hits my ear like a gentle rain.

'I'm sure.'

'I'll call you tomorrow. So if it's a number you don't recognise, it's just me, okay?'

63

'Okay,' I maffle.

Just him, I think to myself with my head heavy and flopping to one side. The weird messages from last night suddenly carnival around my head.

'Bye, baby. I love you,' David whispers.

'I love you too. Bye, bye.'

I hang up and sit still on the end of my bed for a while. The usually comfortable mattress feels like rocks under my arse, and I shuffle and twist, but I can't contain my restlessness. The message from last night won't dissipate. I replay each one clearly now, and I'm as unnerved as ever. Deleting them from my phone hasn't deleted them from my head. Suddenly, my neat, three-bedroom semi-detached house grows to enormity in my imagination, and I'm overly aware of being all alone. I can't take my eyes off the bedroom door. My heart pounds in my chest as I imagine someone charging up the stairs at any second. I think about calling Kim, but I remember her date. I can't call Liz or Ruth; they're both pissed off with me after my weird behaviour last night. My shoulders round and shake as large, uncontrollable tears trickle down my cheeks and splash against my knees. I miss Danny so much. It's a physical pain as if my ribs are shrinking, and soon, there won't be any room left inside for my heart, and it will implode under pressure.

I reach behind me. My hand pats around the mound of tangled duvet searching for the bottle of wine. I beam brightly as the noise of my wedding ring clinking against the glass bottle kisses my ears. I thank God for screw caps and slug huge mouthfuls, barely taking the time to catch my breath between.

Chapter Eleven

AMBER

I potter about in the kitchen making as much noise as I reasonably can. It's past seven thirty a.m., and if I don't leave the house in the next ten minutes, I'll be swallowed up in Monday morning traffic and almost certainly be late for work. I clink cups off each other and bang cupboard doors, hoping to wake David. When he asked me if he could stay over for the rest of the weekend, I didn't know what to say. I definitely didn't see that question coming. He said he couldn't go home and face his wife, considering what we'd done. *Fair enough*. But staying with me? *Wow, I couldn't make this crap up.* I suggested he stay in a hotel, but he was one step ahead of me and had already thought that idea through. He said the booking would show up on his credit card bill, and Emma would notice. He was right, but I couldn't help but be disappointed to realise he's more astute than I give him credit for.

Seconds later, the double doors between the kitchen and sitting room slide open, and David appears in the alcove. His suit is crumpled, and he isn't wearing a tie. His messy hair and pale face are evidence that he didn't sleep much on my couch last night. He must not have taken the sleeping tablets I gave him. I recall the disapproving shake of his head when I offered them to him. But I'd breezily made up some excuse about being a nervous flyer, and with the amount of traveling I do with work, I thought he'd believed me. It's bothersome to know he didn't take them and instead spent a restless night tossing and turning. It irks me to know he was awake and listening to every move I made in the room above him. He looks like crap, and I can tell his head will be all over the place today at our meetings. He'll be a liability. I can't hide a smirk as I look him up and down. If today's meetings don't go in our favour, the team will look at David, not me.

I turn my back on him and make some coffee. I can hear him walking closer to me, and I know to suspect him sitting comfortably at the kitchen table when I turn back.

'Here,' I say, spinning one hundred and eighty degrees on the spot and stretching my arm out to pass him a cup of coffee.

I'm taken aback to find he's actually in front of the back door using the glass panels as a makeshift mirror to tidy his appearance. He runs his hands over his suit jacket and straightens it out, and he pulls a grey and navy striped tie out of his back pocket. It's the perfect complement to his sky blue shirt. He's scrubbing up rather debonair.

'Here,' I repeat, this time gaining his attention. 'I made you some. It looks like you need it.'

'Thanks,' he murmurs, meeting me at the table to take the cup.

I retrieve another cup from the countertop for myself, and we both sip in silence. He checks his watch a number of times, and I wait to see if he'll suggest we leave soon. He should. We only have minutes left if we're going to make it into the office on time, yet he doesn't say a word.

I drop my cup into the bubbly water in the kitchen sink. He walks over to the sink to copy.

'You should lead today's pitch,' I say randomly.

I throw him off-guard, and he misses the sink and cracks the cup off the granite countertop. The cup remains surprisingly intact, but David's face is glowing red.

'Oh Jesus, Amber. I've nothing prepared. I thought you were leading this one.'

'Well, I was … but …'

I sigh for good measure. I consider crying but then decide against it. I don't want to exhaust every display of emotion in one sitting.

I eyeball David. He needs to say something, but he's looking at me like a rabbit in the headlights. *Christ, he makes my skin crawl.*

'I can't do it now. Not after … what we've done,' I whinge. 'I just … I'm just not in a good place.'

'And what? You think that I am? Amber, I cheated on my wife, for God's sake. Work is the last thing on my mind right now, to be honest.'

'Well, it's a fine mess we've gotten ourselves into, isn't it?' I sniffle, not so much for effect this time as for a noise to mask the grinding of my back teeth.

The pitch will fail today, and I will not be responsible, I decide calmly.

'I'll have to call in sick then.' I throw my hands in the air and shake my head. 'I can't. I just can't.'

'Okay. Okay,' he says, pulling himself to stand straighter and taller. He almost looks attractive like that. Ben Affleck like, only without the American accent and great teeth.

I throw my arms around his neck, and I feel him brace himself. 'Thank you. Thank you,' I say. I even dare to kiss him

67

on the cheek, and it startles him so much I can hear his breath catch in the back of his throat.

'We can go over your notes in the car,' he says, impressively together. 'But first, can I borrow your phone again?'

I look at him like he's just asked me to donate a kidney.

'I need to check on Emma. I want to catch her before she goes to work?'

I drag my phone out of my trouser pocket, grunt, and pass it to him. I would warn him not to tell her anything again, but I already know there's no need. He's making the face he pulls every time he's getting ready to lie. I'm used to it. He pulls that same dropped lip crap with me when he attempts to cover for some incompetent member of the team. I know him better than he realises.

Three hours later, I'm standing outside the main doors of the canteen smoking and mulling over memories of this morning's meeting. I haven't lit up in years, but the pitch went perfectly, and the Boston guys were throwing their business at us before they even left the boardroom – thanks to David.

One of the younger ones noticed David's odd slipup, and for a moment, I was certain he'd wise his partners up before they walked away, but instead, he shook David's hand and congratulated him on what came off as David's first ever pitch.

David took the praise like a gentleman. He even manged to slip in an apology for appearing so distracted, explaining that he and his wife had lost a close family friend recently. It was genius, really. It was also a cheap shot, but it worked, and David knew it would. He's actually more difficult to predict than I thought, which certainly makes things interesting. The Boston boys rallied round, offering their condolences on the loss of the man I know David was barely acquainted with and didn't particularly like. I actually can't believe it. He had them eating out of his hand.

The money about to be thrown our way in bonuses will come in useful, but it also means David's position with the company is more secure than ever. That's the last thing I want.

Thinking on my feet, I take my phone out of my pocket and head back inside. I begin shaking as soon as I step into the elevator, and by the time I reach my desk on the fourth floor, I'm a quivering mess. My cheeks are rosy where the wind outside has pinched them. But I'm holding my breath for long intervals, and I'm convinced it's making the rest of my face pale. I slink into my high back leather chair and keep my head down. I swing my chair from side to side as I toss my phone onto my knees and scroll through the notifications blinking at me.

I find a Facebook friend request pending approval, and I click to accept it. The photo of a well-groomed Asian male trying to look sexy makes me giggle. It's painfully blunt to me that it's a stock photo taken from the internet, but I doubt others would be as observant. *Half our clients are from Singapore and Malaysia*, I smirk. It's not unlikely that some of them would reach out on Facebook. People won't think twice about it. I click through to the profile, and it's glaringly obvious I'm Sun Lee's only friend. I run my hand through my long, straight blond hair, and it must be screaming to any of my onlooking co-workers that I'm agitated. I screenshot the Snapchat messages before they disappear, and I download the photos attached. I breathe in through my nose and out through my mouth and squeeze my eyes tightly, sending tears trickling down my cheeks.

Some of my female colleagues race over to me. Inapt at sniffing out gossip, they pry into my wellbeing.

'Oh, Amber. Are you okay? You don't look well,' one of them says, draping her arms around my neck like a shawl. 'Has something happened?'

'Something terrible,' another adds, her hunger for a juicy scandal practically salivating from her lips.

'Are you ill?' a third colleague finally probes.

I shake my head and continue to quiver all over like a leaf in the breeze.

David finally notices the commotion at my desk and pries himself away from the Boston team, who are busy patting themselves on the back. They stop short of measuring testosterone levels as they congratulate themselves on a job well done. He scurries towards me. I can't tell if the look on his face is concern for my welfare or fear that I've shot my mouth off. *How interesting.*

'Amber, what's wrong?' he says, pushing his way through the girls surrounding me to place his hand on my shoulder.

I spin my chair around to face him. The girls beside me step back but stay close enough to watch the drama unfold. I throw my arms around his waist. His suit jacket is open, and I bury my face in his shirt against his belly. He's warm. Too warm. I can tell he's hot and sticky under his clothes. My stomach heaves as his touch repulses me, but I don't move.

'What is it?' he asks, peeling me away from him.

I sit upright. Rigid. And drop my bottom lip. I pick my phone up from my knees and pass it to him.

He shakes his head, unsure what he's supposed to do. His blank face is comical, and I have to disguise a laugh with crying.

'Someone is watching me. Look,' I say, pointing at the screen. 'Read the messages. See what they're saying. They know what I did.'

David drops his head and stays silent for a moment as he reads.

'Who is this?' he asks, flicking his eyes up to meet mine.

'I don't know. Some stranger.'

'It can't be a stranger. It has to be someone you know. How else can they know what we …' David cuts himself off mid-sentence, turning to face the group of our female colleagues staring at us.

'Just ignore it, Amber. It's bullshit, okay,' he says impressively casual, but I can feel his hands shake as he passes me back my phone.

'I had some weird text messages a few years ago,' one of the girls pipes in. 'Turns out it was an ex-boyfriend. Freaked the hell out of me at the time, though, so I totally understand how you must be feeling right now, Amber.'

My eyes narrow, and she takes another step back. I don't give a shit about her domestic problems. Her unsolicited opinion isn't helping.

'There's more,' I whisper. 'On Facebook. A photo. It's of the two of us.'

David coughs loudly. It makes me jump.

'Why did you post a photo of us on Facebook?' He grunts.

I don't answer straight away. Redness is creeping from his ears, across his cheeks, and down the sides of his nose. I can't tell if it's temper or terror. David and I are Facebook friends.

And, of course, he is friends with his wife. Any photo David is tagged in, Emma will see on her feed. But he's not tagged. Well, not yet, anyway.

I allow myself a couple of deep breaths before I mumble, almost incoherently, that I didn't post it. Someone else did.

'Who?' David barks, the redness of his face turning to purple.

I shrug. 'Sun Lee.'

'Sun who?'

'Look.' I scroll through my phone and show David the profile picture on the account.

'A client?' David asks, just as I assumed he would.

I don't say anything and let him draw his own conclusion.

'How did he get a picture of us?'

David snatches the phone out of my hand. His aggression and urgency make our colleagues gasp. This is the best gossip they've been privy to since the janitor was caught having sex with the foreign intern on the photocopier at the Christmas party last year. David had laughed about it with the team until mid-March. I bet he never thought *he* would be the laughing stock of the next scandal.

'This was taken at the weekend.' David snorts angrily as he glares at the photograph of us sitting next to each other in the hotel dining room.

'I don't remember posing for a photo, do you?' he says, his eyes burning into me. 'Did you take a selfie or something without me noticing?'

'You don't remember a lot of things about that night,' I snarl. 'Your selective amnesia is rather convenient, isn't it?'

David's bottom lip drops, and I hope he heeds my warning not to belittle me in front of our colleagues again.

'This isn't a real account,' David says. 'This guy has no friends except you. And look at this profile photo. It's bollocks. Something taken off the internet, I reckon. Sun Lee is not a real person. It's a troll. Just delete them as a friend and forget about it.'

I'm about to say something to highlight how shaken I am by the whole ordeal, but David cuts across me. 'And don't accept friend requests from people who you don't actually know in real life, okay?'

'I never understand that,' another one of the girls says. 'Like, I mean, all these people with three thousand friends.' She stands with a confident hip out and twirls a strand of curly hair around her finger. 'And I'm just here like, *oh no, you don't.* There's no way you've got that many friends.'

'Yeah, I know, right,' the third girl finally joins the conversation. 'I mean, it's actually just desperate. Like the internet can be super scary. It's totally freaky when someone is sending you messages and stuff like they know you, but they could be some random weirdo who just wants to murder you or something.'

As irritating as their juvenile attempts to explain themselves are, they actually add a dimension to the situation that is really very helpful.

'I think that's a little dramatic, don't you?' David says, his arms making a shooing motion towards the girls, so they distance themselves from us even more.

'Oh, David,' I cry. 'It's scary. Someone knows. Someone knows everything.'

'No one knows anything, Amber.' David grits his teeth. 'There's nothing to know, anyway. You're not the type of girl with skeletons in her closet and as … as …' David points toward the girl nearest us.

'Giselle,' she says, telling him her name with an unimpressed raised eyebrow that he didn't already know it.

'Yes, of course. Giselle.' He blushes as if he momentarily forgot it, but I know better. 'As Giselle says, it's probably just a disgruntled ex. Look at you, you're gorgeous. Any man who lost you would be beating himself up.'

All the girls nod and smile, like I need the encouragement. I pull a face at David, wondering if he's secretly referring to us. My skin actually crawls. He'd better not be developing feelings. That would ruin everything.

'I can't be here. I just can't,' I say, standing up, my knees knocking.

'Okay, well, you can't drive in that state,' David says. 'I'll take you home.'

I swallow hard. 'Thank you.'

Chapter Twelve

EMMA

The smiling faces of thirty-two five-year-olds stare up at me as I stand at the top of my classroom. Their arms, some still chubby from baby fat they've yet to lose, are folded and resting in front of them on their school desks. They're silent at last after finishing the usual morning routine of giggles and chatting while they take their coats off and stuff their schoolbags under their desk. It's around this time every day that I reach for my three-hundred-and-sixty-five page book of one-page stories, open it at random, and prepare to tickle their imagination with my enthusiastic character voices. But not today.

My classroom is my haven. I love my job. I love the kids. Thirsty for knowledge, their inquisitive minds fascinate me every single day. I'm a good teacher, or I certainly try to be. I give my all. I dry crying eyes when little legs trip on the playground. I encourage small hands to keep trying, and soon, they'll manage to colour inside the lines. I cherish the rewards; their beautiful smiles, or a pair of sneaky arms wrapped around my leg stealing a cheeky hug.

But today is different. Today, my brain pulses in my skull. Their young, high-pitched voices are like tiny spears attacking my head. It's not their fault, I know. The wine is to blame. The fuzziness that I welcomed last night must be paid for with a searing headache this morning.

The silence begins to break into giddy mumbles, and I know their angelic posture won't last much longer.

'Okay,' I say, clapping my hands just once to gain their attention. 'You've been so good all morning; I think you deserve a special treat.'

A loud chorus of approval erupts, and it's hard to believe that such tiny bodies can create such a big noise.

'Shh,' I warn, placing my finger against my lips.

Silence only takes seconds to return, and I smile. I remind myself that it's not their fault I feel so awful today.

'How about we spend the morning watching a movie?' I suggest.

More cheering follows. I press play on the remote control I've been hiding behind my back until now and wait for them to settle down before I take my seat.

There's some arguing between the girls about who really is the best the Disney Princess. The boys are more united in their stance that all princesses suck. But within a minute or two of the theme song serenading the classroom, all their little mouths close and their eyes are fixed on the screen.

Friday is usually treat day, and that's only if the childrens' behaviour all week has earned it. Monday morning is most definitely not treat day, and I know I'll have some overbearing parents knocking on my door tomorrow morning, furious that their little one's brains are being neglected. But tomorrow feels like a lifetime away right now.

I spend the time the kids are engrossed in the movie sitting with my arms folded across my chest and my eyes closed. I don't dare drift off to sleep, even though I'm exhausted. I'm not sure I could sleep even if I wanted to because I've too much on my mind. I had another weird Facebook friend request this morning before I left for work. This time from some girl in Boston. The profile picture was a bouquet of white roses with droplets of blood on the petals. It was depressing and morbid, and I don't know why anyone would want that as the image representing their account. The cover photo was an overhead shot taken at some heavy metal concert—the type where everyone wears black and paints their faces or wears creepy masks, and the songs are all about killing yourself. Ironically, I hate that kind of music. I have enough demons in my soul telling me to hurt myself, so I don't need some underweight, overexcited band screaming hateful words at me, encouraging me to slit my throat.

No other telltale signs existed about who this person might be. Her account was set to private, so I couldn't even investigate to find clues. All I know is we had no friends in common, and her name, which I've forgotten now, wasn't familiar. Ordinarily, I'd assume the request was an error and forget about it. *Ordinarily.* But not after the weekend. A second request from a stranger in as many days is an unnerving coincidence. And Boston, of all places. I know David's client is a big Boston company. Maybe Kim was right; maybe all of this is just one of David's colleagues thinking they're being funny. It's possible Boston is supposed to be a clue; a hint to their identity. It's distasteful and pathetic, but perhaps, it's all a sick joke. I begin to hope one of David's co-workers really does have a twisted sense of humour because thinking about the alternative is really freaking me out. I know celebrities get stalked online all the time. Crazy trolls get their kicks as they hide behind a laptop screen just waiting for someone famous to snap and reply, if only to tell the troll to piss off. I've seen the strange spats on Twitter, the ones that make entertainment news, and I've laughed at the stupidity of it all. It doesn't seem so funny now. *But why me?* I'm a nobody. Why would anyone want to troll me?

I jump as the bell rings, announcing morning class is over. Some of my more eagle-eyed students notice my jitters and giggle. All the kids wait for my nod before they hop up from their desks and race outside to play.

I normally relish the opportunity to snatch a quick cup of coffee from the staffroom while the kids are outside, running off some of their built-up energy. This morning, I don't move from behind my desk. I can't face my colleagues. I know everyone will be chatting about their weekend, and I don't want to talk about mine. I've already overheard some of the older teachers condemn my marriage due to David's lack of presence.

'Modern men,' they often complain. 'They don't know how to be a good husband. It didn't happen like that in our day. No wonder so many marriages end in divorce these days.'

None of them ever say anything to my face, of course. They're too polite. When the rumours do finally make their way to me, I can usually brush them off with a giggle and an insincere platitude that at least I'll never get bored of David. I'd struggle to brush anything off today.

I've barely had five minutes alone when a stern knock sounds on my classroom door, and it creaks open slowly.

'Emma.' Richard, the principal, says my name like I'm a naughty pupil.

'Good morning, Richard.'

'Is everything all right in here?' he asks, his voice choppy and agitated.

Richard is a nice guy on a personal level, but we've clashed in the past professionally. We're both pretty passionate about our work, and we don't always agree about what's best for the kids. But even in our most heated discussions, Richard hasn't worn an expression as sour as the one he sports right now.

'Everything is fine. Why do you ask?' I defend.

'Your class was missed at assembly this morning.'

I close my eyes. *Oh God, bloody assembly.* I completely forgot. My class was supposed to be reciting a poem about winter. I must be the laughing stock of the school. If I thought the parents would be annoyed about their kids spending the day watching movies, that'd be nothing to their fury tomorrow when they realise my mistake.

I shake my head. 'Oh, Richard. I'm so sorry. I completely forgot.'

'Emma, go home.'

'Excuse me?' I say, my breath catching in the back of my throat.

'You're not yourself at all. Some of the other teachers told me about your friend. The old man from the train station.'

'Oh.'

'I read about it in the papers,' Richard's shoulders roll forward, and his height shrinks by a couple of inches. 'Shocking stuff. I had no idea you knew him.'

'Yeah.'

'Well, listen, don't worry about work right now. Take some time for yourself. I'll get a substitute in to cover for you. You need some head space.'

'Are you sure?' I smile.

Richard places his hand on my shoulder and gives a little squeeze. 'Emma. Go home.'

*

An hour later, I'm standing in the middle of the biscuit aisle in the supermarket. I came in to grab something for lunch since I didn't get around to grocery shopping last week. Eggs and bread were all that were in the house, and Kim and I polished those off yesterday morning. I've survived on a couple of slices of toast since then, and I'm famished. I'm not sure I'll even make it up to the counter before I rip open the packet of chocolate chip cookies in my hand.

I find myself diverting through the wine aisle. I stood in this same spot at this same time on Saturday. Picking up a bottle of chilled white wine on a Saturday morning is socially acceptable. Scanning the wine aisle on a Monday morning is decidedly less so. And I'm uncomfortable as I feel a pair of eyes blister into me. The owner of the eyes is a woman about my age. She's wearing dark coloured tracksuit bottoms with a noticeable yoghurt or milk stain on the thigh, and her hair is greasy and hangs lifelessly by her face. She's overweight, but that doesn't stop her from sharing a packet of crackers with her toddler son who's sitting in the front of her trolley. She's judging me. The disapproving shake of her head tells me so. And I should be annoyed. I should judge her sloppy appearance and her haphazard attitude towards healthy eating, but I don't. Instead, I'm pinched with jealousy. I want to be a mother like her. I should be a mother. Suddenly, I'm transported back to being a scared seventeen-year-old again. And the guilt I still feel about the decision I made at the time is momentarily strangulating.

I shake my head as if the movement will spill the memories I hate out of my brain. I grab the nearest bottle of Sauvignon Blanc and hurry towards the counter.

My phone is beeping frantically in my bag as I stand in line. Inquisitive heads turn towards me, investigating the irritating noise. My cheeks heat as the bottle of wine takes pride of place in the centre of my folded arms as people wash their eyes over me. The remainder of my groceries lines the rest of the length of my arms so I can't even reach into my bag and hit mute on my phone.

'Here, let me take some of that for you,' the elderly lady in front of me says.

'Oh, no. It's okay,' I mumble, mortified that she's reaching her hands out to take my groceries from me.

'C'mon. C'mon. Pass them here.' She's smiling brightly as she practically wrestles the wine and cookies out of my grasp. 'There's no point in having a phone on you if you don't answer it. Or at least that's what my grandson always tells me. He's only six and already knows how to work the silly thing better than I do. He can watch videos and whatnot on it. I can just about figure out texting. My daughter says it's because he's growing up with the technology. I don't know. I think kids' brains will be fried by the time they're teenagers. Either that or they'll have square eyes.' She laughs. It's a real hearty belly rumble, and I know she means to be friendly and chatty.

I force a smile. My phone has stopped beeping, so I stand still and wait for her to pass me back my stuff.

'Aren't you going to check your message?' she pries.

'Not right now. If it's important, they'll call back later.'

'S'pose.' She shrugs. Her eyes drop to my wedding ring. 'But it could be the man in your life trying to get in touch. Men have no patience, you know. My husband, God rest his soul, couldn't wait two minutes for his tea. Six o'clock on the dot, he wanted his dinner. If it was a minute late, my God, there was hell to pay.'

I can feel my eyes widen as her words shock me, and I've no idea what to say. I hope she didn't mean that he was violent, and if she did, I'm glad for her sake that he's dead. She doesn't realise it, but her ramblings have actually given me some healthy perspective. I'm pissed off at David because he's working his arse off to provide me with a great life when really I should be grateful. *I'm a bitch.* I decide on the spot to welcome him home with a delicious dinner. I have some new lingerie that I bought before our wedding that I haven't even shown him. I'll wear it tonight, and it'll be a nice surprise. I can feel the warm buzz of excitement tingle in the base of my spine.

'Excuse me,' I say, finally taking my wine and cookies back from her. 'I've forgotten something.'

*

Alone at the back of the store, I tumble the groceries from my arms into a shopping basket and wander around, gathering up the ingredients to create a culinary masterpiece when I get home. I toy with the idea of buying an apron just so I can wear it, and nothing else, as I cook. That really would surprise the hell out of David when he walks in the door.

The basket grows heavy, and I put it down on the ground and stretch my back. I smile. I'm in a much better headspace now than when I first walked into the store. My hangover doesn't even feel as bad anymore. I open my bag and fish out my phone, remembering I have messages.

My grasp tightens around my phone until my fingers ache. It's not David. I feel my mood sway the other way again. Suddenly, I'm aware of the skin covering my bones, the blood rushing through my veins, and the beating of my heart. It's not quite like an out-of-body experience, but I do feel like my mind has been severed from my body.

I close my eyes, sucking in air sharply through my nose and forcing it back out through a narrow gap between my teeth in short, even pants. I repeat. Over and over. Accepting that my moods sway like a pendulum was hard. Accepting that would possibly never change was even harder. Learning how to draw myself back from the darkness was almost impossible. But I was willing to learn. It took a lot of practice, but I've become steadily more and more adept at keeping myself calm when I'm alone.

Steadier, I read the WhatsApp message from Peek-a-boo. *Who the fuck is Peek-a-boo?*

Hello.

Hello! I roll my eyes. A little vomit sits like a lead brick somewhere between my stomach and my chest.

I reach down and hook my arm under the handles of my heavy basket. The metal eats into me, even through my coat, as I hurry back towards the main body of the shop.

Another beep from my phone summons my attention. Despite pausing as a nervous breath catches in my throat, I read it anyway.

Tut. Tut.

Don't u know it's rude 2 ignore someone?

Let's be friends.

A man appears from behind a mound of stacked cereal boxes in the centre of the aisle. I freeze. But he walks past me, pushing his trolley. Within seconds, he disappears around the corner at the end of the aisle.

I look back at my phone in my shaking hand and toss my head. I flick my finger from bottom to top on my screen and hold my breath as I read the next message that appears.

My friend is pretty.

'What the hell?' I hiss out loud.

My finger jars at the knuckle as I press the letters on my touchscreen with unnecessary force. I can't ignore this crap any longer. I have to reply. This idiot isn't taking the hint.

I think you have a wrong number.

We are not friends.

I don't know you.

I hit send and stand still, staring at the words I've just typed. I can tell whoever this is wants me to engage, so when they reply, I'm expecting it.

That's not nice.

I just want 2 tell u something.

Seriously? Tell me something? Maybe whoever is on the other end is just lonely. But this isn't how you go about making friends. I know we're in the age of technology and all that, but there are websites for meeting people. Normal people don't randomly troll strangers. This has to stop now. My instinct is telling me to block them, but I fight against it and type another reply, hoping I can let them down gently.

I'm sorry.

I have all the friends I need.

Please don't contact me again.

I read back over my own words a couple of times, content that I've made my point. It's over. I slide my hand into my coat pocket, and before I even pull it back out, my phone is vibrating against my palm.

Oh, come on!

I jerk my hand out of my pocket, still clutching my phone, and shake my fist as if the motion will spill the words to tumble around in cyber space and I won't have to deal with them.

'Consider yourself blocked.'

I blush as I realise I'm talking, rather loudly, to thin air. I open the app once again. I've no idea how to block someone, but I'm about to find out.

It's no surprise to find another message waiting for me, but it *is* annoying. I asked them to leave me alone. And I was nice about it. I toss my eyes up and around. *Obviously too nice.* This is edging towards ridiculous now.

I click on different icons here and there, trying to delete, or at least block, this weirdo. But the app settings are confusing, and all I manage to do is change my profile status. I try again, this time losing patience. I accidentally open the waiting message in frustration as I tap on just about every icon hoping to get rid of them.

Oh, my God. Oh, my God. I almost drop my phone. It's me. It's a picture of me. They've sent me a photo. Something is written below. I scroll down.

I told u I had something 2 tell u.

I like your blouse.

The hairs on the back of my neck stand like soldiers to attention, and throaty crackles lace my breathing. My coat is zipped closed right now, but if I opened it, I'd reveal a blue and white striped blouse. The same blouse I'm wearing in the photo. The picture was taken today. *Today. Oh, my God.*

David's colleagues would never take a joke this far. And they're all at work anyway, so they wouldn't get an opportunity to take my photo. My whole body shakes. *Who the hell is this freak?*

I spin around on the spot. Circling a full three-hundred-and-sixty degrees with my eyes open so wide my brows ache from the stretch.

'This isn't funny.' I pant. 'Do you hear me, whoever you are? Not funny.'

No one is here. I spin around again. *No one.* But I don't feel alone. I can virtually feel hot breath on my neck and hands on my skin. I can feel someone watching me. *Shit.*

Skidding on the floor tiles a couple of times, I race to the top of the shop. The metal basket laden with my groceries wallops against my hip over and over. It'll leave a nasty bruise tomorrow, but I don't think about that now.

Reaching the hub of people at the checkout, I come to an abrupt stop and stand poker straight. The checkout area is a lot busier than it was a few minutes ago. People are everywhere – young, elderly, and children. I look everyone up and down as my heart beats so fast I feel like it can't cope with the pace. There are too many people. Strangers. Everywhere. Any one of them could be this freak. They're probably watching me right now. Laughing on the inside. I hate them. I don't even know who they are, and I hate them.

I have to get out of here.

I drop my basket onto the ground at my feet, a little too roughly, especially as quite a few people have begun to stare at me. I guess my shaky persona is drawing attention. The security guard at the door straightens his round shoulders and glares at me.

Does he think I'm going to steal something? He must. He's walking towards me.

The door is in view, and I'm desperate to abandon my shopping and race to my car. Panic is belting against my skull as if a tidal wave of blood is building up inside my head and the pressure could force my eyes to pop right out of their sockets.

I look through the glass doors. If I squint, I can just about make out my car in the carpark. The impulse to run is overwhelming now. It's messing with my breathing. The effort to suppress the urge is bullying all my other senses into submission. I can't think of anything else, and my lungs are feeling the pressure as they plead with my brain to remember to inhale.

Long, even breaths. *I've got this.* I know what to do. It takes me a few seconds, but I regain control.

Calmer, I eye up a five kilogram bag of potatoes on special offer near the checkout. I join the queue and concentrate on keeping my breathing steady. Any lapses in concentration and I'll lose it again. Only three people are ahead of me with a couple of items each, but we're barely moving.

'Hi, how are you?' the girl behind the till says, as I finally pick my bits and pieces out of the basket and place them on the conveyer belt.

'Hello,' I mumble. 'I need potatoes too.'

'Potatoes?' She looks at the items between us.

'Yeah.' I cringe. 'I hurt my back in Pilates, and I can't lift anything heavy. I was wondering if someone could carry them out to the car for me, please? Sorry to be a pain.'

'No problem. Hang on.'

I can feel my face redden. I wonder if she can see straight through my pathetic lie, but I could hardly admit that I'm scared senseless to walk out to my car alone in case a freak is waiting out there to murder me. *In broad daylight. Yeah, right!* I try to scold myself and get a grip, but I'm beyond paranoid.

'Frank.' She leans forward and calls out, summoning the security guard. 'This girl needs some help with her spuds.'

The security guard turns around and smiles. 'Sure. Do you want the big bag or the little one?'

I hate potatoes, but I must opt for the heaviest bag there. I need him to carry it all the way to the car so I won't be alone.

'Big.' I flash an overzealous toothy grin. 'Thank you.'

Chapter Thirteen

DAVID

I sit on the edge of my bed and rub my knees. The soft bit just above my kneecap is red and sore from my elbows digging into them, and my left calf is threating to cramp up. I must have sat statue-like for at least an hour with my elbows on my knees and my hands clasped with my chin resting heavily on top. My back hurts now, and it clicks and creaks as I straighten up. The duvet and sheets are balled up and messy underneath me, so I can tell Emma had a restless night tossing and turning. And she must have left for work in a hurry this morning; she'd never leave the bed undressed otherwise. She likes it perfect, with cushions that match the curtains dotted across the pillows.

I stand up when I hear a car pull into the driveway. For a moment, I panic that it's Amber. She insisted on dropping me to my goddamn front door regardless of my constant reassurance that I didn't need her to. She even pulled into the driveway, for Christ's sake. Somehow, offering to take her home turned into her asserting that she wanted to be alone, but not until after she dropped me home. She didn't even realise that it made no sense for me to be out of work if she was okay to drive by herself. I tried to bring the topic up and suggested I head back to the office, but she shot the notion down. And I wasn't about to complain about getting the afternoon off. It was all a bit weird. She was obsessed with chaperoning me home.

Amber's not a gossip. She pisses off the other girls in the office with her snobbery and keep-to-herself demeanour. So I doubt she was desperate to see where I lived so she could go back and report to the other girls. But I can't think of another reason for her adamancy. And then, for someone who was apparently so desperate to be alone, I thought I was never going to get rid of her. For fifteen minutes, we made awkward small talk parked outside my sitting room window, and the whole time I kept looking at Amber and thinking, *I've fucked you, and now, I have to tell my wife.*

My personal life is about to come crashing down as soon as I tell Emma about the one-night stand. But oblivious Amber just kept going on and on about her bloody Facebook troll. I reiterated that the internet is full of weirdos. I told her that all she has to do is block them and move on. She finally got pissed off and left. *Thank God.*

I walk reluctantly to the window and part the drawn curtains just enough to peek out without being seen. I exhale heavily when I discover Emma's car parked in the driveway. She's still sitting behind the steering wheel. It takes me a few seconds of staring at her motionless body to realise she's home from work early too. I twist my wrist, still clutching the curtain and check my watch. It's not long past noon. Emma's home unusually early.

A dull pain coils in my stomach, and I actually want to be sick. Maybe then, I can throw up some of the guilt weighing me down. In spite of gagging every couple of seconds, I stay standing on the spot, watching my wife through the narrow gap in the curtain like some demented pervert. But I just want to see her. Her ivory skin is emphasised by her rosy cheeks, and her shoulder-length mousy brown hair falls in soft waves around her face. She's beautiful, and she's probably the only person in the world who would disagree. Emma's confidence is rock bottom. No matter how many compliments I give her or how many men offer to buy her a drink on a night out, she doesn't see her own beauty on the inside and out.

Oh Christ, what have I done? Sleeping with Amber may be the final nail in my wife's coffin. It could destroy her. *Maybe Amber's right. Maybe I shouldn't tell her.*

Ten minutes or so tick by painfully slowly and Emma still hasn't moved. *Maybe she knows?* The pain in my stomach worsens, and I drag myself to the en suite. I lean over the loo for a few minutes, retching. I forget my dodgy stomach when I notice the empty wine bottle stuffed behind the shower curtain. I can't tell if Emma was drinking in the shower, or if she was so pissed, she thought the shower was the bin and dumped the empty bottle there. Now I know for certain that I never should have left her alone this weekend. The guilt is so bad now that I finally manage to hurl, barely turning my head back around in time to aim for the toilet bowl.

I brush my teeth, pick up the empty wine bottle, and make my way out to the car where Emma is still sitting. She's staring at her phone and doesn't notice me. I open the driver's door, and she screams. I jump back instinctively, yelping in response. Taking a second to straighten up and step forward again, I laugh, imagining how ridiculous I must look to the neighbours. Emma doesn't laugh. But I wish she would.

'Hey,' she squeaks; teary green eyes peek out at me from under her heavy fringe.

'Hi, Ems. I'm sorry. I didn't mean to give you a fright. You okay? You've been out here for ages.'

Emma shakes her head.

'Are you sick?' I think of the wine bottle I'm clutching behind my back. 'You never come home from the school early.'

'I'm not sick,' she says, twisting her legs out of the car as she stands up.

I believe her. God, I wish I hadn't brought the wine bottle into the garden. What was I thinking? *That I was going to scold her for drinking?* How dare I? I just worry that there's always the chance she'll do something to hurt herself when she's drunk and alone.

'You're home early,' she says, leaning into the car to fish out a bag of groceries.

'Yeah. The meeting ended sooner than expected.'

'So they let you go home? That was nice of your boss.' Emma pulls her head out of the car and stands up straight again. She drops the bag at her feet. 'Well, s'pose you've been working all weekend. It's just time in lieu really, isn't it?'

'Yeah. I guess you could say that.'

Emma's right. The whole team should have gotten the afternoon off. Or tomorrow. I'm exhausted. Maybe I'll phone in sick in the morning. At the very least, it would mean I wouldn't have to face Amber for a while.

'You're home early too,' I point out, tossing the wine bottle onto the grass verge when Emma sticks her head back into the car again. It doesn't make a sound as it hits the ground.

'Yeah. I got upset in school, and Richard told me to go home. He was actually really sweet about it. I'm probably going to take the next couple of days off.'

I place my palm on the small of her back and rub it around in little circles. 'I think that's a good idea. You could do with

92

some space. Actually, I think I'll take a couple of days leave too. We could spend some time together, yeah?'

Emma pulls her head out of the car again; this time, she turns around as she swings her handbag over her shoulder. We're so close that even through her thick winter coat I can feel her tits press up against me. She hasn't done it on purpose, but it's nice. I don't want her to move. I don't want to move. I wrap my arms around her waist and kiss her forehead. I take a picture in my mind. After I confess, I may never get to hold her like this again.

I wish I could do as Amber suggested and just not tell Emma, but I can't. She doesn't deserve to be cheated on, and she doesn't deserve to be lied to. Unfortunately, I can only remedy the latter. *I have to.*

'There's a bag of potatoes in there too. Will you lift them out please?' Emma says, breaking away from me to fetch the bag of groceries on the ground beside us.

'Potatoes? You hate potatoes, don't you?' Emma and I switch places, and I lean into the car to retrieve the large, heavy bag waiting on the floor in front of the passenger seat.

'It's a long story.' She sighs.

'Well, I've got all afternoon to listen.' I grunt, my back objecting to dragging the bag across the seats and out the driver's door.

Emma tilts her head towards the open front door. 'Not out here.'

'Sounds serious.' I swallow.

'Come on. I'll make us some coffee.' Emma wrestles with the green carrier bag and paces towards the house. She doesn't look back to see if I'm following.

Chapter Fourteen

EMMA

David's face is redder than usual. The bag of potatoes can't be that heavy that it's leaving him breathless. He's forever lifting weights in the gym, for goodness sake.

'Where'll I put these?' he asks when we reach the kitchen.

'Um …'

David opens one of the cupboards we never use and stuffs the huge, awkward sized bag in. 'There,' he announces, proudly dusting off his hands. 'So do you have a craving for carbs all of a sudden or what?'

'David, sit down.' I puff out.

David's face loses all colour, and for a second, I think he's going to fall over. I've never seen him so jumpy. It's making me nervous.

'What? What is it?' He twitches.

'Just sit, okay. I'll get those coffees.'

David pulls out a chair from the kitchen table and plonks roughly down. He slides out the chair next to him for me and pats it with his hand.

'Don't drag this out, Emma. Please. Just tell me?'

I half fill the kettle and flick it on all the while keeping my eyes on my husband. His fair hair is tossed and spikey like he's been running his fingers through it. His usual dapper appearance seems tarnished, almost grubby. The top button of his sky blue shirt is open, and the knot of his navy tie is slack and hanging looser than normal. I suspect the meetings with the client haven't gone as well as David would like to pretend.

94

Maybe the whole weekend was a bust, and he's feeling the strain.

The kettle whistles, and I set about making two cups of instant coffee. I walk to the table, my hands shaking, and place both cups down. I take a seat next to David and wait for him to say something. But he's pensive and silent, and it's obvious he wants me to talk first.

'How was your weekend?' I blurt.

'Okay. Fine, I guess.' David runs a hand through his messy hair. 'We already talked about this on the phone. How are you? Is something wrong? You're not yourself.'

'Yeah,' I admit, bouncing on the spot as I scald my tongue with the piping hot coffee.

'Emma,' David barks, ignoring that I nearly fried my face.

'What?' I retaliate way more snarkily than I intended. 'Sorry, I'm sorry. I didn't mean to bite your head off. I'm just freaked out.'

'Why? Will you spit it out?' David's face is ashen, and he's sitting so far over on the edge of the chair I'm surprised he can keep his balance.

'I think I have a stalker,' I mumble, somewhat mortified to say those words out loud.

I know how diva like they sound. Stalkers are reserved for celebrities and figureheads. *What the hell does someone want with me?*

'A stalker?'

David is grinning. His whole body appears lighter all of a sudden. His eyes are dancing brighter than an excited five-year-old on Christmas Eve. It's almost as if I've just told him he won the lottery or something equally as awesome. I thought he might be at least surprised. I certainly didn't think he'd be bizarrely elated.

'David, I'm serious,' I growl. 'Someone has been sending me weird messages on the internet all weekend.'

David rolls his eyes, and his smile grows. He's really starting to piss me off, and once again, I suspect that maybe this is some weird joke.

'Did you know about this?' I grunt, struggling to hold back tears.

Is he sniggering at *me* or at the *idea* of a stalker? I can't tell, and I'm embarrassed to ask.

'No. I didn't. But c'mon, Ems. You can't actually be taking this shit seriously.'

'It's not funny. And I *am* serious. I was so freaked out earlier that I couldn't walk to the car alone. That's how I ended up with potatoes.'

'What?' David can't hold back the laughter now.

I can hear myself. I know my mixed-up ranting is making no sense. I try to calm down. I'm not worried about having a panic attack now; I'm home and safe, but I know my speech is racing, and I'm hard to understand when I'm like this.

Consciously speaking softer and more controlled, I try to explain. 'I was at the shops earlier picking up a few bits for lunch. My phone was going crazy. Some weirdo was messaging me. Watching me. The shop was jammers with people. Any one of them could have been this guy. So I picked the heaviest thing I could find to buy, and I told the girl behind the till I needed help carrying it.'

'Facebook, yeah? Was some werido trying to be your friend?'

'Yeah … and …'

'Oh Emma, baby. Stop. You're working yourself into a state. It's just your anxiety running away with you. I never should have left you alone this weekend. I'm so sorry.'

'No. It's not that. I was fine on my own. Honestly.'

'Well, clearly you weren't fine if you are going around buying random bags of spuds. Jesus, we'll be eating shepherd's pie for a month.'

I giggle. My chest is still painfully tight, but David is slowly making me feel better.

'Anyway,' he says, taking my hand and giving it a little squeeze. 'You wouldn't believe the amount of crazy people who try to reach out to me on LinkedIn. I've no idea who they are, and I've definitely never worked with them. They're just attention seekers or something. I was saying the same thing to Amber earlier.'

'Really?'

'Yes. Really.' David grins. 'She had some creep on Facebook try to friend her too.'

I grunt. I know the internet is a playground for the odd and creepy. Almost everyone has been on the receiving end of a keyboard warrior at some point. Nerdy types who wouldn't say diddly-shit to anyone in real life, but stick them behind a laptop, and they become trumped-up bullies. It's how they get their kicks. But this is different. This is personal.

'Yeah.' I mellow. 'And I know that happens all the time but—'

'Yes, it does. Exactly.' David nods. 'Look. Maybe there's some horny bastard out there going around checking out all the pretty girls on Facebook, hoping one of them will be stupid enough to sleep with him.'

I raise a sceptical eyebrow, and David's bottom lip droops, realising that he's inadvertently told me his boss is attractive.

'Block and move on,' he says, dragging his finger across the air as if he's reading invisible words written in the wind. 'Block and move on.'

'Yeah, fine. I would. Except that doesn't explain how someone out there has a photo of me?'

'A photo? Of you.'

'Yes. Me. That's what I'm saying. This is more than just a friend request here and there. It's actual stalking, and yeah, I know how dramatic and stupid that sounds, but someone is actually watching me. How else would they have my picture?'

David's whole face scrunches as if my story is a horrible smell hitting him in the face. I hate when he does that. Looks at me like he thinks I'm overanalysing everything.

'They probably googled you and downloaded the first hit they got. It could be a scam or something. Try to friend you and then tell you they're from a war-stricken country and they need money to get their family out or whatever. You know, you hear about these con artists all the time.'

I zip open my coat and slide my arms free.

'This blouse is new.' I swallow. 'Today is the first time I've worn it.'

'It's lovely,' David interrupts.

'I'm wearing this exact blouse in the picture they sent me.'

David's stupid grin falls away.

'Explain that?' I toss my head to the side and wait.

'Okay, this *is* weird. Show me?' David's tone is softer now, and several concerned lines are etched into his forehead.

'I can't.' I grimace. 'I deleted it.'

'Okay. Show me the rest of the messages, then?'

'I deleted those too.'

'What?' David snips. 'You deleted everything?'

'Yeah. It was creepy. I didn't want to keep that shit on my phone. And anyway, Kim said I should just get rid of them.'

'So Kim knows.' David sighs.

'Yeah. I got the first message on Saturday night when we were out for drinks. And things kinda continued from there.'

'Okay.' David slugs some of his coffee. 'But Kim saw the messages too, right?'

'Yes,' I snap. 'What? If Kim hadn't seen them, you wouldn't believe me? Jesus. Thanks, David.'

'No, Ems. That's not what I mean.'

'Well, what do you mean?'

David stands up and paces the floor. 'Fuck, Emma. I don't know. You've just thrown all this at me. How do you expect me to have an answer to that?'

'I don't.' I soften. 'I just want you to know. That's all.'

'Okay. And now I know.'

'Well?'

'Well what, Emma? What the hell do you want me to say here?'

'I dunno. I just want you to care.'

'I do care. Of course, I care.' David's stiff shoulders relax, and he paces back to the table and sits down beside me again.

'I can't do this,' he says, dropping his face into his hands. 'I'm sorry. I'm so sorry.'

I can't see his face, so my eyes dart all over every part of him looking for a clue about what the hell he means.

'Can't do what?' I exhale. 'Listen?'

'No. God no, Ems. I've done something terrible.'

My eyes widen, and I feel the burn of coffee making its way up the back of my throat.

'Do you know who this person is?' I quibble. 'This internet freak. Do you know them?'

David tosses his head from side to side, his body swaying in sync. 'No. I'm not talking about that.'

'Well, what then? David, you're not taking this seriously at all. I'm not just being paranoid, you know?'

'Christ. Ems,' David spits. 'Will you shut up for two seconds?'

My jaw gapes. David never speaks to me like that. He tiptoes around like he's on eggshells, so much so it's actually annoying. This isn't like him.

'Baby, you're freaking me out,' I murmur. 'I know you think I'm mad, but why are you so angry? I don't understand.'

'I'm not angry with you, Ems.' David drags his hands up and down his face, pulling his skin so roughly it looks like it hurts. 'I'm not angry with you at all. It's me. It's all me.'

'It's you?' I yelp. 'The stalker, you mean?'

'Will you forget the fucking stalker? Fucking forget it,' David shouts, throwing his hands above his head. 'Some asshole online is the least of our problems right now.'

My head drops to one side, almost meeting my shoulder, and I eye my husband up as if he's a stranger. He's acting so odd he might as well be.

'What happened this weekend?' I whisper.

100

A sharp shiver runs the length of my spine, letting me know I'm afraid of the answer.

'It's Amber.' David swallows.

I straighten. David's eyes lock on mine. Usually just looking into his big, round, baby blues soothes me. But I see something now I've never seen in him before. His eyes are glassy and dull as if winter clouds have collected and pushed away his usual summer sparkle. I swallow hard, recognising those clouds. It's guilt. I know it because when I'm having a bad day, I gaze into the mirror and those same clouds stare back at me.

I try to remain sitting upright, but it's as if an imaginary weight is tied to my shoulders, dragging me down. Tearless, panicked sighs shoot out of my mouth like a wounded animal. I try desperately to close my mouth and to catch my breath, but my body disobeys me and cries harder. I know what David is going to say. I know it, and I hate it.

'Amber,' I pant between jagged coughs.

David slides off his chair and drops to his knees on the kitchen tiles in front of me.

'I'm so sorry, Ems. So sorry. I don't know how it happened. Oh, Christ,' David cries, placing his hands on my knees.

His fingertips feel like acid against my skin, and I want to push him away, but I'm frozen. Seconds tick by in painful slow motion.

'Emma, please. Say something. Please, baby. Anything.'

I begin to jerk back and forth like a child on a rocking horse.

David scurries backwards, his knees still on the ground. He's watching me, not daring to take his eyes off me. He's afraid, I can tell. He's afraid that he has broken me. Maybe he has.

My body sits on the kitchen chair, but it's just a shell. I'm not inside right now. I'm down at the train station having tea with Danny. My mind can see it so vividly, it's real. I could swear it's real. I sit in the freezing Porto cabin with my friend. And it's good. It's good because my friend is alive and well, and my husband isn't a cheating bastard. I shake my head as the memory fades, and my mind travels back to reality. David was right. Some asshole on the internet really is the least of my worries right now.

'Say it, David,' I growl; my eyes round and glassy like two china saucers.

'Emma, please?' David whispers, dropping his head.

'Fucking say it. Say it. Say it. Say it!'

'I slept with Amber,' David shouts. 'I slept with her.'

Chapter Fifteen

EMMA

I pause outside the huge, black, wrought-iron graveyard gates and finally look up from watching my feet. I don't remember how I got here. The graveyard is a strong five miles or more from my house. The maze of roads along the way is always busy, heaving with pedestrians and traffic. But I don't remember passing a single person or car. I don't even remember consciously setting out to go to the graveyard, yet here I am, meters from Danny's grave.

The wind nips against my skin like hungry wolves at a carcass. I stormed out of the house in such a hurry I forgot to take my coat. It's barely above freezing, and all I'm wearing is a pair of skinny jeans and a satin blouse. I wrap my arms around myself and rub my hands up and down my arms, trying to keep my shivering under control.

I look up at the sky, willing a little blue to peek out from behind the clouds, but all I see is thick grey rain clouds. The gloomy, miserable weather clones my mood to perfection.

I think about turning around and going home, but I quickly dismiss the option. My house doesn't feel like home right now. I think about calling Kim. Glancing at my watch on my shaking wrist, I realise she's still at work. I know she'd leave early if I asked her to, but that wouldn't be fair. My only other choice is my mother. Her house is on the far side of town, but it's within walking distance. The thought of calling her and asking her if I can pop over out of the blue makes me sick. Even if I plaster on my best fake smile, she'll see straight through it, and she'll worry. She always worries about me. Then I'll feel guilty on top of everything else. It's a vicious cycle, but right now, I have no reasonable alternative. I reach into my pocket, and I could cry when I realise I've left my phone on the kitchen table. I can't contact anyone. I can't even call a taxi, not that I could pay for one either. My handbag and wallet are at home too. All I have with me are the clothes I'm wearing and an agonizing headache.

I'm so caught up in myself that I barely notice the little old lady who walks past. She only catches my attention because she passes by so close to me that I can feel the warmth of her body for a split second. I watch as her tired frame, hunched like a question mark, shuffles along the footpath as she makes her way through the main gates. A plastic bag dangles from one of her hands, and she has a bunch of pretty, white lilies tied together with a blue ribbon in her other hand. I follow her. I don't really know why. Something about her intrigues me. I wonder whose grave she is visiting. Her husband, perhaps. She walks with her head down, and from behind, she looks lonely and heartbroken. She looks like me, just much older. I bet she lived a long, happy life married to a wonderful man she loved with all her heart. I hope so anyway.

I keep my distance so as not to startle her, but I continue to follow her as she weaves in and out amongst the headstones. I find myself worried she'll slip on the icy grass, but she seems to know every blade and stray pebble like the back of her hand. She finally comes to a stop at an unmarked grave. A new grave. *Danny's grave.* The cold air wedges in my throat like an oesophagus-sized rock. I'd been so busy hoping she wouldn't fall that I hadn't noticed we were walking towards a familiar part of the graveyard.

Finally, the pain that I've tried to keep inside spills over in uncontrollable, salty tears. I don't make a sound. My shoulders don't heave, and my body doesn't shake, but tears flow like raindrops in autumn. I miss my friend. I miss my husband. I miss my life. I am so alone.

The elderly lady bends down and places the lilies on the raised mound of earth. She wobbles on her hunkers as she roots in the plastic bag. She pulls out a flask, a teacup, and a packet of digestive biscuits. I'm pleased Danny has a friend. But I don't remember seeing her at the funeral. Maybe she couldn't make it or only found out about Danny's passing later. It doesn't matter, I decide. She's here now. *Danny has a friend aside from me, and she's here now.* That means she was probably at the station sometimes too or at his house. It means Danny wasn't as lonely as I thought. Today has been horrific, one of the worst I can remember in a long time, but this little ray of light has lifted me. And I smile through my tears as I realise that even after he's gone, Danny can still make me feel better.

I back away slowly. I want to allow the little old lady time to enjoy her tea undisturbed. But I've barely taken five paces backwards when she calls out.

'Aren't you going to come and say hello?' she says without looking up.

I glance around. There's no one else here, so she's definitely talking to me. I cringe. She must have known I was following her the whole time.

'Oh, come on now. Stop that,' she scolds. 'The cat got your tongue or something? Where are your manners? Come say hello.'

I clear my throat with a dry cough and take a large step forward.

'Hello,' I say.

'Ah, that's better,' she replies.

She roots in her bag and pulls out a second teacup. 'Tea?'

I shake my head.

'Okay. Suit yourself. But it's warm. And you look positively frozen, child.'

'Okay then,' I consent; the Deja vu of this tea-accepting ritual is making me both miserable and excited at the same time.

She nods and doesn't bother to stand up as she reaches around for her flask and pours tea for me.

'Here now,' she says, lifting the cup over her wobbly head.

I scamper over to her and grab the cup before she scalds herself. I wonder if I should crouch down to her level or offer to help her up. It feels odd to be at such mixed heights.

'You're a friend of Danny's,' I say, finally making the decision to squat beside her.

'No man should be alone in death. Just as no man should be alone in life,' she says before biting into a digestive with a loud crunch.

I hope she'll offer me one. I never got around to eating lunch earlier, and my stomach is pleading with me to feed it something.

'Do you think Danny was lonely?' I choke back more tears.

She shakes her head. 'It's not my place to judge.'

'But he had me.' I tap my fingers against my chest, accidentally jerking the cup in my other hand and spilling some tea over the edge. 'And he had you. He must have had other

106

friends too. I hate to think he was so lonely that he … that he …'

I stop and sniffle back some snot. I can't bring myself to say the word suicide out loud, but I don't have to. She says it for me.

'I read about his death in the paper. He jumped, they said. How very sad.'

'Oh God,' I stutter. 'I'm so sorry you had to read about Danny's death in the paper. Did no one tell you?'

The lady puts down her teacup, and it falls to one side unsupported by the flaky clay.

'I'm sorry,' she whispers. 'I think I've misled you. I didn't know Daniel, sorry, Danny, when he was alive.'

My stomach knots, and my eyes narrow as I take in the look on her face. 'Then why are you here? You've laid flowers and everything.' My gaze drops to the pretty white lilies.

'Because, like I said, no one should ever be that lonely. There are no other flowers here. I thought it would be nice to leave some.'

'We weren't supposed to leave flowers,' I snap, defensively. 'It said so in the text message I got when Danny died.'

The lady's face scrunches, and she looks even older. I can't tell what she's thinking, but her eyes are burning into me, and I suspect she's judging me.

'I got a text when Danny died. I'm not sure who from, really,' I explain. 'I thought it was someone in his family, but then I couldn't find any family at the funeral.'

I stop abruptly and bow my head. I've no idea why I feel the need to defend myself to a perfect stranger.

The lady pulls a folded white tissue out of her coat pocket and passes it to me.

'I'm sorry,' she whispers. 'The last thing I meant to do was upset you. I work here, at the graveyard, you see. Well, I volunteer. Just a little cleanup here and there. I pull up the odd weed, and I sweep the leaves off the paths. That sort of thing. Every now and then, I spot a lonely grave, and I leave flowers or maybe a candle. I certainly never meant to interfere or hurt anyone. I really am sorry.'

I dab under my eyes with the tissue and sniffle. 'So you really aren't Danny's friend?'

'No,' she says. 'I never had the pleasure of knowing him.'

'But you brought tea. And digestives.' I point. 'They were Danny's favourite.'

'Just a coincidence, I'm afraid.' She sighs. 'The hot tea keeps me warm inside on a day like today.'

My breath is jagged and laced with tears. I try to hide my disappointment, but I feel like she can see through me as clear as if I were made of glass.

'But Danny sounds like a man with good taste. Digestives are my favourite too,' she soothes.

I slug some tea, desperate for the warmth in my mouth.

'Are you related?' she asks after a brief, awkward silence.

'Danny and I?' I beam, realising that just saying his name makes me warmer than the tea ever could. 'No. We were just friends. But Danny was like a father to me.'

The lady nods and munches on another biscuit.

'My father died when I was a baby,' I explain.

'Oh, I'm very sorry,' she says, her mouth full of mushy biscuit. 'That must have been very hard for you. And for your mother.'

'I don't remember him,' I confess. 'My mother remarried when I was eight. We get on okay, I guess. But she's closer to my younger sister, Lucy. Lucy, my mom, and my stepdad are a family. I've always been the spare part on the edge of that. Danny was the nearest thing to family I had. He helped me though a very hard time when I was young. He helped me a lot.'

I shake my head and cover my mouth with my hand. I'm desperate to stop my rambling. In spite of the freezing wind, I feel the heat in my cheeks as they flush with embarrassment. I'm usually painfully reserved, so I've no idea why I just blurted out my family sob story to a complete stranger.

'Danny sounds like a wonderful man,' she pacifies.

'He was.' I sigh.

She finally twists the open end of the biscuits towards me and shakes the packet as she offers me some. I grab one just as it falls out and devour it.

'May I have another,' I say, blushing.

'Here, have them all,' she says, passing me the packet. 'You look like you need them.'

She takes my empty teacup from my other hand and tosses it gently into her plastic bag and begins to tidy away her flask and her own cup. I feel a sting of disappointment as I suspect she's getting ready to leave.

'You need to take care of yourself,' she says, standing up and placing her hands on the small of her back as if it aches. 'I know losing someone you care about is very hard, but it's no

109

reason to skip meals. You and that other girl look like you're fading away.'

'That other girl?' I echo, standing up.

'Yes,' she says, concentrating on checking her little plastic bag and only offering me a fraction of her attention. 'I thought you were sisters, at first. You're both around the same age, I think. And you both look too skinny to be healthy – no offence.'

I shake my head. 'None taken.'

Silence falls over us again, but this time, it's more frustrating than awkward.

'This girl,' I pry shamelessly. 'Does she visit Danny's grave too?'

'Yes. A lot. That's why I assumed she was a daughter. She was even here in the middle of the night on Saturday, apparently. One of the Neighbourhood Watch men spotted her. Poor girl.'

'That's odd,' I say. 'To come to a graveyard in the middle of the night. I'd be scared.'

'Of ghosts?' she teases. 'It's not the dead you need to be afraid of; it's the living that you need to watch out for.'

I scrunch my face. Her cliché rings a little too true with me now as I think of David and his boss making love all weekend.

'Do you know her name?' I ask, trying to block out the images of my husband that are coming to mind.

'No. I tried introducing myself earlier this afternoon, but she literally ran away as soon as she heard my voice. I thought she was going to break her neck. She had a big floppy hood covering half her face. She couldn't possibly see out properly under that thing. I don't understand the way young people dress nowadays. Anyway, I hope I didn't scare her off. I hope she comes back. I'll try offering her tea next time.'

A big floppy hood, I think, remembering the girl in the church at the funeral. It must be her. I wonder who she is. Danny never mentioned anyone, but she must know him well. Otherwise, she wouldn't visit his grave. I wish I knew her name or where to find her. It would be great to have someone to reach out to who knew Danny too. Maybe we could reminisce. I find myself growing pathetically excited about the possibility that someone out there knew Danny the way I did.

'Anyway,' she says, her quivering voice cutting across my daydreaming. 'I'd best be on my way. You hang on to those biscuits and eat up. Maybe, I'll see you again soon.'

'Yeah, maybe. And thanks. For the biscuits. And for the tea. It was nice to meet you.'

I watch as she shuffles away; she's even more hunched now than earlier, and I find myself genuinely hoping we meet again.

I wait until she's completely out of view to allow myself to cry. I lean over the grave and gag on bubbles of my own spit and mucus. The raised mound of clay doesn't look anything like a grave yet. It's obvious at a glance that it's freshly dug. Obvious that the body committed to the earth was a real person, alive and breathing just days ago, and now, it boils down to nothing more than dark brown soil piled loosely in the shape of a rectangle. If I didn't know Danny's coffin was buried here, if I hadn't seen them lower the pine box into the ground with my own eyes, I wouldn't believe he was down there. And even after seeing the coffin, I'm not sure I trust Danny was inside. Danny was just so full of life and love.

People like that don't die. Not suddenly. Not without saying goodbye.

It was a closed coffin at the church. There was no opportunity to lean over the side, kiss Danny's forehead, and tell him I'll miss him. There was no chance for one last look at his face. No time to make one last memory. Trains don't leave pretty corpses.

Clouds of dark thought close in on the corners of my mind, like a sudden storm. I try to block them out, try to claw my way back to brightness, but I'm fighting a losing battle. I know to let the hurricane ride its course inside my head. Fighting will only leave me exhausted, and in the end, I'll succumb to the power of my mind anyway.

I scurry backwards to the bench I'd caught out of the corner of my eye on the way in. My knees are beginning to give way, and I need to sit. The bench is dilapidated and in need of attention where the varnish has chipped, and the weeds are almost as tall as the four wooden legs they hug. The timber slats are damp and freezing, and I buck away a couple of times before committing my full weight to sit. The cold pierces through my jeans and burrows its way into my bones. But the icy bench is a calming contrast to my burning thoughts as my mind races. My breath catches in my throat as if it's laced with glue. I'm an inferno on the inside, but outside, my body is cool and calm. That's a first. Usually, when I lose it like this, I'm a complete mess all over. But anyone looking at me right now would have no idea of the torment going on inside my brain.

I think about Amber, and I shake my head. I've never met her. I only know what she looks like because of that photo I received of her and David cuddled together. I dry retch thinking of it. I hate that she looked pretty in it. And confident. She definitely looked self-assured. The total opposite of me. David said she's not much older than we are, so thirty-five—maybe. She's senior management, so obviously, she is as ambitious as she is attractive. Amber seems like the type of woman who could have whatever or, in this case, *whoever* she sets her mind to. Why the hell did she set her sights on a married man? *Bitch.*

My thoughts drift to the stupid troll getting their kicks out of tormenting me online. I don't know what they look like. I don't even know if they're male or female or what age they are. Two strangers. Two intruders dare to wreak havoc on my life. *Screw them*, I decide, suddenly defiant. The fire inside me grows until even the tips of my fingers tremble and burn. And it takes me a moment to realise that what I'm feeling is different from usual. This fire isn't guilt or self-disgust. I don't burn with hatred for myself. *I hate them.*

I've hurt myself too often. I've damaged my flesh and my soul. Danny spent years piecing my fractured mind back together. Two strangers don't get to tear me down again. I'll be brave, and I'll get through this. And I'll do it for Danny. It's then I realise; it's time to go home.

Chapter Sixteen

AMBER

The sitting room couch feels lumpy beneath me. I've been sitting in the same spot for a couple of hours without moving. The same spot David slept in last night. I shudder just thinking about his restless, clammy body lying on my cream leather.

My thumb aches from repeatedly refreshing my Facebook newsfeed on my phone and scrolling through reams of text messages. I've a tonne of messages from the girls in the office. But I don't have a single one from David. I thought he'd at least text to check if I'm okay. But he was a mess when I dropped him off at his place earlier, so I doubt he knows his arse from his elbow right now. There was no way he'd be able to hold it together in front of his wife. I suspect he's crumbled and told her already.

I was surprised by how boring and normal David and Emma's house seemed. A red brick, semi-detached, two-story in a tidy cul-de-sac. It's nestled in a sleepy part of an old estate with mature trees, well-kept gardens, and kids running around on the green. It's no doubt a tight-knit community of family homes. I bet their neighbours like them. I bet they are invited around for dinner parties and summer barbecues. I bet they know all their neighbours by their first names, and they wave to each other every morning. I snort as the bitter sting of jealousy hurts my head. But their neighbours don't know them. Not really. Not the way I know them. Their neighbours only see what's on the outside. They see what David and Emma want them to see. The picture-perfect couple. Young, newly married, and so in love. They don't know what they're capable of. They don't know what *Emma* has done. But I do.

Evening falls outside my window, slowly sweeping away the brightness of daylight. There's a light rain out there, and it's getting dark earlier than usual, even for November. I stand up and draw the curtains. I spin around and take a moment to savour the darkness and silence. But my phone begins buzzing, and I remember what I'm supposed to be doing. I remember my plan. I read the most recent text.

Hi, Amber.

Just checking in, hun.

Are you okay?

Hun? I roll my eyes and practically gag on the stupid terms of endearment women use for each other. I barely know this girl. Giselle something-or-other. Even seeing her name appear before her text, I struggle to put a face to the name. But I know her nosy streak will work to my advantage. I flick on the lamp on the low, corner table next to me and sit on the floor just inside the window. I try to get comfortable, knowing I could be here for a while if all goes according to plan. Another message follows.

Sweetie. Seriously.

I'm starting to worry.

Just let me know you got home okay?

I grin so brightly I can feel the muscles beside my ears twitch. Giselle saw me leave the office with David. She knew he was driving me home. Does she really think something might have happened along the way? Without me even saying a word, she already doubts his character. *Oh, this is too easy.*

I close my eyes and breathe out heavily through my open mouth. My reply is paramount. I need to steer this in the right direction, but I have to be subtle. Giselle isn't the brightest bulb, but when it comes to gossip, I get the impression she's goddamn Einstein at sniffing out bullshit.

Hey.

Thanks for your messages.

I'm okay … I think.

I hit send and realise I'm twitching nervously as I wait for her reply. Seconds tick by slowly, turning to minutes. She doesn't reply. *Shit. Was I too subtle?* I can't send another message. It'll look like I'm trying too hard. I stand up and kick the corner table, sending the lamp crashing to the ground. I wish someone less dim was prying into my life. Giselle is no use. I need an alternative.

I remember the Facebook friend request earlier. *That'll do nicely.* I pick up the lamp, am relieved the bulb didn't crack, and place it back on the table. *No harm done.* I scurry to the sideboard under the television and open the top drawer, pulling out my laptop excitedly. I can't wait to get typing. Giddy bubbles fizz in my stomach, and I wonder why I wasted an afternoon waiting for David to make the first move when I could have been in control all along. I'll beat myself up about that later; right now, I'm too enthused to think about that.

I make my way back to the couch, and by the time I sit down, I have my laptop open, turned on, and ready to go. I chew my bottom lip as I try various combinations of emails and passwords to log in to Facebook. None are right. I set the Sun Lee account up in such a hurry earlier I can't remember what the hell security I used. Frustrated at my own stupidity, I open the spreadsheet I created over the weekend. I scroll through the list of identities, photos, and the corresponding emails and passwords. Each set creating a fake person. I've been meticulous in my detail, so I don't trip myself up. The accounts are nothing more than a name and a basic profile picture, usually scenery or something equally non-specific.

I'm wasting my time because I know the Sun Lee account won't be on the list. I created him in a fit of blind panic, and I'm paying the price now with no login details. *Dammit.* I try one last attempt, but when I'm still denied access, I begin to lose my temper. I need to be consistent. I need a single account following me. Just one simple name. Anything more is messy and makes me look paranoid. Paranoid like Emma. I smirk as I remember all the fun I had tormenting her over the weekend, right under her husband's nose.

Finally, I remember the login details and access the Sun Lee account. *Eu-fucking-reka!* I slide my laptop off my knees and rest it down next to me, relieved as the cool air hits my sweaty calves. I pace to the kitchen and fling open the cupboard under the sink. I crouch and pull out air freshener, bleach, and a box of dishwasher tablets and let them fall messily on the tiles. My eyes widen, and I purr loudly as I spy the bottle of vodka nestled behind some washing up liquid and grab it. I don't bother to waste time searching for a glass. I unscrew the cap and throw it away. Sticking the rim right under my nose, I inhale until the pressure makes my eyes want to pop. My mouth salivates as I begin to imagine the burn of alcohol as it flashes past my tongue. I fumble on the floor with my free hand and find the cap. My shaking fingers create a tedious task as I try to screw the cap back on. Finally, I succeed. I stuff the cuboid glass bottle back into the cupboard, only relaxing when I feel the resistance of the wall back against my force. I pick up all the cleaning agents off the floor and place them back in order of height, tallest first, in front of the bottle of vodka. I'm hiding the vodka from myself. It's routine.

I make my way back to the sitting room, stopping every couple of steps to toss my head over my shoulder and eye up the cupboard. I sit in the same lumpy spot on the couch as I did earlier and once again, rest my laptop on my knee. I type Emma's full name into the Facebook search box, and her profile picture is the first to appear in the dropdown menu below. Her cheesy grin in her profile photo, as she sits cross-legged on a sandy beach somewhere sunny and tranquil, irritates the shit out of me. Her clear skin and green-brown eyes mean she always comes out better in photos than in real life. Just another thing to hate about her, I guess. I imagine David took the photo on their honeymoon. It's dated six months ago, so that adds up. I can't access her photo albums because the paranoid freak has everything she possibly can set on private. But I can see her profile pictures. All of them. Past and present. *They will have to do.*

Clicking through, I'm disappointed to discover there aren't many. Emma appears to have only joined Facebook in the last couple of years, and she doesn't change the image representing her account often. I flick through more of Emma's boring, smiling poses, but I stop on one, very distinct photo. It's a generic image that she's probably downloaded from the internet, but she's tagged David, and I know why. The picture is somewhat blurry; a pink cushion resting on a cream sofa, but it's the writing on the cushion that catches my eye. *Sometimes a hug says more than words ever could.* It's a corny cliché, but it obviously has some sweet, deeper meaning between the two of them. It's perfect and exactly what I'm looking for.

I save the image to my desktop and immediately upload it as Sun Lee's new profile picture. Emma shared the photo almost two years ago, but it didn't garner many likes. Most people will have forgotten or never have noticed. But I'm counting on David to remember. I cross my fingers that he'll recognise the slushy words as soon as he sees them.

My phone buzzes, and I reluctantly pull my attention away from my laptop to check my messages. Giselle again. *Good.*

You only think you're okay?

Amber, that doesn't sound good.

Did David Lyons upset you?

He was acting really weird today.

Giselle doesn't know it, but her message has just made my day, and we're about to become very, very good friends. Another follows.

He didn't come on to you or something, did he?

I shuffle on the spot and squeal excitedly. Giselle is suddenly my new favourite person. *Lucky girl.* I consider hitting the green call icon beside her name, but crying down the phone to her is a bit too nineteen nineties rom-com to be believable. I need to be classy and reserved. If Giselle has to drag the story out of me, it will work to my advantage down the line. I decide to allow my silence to give her time to draw her own conclusions. I'm confident about what the nosy bitch will decide. As predicted, a third text comes through in as many minutes.

You can tell me.

You know I won't tell anyone.

119

'On the contrary,' I say out loud as if I'm not alone. 'I'm relying on you to tell everyone.'

My fingers punch a reply. I'm so excited; I hope autocorrect can rescue my ramblings and make sense of my letters.

I don't want to talk about it.

I'm too upset.

I send my cryptic reply and switch off my phone. I know Giselle will be bursting to talk it over. When I'm not available, she'll presumably try, but fail, to keep the secret. She'll have to tell someone. Even if she only tells one other person, they may just be enough to get the rumour started.

The fan on my laptop kicks in loudly, summoning my attention back to the screen. Just in case braindead Giselle doesn't shoot her mouth off, I decide to back up our last text with some viral evidence.

Still logged in as Sun Lee, I search for myself on Facebook. Surprisingly, there's quite a few Amber Hunters, and it takes me a while to find myself. Having deleted the Sun Lee friend request earlier under David's watchful eye, I can't simply send myself another. I could make up some bullshit excuse about thinking Sun Lee was one of our Asian clients, but I've underestimated David before. He's not the pushover I suspected, and I know he wouldn't believe that reasoning. The only alternative is to make my personal account public and visible to everyone. I'd rather not go there, but it's the only inconspicuous solution. I lean forward and pick my phone up off the low coffee table directly in front of me. I open the Facebook app and casually scroll though my settings. I make the necessary amendments and sit back and relax with a pronounced sigh. My account is now an open, internet scrapbook of photos and comments. Anyone and everyone are free to flick through with the click of a button and spy on everything I share. I feel painfully exposed, like leaving the house naked, but bare and vulnerable is exactly what I'm aiming for online.

Many people have open Facebook accounts. Bloggers, vloggers and general attention seekers. It's all about having one thousand followers these days. Amber Hunter is just on trend. People will believe that.

I rest my phone down on the cushion next to me with the screen facing upwards. My wrists hover over my laptop keyboard, poised and ready to type. Choosing my words is causing my tongue to tingle as I repeatedly flick it over and back across my top teeth. It's exhilarating being someone else. The freedom to do and say as I please is addictive. My mind wanders to the bottle of vodka under the kitchen sink. I smack my lips together, almost biting my tongue as I remember the taste. It's been so long. Five years next month. Five whole years since I tasted so much as one drop of alcohol.

Addiction is my least favourite word. That word has defined me almost all my life. *Once an addict, always an addict.* I shrug and roll my eyes. *Fuck that!*

Sun Lee is only a figment of my imagination, but he's having a more profound effect on me than drugs or booze. He's the greatest weapon I possess. Emma Lyons ruined my life. Revenge will taste so much better than a five-year-old bottle of cheap Russian vodka ever could.

My fingers take on a life of their own, and I smirk as the sublimely rootless words appear on my laptop screen as I type. I'm logged into Facebook as Sun Lee on my laptop, and I'm logged in as Amber Hunter on my phone. This is too much bloody fun.

YOU CHEAP HUSBAND-STEALING WHORE. I'M WATCHING YOU!!!!

My phone beeps obediently. I laugh out loud as I pick it up and read the slanderous words plastered across my real Facebook page by, what convincingly appears to be, some Asian guy with a profound proverb as his profile picture. *It's fucking perfect.* I drop my head back, exhale deeply, and wait for someone to notice that Amber Hunter is a helpless victim of cyber bullying.

Chapter Seventeen

EMMA

Dusk falls, causing obedient street lamps to flicker as I make my way home. Traffic is heavy in the town square, and chaos at the traffic lights erupts as everyone loses patience on their commute home from work. David regularly complains about the backlog of traffic getting through the junction close to our estate. I see what he means, and it makes me smile as I recognise I'm close to home.

I'm walking quickly. My hips waddle as they try to keep up with my feet. I've passed feeling cold. I'm almost numb. My jeans are soaking from the knees down because some idiot in a 4x4 drove through a giant puddle and splashed a small tsunami all over the footpath and me. I can feel the denim start to harden, and I suspect some damp patches are turning to ice. They scrape against my legs like sandpaper. It's becoming a physical battle with my body to continue propelling myself forward. Part of me just wants to lie down, in this exact spot, and maybe never get up again. But I'm so close to home. When the wide mouth of my estate comes into view, despite being exhausted, I begin to run. Slowly at first, but by the time I hit my cul-de-sac, I'm really sprinting.

I jump onto the low step at my front door with renewed energy. Clenching my fist, I pound on the green, timber door until it rattles on its hinges. Nothing happens. I bang harder. I pause, bend forward, and suck huge gulps of air in through my open mouth. I scurry off the step and shuffle to one side, eyeing up the hideous, potted plant David's mother gave us as a

Christmas present last year. I'm certain I'm going to throw up, so I decide I'll aim there. But vomit doesn't come, and neither does an answer at the door. It takes me until now to realise David's car is missing from the front drive, and no lights are on inside the house. David's not home. He's left me. *Oh. My. God.* I have no key. No phone. And no composure. I make my way back to the front step and sit down. I drop my head between my legs and hope that it will help to ease the palpitations in my chest. It doesn't. Sudden, loud ringing assaults my ears. Darkness swoops across my eyes as if someone is closing a tiny, black-out shutter over my face and I have no way of opening it again. I know fainting is imminent and impossible to fight off.

When I open my eyes again, I scream. A hand is gripping my shoulder tightly, shaking me.

'Emma. Emma, wake up! Jesus Christ, you're freezing. How long have you been out here?'

I recognise Kim's voice before my eyes adjust and allow me to take in her face. It takes me a while to notice she's frantic.

'Eh … eh …' I stutter, the noise rattling up from somewhere between my stomach and my throat.

'C'mon,' Kim says softly as she slides her arms under mine as if she's a mother scooping up a toddler.

I try to cooperate, but my limbs are floppy, and I make her task almost impossible.

'Here, let me help,' a male voice suggests.

Kim steps to one side, and a broad, tall man takes her place.

'Should we take her to the hospital?' Kim asks.

'No.' He shakes his head.

'But she could have hypothermia or something.'

'She'll be fine.' He crouches, and even though he's a big guy, he makes it right down to my level so his eyes can meet mine. 'We just need to get her inside, Kim.'

He reaches out to me, but I jolt away, and my back stiffens like a startled cat.

'C'mon now, Emma.' He sighs. 'You're really cold. Too cold. Let me help you.'

I shake my head.

'Emma, this is Andy,' Kim explains. 'You met him in the club, remember?'

I nod.

'Good. Now, let him help you.'

I nod again.

'Okay, Emma,' Andy says. 'I'm going to pick you up now, all right?'

'Yeah. Okay.'

Andy slides one arm under the back of my knees and his other arm wraps around my back. He raises me into his firm arms and holds me against his chest as he stands up. I instinctively nestle against him. His body feels like a furnace against me, and I shamelessly take comfort in his touch.

Kim brushes past us and jiggles a key in the lock. I'd given her a spare key when David and I went on our honeymoon so she could check in on our place. I'd been meaning to ask her for it back, but I kept forgetting. *Thank goodness.*

The front door swings open, and the heat of the house wafts towards me like a warm summer breeze. Kim and Andy waste no time hurrying inside. Kim feverishly drops her arm behind her and presses her palm against the door shutting it with a loud bang. I stiffen instinctively, and Andy's safe arms tighten around me, attempting to silently settle me.

'The bathroom is upstairs, second door on the left,' Kim says.

Andy makes his way up the stairs with me securely cradled against his warm chest. Kim trots closely behind us. Reaching the bathroom, Andy uses his foot to push the ajar door wide open. Kim races over to the bath, bends down, and twists on the tap while Andy makes his way towards the loo. Using his foot again, he gently kicks the lid down and lowers me to sit on top.

'The water's hot, thank God,' Kim gushes.

Andy grabs the clean towel hanging over the edge of the bath and wraps it around my shoulders.

'Okay, great,' he says. 'Fill it up as fast as you can. Turn on the cold tap too. It'll speed it up. Lukewarm water is fine to start. She's so cold that we need to build her temperature back up slowly anyway. Don't want to shock the shit out of her.'

'Yeah, okay. Good idea,' Kim gasps.

'You're really cold, Emma,' Andy explains. 'It's not good.'

I like Andy, I decide. His voice is soft, and he sounds like he really cares about making sure I'm okay.

'Kim, stand here, yeah?' Andy says.

He has a hand on each of my shoulders, and he doesn't let go until Kim is right beside me ready to grab on.

'I have her,' Kim says, triumphant.

'Right! Good. Let the water keep running.' Andy tosses his head over his shoulder and looks at the bath filling up quickly. 'I'm going downstairs. I'll make some soup or something.'

Warm her up from the inside out too.' Andy turns back to face me, and his whole face smiles. 'You hungry, Emma?'

Food. Oh, my God, I'm starving. Just the mention of food makes my mouth water.

'Yeah,' I manage.

'Good. That's good.' Andy winks. 'I'm going to root around in your kitchen and make something to warm you up, okay?'

'Okay.'

'Kim. You good with her?'

'I got her,' Kim blubbers.

'She's fine, Kim,' Andy promises. 'Stop worrying!'

Kim agrees with such excessive head jerking that I can feel her hands shake as her fingers dig into my shoulders.

'Emma, you're fine,' Andy calms me. 'Just cold and hungry. But fine. I'll be back in a few minutes.'

Kim waits until Andy is out of earshot to berate me. 'Sweet God, what were you thinking? You're like a feckin' ice cube, do you know that?'

My head bobs up and down like a child in my class whom I scold for pulling another child's hair.

'Sorry,' I mumble somewhat incoherent.

'Oh, Emma,' Kim softens. 'I was so worried.'

Guilt weighs my stomach down like an anvil. My whole intestines tighten and a loud rumbling noise rattles around inside me. I pray I won't have a sudden onset of diarrhoea.

'I really am sorry.' I drop my head. 'I didn't mean to freak you out.'

'It's okay,' Kim says, sliding her finger under my chin and tilting my head up again until I've no choice but to look at her. 'David told me.'

I close my eyes. The noise of the bath running imitates the pounding of my blood coursing through my veins.

'Told you what?' I say, my eyes burning I slam them so tightly shut.

'Oh, Emma. Don't. Don't torture yourself. We don't have to talk about this now. David was worried about you. He still loves you.'

I snort roughly, dragging my upper body forward. Kim steadies me.

'So David phoned you, then?' I say.

'Yeah.'

'When? He doesn't have a phone? He lost his at the weekend.'

'Really? Well, he must have bought a new one because he called a while ago. He had no idea where you were, and he was freaking out.'

'He thought I'd be with you?' I roll my eyes, pissed off that he has no doubt dipped into our house savings to buy the latest goddamn iPhone.

'Yeah, I guess so. He got really upset when you weren't with me. And when you weren't at your mother's either, he called back and asked me to help look for you.'

'He called my mother?' I squawk. 'Oh, great.'

'Emma, he was beside himself. I could hear it in his voice.'

I run my hand over the top of my head and down my hair. 'He thought I might do something stupid, didn't he?'

Kim nods slowly. 'Yeah. Maybe. I guess.'

'And did you? Did you think I'd run off and try to top myself?'

'No. But at least I know why you freaked out and tried it years ago. David doesn't. So he can't possibly understand.'

'Yeah.' I sigh.

The sting of hypocrisy blisters. David couldn't keep his affair secret from me, and I hate him for it. I resent him for telling me as much as I resent him for sleeping with Amber. Yet all these years, I've been hiding a huge secret from him. *I'm a bitch.* I tell myself that I hide the truth because I'm protecting him. Maybe I'm lying to myself as much as I'm lying to him. Perhaps, I should tell him. I should just phone him up right now and confess. It would put us on equal ground. One terrible mistake versus another. Would they cancel each other out then? Could we just go back to normal then? Could we just forgive each other and pretended like we're both okay? But I know life doesn't work that way. Even if David could forgive me, I could never forgive myself. And I could never, ever forget.

'Emma. Emma, you okay?' Kim clicks her fingers close to my face.

'Yeah. Just cold,' I lie.

'I know what you're thinking.'

I stare at Kim, raising a sceptical eyebrow.

'No need to look at me like that,' Kim moans. 'Emma, you were seventeen. You were just a kid, and you made the right decision. Seriously.'

'He cheated on me, Kim. David cheated on me.'

'I know. It's shit.'

'But I don't deserve to be mad.'

'Eh, Yes. You. Do. You should be furious. I am.'

'But what I did was worse. Way worse.'

'It was different. Very different. It was a long time ago, Emma. You can't keep beating yourself up. It won't change anything.'

I clasp my hands and bang them gently against my nose. I can't think; my mind is like quicksand and every rational thought is sinking.

'What did you say?' I finally ask, concentrating so hard my eyes bulge as I look at Kim.

'I said guilt won't change anything.'

'No. I mean what did you say to David? What did you say when he told you he'd cheated on me?'

'Nothing. There was nothing to say, and it wasn't my place anyway.'

'Were you angry?'

Kim lets go of me for the first time to shrug. 'Dunno. I honestly didn't think about it. I was just concerned with finding you. That's all.'

I smile, but it does little good to hide the tears collecting in the corners of my eyes. I must look ridiculous as I try not to blink, hoping to hold the waterworks at bay.

'Andy and I drove around for ages looking for you,' Kim explains. 'David was doing the same.'

My cheeks burn, and it's becoming increasingly difficult to hide my embarrassment.

'You okay sitting there if I check on the water?' Kim asks.

I nod, relieved when Kim turns her back and I can wipe my eyes unnoticed.

'Where's David now?' I ask, as Kim rolls up her sleeve and dips her elbow into the bath as if she's testing the temperature for a small child.

Kim pauses, turns around, and takes a deep breath. 'At his mother's.'

'Of course, he is,' I growl, the realisation twisting in my stomach like a blunt knife. 'I bet his mother is loving this. Her favourite goddamn words are I told you so.' I jerk from side to side on the loo. 'I told you not to marry her. I told you she was crazy,' I mimicked in a painfully high-pitched voice.

'Yeah well, he told her to fuck off and married you anyway, so that's all that matters in the end.'

I'm about to add something bitchy and sarcastic about him sleeping with his boss when I hear Andy at the top of the stairs.

'That looks full enough, Kim ' he says softly, looking into the bath from the doorway. 'I couldn't find any soup, so I just made some tea. I hope you like tea, Emma.'

I drop my face into my hands, and I can't battle my emotions any longer. Tears fall uncontrollably. I can't see the expression Andy makes, but I guess he looks confused because Kim begins to explain about Danny and tea and our ritual at the train station.

I feel a warm hand on my knee, and I look up to see Andy crouched next to me.

'I'm sorry,' he whispers. 'I didn't know.'

His eyes are glassy, and his whole face, even his ears, is pale. He seems genuinely distressed that he has upset me. Although I barely know the guy, I suspect Kim may have found a keeper.

'I just miss him,' I explain with a rough cough.

'Of course.'

'C'mon, Emma. Let's get you into the bath,' Kim says.

I suck air roughly through my nose until it makes a squeaking sound, and my whole body stiffens. Andy sets the cup of tea down on the back of the sink next to us. My eyes follow his every move.

'Maybe I should help her by myself,' Kim says, moving closer.

I drive my spine into the back of the toilet and sit rigidly. My eyes dart from Kim to Andy and back to Kim. I repeat, giving myself a headache.

'It's okay.' Andy softens even more. 'You can keep all your clothes on, Emma. We just want to bring your body temperature up. The only things we need to take off are your shoes. Is that okay?'

My hands ache where the cold has bitten my fingers, and the heat of the house attempts to thaw them out again.

Andy slides his arm around my waist and hooks his other arm under the back of my knees. He's pretty strong, and his calm demeanour helps to make this all feel a fraction less awkward. I'd like to tell him I'm okay and at least make my own way into the bath, but my legs are cramping like I've run a marathon and every little twitch burns. Before I have time to overthink it, Andy is lowering me into the bath. I can't help but let out a relieved groan as the warm water instantly softens my stiff jeans. The water soaks through my blouse and caresses my icy skin. I drop my head back on the ledge and close my eyes.

'Thank you,' I whisper, sliding a little lower, submerging my shoulders.

Silence reigns, and I open my eyes to find Kim sitting on the edge of the bath, the cup of tea in her hand.

'You'll be okay, Emma,' she says, waiting for me to sit up straight before she passes me the cup. 'You always have me. No matter what.'

Chapter Eighteen

EMMA

I throw back the duvet and slide my legs over the edge of the bed. Kim had insisted I go for a lie down after my bath, and even though I protested that I wasn't tired, I'd manged to sleep for a while. It's pitch black in my bedroom—the wonky street lamp at the end of the cul-de-sac must finally have given up—as not even so much as the moonlight shines in through the heavy curtains. I pat my hand around on the bedside table, searching for my phone to check the time. Groggily, I remember I left it downstairs and haven't had it all day. I stretch my arms out in front of me at shoulder level, patting the air all around me. Making my way towards the door, I hope I don't crash into anything along the way.

I'm relieved to find the landing light is on, and I squint as I adjust to the brightness. My legs are wobbly, and my calves are so bruised and achy, I feel like someone has beaten me up. I'm wearing one of David's old rugby jerseys, and it comes down to my knees, but the timber floorboards drive cold through my bare feet all the way up to my knees. I'm about to dash back into my bedroom to grab my dressing gown when voices coming from downstairs distract me. The words are muffled as they carry through the ceiling, but I can tell they're male voices. Two men, and they're arguing, I think. I scurry downstairs, forgetting about my bruised muscles, and stop outside the closed kitchen door.

It's David. I recognise his voice straight away. *He came home.* He's hysterical. I think he's crying. It's hard to tell. I press my ear against the door and try to garner a better picture of what's going on.

'Emma's fine, man. Calm down,' Andy comforts.

My eyes narrow. I'm not fine. I'm healthy, if that's what Andy means, but my husband slept with his boss on the day I buried my best friend. I am definitely not bloody *fine,* and I don't know how I feel about a stranger telling my husband that I am. I know Andy's only trying to help, but it's mortifying that Andy is meeting us for the first time under these circumstances. He must think we're insane.

'Thanks. Thanks for your help,' David says firmly.

There's a moment of silence, and I wonder if they're shaking hands or something. They don't know each other so a hug would be too much, and David's not the physical type anyway. I'm really the only person he ever touches. Or I was. Until Amber.

The silence continues, and I wonder if I should go in and rescue David from the awkwardness. But I'm not sure I can hold it together if I see him, and I don't want to be a mess in front of Andy. Not again. I wait and hope I'll hear Kim's voice trying to lighten the atmosphere. I don't.

Footsteps make their way towards the door on the other side, and I panic, knowing that someone is going to open it and find me standing in the hall. I scurry to the bottom step of the stairs and sit, pulling my knees into my chest. My heart is pounding, and my palms grow sweaty. I'm hiding like a scared child from a monster. David's not a monster, and I know it. Any normal person would march into the kitchen and kick his cheating ass out. But I'm not normal, and I know that too. I don't want him to leave. He's all I have. He's my everything. I can't lose him. I won't cope. I slide my hand inside the neck of the rugby shirt and pull it away from my skin; even with the top buttons open and me tugging at it desperately, it doesn't help relieve the pressure as it becomes a struggle to breathe. I open my mouth wide and gasp. I feel the air come into my mouth, but it can't make its way down my throat. My heartbeat quickens and ribs shrink until they're so tiny and tight I worry they'll pierce straight through my heart. I want to call for someone to help me, but just as air can't make its way down, words can't make their way out. Beads of cold perspiration trickle down my spine and rest on the band of my knickers. Shaking, I spread my legs and drop my head between my knees. Close to passing out, I begin to count backwards from fifty. I attempt to inhale on the beat of every fifth number. I breathe out again on the next five. I make it all the way down to twenty before the tightness in my chest eases and the pain subsides. I keep counting down, following the breathing pattern, and at zero, I sit up again. I can breathe. It's still tight, but I'm not suffocating. I have some control. But I can't control the emotional pain boiling in my stomach and bubbling like lava into almost every part of my body.

I rush up the stairs; the heavy beat of my feet against the solid oak pounds loudly, creating the impression that I weigh much more than I do. I scurry into the bathroom, and with my fingers shaking uncontrollably, I fiddle with the key and lock the door behind me. No one remembered to pull the plug on the bath earlier, and a weird, blue-grey scum wraps all the way around the inside of the bath, settling at the rim of the water. *It must be the dye that bled from my jeans*, I think. It's disgusting, and I don't relish the thought of having to bleach to the foamy stain tomorrow.

For a brief moment, I think about sliding under the water with my head down. *How easy all my problems could be solved. I could close my eyes and never open them again.* I notice David's razor on the back of the sink, and my eyes seek out the slender, silver blade. I jerk my eyes away and settle them on the nearest bright colour. My makeup bag. I think about the tweezers I know are inside. Nail scissors, too. My dressing gown is stuffed into the laundry basket and the belt dangles over the side of the cream wicker basket like a sky blue fleece rope—teasing me. It begs me to wrap it tightly around my neck. I slam my eyes shut, wobbling on the spot just inside the door. *Easy options*, I warn myself. *Easy options.*

At some point, I must have leaned my back against the door and slid to the ground because when the pounding comes on the other side, I realise I'm sitting with my knees tucked tightly against my chest, and the bony parts are digging into my boobs.

'Emma. Open the door,' David orders.

I put my hands over my ears.

'Emma!'

The door rattles behind me as David jerks the handle up and down so roughly I'm certain he'll break it.

'Emma, Emma, Emma,' he shouts, pounding his fist against the door furiously.

I stand up and turn around to face the shaking door. I instinctively scurry backwards, half-expecting David to break the door down any second.

'Oh God, Emma. Please. Please just open it.'

My tense shoulders fall, and my head feels too heavy for my neck to support. I understand. David's not angry, he's desperate. He's afraid.

I take a large step forward and turn the key counter clockwise. David's still pounding his fists against the other side and doesn't hear the key turn.

'Baby. Please. Just answer me. Tell me you're okay.'

I don't reply. I can't tell him I'm okay. I'm not okay. But I'm still alive. I haven't hurt myself. Danny would be proud of me today. I cling to that thought.

'Emma. Oh God, baby. Please just let me in. I'm sorry. I'm so sorry. Please open the door.'

My lips are suddenly dry, and they sting and crack as I open my mouth. 'It's open.'

The handle twitches, and before I have time to draw the breath that I desperately need, the door swings open and David charges towards me. He grabs me roughly and gathers me into his arms, pressing my whole upper body into his. I stiffen. I can't bring myself to wrap my arms around him too, even though I'm desperate to feel a tender hug.

David sniffles and snorts, kissing my head over and over between shaky exhales.

'I'm sorry. I'm so sorry. I love you,' he whimpers.

I believe him. I know my husband loves me. I love him too. But the puncture of betrayal is taking its toll. Just like the air seeping from a tyre, the love I feel between David and me is slowly seeping from my heart. David is my air. And just like a tyre without air, I feel deflated and low without my husband's fidelity.

'Emma, say something, please?'

I break away and look David in the eye. His usual sparkle is missing, and his bright, blue pupils look dull and grey like the ocean during a storm. He seems shorter too. As if what he has done is weighing him down so much he's actually shrinking.

'I never meant to hurt you. I swear. You are everything to me, Emma.' David drags his arm under his nose and snivels. 'You're everything. Please forgive me. I'm begging you.'

David stands between the sink and me. Even tilting my head to one side, I can't see around his broad shoulders to catch a glimpse of white porcelain. I can't see my makeup bag or his razor. The laundry basket is behind me, so I can't see that either. David stands between me and all the things that I could use to hurt myself, and I wonder if it's some sort of metaphor. I think I want it to be. All I can see is the bath full of murky water. I force the sleeve of David's rugby shirt up my arm as I step closer to the bath. I lean over and plunge my arm all the way to the elbow into the cold water and pull the plug. I watch as the drain guzzles the water down.

'Okay,' I say, just about audible over the noise of the water draining.

'Okay,' he echoes, uncertain.

I pull my arm back out of the water and shake it off as I stand up straight. 'Okay, I forgive you.'

It's not a complete lie. I *want* to forgive him. But just because I want to doesn't mean I can.

'Oh, Emma.' David grabs me again. This time, I don't balk, but I still don't wrap my arms around him. 'I'll make this up to you. I promise. We'll be okay. We'll be okay. I love you.'

His desperation to make it all better is etched into every worried line of his face. I know how he feels. I've spent the last fourteen years trying secretly to make it up to him.

'David. I … I … I have to tell you something …'

'There you are,' Kim says, appearing at the door. 'C'mon. I've made dinner.'

Kim can't possibly know she's interrupted us just as I was about to confess everything to David. I'm sure she senses the stagnant atmosphere, but I'm also sure she blames David for it. She's glaring at him like she wants to rip his skin off his bones with her bare hands.

'Well, it's takeaway, actually, but I did put it on plates, so it's almost like cooking it myself,' Kim flutters.

David shuffles on the spot like just being near Kim is making him nervous.

'There's some for you too, David,' Kim says, knowingly. 'And I asked Andy to stay too. I hope that's okay. He works tonight, and he won't have time to get home and grab anything before his shift starts.'

'Of course.' I nod. 'He was great today. I need to thank him.'

Kim shrugs. 'Ah, don't worry about it. Andy's cool. It's no big deal to him.'

David grows pale, and I can't read him. I wonder if another man having to all-but-rescue his wife is sitting uncomfortably with him.

'Thanks for today, Kim,' David mumbles.

'You're welcome. But I already know I rock.' Kim jiggles on the spot and uses the back of her hand to jokingly toss her long strawberry-blond hair over her shoulder dramatically. She can't keep a straight face as she laughs.

'Not to mention you're so humble,' I add, reluctantly reaching for David's hand.

He slides his fingers between mine and squeezes, causing my wedding ring to pinch the flesh a bit at the base of my finger, but I don't flinch. The pinch stings, as if it's mocking me. Reminding me of the sting of David's infidelity. But it also reminds me that I'm the one David made a vow to, not that bitch Amber. *For better or worse.* David has seen me at my very worst. *Maybe this is his.*

My thoughts circle in my head like a spinning top. I try to grab on and stop it as it tears through my brain, but I can't. It gains speed with every passing minute, and eventually, it will burst through my skull, and my mind will explode. Maybe that wouldn't be such a bad thing. If I explode, I'll be done. Finished. Gone. Dead!

My moods have always swayed like a pendulum. Dr Brady and David have pleaded with me over the years to try medication. I told them both, more than once, to shove the drugs up their arses. David laughed and said that's exactly the response my bipolar forced me to give. I laughed more and told him to fuck off and stop relying on the internet for information. Google isn't medical school, I've bitched countless times. Of course, Dr Brady wasn't as easy to argue with, and I have about ten unfilled prescriptions stuffed into my sock drawer. I knew I wasn't ill. I was just fucked up in the head because I'd made a huge mistake. But I couldn't tell my husband or doctor that. I've been in a much better place for ages. Years. David and Danny helped me much more than any medication ever could. But my head is all messed up again now.

'Oh, before I forget,' Kim chirps, drawing my attention back to the here and now. She reaches her arm around her hip and pulls something out of her back pocket. 'You left this on the window sill in the kitchen, and it was ringing a few minutes ago.'

'Oh, that's where it was.' I swirl my eyes and take my phone from Kim's hand. 'Thanks.'

'When was it ringing?' David asks.

'Eh, I dunno. Andy heard it. He told me when I got back from picking up the Chinese. He didn't want to answer, and he didn't want to come up and disturb you both, so he just let it ring out.'

'It rang out?'

'Yes. I just said that.' Kim turns her glance towards me and pulls a face.

'So Andy was the only one who heard it ring?' David growls.

The sides of David's nose are growing an unflattering purplish-red, and I know he's slowing losing his temper. I just don't understand why.

'Yes. Well, I wasn't here, was I? And you two were upstairs.' Kim's eyes darken. 'Obviously, Andy wasn't going to come barging into the bathroom, now was he?'

'Can I see that for a minute, Ems?' David stretches his arm out to me and opens his hand.

I pass him my phone. He studies it for a couple of seconds before turning the screen around to show Kim and me.

'It's not showing any missed calls.' David jerks his head to one side. 'Look.'

Kim glances at the phone but quickly turns her attention back to me. She's wide-eyed and obviously looking for a clue about David's strange behaviour from me. But I have no idea why he's acting like this either. I shrug.

'Andy turned the sound off,' Kim says. 'He probably messed up the call log. Sorry, Emma. His phone is an Android, so he's not used to the settings on an iPhone.'

David pulls his chin between his thumb and index finger, and his eyes are rounder than usual with his pupils burning into me. I wish I knew what he is thinking. Maybe Andy makes him suspicious, which is fair enough. We don't know the guy, and he's suddenly become very involved in our life. But that's my doing. And I have an inclination that David's attitude is less about misgiving and more about embarrassment.

'Look, I'm sorry, Emma.' Kim stiffens. 'Andy wasn't snooping or anything. He just didn't want your phone ringing and giving you a fright. I didn't know you were expecting a call. Was it your doctor or someone?'

I squint and glare at Kim, mildly insulted. I don't need to call a doctor because I flipped out earlier. Jesus Christ, anyone would have lost it under the circumstances. I can never get away from the goddamn stigma of crazy bitch.

'I wasn't expecting any important calls,' I calm.

I try to appreciate that Kim is just worried, and I realise how lucky I am to have her as a friend.

'Don't worry about it. It was probably just work anyway. I left early today.' I flick my hand as I throw the suggestion away.

'It can't have been the school calling you.' David snorts. 'It's a new number. I got you a new SIM earlier.'

'What? Why?' I twitch.

'You were all freaked out about that stalker thing, and I just thought it might help.'

'Help take the heat off you,' Kim mumbles.

Kim's jaw squares, and I guess it's from pressing her back teeth together tightly. I can tell David's odd behaviour on top of his infidelity is pushing Kim's temper close to breaking point. Usually, I'd jump to his defence but not today. He deserves every dirty look Kim throws his way. However, I'm glad David doesn't seem to hear her. Kim means well, but I really wish she'd go back downstairs. I don't know how much longer she'll keep her feisty side under control, and I can't handle any more drama today. David and I need some privacy.

'I'm sorry, Ems,' David mumbles. 'I thought I was doing the right thing. I hate seeing you like that.'

'But my phone has all my contacts. All my numbers. They'll all be lost now,' I protest.

'No. No, they won't. We can transfer them over.'

My forehead scrunches, and I don't make any effort to hide how unimpressed I am. 'So you've done that already, then?'

'Well, no. Not yet. I didn't get a chance.'

'Okay, right. Well, obviously someone knows the new number or they wouldn't be calling me.'

'But that's just it.' David uses his free hand to ruffle his hair. 'No one knows it. So I don't get why Andy thinks your phone was ringing. It's weird.'

Kim's expression is so beastly she's practically growling from her pours. 'Eh, not that weird, David. It's probably just the phone company cold calling to check if you got set up with the new number okay. It's just marketing. We do this in work all the time. I wouldn't worry about it.'

143

David's irritation is reaching his breaking point, and I have to pull my hand free from his. His tense grip is cutting off my circulation.

'It's a pay-as-you-go SIM, Kim. Just a packet I picked up off the shelf. The phone company would have no clue who bought it or when. And I doubt they care, either.'

'So who is it then?' I stutter.

My back cracks as I tug my hand away from David and jerk backwards, my feet still cemented to the spot.

'Probably just your mother, Ems. I'm sorry,' David backpedals. 'I called her when I couldn't find you.' David's efforts to sound breezy make his whole body stiff and awkwardly; it would be comical if he wasn't so patronising.

'And you gave her the new number?' I clip.

'There we go. That explains it,' Kim interrupts. 'Now seriously, can we eat? I'm bloody starving.'

'Sure.' David walks out of the bathroom first.

I stuff my phone into my pocket and walk after him. I'm not hungry. In fact, despite only having some digestive biscuits in my tummy, I feel bloated and full. It's odd to think David couldn't lie to me about something as world imploding as sleeping with his boss, but he's confidently lied straight to my face about something as simple as giving my new phone number to my mother. I begin to wonder if I really know my husband at all.

Chapter Nineteen

EMMA

My jerky, dangerous driving pollutes my journey to work. I run a couple of red lights, and it's as if I've completely forgotten indicators exist. Other drivers flash their headlights at me or honk their horn to voice their fear or frustration. I cross my fingers that the cops won't spot me and pull me over. I'm screwed if they breathalyse me because I'm sure I'm still over the limit from last night. I cringe, thinking back on my behaviour at dinner.

Kim had bought a couple of bottles of wine to go with the Chinese takeaway. King Prawn Szechuan and red wine are my favourite combination, so I often overindulge but never quite like last night. I practically raced Kim and David to drain each bottle. By the time they were halfway through their first glass, I was finished and helping myself to another. And another. When Andy explained that he couldn't drink when working, I was delighted and warned everyone rather loudly that I planned to drink Andy's share. I did. And then some. By the time Kim reluctantly left to go home, I was ready to pass out on the sitting room couch. I woke up in my own bed, so David must have carried me upstairs at some point during the night.

I think back on David's sour face when I walked into the kitchen this morning, and I'm so distracted I almost clip the ankles off an elderly lady crossing at pedestrian lights. I raise my hand by way of apology, but she's not impressed and scowls at me. I'm less than ten minutes from work, and I can't wait to get into my classroom and put my head down on my desk. I try to concentrate on the road ahead, but my conversation with David in the kitchen this morning is playing on repeat in my aching brain.

'I think you should call Dr Brady,' David said.

I glared at him with contempt.

'Why?' I snorted as I slid two slices of semi-stale bread into the toaster.

'Emma, you're in a bad place. I'm really worried about you.'

'And what does that have to do with Dr Brady?'

'Well, you said Dr Brady helped you a lot in the past. Will you call him?'

That was when I lost my temper. I threw the tub of butter in my hand across the kitchen, narrowly missing David's head. I don't think I would have even felt bad had I hit him.

'Dr Brady is a medic not a fucking magician, David,' I snapped. 'Unless he can somehow turn back time and stop you from sleeping with Amber, then I don't think he can help me.'

My grip on the wheel tightens, and my hands cramp, my fingers turning white. I turn in the gates of the school, and I'm actually relieved to be running so late. There are no kids running around outside. My head is so fuzzy; it would be terrifying to try to navigate my car around their giddy bodies today.

'I'm so sorry I'm late,' I mutter as I barge into my classroom.

Thirty-two little heads turn around to smile at me, and without overthinking it, I smile back.

'You okay,' Liz says as I make my way to the top of the class. 'We weren't expecting you in today. Richard said you were feeling ill yesterday.'

Liz started as a classroom assistant last year, and we became good friends quickly.

I scrunch my nose and toss her a look that suggests it's a long story. 'I'm much better now,' I lie.

'You sure? You look very pale.'

'Does Richard know I'm running late?' I ask, sidestepping her question on my wellbeing.

'He's not in today,' Liz beams, knowing she's just made my day.

'Phew,' I joke, sliding my handbag under my desk. 'Thanks a mill for looking after my class. I hope they were good.'

'Ah sure, they're little dotes,' Liz says.

I open the rollcall book on my desk and fish around for a black pen.

'Oh, I called the roll already.' Liz grins, triumphant.

'Oh. Okay, thanks.'

'Three absent and one coming in late. His mother called.'

'Okay.' I grimace.

I'm painfully regimental calling the roll, and as I glance at the open book on my desk, I can already see that Liz has used a blue pen and ticked each child's name off the list instead of placing a little x in the boxes provided that correspond with the date. It'll grate on my nerves all day. But I console myself that I'll wait until break time, and I'll fix it then.

'Okay, kids,' I say with a single loud clap of my hands to gain their attention. 'Take out your maths copies and let's go over last night's homework.'

I glance at Liz, smiling, and wait for her to say goodbye.

'I've already gone over their maths homework with them. And their spellings.'

147

I sigh heavily and pull out my chair from under my desk. I need to sit.

'Emma, you sure you're okay?' Liz crouches close to me and softens.

Some curious necks stretch as little eyes stare up at us, but the majority of the children are whispering and chatting among themselves and pay us no attention.

'Yeah. I'm fine.' I shrug.

'It's just …' Liz shuffles on the spot. 'Were you out again last night?'

'Sorry?'

'It's just … oh God, now, don't take this the wrong way, but I can smell it on your breath.'

My hand covers my mouth, and I blush. 'Oh, my God. I'm sorry. I had takeaway last night, and it was loaded with garlic. I've chewing gum in my bag. I'll use that.'

'Actually …' Liz looks even more embarrassed than I am. 'I mean alcohol. It's quite strong, to tell you the truth. Look, Emma, I'm not having a go at you, but it's just if Richard pops by later and gets a whiff, well, you know yourself. He won't be too happy.'

I don't know whether to be pissed off or grateful that Liz mentioned this. I brushed my teeth this morning, of course, and I drank a tonne of water in the car on the way to work. I can't believe I still stink of booze.

'Ah Emma, don't be getting upset. We've all done it from time to time. I just don't want to get you in trouble with the principal.'

'Well, then don't tell him,' I bark.

148

Liz jerks her head back without moving her body; it gives her a stocky double chin, and some of the children begin to laugh.

'Emma. I meant well.' Liz snorts.

'Yeah, I know. Sorry. I'm probably just hungover. Kim was around for dinner last night, and I think I overdid it a little.' I toss my head to one side, smile, and wave my hand in the same direction as my head, hoping to come off as breezy and sociable and not an alcoholic and incompetent.

'God, I know the feeling.' Liz chuckles. 'But I'd definitely munch on some of that chewing gum if I were you. Actually, could I have a piece?'

I duck my head under my desk and rummage in my bag. I pull out my last piece of gum and pass it to Liz. She finally leaves, and I suspect that by the time lunch break comes around, almost every teacher in the school will have heard the gossip about my boozy breath.

Forty minutes later, the children are quietly working away on a tricky word puzzle. It's been an unbearably long morning. I spent most of my time avoiding getting too close to any of the children. The last thing I need is a curious five-year-old telling their parents that Ms Lyons smelt funny in school today. When the bell finally rings, and the children make their way outside to play, I decide to avoid the staffroom. I'm desperate for a coffee, but I can't face the rumour mill. I already struggle with some of the older, more interfering teachers constantly prying about when David and I are going to start a family. Before the wedding, they regularly nagged me about when David was going to pop the question. It's as if they're ticking off milestones in a life events handbook. It's harmless foolery, really, but I can't cope with any jokes today.

I stay sitting at my desk instead, checking my phone. I've lots of message from David. Most are of him telling me how sorry he is for upsetting me again this morning, and the rest are a series of various funny emojis.

I don't know how I feel about his apology. I don't want to get into an argument about seeing a doctor, and I definitely don't want to talk about Amber, so I reply with more emojis. None of a smiley face, though.

In spite of the whirlwind that was the last twenty-four hours, I feel somewhat lighter knowing I can check my phone without the fear of some creep out there trying to get in touch. A new SIM was a good idea. David definitely got that much right. And Kim's suggestion to stay away from social media was logical. No Facebook or Twitter or any of it. My fingers are itching to log in, but I suspect I'll find a tone of nastiness waiting for me in the virtual world. It's a difficult detox. My life has become so entwined with the internet. Checking in on what friends are up to and seeing pictures of their travels or babies. It's part of my everyday routine like brushing my hair or getting dressed, and I feel the loss. Without the online world demanding some of my day, I'll have more time than ever just to think. And right now, I've way too much to think about.

Chapter Twenty

DAVID

I sit behind my desk and glare at the empty seat where Amber's arse should be. I'm not surprised she's not here. I didn't want to come in today either. I needed to talk to Emma and explain everything properly, or as best as I could. But she wouldn't take the day off, even though I knew she was dying with a hangover this morning. Her eyes were practically falling out of her head, but she wouldn't hear of taking a sick day. I don't think she can bear to be around me.

I'm surprised she didn't throw up last night with the amount she drank. I carried her upstairs sometime after four in the morning, and she didn't even stir. I didn't want to get into bed with her because I wasn't sure how she'd feel about waking up beside me after everything I've done. Instead, I sat on the rug at the end of the bed and watched her. I'm beyond exhausted now, and I have to fight the urge to fold my arms across my desk, put my head down, and sleep.

I'm oddly aware of more whispers than usual carrying around the office today. Intimate groups of people nattering constantly surround the watercooler, and every now and then, the odd brazen co-worker will stare directly at me as if to tell me they know what I've done. I suspect I'm being paranoid. I'm stressed out about Emma, and combined with no sleep, I am totally on edge.

I grab my coat off the back of the chair, tell the new guy beside me that I'll be back in ten minutes, and make my way outside to get some fresh air. I check my phone in the lift and

151

chortle when I find a series of brightly coloured emojis from Emma's new number. I'm glad she's using the phone, and I'm fucking delighted she's even talking to me at all. I type out *I love you*, but I delete it without sending. At times like this, I wish I still smoked. I could definitely use a cigarette now. But I gave that up fourteen years ago. Emma and I had a deal. She'd get the help she needed for her head if I quit smoking. And it worked. For a long time. But I think I've broken us both again.

The blast of cold air smacks me in the face as soon as I step outside. I don't even think about whether to turn left or right; I just begin walking at a quick pace to keep warm. A blanket of ice covered the ground last night. It's mostly thawed now, but the shaded part of the footpath where the buildings tower over is quite slippery. I cross the road and walk on the same side as the River Liffy, where the winter sun is attempting to shine. I make my way past the bubble of offices and into the retail area of the city. I pass a florist, and I realise I never got around to buying flowers and jewellery for Emma at the weekend, and I'm devastated that the idea is redundant now. I may be a cheating bastard, but I'll be dammed if I'll live up to the stereotype. No amount of flowers can change what I've done.

I dart in and out of a tiny corner coffee shop and pick up a takeaway Americano. I feel less shaky after a couple of hot mouthfuls, and I resign myself to heading back to the office. My phone rings, and the only reason I take it out of my inside jacket pocket and answer it is because I'm hopeful it's Emma. I picked up the cheap heap of shit yesterday, and I haven't had time to figure out the settings. But it doesn't take much to understand how to answer a call. I'm deflated when I hear the new guy in the office's country lilt on the other end.

'David, you need to come back.'

I squeeze the paper cup in my hand and some milky coffee dribbles over the edge and scalds my fingers. *Dammit.*

'What's wrong,' I groan, shaking my stinging fingers. 'Is something wrong with the Boston account?'

I tense, remembering the thirty-day cooling off period hidden in the fine print.

'Human Resources is on a manhunt for you.'

'What? Why?' I snarl.

'I dunno. No one is saying much, but it looks like it's serious. One of the head guys down there actually came to our floor looking for you in person. I'd say he even checked if you were hiding in the jacks. And his face. Oh man, he looked pissed.'

'Okay, okay,' I pacify. 'I'll be back in ten minutes.'

I hang up and notice my fingers are trembling as I slide my phone back into my pocket. I throw my almost full coffee cup into the nearest bin, and the stench of rotting rubbish makes my stomach heave. My first thought is that Amber has resigned, but even if she has, that wouldn't explain why HR is looking for me. I go back to worrying that the Boston contract has gone tits up, but that's definitely not an HR issue. *My brain hurts.* I walk faster. Thoughts of a promotion cross my mind, but I dismiss the notion quickly. That kind of thing is all corresponded via email and confirmed with your manager. Human Resources never has any physical contact.

Physical contact. Physical contact. Physical contact. The words claw at my mind like a jagged rock. *Oh, my God. Emma! Has she hurt herself? Oh, sweet Jesus, that's it.* Why didn't I cop on sooner? HR must need to break the news in person.

I lunge forward, and I just about make it around a quiet street corner before coffee sprays out my nose and mouth as I projectile vomit. I wipe my mouth with the back of my hand and spit a couple of times, trying to expel the taste of acidy puke. I try calling Emma, but she doesn't pick up, and it's only as I race back to the office with my phone against my ear that I realise I've been dialling her old number the whole time.

I plunge through the main office doors, frustrated with the time it takes to swipe my security pass. I avoid the lift; it's on the top floor and waiting for it to come down will take too long. I take the stairs two steps at a time. I'm back at my desk, on the fourth floor, in minutes. A layer of perspiration sticks my shirt against my back, and I dare not take my jacket off and reveal the dark patch I'm certain hangs under my arms. The new guy is on the phone. His chair is twisted around to face the window, and his back is to me. I tap him on the shoulder, but he doesn't spin around. I glance around the office quickly, and no heads turn to look at me. I was expecting a lot of staring and whispers. Our office is predominantly female. For every one man who works here, there are at least three women. Gossip and rumours are as everyday as spreadsheets and conferences. HR can't have made that big a scene, or all eyes would be on me now, hungry for their next juicy story. Maybe the new guy talked the drama up.

I exhale somewhat too sharply for my tired lungs, and I feel lightheaded. I sit down, mortified. I place my phone on my desk next to my PC and scroll through my messages as I simultaneously cast an eye on my computer screen. I've no urgent emails and nothing at all from HR. I also notice Emma's last text message came in less than thirty minutes ago. My hands fall off my desk and drop by my sides. *She's okay,* I console myself. My shoulders drop, and I slouch as I realise that's all I care about. *My wife hasn't tried to kill herself because I'm a cheating bastard.* Compared to the panic I felt moments ago, no matter what HR wants to talk to me about, I'll be okay. I close my eyes and allow my head to flop forward until my chin touches my chest.

I must have briefly fallen asleep because my eyes flare open and I jolt upright when I feel a hand squeeze my shoulder.

'David,' Giselle says.

'Um. Em-hm,' I reply, groggily.

I force my lips to remain closed while I yawn. It hurts, and I must look like I'm having a stroke or something because she pulls a face and takes a step back.

'What is it, Giselle,' I say, fully awake and irritated.

She tosses an eyebrow then narrows her glare. 'I'm surprised you showed your face here today.'

'What?'

'There's no need to look at me like that. I know everything,' Giselle snipes.

'Really?' I growl. 'And what is everything?'

'You and Amber. I know what you did.'

'You've spoken to Amber?'

'Of course.' Giselle eyes me with utter disgust.

'And what did she say?'

'Not much because she's so upset, understandably. But I could read between the lines.'

Temper boils in the depths of my stomach, and if Giselle were a guy, I'd probably throw a punch.

'Maybe you should spend a little less time with your nose in other people's business, Giselle.'

'Oh, you'd like that, wouldn't you?'

I smirk. 'Yes. Actually, I would.'

'You're disgusting. Do you know that? You're married, for fuck's sake. Amber is in a state. How could you take advantage of her like that?'

I stroke the bridge of my nose and struggle to stay calm. '*I* took advantage of *her?*'

'Yes. And you know it.'

'And how do you come up with that little theory? Is it simply because I'm the one with the penis? Maybe she took advantage of me, Giselle. Maybe I have everything to lose, and maybe I'm upset. Maybe, you know, just maybe.'

'Well, I've reported the sexual harassment to HR anyway, so ...' Giselle shrugs as if she isn't a vindictive bitch.

'Fuck you.' I stand up and toss some paperwork off my desk into Giselle's direction.

'Oh, you'd like that, I bet,' she moans, stepping back and staring at the pile of paper that fell at her feet. 'You bloody pervert.'

I hate her. I actually despise the overweight, over-made-up bitch standing inches in front of me. I remember my first week in the office. Giselle was over at my desk every lunch break, offering to introduce me to the other girls and suggesting I give her a shout if I needed an induction. She put herself out there as my go-to girl, and she was royally pissed off to discover I was married, or so I heard. We haven't really spoken much since. Until now.

'Actually, I'd rip my knob off and stick it in a jar of vinegar before I'd give you so much as a slap with it.' I berate, my temper lost.

'Oh, piss off, David,' she spits.

'Good idea.'

I pick my phone up off my desk and stuff it into its usual spot in my inside jacket pocket. I tilt my head to one side, raise my right arm, and toss my middle finger towards Giselle. Slowly, I walk away.

'Oh, and, tell your psycho wife to leave Amber alone. We all know those messages are coming from Emma,' Giselle shouts when I'm halfway across the office.

I turn around, venomous. I'm back in front of my obnoxious co-worker in seconds.

'What the fuck did you just say?'

Giselle, completely unintimidated, stretches to her full height. And in her stupid, unprofessional heels, she has an inch on me. 'You heard me, David.'

'My wife doesn't work here. You don't know her, and she has nothing to do with you,' I foam.

'She *had* nothing to do with me. But when she starts harassing my best friend online, that's a problem.'

'Your. Best. Friend?'

'Amber.' Giselle pouts. 'Yes, David. We're very close, actually.'

Amber doesn't have friends, just people she can tolerate, and Giselle isn't one. I've only worked here a matter of months, and I've observed that.

'And what the fuck does Emma have to do with Amber?' I quiz.

As soon as the words leave my mouth, I regret the question. If Giselle states the obvious, I know I'm not going to be able to keep my temper under control. I'm struggling as it is.

'Oh, c'mon. You must have seen the Facebook status. They're not even subtle. Oh, and not to mention Emma stupidly used one of her old photos as this Sun Lee dude's profile picture. Hastag. Epic. Hilarious. Fail.'

'Giselle, what the actual hell are you on about?' My back teeth grind.

Giselle wrinkles her top lip, and her teeth, with something brown caught between the top front two, twinkle at me. My stomach churns.

'Do you genuinely not know?' Giselle sniffs. 'Okay, then I really *am* sorry to tell you …'

I'd possibly believe her sincerity if she could manage to keep a straight face. But she's so ecstatic that her eyes are practically dancing in their sockets.

'Your desperate wife is trolling Amber on Facebook. And Emma sucks at it. I totally knew who she was straightaway. Not cool. I mean I get that she's upset because of everything. Anyone would be. But this is not how you deal with this kind of stuff. It's stinks of desperate teenager fighting over a boy.'

'Only Emma's not a teenager, Giselle. And I'm not a boy. There's no fighting. Emma and I are husband and wife. Emma has nothing to fight for. I belong to her. One hundred percent.'

I hate the tired oxymoron that just dribbles past my lips. But Giselle looks positively fucking delighted with herself, and it takes me a few seconds to realise I've accidentally confirmed that Emma has sent Amber messages.

'Giselle. Look,' I spit, furious. 'Emma isn't trolling Amber.'

'Really?' Giselle snorts. 'Well, this says she is.'

Giselle shoves her phone screen in my face. I snatch the phone and read the latest post to Amber's profile.

You can't have him.

Touch him again and I'll kill you.

'Oh, come on,' I growl. 'This isn't Emma.'

'Well, yeah, I mean she's hardly going to say freaky stuff like that to Amber as herself. This is a fake account. It's obvious. Look at the profile photo. I flicked through Emma's old profile photos, and she used this exact one herself six months ago.'

'Giselle. It's not Emma. I'm telling you.'

'And I'm telling you it is.'

Emma was so drunk last night she barely knew her own name. She certainly wasn't posting obnoxious shit on the internet.

'Well, if you could take the time to snoop through Emma's previous profile pictures, then anyone could,' I growl. 'Anyone could set up this fake account using this picture. I won't tell you again. This. Is. Not. My. Wife!'

Giselle's face falls, and I hope what I've just said gets through to her tiny gossip-fuelled brain. 'These rumours are slanderous and dangerous. Don't you get that?' I spit. 'Actually, if anyone needs to speak to HR about harassment, it's me. You need to stop accusing my wife of trolling.'

'And you need to calm down,' she mutters; her cocky arrogance is fast being replaced with worried jitters.

'Oh, I am calm,' I lie convincingly.

Giselle takes another step back. Unflattering red bubbles are appearing under her chin and climb up onto her jaw. It looks raw, and I'm guessing it's a stress rash or something. I bet she regrets shooting her mouth off now.

'Sexual harassment is serious, Giselle. It's not office entertainment. I have no worries about setting HR straight that this is all bullshit.'

'Are you saying you didn't take advantage of Amber when she was drunk?'

'I'm saying you should mind your own fucking business.'

'You can't intimidate me, David.' Giselle quivers, her body language making a mockery of her argument. 'I'm not worried.'

'I'm not trying to. But I would be worried if I were you because when HR does speak with me, I'll be certain to let them know exactly who started the slanderous rumours. I'll even let them know you tried to drag my wife into it. So this is the last time I'll ask you. Back the fuck off.'

Giselle throws her hands dramatically in the air above her head like she's seen one too many reality cop shows and this is the only way she knows how to surrender.

'I'm out of here.' I turn and walk quickly away.

Chapter Twenty-One

DAVID

The train is quiet at this time of day. It's after lunch, but the manic rush of commuters making their way home is more than an hour away, so many of the seats are unoccupied. Most of those which are in use are taken by young kids in school uniforms sitting next to their au pair or a parent, and they're on and off after a stop or two. Emma gets the train home after work most days at this time, but I know she won't be here today. I watched with trepidation as she sped out of our driveway this morning. I don't even know why I find myself on the train now. It's weird, but it makes me feel close to her. I sit with regret that I never took the time to do it before. Maybe I could have gotten to know Danny too. Emma loved him so much. He was such a huge part of her world, and it pains me now that I missed that.

By the time we're four stops outside the city, I have the carriage all to myself. The rattle of the train as it trundles down the line plays like an even drumbeat, as if attempting to offer some rhythm or order to my racing thoughts. I'm still seething about Giselle's dumb and dangerous comments earlier. I didn't want to have any contact with Amber if I could possibly avoid it—even just saying a passing hello in the office would feel like a further betrayal of Emma—but I can't ignore all this sexual harassment nonsense. Amber has no right to drag my name through the mud. I need to speak with her and find out what the hell she's been telling people.

Amber's phone rings out three times, and that boils my temper. I know she's ignoring me. I can see she's live on Facebook messenger at this very second. I bet she's sitting on her couch with her phone in her hand laughing as my name appears on her screen. I call again. I'll keep calling all day if I have to. She can't ignore me forever.

'Hello,' Amber groans, on the first ring of my fourth attempt.

'Hi,' I bark.

'David?' she mutters as if hearing my voice shocks her.

'Yeah. It's me. I've been trying to call you for ages.'

'Sorry, I was in the other room. Are you okay? You sound tense.'

'Tense?' I echo, irked by her reflection of the obvious. 'Amber, what the hell have you been telling people about us?'

'Excuse me?'

'You heard me. Giselle thinks I fucking assaulted you or something. She reported it to HR, for God's sake.'

'Oh, David.'

'So what is it, Amber? It's not enough for you that I could lose my wife, so you want me to lose my job now too?'

'David, calm down, please? Where are you? There's a lot of background noise. It's hard to hear you. Are you driving?'

'I'm ...' I cut myself off and drill my top teeth into my bottom lip.

I don't want to tell her where I am. I don't know why, but my gut is telling me not to share anything more than absolutely necessary with her.

'Amber, will you just answer my question? What did you tell Giselle?'

'Nothing, David. Honest. We're not that close. I barely know her.'

'Really?' I snort. 'Well, that's not what Giselle thinks. She seems to think you're goddamn best buddies. And that I'm some sort of perverted predator.'

'Where are you?' Amber asks again. 'I'll come meet you. We can talk.'

'No,' I snarl. 'We can talk now.'

'I think anything that needs to be said would be better done in person.'

'Amber, I said no. Christ, that's the last thing Emma needs. You and I meeting up for a cosy chat.'

'Of course. Sorry. We have to think of Emma.'

Amber's words are kind, but she can't seem to hide the malice lacing her tone. It shakes me. And the way she says Emma's name is unsettling. I will the train to go faster. I want to be at home desperately. I hope Emma is there when I get in.

'*I* have to think of Emma,' I correct.

'How is she?' Amber asks.

I shake my head. *How the hell do you think she is?* I sidestep Amber's uncomfortable prying.

'Amber, I need you to explain to HR that the accusations Giselle made are false, okay?'

'Yes. Absolutely. If I can help at all, I will.'

Amber's tone is freaking me out because I can hear the undercurrent of sarcasm. And I suspect more than ever that she's the driving force behind Giselle's misconceptions.

'David. You know I would never tell anyone about what happened between us, right? Especially not Giselle. She has the biggest mouth in the office.'

163

'Well, you must have told someone, Amber. I've seen the posts on your Facebook page. Someone really doesn't like you,' I say, smirking as I gain the upper ground.

'It's just a stupid internet troll, David. Hardly someone I know or talk to.'

My eyes narrow. Maybe this troll has Amber more freaked out than she's letting on. Maybe that's why she sounds so strange.

'It can't be a stranger, Amber. Someone clearly knows what we did. Whoever you told has a big mouth.'

'As I said, David, I didn't tell anyone. We made a mistake. It's not something I'm proud of and want to talk about. Maybe the problem is whoever *you* told.'

'It's not Emma, Amber. If that's what you're implying.' I'm incensed that Amber is trying to suggest Emma is behind those crazy messages.

'I never said it was, David. You came up with that all on your own.'

'Oh, Amber. Stop with the mind games. Emma is being trolled too. So obviously, it's the same person. If someone out there has a grudge against you, I wished they'd leave my wife out of it.'

Amber clears her throat, like what I said has really shocked her, and I genuinely believe she didn't know.

'Oh shit, really? Okay, this is getting scary now.' Amber's voice quivers. 'Who is this person?'

I pause, processing. The rumble of the train seems to grow louder, like a tiny hammer tapping against my brain, but it helps me think rationally. Something about the way Amber is acting doesn't sit right with me. Amber oozes confidence. Some of

164

the lads at work say that it's the most attractive thing about her. Others are less full of shit and admit her long blond hair and gigantic tits turn them on. Ironically, I don't fine either eye-catching. Amber is too superior and cocky for my taste. However, it's not difficult to gauge that a stalker on the internet would genuinely shake even someone with Amber's self-assurance.

'David, say something. Please. Do you think this troll thing is serious? Tell me,' Amber shouts. 'I'm home on my own. I'm scared.'

'Look,' I stumble. 'I bought Emma a new SIM for her phone, and she's avoiding the internet for a while. Maybe you should do the same until all this blows over. I'm sure it's just an asshole with too much time on their hands, but still, there's no harm in being careful.'

'Emma has a new number?' Amber is oddly surprised by the idea.

'Yes. And maybe you should do the same.'

'Okay, okay. Good idea.'

'I'm taking the rest of the day off,' I say, telling not asking. 'I need to take care of Emma.'

'Yeah. I understand. Thanks for letting me know about the new phone number idea. I'm going to make sure to get myself one too. Do tell Emma I was asking for her, won't you.'

What? I guess that's a figure of speech, but even still, it's a weird thing for Amber to say. Obviously, I'm not going to tell Emma that Amber and I spoke at all.

'And don't worry about HR, David. I'll speak to them. And Giselle. I'll explain everything. You just concentrate on your family. Emma. Family really is the most important thing, isn't it?'

'Eh, yes. It is. Goodbye, Amber.'

I end the call and look out the window. *Family is important. Emma is important.* What a strange thing for Amber to say. But our whole conversation was odd; it's probably just how things are going to be now. Every conversation tinged with regret. I try not to dwell on thoughts of Amber because I'm only two stops from home. It's just enough time to make another call while everything is fresh in my head.

'Hey,' Kim's chirpy voice answers after just a couple of rings.

'Hi, Kim, it's David. I was hoping I could ask you a favour.'

'What is it?' Kim squawks, instantly on edge. 'Is Emma okay?'

The corners of my lips twitch, slowly making their way into a subtle smile. Kim worries about Emma just as much as I do. And even though Kim drives me mad, I'm glad Emma has her as a friend.

'She's fine, Kim. Don't worry.'

'Okay, good.' Kim sighs.

'You free to talk?' I ask.

'Yeah. I'm at work, but it's okay.'

'Umm …' I close my eyes, embarrassed that I'm calling Kim twice in as many days and asking for her help. And even more ashamed that I behaved pretty crappy last night when she and Andy were at our house. I won't be surprised if she tells me where to go with her next breath.

'David, what is it? I'm working; I can't stay on the phone long.'

'Oh, yeah, sorry, it's just … look, Andy is a cop, right?'

'Yes. He told you that last night.' Kim grunts, and I know for sure she's still upset about my attitude last night.

'I know, yeah. It's just, I was wondering if he could do me, eh, us a favour.'

'Andy and I are only going out a few days. It's all pretty new. I can't be asking him to quash speeding tickets or anything like that. I mean I haven't even seen him in uniform yet.'

'Really? I thought you'd be into that kind of thing,' I joke, desperate to lighten the atmosphere.

'Okay, David, seriously. What do you want?' Kim half scolds, half laughs.

'This troll crap with Emma …'

'Yeah, what about it?'

'Well, it turns out Amber is getting trolled too.'

'Oh, you are kidding me,' Kim screeches. 'All this is because you're worried about your girlfriend. Jesus bloody Christ, David, your wife is a mess, and you're phoning me about Amber's problems. Not cool, man. So not fucking cool.'

'Kim, calm down. This is about Emma. Trust me. Emma is my priority.'

'But it's Amber's troll you're worried about.'

'No, that's not it. Well, actually, that is it. Sort of. Just listen. I think it's the same troll. The same person. But it's more than just online. It's someone following them. Amber, Emma - linking them together. I don't want to say anything to Emma and freak her out even more, but someone knows everything. Someone is watching them. Watching us.'

'Okay, crap. That's scary. I don't actually know what to say.'

167

'Say you'll ask Andy about it? Get him to trace the messages. He can do that, can't he?'

'I don't know.' Kim gulps. 'He's not a detective or anything, and he's definitely not techie minded, so figuring out computer stuff wouldn't be his thing.'

'Okay, but can you at least ask him? Maybe one of his colleagues can help. Please, Kim?'

'David, if this is all as serious as it sounds, don't you think you should just file an official statement with the police yourself?'

'No. Jesus. No. That would scare the crap right out of Emma. No. I don't want her to know this is something to worry about because she doesn't need this stress. Please don't tell her.'

'Yeah. Okay. I getcha.' Kim sighs. 'I'll talk to Andy. I'm meeting him for dinner tonight. I'll mention it him then.'

'Thanks, Kim. I owe you one.'

'David, I'm doing this for Emma. I'm still super pissed off with you, you know.'

'I know. But still, thanks.'

'I'll let you know what Andy says.'

'Okay, great. Talk to you soon.'

'Bye, David.'

'Bye, Kim.'

I hang up and tilt my head until my ear is as comfortably close to my shoulder as possible. I do the same on the other side and exhale deeply at the sound of the pop as the tension in my neck and across my upper back eases. My stop is coming up next. I slide my phone into my inside jacket pocket, and I make my way towards the doors. The train slows and jolts as it approaches the station and throws me off balance. I lunge forward and grab the top of the seat nearest to me to steady myself. Straightening back up again, I notice someone sitting next to the window at the extreme back of the carriage. Something about them piques my interest. Maybe it's the silence between us or the poignant air that seems to seep from them and slowly waft towards me. The fine hairs on the back of my neck prickle, sending an eerie shiver down my spine. I didn't notice them get on at any stage, and I'm certain they weren't there before me. I blush, realising I was speaking quite loudly on the phone moments ago. The train steadies as it pulls painfully slowly into the station. I stretch my neck and roll onto my tiptoes. Whoever is down there seems oblivious to me as they sit slouched next to the window. I can just about make out a hood pulled over their head, and I assume it's a teenager. They probably have headphones stuck on their ears and music blaring. I relax as I doubt they heard a word I said on the phone. The doors open, and I step onto the platform. As the train pulls away, I can't shake the feeling of eyes on my back. I spin around and stare back at the carriage where I was sitting. The hood is turned facing the window now. Facing me. I can only make out a chin because the hood flops so far over the face, but I know they can see out underneath. They can see me. The train picks up speed as it pulls away from the station, and it's only when it trundles around the bend in the tracks and out of view that I realise I've been holding my breath. *Christ, Emma and Amber's paranoia is rubbing off on me.* I roll my eyes and snort at my own foolishness.

Chapter Twenty-Two

Four weeks later

EMMA

David leaves for the office at ridiculous o'clock every morning, but today, he's pottering around our bedroom and getting ready for work even earlier than usual.

'Go back asleep, Ems. It's early,' David says, noticing I have one eye partially open.

'What time is it?' I groan.

It's dark outside. The temperamental street lamp at the end of our cul-de-sac endeavours to shed light through our heavy bedroom curtains.

'It's just before six. I've some stuff I need to sort before work. Go back to sleep.'

I roll over and flop onto my belly. My back is stiff and aching from sleeping on the extreme edge of the bed all night. It's a position I seem to have subconsciously adopted in recent weeks. Sometimes, I wake up with pins and needles where my arm has flopped over the edge and dangled unsupported all night.

'I won't be late home tonight,' David promises. 'Let's get a takeaway and a bottle of wine, yeah?'

David leans over me, gathers my hair to one side, and kisses the part of my neck he exposes. 'See you later, baby.'

'Okay, bye.' I drool, closing my eyes.

An hour and a half later, when my own alarm goes off, I'm wide-awake. I couldn't go back to sleep after David left despite being exhausted. I know if we're ever going to get our relationship back on track, I have to stop suspecting he's up to something anytime he deviates even slightly from our daily routine. But I'm struggling. I can just about tolerate his kisses, but at the same time, I'm desperate to feel him beside me, to know I haven't lost him. It's the weirdest mix of emotions, and constantly trying to figure out my feelings is leaving me drained.

Downstairs, I flick on the kettle and rummage around in the kitchen, looking for the instant coffee. I finally find it hidden behind the milk in the fridge. David put it there this morning, and I guess our relationship problems are leaving him just as exhausted as I am. I hear him toss and turn at night while I pretend to be asleep.

Finally, with a cup of hot coffee in my hand, I sit at the kitchen table and read over the letter I received in the post three days ago. It arrived in a long, cream envelope. The kind made of thick, expensive paper. Stuck evenly in the centre is my name and address printed on a rectangular ivory sticker. At first, I suspected it was a wedding invitation, but none of our friends are engaged. I balked uncomfortably when I first opened it and discovered a solicitor's office in the city centre had sent it. Mullins and Company. I'd never heard of them, but I'm familiar with their address close to Stephen's Green. They're just around the corner from David's office. The bottle green lettering of their name styled into a logo at the top right of the letter is assertive and almost aggressive, and of course, my first thoughts were that I'd done something wrong. Why else would a solicitor be in touch with me?

Bradly Mullins & Co.
23 North Edgeworth Street
Heaton Road
Dublin 2

Ms Emma Lyons,
14 Earl Lawn Manor
West Town
County Dublin

Re: Last Will and Testament of Mr D. Connelly

Dear Ms Lyons,

My name is Bradly Mullins. I am a solicitor here at Mullins and Company.

Firstly, please allow me to offer my sincere condolences on the passing of your close friend Mr Daniel Connelly.

I had the pleasure of becoming acquainted with Mr Connelly two years ago when he approached me to draw his will. And that, Ms Lyons, is the reason for my unsolicited letter to you today. Mr Connelly named you as a beneficiary. However, Mr Connelly also advised me that you would not be aware of this and requested that in the event of his passing, I reach out to you personally.

Perhaps, you would be kind enough to contact my secretary on 01 67584734 to arrange an appointment at your earliest convenience.

I look forward to meeting you, and once again, my very sincere condolences on your loss.

Kind regards,

B. Mullins

Bradly Mullins

I read and re-read the letter until the letters blur and no longer form words. I've read it so often over the last three days I know the wording by heart now. I'd phoned Bradly Mullins's secretary the same afternoon I received the letter, and she gave me an appointment for this morning at eleven a.m. I've taken the day off school, and I haven't told anyone why, least of all David. He'd probably suggest coming with me, and I don't want that. I'm shocked Danny named me in his will; I'm even more surprised Danny has a will at all. He wore the same pants with a hole in the back pocket for nearly two weeks straight until I bought him a new pair. I doubt he has much to leave behind. Perhaps, it's something small and personal. Something that meant a lot to him, and he wants me to have it. I really hope so.

I have no idea how the legal side of leaving something to someone works. I want to Google it before I go to the solicitor's office, so I don't sound like a complete idiot when

Bradly Mullins starts spraying legal jargon at me, but I can't use the internet on my phone. My new number isn't in a contract, so it would gobble a huge chunk of my prepaid amount to log on even for a minute or two. My laptop is at school, but I run upstairs and check if David has left his at home today. I'm delighted to find it in the usual spot under David's side of the bed. I sit cross-legged on the floor, open the laptop, and place it in my lap. David set up both our laptops, and for convenience, he used the same password, so when I type in the familiar combination of letters and numbers, I assume I've made a mistake when the desktop doesn't come to life.

I try again. Typing slower this time. Access still denied. *What the hell?* When my third attempt fails, I realise David has changed his password. It stings. I don't know when he changed it, but I'd be willing to bet it's since he slept with Amber. My chest tightens, as if someone has punched a fist through my ribs and has a powerful grip on my heart. I push thoughts of my meeting with Bradly Mullins aside and wonder what the hell is on David's laptop that he doesn't want me to see.

I punch in numerous words that I think David might use. I try birthdays and anniversaries. I'm close to tears of frustration when nothing is successful. Finally, I try combinations of words. His favourite food followed by the name of his favourite football team, and I laugh out loud when the ridiculously simple combination works.

His desktop looks normal. The beautiful white sandy beach of Barbados with its turquoise sea is his home screen wallpaper. I remember taking the photo on our honeymoon. I had to squeeze between two large palm trees to get the perfect shot and seeing the image now brings back a flood of happy memories. There are minimal icons on the screen, all stacked vertically on the left. Nothing suspicious jumps out at me.

I don't have a moment where I pause and think I shouldn't snoop through my husband's stuff. I feel I have every right to find out if he's hiding something from me. Maybe he's still sleeping with Amber. He tells me she hasn't been to the office in weeks, but how do I know that's true? He could be shagging her ten ways until Sunday on their lunch break for all I know. I feel sick that this uncertainty hangs over me every day. The minute David is out of my sight, a cloud of anxiety descends, and it doesn't lift until he comes home again and I know where he is. As if I'm a worrisome parent trying to keep tabs on a teenager.

My fingers shake as I click to open his email. There are a tonne of work-related stuff. Some online purchase confirmations and a hotel reservation that he cancelled. My heart races as I read the email from the hotel. But I relax when I realise the booking was made two months ago and the dates coincide with my birthday in three weeks. Then my relief is matched by the bitter sting of disappointment. David isn't planning a sneaky weekend away with Amber, but he doesn't want a romantic getaway with me anymore, either.

Amber's name isn't showing anywhere in his recent emails. I search for her, but all that pops up are some work emails where she's been cc'd. I exhale sharply, and the guilt of snooping that was absent moments ago begins to niggle at the pit of my stomach. I'm about to shut the browser when I spot an email dated last week from Andrew Flynn. *Andy? Kim's Andy?* I open it and practically gag on my own spit when I discover it's a chain, and David and Andy have been chatting back and forth quite a bit.

From: Andrew Flynn <andy.flynn@gotmail.com>
To: David Lyons <davidLucasLyons@mail.ie>
Date: 24 November 13.42
Subject: Number check

Hi David,

Kim told me you are worried about the messages Emma has been getting. Not sure how much help I can be, but I'd be happy to look into it for you. Do you still have Emma's old SIM? Can you drop it in to me at the station?

Best,

Andy

_____

My hand covers my mouth as I re-read the date. The email was sent almost three weeks ago. David pleaded with me not to get worked up over the stalker thing, but he's clearly concerned about it himself. I thought changing my number had sorted it all out, so I don't understand why David would be asking Andy to look into it. My cheeks burn as I realise I never asked David for my SIM back. There's personal stuff on it. Text to friends, photos from our honeymoon, screenshots of David and I sexting, for Christ's sake. I'm mortified. I read the next email, cringing.

From: Andrew Flynn <andy.flynn@gotmail.com>
To: David Lyons <DavidLucasLyons@mail.ie>
Date: 24 November 16.15
Subject: Number check

Hey,

Thanks for dropping in the SIM earlier. I'm pretty crappy at
the techie stuff myself, but I've got someone looking into it.
Should have some answers for you really soon. I'll be in touch
as soon as I know more.

Cheers,

Andy

Oh God. Oh God. I rack my brain and try to remember if I
have any naked photos on my phone. I know David and I took
some when we were goofing around in Barbados, but I'm
almost certain I deleted them. *I really hope I did.* I read the third
and final email.

From: Andrew Flynn <andy.flynn@gotmail.com>
To: David Lyons <DavidLucasLyons@mail.ie>
Date: 26 November 10.37
Subject: Number check

Hi David,

My guy in IT got back to me. Unfortunately, we didn't get as much info as we were hoping for. There was little to nothing saved on Emma's SIM. She must use the storage on her phone, not her SIM card. I looked into the Facebook accounts, but whoever this stalker is knows their stuff. They used a proxy server so we couldn't trace the IP addresses for any of the Facebook accounts. We've no idea what PC set them up. But it does seem to confirm your hunch that all the messages are coming from the same person. We had a little more luck tracing the WhatsApp messages. We ran the phone number. It's an old account belonging to a loyal customer. They first signed up about seven years ago. A Jane Burke. Does that name ring any bells? We got an address too, but when we checked it out, it's rented accommodation. The landlord remembered the girl from about five years ago, but he doesn't have any forwarding address. I'll keep digging, but to be honest, stuff like this on the internet is a nightmare. It's why cyberbullying is rife. It's almost impossible to get to the bottom of.

Kim tells me you're playing football tonight? Is it on the pitch around the corner from the station? I could meet you there around 9 p.m. to talk more. Let me know if that suits you.

Andy

———————————

My back teeth lock. David was late home after football two weeks ago. He told me he went for a couple of drinks with the lads from the team. He keeps lying to me, especially about this internet stuff. He's changed so much I barely recognise him anymore.

I shut down David's laptop and slide it back under the bed. I need to leave soon if I want to be on time for my appointment at the solicitor's office. I'm no longer concerned about Googling anything about inheritance. All I can think about is my husband constantly going behind my back, and my paramount concern, *who the hell is Jane Burke?*

I rush down the stairs, almost stumbling over my handbag lying on the last step. I grab two paracetamol from the cupboard above the fridge and swallow them without even water to wash them down. I stuff the almost full box into my back pocket, as if just having them there acts as some sort of pacifier for my shaky mood. I pick up my coat and handbag from the stairs and hurry out the front door.

Today is my first time at the train station in longer than I can remember, and I repeatedly pat my back pocket every few seconds as I wait behind the yellow line on the platform for the train. I don't face a long wait. The overhead sign, glowing amber, states the next train is due in three minutes. But for me, three minutes stretches on to eternity. I'm overly aware of my own presence. Every sharp inhale sounds as loud inside my head as a stampede of charging rhino. Only three other people are on the platform, and despite not a single head turned towards me, I feel they're judging me, watching me. When the train arrives, surprisingly on time, every step toward the open doors is a challenge. My legs are shaky, and my feet twist in clumsy, awkward angles. I'm sure I'm going to fall flat on my face, and everyone will see. Or even worse, I'll catch my legs in the gap, and the train will take off, dragging me down the track.

The hairs on my arms stiffen and spike against my jumper. I want to drop my handbag and run back to my house. But I beg my legs to keep moving forward.

The train doors close behind me with a whooshing sound, and I flop on the nearest seat and drop my head. The train is busy but not overcrowded. I'm getting off at the last stop, so I'm relieved I don't have to look up and accidentally make eye contact with anyone while watching for my stop. I pull my bag onto my lap and hug it into my chest. I close my eyes and count backwards, slowly and evenly, from twenty. I make it to seven when my phone beeps. The distraction is fortunate, and I instantly feel my chest loosen as I root in my bag for my phone. I'm disappointed I didn't think of calling someone sooner. Dr Brady always advised me that when self-soothing failed, a familiar voice could really help. I used to call David or Kim just to listen to them drone on about their day. I never told them how much the sound of their voice helped me. But I haven't made a call like that in years.

A number I don't recognise waits on my screen, and I balk and crane my neck to look around, suddenly feeling the familiar sense that someone is watching me. The other passengers are busy with Kindles or phones in their hands or listening to music, and no one even glances my way. I calm, remembering that I have a new number, and it might be a friend whose name I haven't yet committed to my contacts. I hold my breath and drop my eyes back onto my screen.

Emma, I'm so sorry to contact you out of the blue. Can we please talk? It's important.

Extremely important.

Amber xx

My lips part and blast of hot air bursts out of me like I've just been slapped forcefully across my shoulders. *What could we possible have to talk about?* I desperately want to text back and tell the husband-stealing bitch to go screw herself, but I remember she's still David's boss, which gives her a power that crushes my soul. I keep my response short.

I don't think that's a good idea.

Her reply arrives within seconds.

Emma, please?
There is something you should know.

I turn my sound off, and with my hands shaking in temper, I stuff my phone into my bag. Does she think I don't know about her sordid night with my husband? *It was just over a month ago, and her conscience is only kicking in now?*

The rest of the train journey is a blur. My mind is racing, and I'm consumed by resentment and confusion. *How dare David's fling reach out to me? How bloody dare she? And how did she get my number? Did David give it to her? Oh, my God.*

I hop off the train and march ridiculously fast down the platform towards the gate. I flinch as I approach the turnstile because a familiar figure catches my eye. A slim girl lurks in the distance. She's slouched with the hood of her jumper pulled up, covering most of her face. I'm certain she's the girl from

181

Danny's funeral. The logical part of me believes it's just a coincidence, but the irrational, more consuming part tells me it's a sign. Maybe it's Danny letting me know he's watching. Maybe he wants us to meet. To talk. To talk about him. I spin around and pace towards her, but as soon as I do, she races to the end of the platform and hops on the train just before it takes off again. I come to a sudden stop and watch with overwhelming regret as the train picks up speed and trundles away. I know she saw me, and I'm confident she recognised me. But I don't understand why she ran away. I stand, alone, on the platform for a few pensive seconds. Foolishly wasting time, I'm willing the train to reverse back up the tracks.

Chapter Twenty-Three

EMMA

'Mrs Lyons,' a pretty, petite woman addresses me as I come through the front door of Mullins and Company.

I'd practiced an introduction in my head, so it catches me off guard to be expected.

'Umm, yes. I'm Emma,' I say awkwardly.

'I'm Sandy,' the woman says, standing up and walking around to my side of reception. 'Mr Mullins is slightly delayed this morning, but he should be with you in ten minutes or so.'

'Okay.' I nod sheepishly.

'Can I get you a coffee or something while you wait?' Sandy points towards a couple of freestanding chairs pushed up against the opposite wall, and I guess that's the extent of the waiting area.

I stare blankly. My heart is racing. I spent so long standing on the platform at the train station that I had to run most of the kilometre and a half here to stand any chance of being on time. It's painfully warm inside. I suspect I have a noticeable sweat patch on the back of my light grey jumper, so I can't take off my coat. I eye up the watercooler.

'Help yourself,' Sandy suggests, smiling and taking herself back around to her side of the reception desk.

A ten-minute wait turns into an hour and fifteen minutes as I sit and guzzle countless glasses of water in an attempt to keep from further overheating. The water doesn't help. I'm close to passing out, and I'm bursting to pee.

'Mrs Lyons,' a deep, male voice eventually says.

I look up and find a man, much younger than I was expecting, towering over me.

'Bradly Mullins,' he confirms, extending his hand.

I glance around awkwardly and notice magazines are scattered haphazardly on a low table next to my seat. I find a space among them and set down the plastic cup of water I've been holding for far too long. I slide my clammy hand along the outside of my coat as I stand up.

'Emma,' I reply, shaking Bradly's hand.

'This way, please, Emma.' Bradly steps to one side and allows me to pass by. 'My office is down the corridor, second on the left.'

Minutes later, Bradly and I are sitting on opposite sides of his huge, almost intimidating, oak desk. We chat about Danny, and for the first time in days, I catch myself smiling brightly.

'I wanted to drop out of college, and Danny wouldn't hear of it,' I explain, happily filling in gaps in the story of friendship that Danny has shared with Bradly.

'Ah, I see,' Bradly says.

Bradly's kind eyes are sincere, and I really believe he regrets that we are both sitting here, having this conversation, so many years sooner than we should be.

'Danny spoke very highly of you, Emma. And now that I've met you, I completely understand his admiration.'

I blush.

'He was like a father to me,' I explain; the heat invading the edges of my face is uncomfortable.

'No doubt,' Bradly soothes, as he crouches behind his desk and roots in a drawer. 'This is for you. From Danny,' he says, sitting back up straight and reaching across the desk to pass me a slender cream envelope.

Bradly's name and address are scrawled messily on the front. I look at Bradly with uncertainty, but he smiles and nods.

'It's okay. It's not for me. It's for you.'

'But it's addressed to you?' I say, pointing at the sloppy handwriting on the envelope.

'I received it in the post just a few days after Danny's death. The sender is anonymous.' He shakes his head and disappointment is scribbled in the tired lines around his eyes. 'I'd seen the coverage on the news, but I didn't put two and two together and realise that the deceased man was Daniel Connelly until this letter arrived. Someone must have found it among his possessions and posted it. A colleague, probably. But it's definitely not for me. It's for you. You can open it now. Or wait until you're in private. Whichever you'd prefer.'

'Um …' I swallow. 'I … I … I'll open it now, if that's okay?'

'Of course.' Bradly pushes his chair back and stands up. 'I'll give you a few moments.'

Tears are forming in the corners of my eyes, and I don't chance words. I just bob my head up and down and wait for Bradly to close the door behind him before I rip the envelope open.

My Darling Emma,

I hope you are reading this with a cup of tea in one hand and a chocolate digestive in the other. For old time's sake, eh?

Oh, Emma, I'm sorry. I know if this letter finds you then I am no longer with you. And for that, I am truly heartbroken. Life is a funny old thing, isn't it? You and I understand that better than most. One day, you can be on top of the world, and the next, the weight of the world is crushing you with no way back up.

I'm a lonely old man. I have no one to blame but myself. I had a family once, but my selfishness drove them away. Days are long and nights even longer. Sometimes, I go days, maybe weeks, without speaking to another person.

I'm almost seventy. I've had a long run, and there were good times. Just not so much anymore. In the years to come, my body will fail me and my mind will follow. I will lose my independence, and without a family to care for me, I will become a burden on the state. A miserable old man with paid help to watch over me until I take my last breath. I can't be that man.

Emma, please understand? I know you will be angry and sad, and I am so sorry that you feel that way. I am sorry that it's my fault, but you have David, and maybe you will have a family soon too. You have lots of people who love and care about you. And even though I am no longer here, I will always love you. You put a smile on this old man's face on his darkest of days. You always thought I saved you, but it was the other way around, Emma. You kept me sane. You kept me company and kept me from leaving this world many years ago.

Don't hate me for what I've done. Love me, miss me, but please, forgive me?

My love to you always,
Danny x

Warm, salty tears stream down my cheeks. My shoulders don't shake, and my body doesn't heave as I hold the thin white paper between my hands. I'm frozen. The only parts of me that move are my eyes as they twist from left to right across the page, reading Danny's words over and over. I can't believe it. The rumours are true. Danny really did take his own life. *I wonder how long Danny has carried this letter around with him. Weeks. Months. Years?* My temper burns inside me. Bubbling up from my tummy, rising into my chest, and finally reaching a scalding point as it burst out the top of my head. *How could he? How could he leave me?* I've descended into a quivering mess when Bradly knocks on his own office door and walks back in.

'I thought you could use this,' he says, carrying two paper cups. 'You do drink coffee, yeah?'

I nod, and he passes me one of the cups. It's hot but not too hot to hold, and I calm as I stare into the tar-like liquid.

'Are you okay?' Bradly asks, taking his seat on the other side of the desk.

'Not really.' I sniffle.

'Sorry. Silly question. Do you need some more time?'

'No. No. I'll be fine. A little embarrassed, but okay.'

'Don't be embarrassed. I lost my mother two years ago, and I still have days when I break down every now and again.'

'Oh, I'm really sorry to hear that,' I say, gaining some control over my emotions.

'Thank you. It does get easier. I promise.'

I smile and scrunch my nose. 'Yeah. I hope so.'

'So,' Bradly says, pulling his neck and shoulders up to sit very straight.

I know the small talk is over, and it's time to get down to business. I'm relieved.

'As I mentioned in my letter, Danny has named you as a beneficiary of his estate.'

187

'Okay,' I reply, dragging my free hand around my face in an attempt to wipe away the streaks my tears have no doubt made in my makeup.

'Unfortunately, there will be some death duties to be paid, but we can help you with all that.'

'Okay,' I repeat, becoming confused. *Death duties on what? An ornament?*

'The most recent evaluation on Danny's house is almost five years old, so it may not reflect the current market value ...' Bradly continues.

'Sorry, I don't mean to interrupt, but what exactly are you saying here?' I slide to the edge of the chair and sit poker straight as if that will help me hear better. 'Has Danny left his house to me or something?' I chew on the words, embarrassed that I've just said something so outlandish out loud.

'Yes. Amongst other assets. Danny has left his estate to be divided equally between you and his grandson, Marley.'

'Danny has a grandchild?' My shock must be evident in my squeaky pitch because Bradly's whole face narrows as if his ears hurt.

'Yes. Did you not know?'

I shake my head vigorously. 'I didn't even know Danny had children, never mind grandchildren.'

'Danny was estranged from his wife, Marley's grandmother,' Bradly explains. 'I don't think Danny had much family contact after they split.'

'Oh.' I slouch. 'That's so sad. Danny never mentioned a wife or children. He never mentioned Marley either.'

'Perhaps it was an emotional topic for him,' Bradly defends Danny admirably.

I shared emotional stuff with Danny, I think, feeling cheated. I shake my head. 'I didn't see a little boy at Danny's funeral. Or a wife. Surely, she can't hate Danny so much she wouldn't come to his funeral. What about Marley's parents? There was no family there. I checked.'

'It's a more intricate situation than usual,' Bradly explains. 'Marley was adopted outside the state as an infant, so there are a lot of legalities to be chased. Unfortunately, Emma, I really can't divulge any more than that, but don't worry, none of these complications will affect you.'

It's affecting me now, I think, pining for the years Danny missed with his grandson. It must have broken his heart. No wonder he couldn't cope with his loneliness anymore.

'Don't look so worried, Emma. I know what I'm doing, I promise.' Bradly sighs. 'As executor of the will, Mullins and Company can go ahead with the sale of the property. Looking for Marley will not cause a problem for you in any way, and it won't delay or complicate the sale. The proceeds will then be divided evenly between you both, and as I said, I can help you with taxes and any other concerns. But I'll keep in touch in the meantime.'

I'm at a loss for words. I hope Bradly doesn't ask me how I'm feeling because I would have no idea what to say.

'I know this is a lot to take in,' he says as if the expression on my face speaks for me. 'But I do this all the time. It sounds more complex than it actually is.'

'Okay.' I barely manage to part my lips and force the word out.

'As I mentioned earlier, we don't have recent value for the house. I'm sure you have an idea of what it's worth, but the

189

first thing we'll do is get an estate agent out there to give us a current market expectation. I'll contact you, of course, with the details as soon as we have them, and we'll push for the absolute best price.'

I blink a lot, but I don't speak. I don't want to admit I have no idea what Danny's house is worth. I've never been in it. I don't even know where it is. But confessing any of that out loud would sound rather weird, considering the circumstances.

Bradly ruffles through some pages on his desk and flashes a toothy grin as he fishes out a piece of paper with some messy handwriting on it.

'Ah, here it is,' he says triumphantly. 'Most recent valuation, dated four years and eight months ago, was one point two million. It's probably worth a little more now that the market is recovering.'

'One point two million euros?' I choke. 'Holy crap, what's Danny selling? A castle?'

Bradly laughs. 'Not quite. But houses in Rathmines do tend to fetch a fair price. It's a good-sized three-bedroomed terrace. It should sell very quickly.'

I sip on some of my cooled coffee and try to hide my complete disbelief.

'Look, Emma. I imagine today has been quite hard for you. Losing Danny is one thing, but suddenly finding out you're set to inherit a large sum of money is possibly rather shocking. I completely understand. But there is something else I must explain. Something Danny requested.'

'Okay,' I say, bracing myself for another surprise.

'Danny has attached a condition to your share of the house.'

My head bobs as I hang on every word.

'Danny wants you to visit a Dr Philip Brady at St. Catherine's Hospital.'

'Excuse me.' I snort. My grip on the plastic cup in my hand tightens, forcing the coffee right up to the rim.

Bradly grimaces awkwardly. 'I'm sorry, Emma. Danny was adamant. He's stipulated that unless you attend a consultation, you don't get a penny. Of course, the choice of whether to make an appointment is yours, but attendance is a condition of receiving the inheritance.'

My eyes glass over as I toss my head over my shoulder and stare at the door. I hope I can hold my tears back until I make it out of Bradly's office at least. I feel hideously exposed. I imagine Bradly must have checked out Dr Brady. He wouldn't even need to Google it; everyone knows St. Catherine's is a mental health hospital. Full of crazies and weirdos, people joke. I can feel Bradly watching me, but my tears are sweeping across my eyes and blurring my vision, so I can't tell what expression he wears. He probably feels sorry for me. Most people do. Or scared. I get that a lot too. As if I might lose my mind at any second and slit his throat like a scene from some dodgy B-list horror movie.

I trusted Danny. I told him stuff I could never tell anyone else. I can't believe he would betray me so easily. *How could he tell a perfect stranger that I'm mad?* Every happy conversation in Danny's station hut, every cup of tea shared, every giggle, every memory—Danny's betrayal has now tarnished them. I feel physically ill. The couple of mouthfuls of coffee that I sipped make their way back up from my stomach and sting the back of my throat like acid. *I have to get out of here.*

191

I stand up, shaking, and clumsily make my way towards the door.

'Emma,' Bradly calls as I reach for the handle. 'Please just think about it. I can tell Danny did his best to look after you while he was alive. Maybe this is the only way he knew how to look after you now that he's gone.'

'If he really wanted to look after me, he'd still be here,' I hiss, pulling the door open.

I don't look back.

Chapter Twenty-Four

EMMA

I don't know where to go or who to turn to. My instinct is to call David, but I still haven't had a chance to think about what all those emails on his computer mean. He promised me complete honesty, but he's been sneaking around behind my back more than ever. I can't call him. Not now.

I can't even call Kim. Chances are she's in cahoots. She's so loved up with Andy, there's no way he's been emailing David and not told Kim about it. I understand Andy's loyalty to his new girlfriend, I even think it's admirable, but I don't understand why Kim wouldn't tell me. I can't fathom why everyone I thought I knew was suddenly like strangers to me.

I can't call Liz; I don't think I got around to putting her numbers in my new SIM. *Dammit.* Besides, Liz is a gossip, and I know my meltdown would filter back to Richard. I definitely don't need the principal worrying that one of his teachers is insane. *Christ,* if the parents got word, it would be an absolute frenzy.

There's no way I'm calling my mother. She'd have a heart attack if she sees me this low, and my sister would relish the drama.

God, I really am alone. Now, I truly understand how Danny felt. I don't want his money. I don't even want an apology for telling Bradly Mullins that I'm bonkers. I just want him back. I want to sit and have tea. I want my friend. I *need* my friend. Panic grips me, and I scan the street for a shop with a window

display with an accommodating low sill where I can sit. I find a
high street store with a sign on the window.

No homeless.

Gardi will be called.

I sit. I breathe. And I worry that a store employee will come
out and warn me to move along. I don't stay long. The eyes of
the passers-by burn into me. Every glance my way is a
judgmental scrape against my soul. I scramble to my feet and
wander the streets with a steady, fast past. I don't know where
I'm going, but I march as if I'm in a hurry to an exact
destination.

An hour later, I find myself leaning over Danny's grave. The
roses I laid at the start of the week have shrivelled and died.
They look miserable and depressing as their previously bright
red petals have aged and turned a grungy brown as if they're
attempting to match the colour of the clay beneath them. Two
new graves are beside Danny's now. They're laden with flowers
and wreaths, and they've been marked out officially with pretty
varnished timber, creating a box around their little patch of
earth. Danny's grave is not so aesthetically precise. It's taken on
the haphazard shape of a rectangle with one side longer than
the other as the clay settles. If it wasn't for the timber cross
with his name on it, marking the top, the grave could easily go
unnoticed. Some weeds have started to grow in the middle, and
I suspect within a few months, it'll be covered in grass unless
it's properly cared for. I crouch on my hunkers and pull up a
stubborn, spiky green weed. The roots drag some clay with
them, and I brush the dirt off my knees where it falls. It's as I
cast the weed to one side that I notice her. I freeze. I can tell
she hasn't seen me because she doesn't run away this time.

She has her damn hood up still, but some strands of blond hair blow out around the sides of her hidden face. Her hair colour is a new clue about her, and it's oddly exciting. Her head is bowed toward the ground, so I can stare without her noticing. She stands with one foot in front of the other, as if she's poised and ready to run if she needs to. And I know if she sees me, that's exactly what she'll do. And I also know I'll run after her.

She's wearing the same faded pink Converse runners that she wore in the church at Danny's funeral. Except now, they're mucky from walking through the wet grass. Her ripped jeans are the same ones she wore in the church too. And her hoodie is the same burnt orange one as always. She only has one outfit, I realise, and I wonder if she's homeless. Maybe she sleeps at the train station. That's probably how Danny got to know her. I know Danny used to leave the station hut door slightly ajar at night, especially in the winter, so anyone who needed shelter from the elements could step inside. Poor girl. She's lost Danny and probably lost somewhere to sleep now too.

Even though I can't see her face, I know she's sad. Her rounded shoulders and slouched body give that away. I'm walking around with the same pose. I suspect she'll look up at any moment and notice me, and a nervous excitement bubbles inside my tummy.

But I'm wrong. She walks deeper into the graveyard and further away from me. She stops under a large tree and crouches next to the headstone beneath the bowing branches. I brush my knees again as I stand up and shake my head at the brownish, grey stain the damp muck has created on my jeans.

It begins to rain. Heavily. The icy drops trickle down my face and soak me within seconds, but I don't mind. The rain is noisy. Huge drops pound the ground masking the sound of my footsteps as I make my way over to the girl in the hood. I stop just meters away from her. She's sobbing so loudly I can hear her over the rain. She bends lower until her knees press against the granite surround of a single grave. She reaches out and traces letters across the white pebbles covering the grave. I wonder what she's writing. Her hands are young, and her beautifully manicured nails defy my theory that she's homeless. I can't figure this girl out. I dare to take a few steps closer as the rain eases, but I lose my footing and wobble off the grass and onto the stony path. She jerks upright and spins around. I stare. She cups her face with her hands, and all I can make out are two dark eyes burning into me. I can't even tell their colour. This girl really doesn't want anyone to know who she is.

'Hi,' I blurt the word coming out of me before I realise it.

She turns her back to me and walks away. I walk after her.

'Wait, please,' I shout.

She stops. I wasn't expecting that, and I freeze.

'Umm.' I cough. 'I didn't mean to scare you.'

She stands still, her back facing me. Her rounded shoulders tell me so much.

'I'm Emma,' I stutter. 'Eh, I was a friend of Danny's.'

Nothing. She gives me nothing. She just stands like a statue.

'I, uh … er … did you know him? I think I saw you at his funeral.'

She nods. It's so subtle I'm not sure if she's just cold or if she's answering my question.

'Umm, are you family?' I say, daring to take a step forward.

196

The stillness of the graveyard amplifies the crunch of the rough ground under my shoes now that the rain has stopped as suddenly as it began. I glance at my feet as I feel cold water drain into my shoe. I look up to catch her running away. I just stand and watch until she disappears behind a maze of headstones.

I exhale sharply, making myself lightheaded. I've a dull ache in the pit of my tummy, and I realise I've needed to pee for well over a couple of hours. I wanted to tidy Danny's grave up a little, pull up the rest of the weeds, and take away the dead roses, but I'll come back later. I cast a quick glance at the grave beside me, my curiosity begging my bladder to hold out a little longer. The branches of the tree hang so low I have to duck under to read the headstone.

Burke
William
Died 16th May 2011 aged 29
Loved, missed, remembered.
Beloved son, husband, and father.

I stand up suddenly, and my shoulders collide roughly with the thick branch of the tree that I'd forgotten was hanging above me. The pound knocks the wind out of me, and I stand, quivering, my mouth gaping wide as I gulp huge mouthfuls of air, desperate to refill my lungs and ease the pain. My whole upper back burns, and I'm grateful for my thick coat that at least absorbed some of the impact. The pain is intense, and it's difficult to process any other thoughts. But I concentrate on deep, even breaths, and finally, I feel like I can walk.

I hurry my way out of the graveyard, a little less careful than usual not to step on any graves. There's a pub across the road from the main graveyard gates. I can use the bathroom there. The pain in my back, the ache in my stomach, and the familiar name on the headstone attack my senses, and I'm so overwhelmed my legs almost forgot what they're supposed to be doing. I stumble awkwardly over loose rubble and almost trip on the edge of a damaged grave surround. Instead of slowing down to watch my footing, though, I speed up because the graveyard gate is in view.

Chapter Twenty-Five

EMMA

I stop outside the main door of the old-fashioned pub. I don't want to go inside. Not on my own. But I'm so close to wetting myself that I have no choice. I drop my head until my chin is close to my chest and pull the door open. I squint, adjusting to how dim it is, and the smells of beer and body odour slap my face like an invisible hand. It's mid-afternoon on a weekday, so it's no surprise the pub is almost empty. I try to find the sign for the toilets without fully raising my head. I spot them quickly at the extreme back. I have to walk past the bar to reach them. I can feel the tiny hairs on the back of my neck stand as I march forward. I don't make eye contact with the barman, but I know he watches me.

I relax when the bathroom door swings closed behind me, and I'm alone. I take a long time washing my hands when I finish. With the urgency of needing to pee gone, the dread of walking back through the bar has free rein to consume my mind now. The smell of alcohol finds me even in here. My mouth salivates thinking about a glass of chilled, white wine. Or a bottle. I'd love nothing more than to walk up to the bar and order, but I won't. Of course, I won't. I'm alone. The barman might ask questions. Like how I am, or why I'm drinking alone in the middle of the day. Or worse, he might say nothing and just study me, judging me. My pulse quickens just thinking about it. I close my eyes and imagine the brightness of outside. It'll only take me seconds to walk from the bathroom, through the bar, and back onto the road, but the longer I wait, and the more I think about it, the path to the outside grows to infinity in my mind.

I assume my regular position of my head dropped and my shoulders rounded as I charge out of the bathroom and powerwalk across the bar. The place is even quieter than before. The two old men who had been nursing a couple of pints while sitting slouched over the bar are gone now. Their absence leaves me even more exposed as the barman once again watches me as he polishes a beer glass. I exhale roughly as I grab the chrome handle of the heavy, mahogany main door and pull it back. Despite the thick, grey, cloudy sky, winter sunlight accosts my eyes immediately.

'Emma, oh my God, Emma Lyons. Is that you?'

I spin around, my hand still firmly gripping the door handle and my shoulder objects to the jerky movement with an audible pop. *Ouch.* I squint as I stare into the dullness.

'It is you. Oh my goodness.'

I let go of the handle and the door swings closed behind me as I take a step back into the bar. A female voice is calling me, but it's one I don't recognise. I take another step.

'What a coincidence,' she says. 'I've been hoping to speak with you. Can I get you a drink or something?'

'Amber,' I say, uncertain.

'Yes,' she replies, shuffling out from behind a table that's too close to the wall; it forces her to lean her belly over the sticky timber and stick her bum out at an unflattering angle as she tries to squeeze past. 'I was worried you wouldn't recognise me.'

I grimace as she stands in front of me. She's much taller than I am. I'm used to most people towering over me, but something about Amber's height is intimidating. Maybe it's the way she rolls back her shoulders, forcing her boobs to perk up as if she's parading a catwalk.

'I recognise you from a Facebook photo,' I say, as I grown inwardly, disgusted with myself for offering her an explanation. Especially one that suggests I care enough about her to snoop on Facebook.

'Oh.' She smiles, revealing straight white teeth. 'I didn't realise we were friends.'

She flicks her hand across the air, throwing the comment away, as if her online social life is just so hectic she can't keep up with her virtual popularity. I don't correct her and explain that we are not friends. I only have thirty-three Facebook friends, and they're all friends in real life too. I don't feel the need to share photos of a lasagne dinner with hundreds of strangers and get excited about how many likes the image can muster. David's the opposite. We laugh about it. Or at least, we used to.

'Can I get you a drink?' Amber's smile grows, and I wonder if she feels awkward or ashamed.

'Um.' I toss my head over my shoulder and eye up the door.

'I really need to talk to you about something, Emma. Please. Can you give me five minutes?'

I honestly think she's going to tell me about her one-night stand with my husband. And my reaction is the oddest thing; I want to laugh in her face. Or scream that I know. That I've known for four long, shitty weeks. But I don't do either of those things. Steadily, I look at her, my eyes meeting hers. She has hazel eyes. They're like mine, except hers have some subtle specks of green dotted unevenly. Goose bumps run the lengths of my arms, and I shiver as I realise they're the same pretty, hazel eyes David looked into as he made love to her.

'Five minutes,' I scowl.

'Great. Thank you. Drink, yeah?'

'Yes. Okay. White wine.'

I sit on the outside of the table, partially because I remember how stupid Amber looked trying to squeeze around the other side, but mostly because this side feels closer to the door and I can convince myself that I can flee at any time. I'm tempted to leave while Amber's at the bar with her back to me. But I've taken off my coat, and I'm desperate for the taste of bitter, sweet wine. I roll my eyes at the irony. *Having a drink with the bitch who's driving me to drink.*

An ivory china cup on a saucer wobbles in Amber's hand as she makes her way towards the table. She's walking slowly, and the concentration it takes not to spill any coffee is written on her face. My eyes switch to the glass of wine in her other hand, and my tongue tingles just thinking about the taste. I'm embarrassed as she places the sensible, hot beverage down on her side of the table and slides the cool alcohol over to me. But as I raise the glass to my lips and take a huge slug, I'm momentarily relaxed, and my whole body softens as the chilly liquid makes its way down my throat. I take another mouthful and then another. Before Amber even sits down, I've drained half the glass.

Amber watches me like an animal stalking its prey, but the wine is taking effect, and I couldn't care less about her. About everything. I allow myself another sip.

'Emma,' she says, finally. 'I ... I ... I don't know what to say.'

'I thought you had something you want to talk to me about?'

'I do. I mean I just don't know how to say it.'

'Just say what you have to say, Amber,' I bark, my patience waning.

'Look, I know you must see me as the enemy.'

I toss my eyebrows and do my best to feign indifference.

'But we have more in common than you think.'

'Really?'

Besides sleeping with the same man, I can't think of anything that makes Amber and me even remotely similar. She's a hungry, go-getter business type. I'd say she's ruthless in the office. I stare at her blankly as I run my eyes over her manicured appearance. Even in December, her blond hair looks sun kissed. I imagine the colour comes from a bottle, but it's elegant and classy nonetheless. Despite the gale-force wind howling outside, not a single strand of Amber's shoulder-length hair strays out of place. She runs her fingers over the side, sweeps a silky lock off her face, and tucks it neatly behind her ear. Her ivory fingers with naturally polished nails catch my attention. Something about her hands and the way she fixes her hair is familiar. So familiar I know I've seen it earlier that day. I know those hands; I recognise the motion as she adjusts her hair. I guess it's a habit; something she does subconsciously. And it's my clue. Bumping into Amber in this pub, at this time, is no coincidence. She's here because she's followed me. I have no doubt that she's the girl from the graveyard. The girl from the train station. And the girl from Danny's funeral.

I deserve to despise the woman sitting opposite me. She took my happiness and trampled all over it. I don't deserve to be afraid of her, but right now, seeing the bitter resentment in her eyes, I'm scared.

I can't remember the last time I ate. I focus on the half-empty glass on the table in front of me. The wine has gone straight to my head, and I curse my fuzzy thoughts. I squint as if it'll help me think clearer. Amber looks on; a smudge of satisfaction etched into the smile lines around her eyes. I want to leap across the table and tear her impossibly perfect hair out.

I clear my throat. 'You think we have something in common,' I say, trying desperately to keep my voice level.

'Yes.'

My eyes narrow to the point of barely open, and I feel myself sway on the spot. I reach for the wine glass and raise it to my lips. I snort. *Amber's not the only one with subconscious habits*, I realise, knowing well that I rely on the pleasure of wine too often. A sharp blade was once my emotional crutch, and now, it's alcohol. I place the glass back on the table with a force that isn't necessary and push it away from me.

Amber hasn't touched her coffee. She sits with her legs crossed under the table and her hands by her sides. The conversation is stilted, but she's confident and comfortable, almost thriving on the stagnant atmosphere. Every so often, I throw my glance towards the barman, but I don't catch his eye. I've gone from anxious to get away from him to leaning on his presence like a security blanket. The thought of being alone with Amber scares me, although I'm not sure why, and I slide to the edge of the chair.

'Here,' she says, suddenly, causing my heart to jump. 'I want to show you something.'

She pulls her oversized handbag onto the chair beside her and rummages around for what seems like an eternity. I crane my neck and try desperately to see over the table and into her bag. I've no doubt she's hiding a burnt orange hoodie and a pair of mucky pink Converse in there. She pulls out her phone and slides it face up across the table to me.

'What?' I mumble, my eyes still on her bag.

'It's our common ground.'

'Your phone?'

'It's what's on my phone.'

My chest tightens. I swallow a lump of air too wide for my throat, and it burns like hell the whole way down. I'm afraid to drop my eyes to the screen. *Maybe she wants to show me messages David has sent her. Texts telling her he loves her or that he's going to leave me.* Tears gather in the corners of my eye, but I don't dare blink. The last thing I could bear is losing it in front of this bitch.

'It's an internet troll,' Amber explains. 'Look.' She leans across the table and taps her finger on the screen. 'They have multiple Facebook accounts all created to harass me. They send me pictures. Call me terrible things. They know about David and me. They threaten me.'

'Oh.' One word is all I manage.

Amber's words have knocked the air clean out of me. I gather the phone into my hands and flick frantically through the Facebook posts. Slanderous messages from many different accounts litter Amber's newsfeed. None of the users have any friends, and they're all new accounts. No posts date back longer than a few weeks. It's obvious, even at a glance, that the accounts don't belong to real people. There are so many nasty posts that I don't bother to read them all.

I run the back of my free hand across my forehead. My skin is sticky and clammy, and some of the wine is making its way up the back of my throat. One account stands out amongst the sea of others. This account posts most frequently and is always the most callous. But it's not the vicious words that draw my attention, it's the profile picture. Or rather, my profile picture. One I used months ago. I downloaded the silly quote from some spiritual healing website. It was an inside joke between David and me. If I could download the quote, anyone could. But I don't believe it's a coincidence. Someone chose that exact phrase on purpose. Someone wants me to recognise it.

'I don't understand.' I sniffle, shaking the phone in my hand as if I can somehow expel the messages.

'Me neither. But two heads are better than one. I thought we could figure this out together.' Amber sighs.

She's calm. Too calm. Surely, this must be freaking her out, but she shows no signs of worry. I glance around. Amber and I are the only patrons in the pub now, and the barman has disappeared somewhere, probably to change a barrel or something.

'Is that why you've been following me?' I soften, thinking I understand and trying desperately to match Amber's cool exterior.

I catch the corners of her lips twitch, but she quickly turns them into a smile. 'What? Following you? Oh, Emma. C'mon. Don't be ridiculous.'

I nod. Certain. 'At the graveyard. I saw you there. Just earlier.'

Amber shakes her head, but I don't miss her left hand drop to her handbag to tuck it closer against her thigh. And I'm one hundred percent convinced she's hiding her jumper with a big, floppy hood in there.

'Look,' she says, still smiling, but acrimony laces her tone. 'This is a stressful time for us both. I know what you mean about feeling someone is watching you. It's this internet stuff. It's creepy. God, I know.' Amber rolls her eyes for dramatic effect. 'I swear I'm a quivering mess sometimes when I think about who could be behind these messages. Like some psychopath who wants to kill us. But I'm not following you, Emma. That would be weird.'

'It would be weird,' I say and try to smile.

I decide to indulge her. She's not going to admit she's been shadowing me. Pushing her on it will only piss her off, and I don't know what she might do.

'What are you going to do about this?' I ask, concentrating to make sure the wobble in my tummy doesn't shine through in my voice. I distract myself by flicking through her phone some more.

'What are *we* going to do, you mean?'

My eyes shoot up to take in her face. Christ, I truly hate her.

'Emma, I'm not stupid.' Amber grunts. 'I know we're never going to be friends or anything. I've hurt you terribly, and I don't expect you to forgive me. I'm not asking that. But whoever this online freak is, they have a grudge against us both. I don't know who they are or what their problem is, but I want to find out. I think our best chance is working together, don't you?'

I shrug. 'It's just the internet, Amber. It's not real life. It's not as if someone can jump through your computer screen and murder you while you sleep.'

'You're right.' Amber nods. 'But what about when real life and online life mixes? What then? What about when the person harassing you on the internet is watching you in real life too? Would you take it seriously then?'

'I know they're watching me in real life,' I growl, some saliva spraying past my lips with force. 'They've told me so. They know what clothes I wear and where I do my fucking grocery shopping, for God's sake.'

'And doesn't that scare you?' Amber eyes are round and wide, and her forehead is turning purple around her hairline.

The rhetorical question gives me the shivers. Of course, I'm scared. It's bloody terrifying to know a stranger is stalking me. Someone is tracking my mundane day-to-day tasks. I don't know when they're watching and when they're not. Maybe they are always there, lurking in the shadows. Maybe they're watching right now. And it kills me a little inside because I know they can sense my fear. They can see it, smell it, and I know they feed off it. My terror gives them exactly what they want. They win, and I lose. Anyone would be scared in my shoes. But Amber isn't scared. *Why not?*

Fear is a natural instinct. Even when I was at my lowest point, I still had fear. Fear of dying, fear of living on. Fear of my secret getting out. But the fear I feel now is different. The internet is infinite. It's all around, like invisible lasers that shoot through the air. A parallel world that sits so comfortable between the spaces of this world that it's become hard to tell where one ends and the other begins. Sure, I can delete my

Facebook account and get a new phone number. But that just masks the problem, it doesn't solve it. I suppose it's a bit like pulling down the kitchen blind and hiding in the cupboard under the sink. It doesn't stop the axe murderer from lurking in the garden, it just stops you from seeing them do it. The vastness of the internet is out of my control, and maybe that's my biggest fear. No control.

Everything I've ever done I've done for myself. I've done it all to try to keep control. Control of my mind. My own selfish urges drive me. I've sliced a blade through my flesh like a butcher gutting a lamb, and I did it for my own satisfaction. The satisfaction of watching my dark red blood pour from my wounds like rain. I always believed rain could wash everything clean. Even someone's soul. But I never thought about the marks my actions were leaving on the souls of everyone who loved me. Psychological bruises that they might never be able to wash away. I'm done causing bruises. I can't be that person anymore.

'Emma, you are afraid, right?' Amber says, her eyes searching mine for clues.

I want to shut them and not let her see. I don't want to offer her any opportunity to read me. I don't want her to see my fear. To feed off it. I pause as a sudden realisation zaps my brain, and I find my eyes wide and stinging and my lips pressed so tightly together they twitch. So many thoughts race through my mind that I shake my head as I struggle to process the information overload. I can't believe I didn't add everything up before. The clues were always there. The conclusion suddenly seems so glaringly obvious. It's Amber. It's all Amber!

All the online stuff started the weekend David went to Kilkenny. When he went to Kilkenny with *her*. I think about the photo I received of the two of them out to dinner. Thinking back, I realise it was a selfie. I don't know how I didn't see that before now. The angle was all screwed up, just like in most selfies when your arm isn't long enough to stretch the camera far enough away from you. I curse myself for deleting the photo. I can't remember if Amber's arm was around David's shoulder or if his arm was around her. I don't know if he took the photo or if she did. If it was Amber, then maybe David wasn't even looking at the camera at all. I try so hard to remember the picture, and I have a feeling David's head was turned as if he was talking to someone beside him. They'd been drinking, so he might not have known she took the photo at all, and if he did, he certainly didn't know she sent it to me.

'There's nothing to be afraid of, Amber.' I straighten my back.

Amber coughs dryly, and I know I'm irritating the hell out of her. *Good.*

Fire begins to burn in my tummy. The wine seems to evaporate, leaving my head much lighter, and I can actually think straight. I'm certain now that David wasn't looking at the camera in the photo.

'Really? You're not worried someone is trying to hurt you?'

I bring my shoulders up to meet my ears and scrunch up my face. 'Oh, I'm certain someone is *trying* to hurt me.' I drop my shoulders again and straighten my back until I feel the base of my spine crack and object to the rigidity. 'I just don't think they'll actually succeed.'

Amber makes a noise like she's about to say something but thinks better of it, and the spit gets caught in her throat.

'What if they're watching right now?' Amber clears her throat, exaggerating her efforts to scan the bar for psychopaths.

'It's just you, me, and the barman over there.' I point. 'It's not me. I doubt it's him, and it's certainly not you, right?'

Amber laughs. 'You're right. Of course. I'm just being silly.' She smiles wryly, showing some teeth. 'I wish I had your mental strength.'

I twitch, and I wonder if that's some sort of a dig. David could have confided in her about his crazy wife. He'd be justified, but it gives her ammunition, and it makes me feel sick.

'Right. So I guess we don't really have a problem here, do we?' I say.

'If you say so ...' A flash of temper gathers in the lines of Amber's forehead.

I place my palms flat on the table, keeping them close to my chest. If Amber comes at me, I'll push hard and pin her to the wall. I flick my eyes to the bar as quickly as possible, afraid to let Amber out of my sight for more than a split second. The barman is back. He's polishing the black granite surface of the bar. He's not paying any attention to us, but I'm okay with that. I can scream if I need to. My confidence grows.

'To be honest, I think whoever is doing this is a coward.' I toss my shoulders and throw the comment away. 'I mean we can all hide behind the safety of a laptop or a phone. I doubt this keyboard warrior would have the courage to say any of this stuff to my face.' I smirk.

'Agreed,' Amber breezes. 'You're only a victim if you let yourself be, right? I mean all these crazy people who jump under trains because life has thrown something shitty their way. They're the real victims, don't you agree? That has to be the worst. At least, you and I have our sanity on our side. This internet troll is bonkers, crazy, nuts.'

I sigh, and I'm tempted to roll my eyes, but I won't give Amber the satisfaction of seeing my frustration. She thinks she's getting to me. Her smug contentment is sickly. But she doesn't realise the deeper she digs, and the more she tries to tear me down, the more desperate she seems.

I slide my coat off the back of my chair and shove my arms into their rightful place. I stand up and flap my arms about, getting stuck in the left sleeve that has turned inside out halfway down. When my hand finally pops out the end, I sigh and look up at Amber.

'Let's just forget about all this troll stuff, yeah? Trust me; the real world is way more scary.' I throw in a wink to really ruffle her feathers.

'Wait,' she says, raising her hand the way the kids at school do when they're desperate to gain my attention over their peers.

'Is there something else you need to talk about?' I ask, turning toward the door.

'Emma, I'm pregnant,' Amber shouts.

I spin around, catching the barman's eye in the process. Amber's outburst has drawn his attention. I sit back down and close my eyes, hoping when I open them again the barman has looked away.

'I'm sorry. So sorry. This wasn't how I wanted to break it to you.'

'It's David's,' I ask, already knowing how she'll answer.

Amber crosses her hands across her chest with an audible slap. 'Emma, I feel awful. You have to believe me. I never meant for any of this to happen. I never meant to hurt you. To hurt anyone.'

'A baby. Oh, my God.' I look up, forcing myself to sit face to face with the woman trying so desperately to destroy my life.

'Oh, Emma.' Amber's voice is gentle, almost sickly sweet, but the venom in her eyes is unmissable. An inferno of hate burns like hot coals in her hazel eyes.

'What are you going to do?' I ask.

I'm calm. Still. Equally as full of hate.

Amber snorts. 'Are you asking me if I'm keeping it?'

I curl my bottom lip down and shrug. I hadn't even thought about abortion, but it's as good a question as any.

'Of course, I'm keeping it. It's my baby, Emma. Just a tiny little person.'

'David's tiny little person,' I say.

'I'm not asking for anything. I don't need money or help.'

'Then why are you telling me?'

'Emma, look, this isn't easy for me. I know you must hate me. But I'm not trying to steal David away from you. I'm not that girl. I just thought you should know. That's all.'

'When are you due?'

'August.'

'Have you had a scan yet or what?'

I push the saltshaker around the table. I can't leave my hands idol for fear they might claw Amber's skin off.

'No. Not yet. It's too soon.' Amber sighs.

'But you're sure. I mean you've done a test. Been to the doctor. Had it confirmed.'

'Yes. I'm sure. I'm having David's baby in August. And I really am sorry.'

'Okay.' I cough and clear my throat.

I stand up and swipe my handbag off the back of the chair, causing the legs to shake and wobble noisily against the tiles. For a second, I think the chair will fall over and smash against the ground. I watch until it steadies.

'Congratulations,' I say as I throw my bag over my shoulder.

Amber's eyes narrow, and I know my sarcasm wasn't missed.

Chapter Twenty-Six

EMMA

I've walked less than a hundred meters away from the pub when my phone begins ringing. I ignore it, certain that it's Amber. *I have nothing more to say to that bitch.* I keep walking, mortified that my phone is blasting the Backstreet Boys classic that is my ringtone loudly from the confines of my handbag. Finally, it rings out, but within seconds, it starts again. On the third cycle, I can't take it anymore, and I drag my phone out of my bag—seething. I'm taken aback to discover Richard's mobile number flashing on the screen, and I groan inwardly before I answer. Richard only ever calls when he wants a favour. Such as chaperoning the school trip or taking on a new extracurricular activity. I'd rather boil my head than sit on a bus with two classes of thirty-five shouting and singing five-year-olds, but saying no to the man who is single-handedly in charge of my career isn't an option.

'Hello,' I answer, breezily.

'Emma.'

'Hi, Richard.'

'Emma. We need to talk.'

'Um, okay. Is something wrong?' Richard sounds upset, and I get the feeling this isn't about a school trip.

'Yes. I'm afraid something is very wrong,' Richard says.

'Where are you? The line is bad. Are you driving?'

'No. I'm walking. I'm in town.'

'I thought you were sick?' Richard snorts.

'I am,' I lie, uncomfortably. 'I'm just on my way home from the doctor.'

'Right. Okay,' Richard says, and I know he doesn't believe me. 'Can you talk now?'

'Yeah. Sure. Do you want me to come in to the school?' I ask, feeling an overwhelming need to oblige. 'I'm only about half an hour away.'

'No. Don't come near the school right now.'

'What? Richard, has something happened. Is everything okay? You sound stressed out or something.'

'Emma, where are you, really?'

My chest tightens, and heat creeps from my neck gradually, making its way to my face. 'I told you. I was at the doctor.'

'When will you be home?'

'I don't know, exactly. I'm not sure what time the next train is at. But I should be home in about half an hour. Why?'

'Good. Call me when you get home. Don't call the school number. Call my mobile. It's very important, Emma. Do you understand?'

'Eh. Okay. Richard, you're freaking me out. Has something happened?'

I notice a dry cleaners meters ahead on my left. It's closed for lunch, so I step into the doorway and lean against the wall. I feel more composed, hiding from the hustle and bustle of the street.

'Richard, I'd prefer to talk now, please.'

I know Richard doesn't believe that I'm ill. I prepare myself for a lecture and a slap on the wrist. I'll have to explain about Danny's will, and I curse myself for not being honest upfront.

'Emma, I don't know how to say this, but it's a very serious allegation, so I'm going to just spit it right out.' Richard stumbles over every second word. 'Have you been drinking at school?'

'Excuse me?' I claw at collar of my coat and pop the top button.

'Emma, this is serious.'

'Yes, Richard, I agree,' I manage. 'Are you accusing me of being drunk at work?'

'No. I'm *asking* you. Have you been drinking on school property? We had a tip off that you were.'

'A tip off,' I echo, furious with Richard's choice of phrase. *A tip off*, as if I'm some fugitive on the loose, and some law-abiding citizen has helped the cops with their search.

I grip the top button of my coat until my fingers curl all the way around and my nails dig into my palm, drawing blood. I spit words though clenched teeth. 'Richard, what exactly is happening here?'

'Look, Emma. A parent got in touch to say they saw you drinking in your car outside the school.' Richard pauses, and for a moment, I think the line has gone dead. 'During school hours. And more than once.'

'Drinking in my car?' I don't know why I keep repeating everything Richard says. Maybe it's because this is all so outlandish I need to hear it twice to believe it's actually happening.

'Yes.' The wobble in Richard's voice is missing now, and I can hear his growing frustration. 'Were you?'

'No. I wasn't drinking in my car. Jesus Christ, Richard. Give me some credit.'

'But you were drinking?'

'What? No. Of course, I wasn't.'

'Emma, you're not yourself lately. You're late more often than you're on time. And I've had parents complain that their kids have spent entire mornings watching DVDs instead of working.'

'Yeah. I know.' I cringe. 'And I'm sorry. I have some personal stuff going on.'

Richard sighs. 'Where are you really, Emma? Have you been to the pub? Have you called in sick so you could go drinking?'

I let go of my coat and allow my hand to cover my mouth. I'm afraid to say another word. Maybe the wine has slurred my speech. My head feels fuzzy again.

'Okay, Emma. I can't force you to admit anything here, but my hands are tied. Liz mentioned you stank of booze a few weeks ago. She was actually really worried about leaving the children alone with you. Good grief, Emma. I can't have a teacher who's a liability.'

I drop my head, and my chin bangs against my chest.

'Oh God, Richard. I don't know what to say.' I snort. 'I explained to Liz that I was hung over that morning. Not drunk.'

I hate that my explanation sounds almost as bad as the accusation. I'm suddenly so exhausted that pulling my head upright takes more energy than it ever should. My shoulders collide with the cold, concrete wall behind me forcing a bubble of spit and air to knot in my throat.

'Liz was worried about you,' Richard softens. 'She's a good friend.'

I growl.

'I had to pry the information out of her, actually,' he adds, wholesomely.

'So who made the accusation? Was it a parent from my class?'

I thought I had a good relationship with the kids in my class, and I always try to be approachable and friendly with all the parents, so I can't understand how anyone would dislike me so much they'd want to complain.

'Does it matter?' Richard says.

'It matters to me.'

'Actually, it was an anonymous tip off on Twitter.'

'Twitter?' I squeak. 'I didn't even know the school had a Twitter account.'

'It's new. We're trying to raise our online profile. It was mentioned at the board meeting last month. You should have gotten the minutes.' Richard hardens.

I blush, and I'm glad he can't see me.

'Look,' I say, concentrating on every word, making sure my vowels are round and not slurred. 'This will sound a little strange, but just bear with me ...'

Richard doesn't say anything, but his silence tells me he's waiting for me to carry on. He's prepared to listen so at least that's something.

'Someone is stalking me. They're following me all over the place online. It's only started recently. I was okay with it at first. I just thought it was weird. But they've starting following me in real life too. I can't even go to the supermarket without them behind me.'

'Okay. Okay,' Richard says, and I can tell he's rubbing his face in his hand or scratching his head or something because the sound distorts as if his phone is shifting around. 'I think you should take some time off. A week or two. I know you're still grieving for your friend, and Liz tells me you were closer to him than I realised. It's okay that it's all too much for you right now, but drinking isn't the answer.'

'Richard,' I snap. 'I wasn't drinking before or at school.'

'Emma, there are pictures.'

'Excuse me?'

'On Twitter. A parent sent photos of you drinking in your car. Emma, I don't know if you realise how serious this is.'

'Oh, c'mon,' I snort. 'They're obviously Photoshopped or something. And Twitter. What parent gets in touch over the internet? Especially if it's something serious. Can't you see this is all a big setup? It's the stalker I'm telling you about. The internet troll.'

'And what about the photos of you leaving the pub just now. Are they Photoshopped too?'

Oh, God. 'Richard, it's not like that, I swear.'

'Emma, stop. Getting worked up isn't going to help anyone.'

'But Richard,' I cry.

'Emma, listen. We have to take this seriously. The children's safety is paramount. As I said, I'm asking you, not accusing you. But it will have to be investigated. And in the meantime, you can't be at the school.'

'So this is how it goes. Some wacko on the internet's word is worth more than mine is.'

'It's not that simple, Emma. I think you know that.'

I close my mouth and sniffle. 'This is wrong and unfair. You must at least agree, Richard. I'm a good teacher. I love those kids.'

'Emma, come on now. Don't cry. You are a great teacher. An asset to the school. Everyone here at St. Kevin's thinks very highly of you, myself included. But at the end of the day, the school has a reputation to uphold. You know how quickly rumours can spread. If this got out, it could be detrimental for the school. And, well, I don't think it would do your career any favours either. So will you please just take some time off? I have to protect the school, but I really am trying to protect you here too.'

'But it's not fair,' I stutter.

'Emma, I don't want to ask again,' Richard scolds. 'To be honest, it sounds like you need the time off. Take the time to recharge. And maybe stay away from the drink.'

'What will happen?' I sniffle. 'I mean what if you can't prove it's all a load of crap?'

'Honestly, Emma. I don't know.' Richard sighs. 'I've never experienced anything like this in my thirty years teaching. It'll go to the board, and they'll take it from there. Try not to worry. You'll be kept informed, and hopefully, it'll all be proved to be nonsense, just like you say.'

'Okay.' I resign.

'Emma, take care of yourself, won't you?'

'Yeah.' I swallow. 'Sure.'

Chapter Twenty-Seven

EMMA

I pound my fist on the button at the pedestrian lights. The barely audible beep-beep-beep of the red man in the box warning me not to cross yet mimics the humdrum beating of my heart. Abruptly, the lights change, and I cross with no real idea of where I'm going. *Maybe I'll go to the train station,* I think. I could hop on board whatever train comes first and just ride it out for the rest of the day. Something is uniquely satisfying about that notion, and I decide it's my best idea in a while. I just need to stop along the way to pick up a takeaway tea. *For old times' sake, Danny.*

A blur later, I find myself heading in the opposite direction to home. The steady trundle of the train rattling down the track pacifies my soul, and I wonder why I didn't think of doing this sooner. I close my eyes and drop my chin against my chest. I sit with my legs crossed, and the paper cup of tea that's growing cold rests between my hands and against my thighs. I don't drink any. I don't actually enjoy the taste of tea. I never have. The paper cup in my hand has nothing to do with the liquid inside; it's all about the person that liquid represents. A friend, a confidant. Sanity in a cup, I guess.

'Last stop Greystones. Mind the gap.'

The generic voiceover announces the stop with such monotonic ease that I barely notice where I am. But something jolts me alive. A memory. I was about three years old, four at most. We built sandcastles. Mom, Dad, and I. We stayed all day, I think. We had a picnic. There were ham sandwiches. And

222

apples. Something fizzy to drink too. I remember a long yellow straw that was bendy at the top. It didn't quite stretch all the way into the cup so some of the time I was just sucking in huge mouthfuls of fresh sea air. And I remember smiling. A lot. All the time, maybe. I had a mother. A father. A family. But not now.

I'm last off the train when it reaches the terminal. The handful of other passengers has gone their scattered ways, leaving me alone. The train springs to life behind me and slowly pulls away, back the way it came. I spin around and take some time to enjoy the silent platform. It's much colder here than it was in the city, and I know to blame the sea breeze. The salty air licks at my skin like sandpaper, and it's so icy I wonder if it's going to snow. Maybe the weather is a sign; Danny's only way of telling me I should go home. If there's heavy snowfall, the trains won't run. I glance at the train timetable overhead. Neon orange letters flash on the screen and tell me there's a train back to the city in ten minutes. I know I should hop on. I *know* I should. But I won't. Noisy seagulls fly inelegantly overhead, and the distinctive scent of salt and seaweed wafts towards me, calling me to visit the shore.

The dark blue-black waves yawn with arrogant confidence meters from the mucky sand. I wander with ease right up to the water's edge and watch as the assertive water dilutes to a foamy hiss as it trickles against the tip of my boot.

A lady walks by. She hugs the shore but never gets close enough for the waves to splash her. Her small white dog darts in and out of the water as he runs circles around her ankles. I watch her walk away until she becomes a barely visible dot of colour in the distance. It's just me, the sea, and a huge open space now. *Perfect.* The wind grows stronger and pinches every exposed inch of my skin. I pull the sleeves of my coat over my hands and shuffle on the spot, desperate to keep warm.

I stare at the horizon as I calmly run through my to-do list in my head.

1. Step into the water.
2. Take a moment to adjust to the bitter cold.
3. Keep walking until the waves reach my neck.
4. Walk farther.
5. Close my eyes.
6. Don't turn back.
7. Peace.

I take a step forward and wait for the cold water to trickle into my boots. But the water runs away from me. I take another step. Nothing. The tide is going out. The water is pulling away. Even the sea doesn't want me to do this. I jump back, and my feet squelch against the soggy sand. I scurry backwards, almost stumbling over my own clumsy speed. The wet sand swallows my footprints almost instantly and wipes away any evidence that I was ever close to the shore. If I run, I'll make the next train. So when I find myself eyeing up a large rock waiting among some overgrown grass where the sand meets land, I resign myself to understanding I'm not ready to go home just yet. But I'm smiling because I know I *will* go home. Soon. And it will be better. It will all be better. I know how to fix everything. I just need a little help.

The rock is surprisingly comfortable as I sit and take my phone out of my bag. I'm not surprised to discover I have an email from Sun Lee. My only surprise is that it had taken them this long to think of email as a way of reaching me when I deactivated my social media.

The subject line is aggressive capitals with lots of exclamation marks, and it tells me *I know what you did*. My fingers shake as I tap on my phone screen. I shake because I'm cold. I'm not nervous, or worried, or even concerned that anyone is watching. I'm past all that. The body of the email is blank except for a YouTube link, which I calculatedly follow. Soft classical music plays as the video begins, and I quickly turn the sound off. A lump forms in my throat as I recognise the sterile environment onscreen; it's obvious from the outset that the video is a short clip of a medical procedure. I avert my eyes as the horror onscreen gradually becomes apparent. I know this procedure. But I don't look away for long. I force myself to watch. The clean, crisp whites of the clinic onscreen are a stark contrast to the bloodied body of a tiny foetus as it's dragged from its mother's uterus unready for life. The thirty-second clip fades to black, and large, gothic red font appears on screen. **Abortion is Murder.**

I hit replay, and I watch the clip over and over. My stomach feeling queasy as the baby, not developed enough to live but formed enough to tell it's a boy, is discarded in a silver, kidney-shaped bowl to one side. The same way a surgeon might remove a tumour or an appendix.

Heavily, I finally close the email and move it into my important folder. I want to be able to find it easily when I go home. I need to show David. And I need to tell him what I've done. I need to tell him what I should have said fourteen years ago.

Chapter Twenty-Eight

DAVID

I stare at my watch. It's only been ten minutes since I last checked the time. Time is ticking by painfully slow as I sit on the couch inside the sitting room window and wait for Emma to come home. I wasn't surprised when she wasn't here when I got in from work. I had a feeling something was on her mind this morning. I didn't ask her about it because I didn't want to upset her, but now, I wish I'd taken that chance.

I try calling her, but it goes straight to voicemail without even ringing. I leave yet another message. I called the school earlier, but I only got their out-of-hours automated response. I don't even know if she turned up to work at all today.

I glance at my watch again. It's coming up on six p.m. It's dark and miserable outside. Emma's car is in the drive, so wherever she's gone, she will be walking at least some of the way home. The forecast is for snow. I've checked the coat rack in the hall and the wardrobe in our room, and her coat is missing, so I cross my fingers that she has it with her and is keeping warm. I decide I'll give it another ten minutes, but if I don't hear from her, I'll call Andy and let him know I'm worried. My instinct is telling me it's time to report her as missing, but if I'm wrong, the drama could tip her over the edge. I resolve not to wait and fish my phone out of my trouser pocket. An email notification flashes onscreen, and I groan inwardly when I realise it's from Amber. She's sent it to my personal account, so I know she's determined to get my attention, and I doubt she wants to discuss anything work related.

From: Amber Hunter <amber12345@mail.ie>
To: David Lyons <DavidLucasLyons@mail.ie>
Date: 15 December 17.37
Subject: I have some news.

Hi David,

I'm sorry to do this in an email, but I just don't know if I could bring myself to say the words face to face. And I don't want to upset you or myself, so I think an email is best.

I'm pregnant. It's yours. I'm sorry to be so blunt, but I just don't know any other way to say it.

I'm not asking you for anything. I don't need money or anything like that. But I am having this baby, and I thought you deserved to know as soon as possible. I understand this must be a big shock (it was for me too) and you'll need time to get your head around it. I would be really happy if you'd like to be a part of this baby's life, but I understand if that's not something you want, and I won't be putting any pressure on you. That decision has to be yours. I've taken some sick leave from work. I'm throwing up like crazy, but I also just need some head space. I know you and the team can handle things without me for a while.

Anyway, please take some time. Think everything through. Talk to Emma. I know this won't be easy for her, and I hope she will be okay. You know where to find me when you're ready to talk.

Love,

Amber

xx

———————

I drop my phone, and it collides with the carpet without a sound. I clasp my hands on top of my head and press down hard until I can't take any more pressure. I love kids. I've always wanted to be a father at some point. But not like this. Once that baby is born, there is no going back. Even if Amber doesn't come after me for financial support, I will still be forever connected to her. We'll have a child together. A human life that we created together. There's no escaping that union. I'm about to become a father whether I like it or not. Amber has all the control. The baby is growing inside her, and I can't do anything about it. My future essentially lies in her hands. I know for sure this baby will cost me my marriage. And if it costs Emma her life, I will never forgive myself.

I need to find my wife. I have to hold her, and I have to try to make this better if I possibly can.

I scoop my phone up off the floor and grab my car keys from on top of the fireplace. I know Andy can't professionally do anything unless I file an official report, and even at that, they'll probably tell me they can't do anything because Emma hasn't been missing for twenty-four hours. The best thing to do is look for her myself. I'll try the graveyard first.

As soon as I open the front door, a blast of angry wind snatches the handle from my grasp and forces the door back until it collides against the wall in the hall, smashing into one of Emma's favourite pictures. The frame cracks and the photo of Emma and me at her college graduation slides down the wall and lands face up. I crouch on my hunkers and use the back of my hand to dust the shattered glass off the picture. I shake it out, stand up, and slide the photo into my back pocket. I roll my eyes at the mess created by the broken frame and the shards of glass. The wind hisses and groans, and I toss my head over my shoulder and notice it's starting to snow lightly. I need to find Emma now. I'll clean up later. I pull the front door closed behind me.

Chapter Twenty-Nine

EMMA

I get caught in the rush-hour commute coming home. Sticky, tired bodies cram into every available space of the carriage. I'm lucky enough to have a seat, but someone still manages to stand on my toe, and someone else elbows me in the shoulder as they attempt to wade through the sea of people between them and the open doors at their stop.

Staring out the open doors, I notice it begins to snow. The lack of space in the crammed carriage amplifies the various moans of disapproval. It's nothing more than a light smattering, and I cross my fingers I'll be home before it gets any heavier. I try calling David to let him know I'm on the way, but the coverage is terrible, and the call drops before it connects.

The blast of cold air every time the carriage door opens is shocking. There's a huge exodus at the last stop before mine, and the carriage takes on a new, almost sedate vibe as the remaining handful of passengers breathe a sigh of relief. I'm so looking forward to the comfort of home. I can't wait to kiss my husband. A nervous excitement bubbles in my tummy as I think about unloading the weight of a secret that's been crushing me for fourteen years.

Minutes away from my station, the train slows, jerks, and comes to a complete stop.

'Sorry about this, folks,' the driver's voice carries over the speaker above my head. 'There's an obstruction on the tracks. We'll get moving again as soon as possible.'

'Oh, for fuck's sake,' the man next to me mumbles into his open newspaper. 'Something on the tracks. It's a bloody train. Can't we just drive over whatever it is?'

I know he's not actually talking to me, more just voicing his frustration, but I can't resist replying anyway. 'It might be an injured animal or something.'

Danny once told me that animals on the tracks cost the rail line a fortune each year. Between delayed trains and staff having to remove injured or dead animals, it's a real problem for them.

'Or a body.' The man snorts, uncrossing his legs and folding his paper across his knees.

I don't reply. I stare out the window and wonder about the day when Danny's body was on the tracks. Did the people on that train moan about the delay causing them to be late for their dinner? Danny's suicide was nothing more than an inconvenience in their day. A blip in the timetable of their evening. I bet most of the people on the train that day don't even remember what day of the week it was or even what month. I wasn't on that train. But the second of November is a date that will remain forever etched into my brain.

'Christ. Are we going to be here all night?' The man beside me huffs. 'And that snow is getting heavier too. A recipe for disaster, this is. Absolute disaster.'

A younger man further down the carriage stands up on one of the empty seats under the window. He slides the narrow glass panel at the top of the window back and tries to stick his head out without severing his nose.

'Oh, my God,' he says, sitting back down, suddenly very pale. 'There's a pram on the tracks. The wheels are mangled, and I think … oh, sweet God …' His lips grow whiter, and I suspect he's about to faint. 'I think there's a baby on the ground. I could see little legs.'

'Oh, no. How awful,' an elderly lady says. 'Not a little baby. How on earth could something like that happen?'

The arrogant man beside me doesn't say a word, but I can see the sadness that sweeps across his eyes.

The delay drags on. It's hard to tell how long we've been at a standstill, but it's easily an hour, probably more, and with no further announcements, frustration slowly replaces the commuters' compassion and concern.

'Are they going to tell us anything?' the man beside me says.

'Maybe there's nothing to tell,' I pacify.

'A baby might be dead,' the elderly lady barks. 'God, I don't know what is wrong with your generation if a dead baby means nothing.'

'That's not what I said.' I blush.

'Well, I'm praying for that little child. I don't care if we have to sit here all night once that baby is all right.' She's snorts, her eyes narrow as she glares at me.

'Praying for a baby that might not exist. Well, I've heard it all now.' The man beside me shakes his head. 'I don't think any of us want to see any harm come to a child, but unless the driver is a feckin' paramedic, he could get up off his arse and tell us how long of a wait we're in for. That snow isn't getting any lighter, and it'll get pretty cold, pretty fast if we're sitting here without the engine running.'

The young man climbs onto the seat again. The snow is falling thick and fast now, and even though he slides his head through the same gap in the window as before, I doubt he can see much.

'Well?' the elderly man says.

He hops down and scrunches his nose. 'Can't see anything. It's pitch black out there.'

'Pitch black,' I echo. 'So no blue lights? No ambulance?'

'Don't think so,' he says.

'We're in a valley,' the man beside me explains, tilting his hand towards each other to form a V-shape. 'Any help would have to come down from the road on foot. You need to look up to see an ambulance. Up at the road, not down the tracks.'

'But we didn't hear any sirens,' I add. 'Even if we couldn't see the lights because of the valley, we'd still hear the ambulance coming, right?'

'Yeah. I guess so,' the young man says, backing his agreeance up with a single confident nod.

'Or maybe the baby is already dead. Sure, what good is an ambulance then?' the elderly lady wails. 'Oh, it's terrible. So terrible.'

'Oh, fucking hell,' the man beside me ushers under his breath, clearly losing patience with the woman's flair for drama. 'An ambulance would still have to come, you know, to pronounce a death. Obviously, this is nothing serious. It's probably a bloody plastic bag or a fallen tree or something. And your man here just needs glasses.' He tilts his head toward the young man.

'Sorry,' the young man apologises. 'I swear I saw a pram, but it was getting dark, you know. Kind of hard to tell what's what, really.'

'Good evening, folks,' the driver's voice finally carries over the speakers, and the entire carriage falls silent. 'Very sorry about the delay this evening. There was a disturbance on the tracks. A baby's pram was tied to the tracks.'

A communal gasp fills the carriage, and everyone turns to look at the young man, who's lost all colour from his face again.

'The pram has now been removed. Thankfully, it was empty, and the only casualty was a doll. Clearly, someone's idea of a joke. On behalf of Irish Rail, I would like to apologise for the inconvenience this evening and thank you for your patience. We hope to be moving shortly.'

'Someone's idea of a joke,' a female voice carries from somewhere, but there's no face to be found behind it. 'A bit of a sick joke, if you ask me.'

I stretch, and try to see over the tops of seats towards the back. Too many heads block my view, and I know that unless I stand up and physically search each seat, I won't find her. I also know I don't need to actually find her to believe that voice belongs to Amber.

A pram. A doll. It's symbolic. I don't miss Amber's efforts. *A baby condemned to die. Abortion is murder. Amber wants me to remember.* She's attempting to mess with my head. I drop my head back until my crown touches the window behind me. Dragging my teeth over my bottom lip, I snort and smile. Amber is on this train. In this carriage. Of that, I'm certain. I'm also certain that her vendetta against me goes way deeper than a drunken fumble with my husband. Amber knows me. I mean really, really knows me. The woman has done her research. She has looked into the darkest aspects of my soul. I have no idea how she's found out so much about my past, but I consider it a challenge to find out. Amber is determined to destroy me, and she obviously thinks dragging up my sordid past will do it. The irony is, the more she tries to break me, the stronger she actually forces me to become.

Chapter Thirty

Fourteen Years Ago

EMMA

The lock on the door is broken, but the cubicle is small enough that I can reach the toilet and still manage to keep one foot pressed against the door to prevent anyone from barging in. I never thought the first time I ever took a pregnancy test would be in the public toilets of Stephen's Green Shopping Centre. I also never thought I'd only be seventeen and still in school or that I would only be going out with my boyfriend for three months. And Kim told me last week that she heard one of the popular girls from the swim team fancies the pants off David. Pregnant and fat doesn't compete with popular and sporty.

I drag the white paper bag from the pharmacy out of my schoolbag, and my fingers tremble as I open it and stare at the bright blue and white rectangular box inside. *Results in one minute,* it says. In sixty seconds, I'll know if my life is pretty much over or not.

I hoist up my skirt and begin to tremble as I pull down my knickers. It's more difficult than usual to hover over the toilet bowl as I try to pee on the stick, making sure to keep it pointing downward according to the instructions. I wince as I get some warm urine on my hand. I place the stick flat on the back of the loo with the window pointing upwards and tidy myself up. It doesn't even take the full minute before two bright blue, vertical lines appear. *Two. Two bloody lines. A positive.*

I'm pregnant. I'm a teenager, and I'm about to be a mother. My eyes sting as fat, salty tears trickle down my cheeks, washing away my heavy makeup with every blink. I stuff the test into the side pocket of my schoolbag, wipe my eyes, and flush the loo.

Kim is waiting by the sinks. She's layering on mascara over already heavily laden eyes. She turns around as soon as she catches my reflection behind her in the mirror.

'Oh shit,' she says, taking one look at me.

I begin to sob loudly. Luckily, it's just after lunch on a Monday, and there aren't many other women in the bathroom. No one except my best friend to notice as I fall apart.

'Oh, Kim, what will I do?'

'Are you sure it's positive?' Kim whispers.

I nod.

'Oh, shit.'

'Kim, seriously. What will I do?'

'I don't know. Do you think you should tell your mom?'

'My mom,' I squeak. 'Eh, no. She'll freak. She'll probably kick me out or something.'

'Well, she's going to notice at some stage, Emma. Like when you start to get a bump.'

I run my hand across my pleated school skirt covering my tummy. 'Oh Kim, this is bad, isn't it?'

'Did you not use protection,' Kim says.

'Well, no, obviously bloody not,' I snap.

'Okay, okay, sorry. Just asking.' Kim softens. 'Right, well, you have to tell David.'

'No way. He'll break up with me.'

'You don't know that for sure.'

My eyes narrow as I glare at my best friend, becoming increasingly more frustrated. 'You're the one who told me what's-her-name from the swim team likes him. Maybe he likes her too?'

'So what if he does. A baby won't change that. Emma, you still have to tell him.'

'No,' I growl. 'I'm not telling anyone. And you can't either. I'll sort something out. But I don't want anyone to know.'

Kim's disapproval is written all over her face, and she turns away from me and goes back to reapplying her mascara in the mirror.

'Kim, I'm serious. You have to promise me you won't tell a soul.' I grip her shoulder harder than I should. 'Promise me.'

'Okay, Emma. Stop freaking out.' She shakes her shoulder free from my grip and wraps her arms around me, hugging me so tight she forces a gush of air to rush out of my open mouth. 'I won't tell anyone. I promise.'

Present day

The vicious wind blows large snowflakes into my face. It's so cold they stick to my eyebrows and lashes without melting. I rattle the key in the front door, and the gust of hot air that rushes to meet me as I push the door open is orgasmic. I peel off my coat and drop it and my handbag onto the bottom step of the stairs. I call out for David, expecting him to appear from upstairs where the landing light is on, but he doesn't come.

An uneven crunch beneath my boots startles me, and I flick on the hall light, surprised to find shattered glass and a broken picture frame on the floor. My breath hitches in my throat, as my first fear is a break-in. But I quickly realise there was no damage evident from outside, the door lock was normal, and there was no open or broken windows, at least none that I noticed. *Amber!* It must be Amber; maybe she called over to tell David about the baby. Maybe an argument broke out. I shake my head. David would never raise a hand to a woman. Not even a bitch like Amber. If anyone got hurt here, it was David.

I drag my hand around my face and accept that my imagination is running away with me. Amber would be no match physically for David, so it would be stupid for her to take him on. And one thing I know Amber is not is stupid. I also know for certain that Amber was on the train home with me tonight. She can't be in two places at once.

I bend down and gather up the twisted, wooden picture frame. I drag the straightest side along the hall tiles to gather the shattered glass into a neat pile. I find the back of the frame, which has come free in the fall and use it as a makeshift dustpan. With the help of the frame, I guide the glass onto it. I don't notice a large, sharp piece of glass wedged next to the skirting board until I lean against it and it rips through the flesh at the base of my thumb. It sweeps all the way across my palm right up to the tip of my baby finger. I scream and drop everything out of my hands. Tiny specks of glass rain down and bounce against the tiles before settling in countless scattered directions. I twist my shaking hand around to inspect the damage. Finding the cut, I watch as burgundy blood floods my palm. It's too messy to see how deep it is, but I guess from the volume of blood that it might need stitches. It hurts. A lot.

Blood trickles onto the floor and dries against the cream porcelain tiles in neat circles. It almost looks as if it's supposed to be there, like it's just a part of the pattern on the tile. I leave the mess of glass and blood and scurry to the kitchen. I flick on the light, and feeling faint, I make my way towards the sink. I grab the countertop with my other hand and run some water. I sway on the spot as I wait for the flow of water to become tepid before I dare to stick my throbbing hand anywhere near it.

'Emma, oh my God, what have you done to yourself?' David's voice behind me startles me, and I let go of the countertop and turn around.

My knees buckle as the familiar darkness dares to creep across my eyes as I lean my back against the press and slowly slide towards the floor.

My husband races towards me from the door arch between the kitchen and the hall. He knocks off the tap with one hand and his other hand slides under my arm as he tucks my chest into his and we slide the rest of the way to the floor together. There's no loud bang as we collide with the ground, but I know David's body has taken the brunt of the fall. He doesn't acknowledge any discomfort or pain. He just holds me. I can feel his heart beat against my breasts. It pounds so ferociously it feels as though it will rip through his chest and jump into mine.

'I'm sorry, I'm so sorry,' I mumble.

'Hush, hush,' he says as he strokes my hair.

'I tried to tidy up, and I made an even bigger mess.'

'It doesn't matter. None of that matters.' David trembles.

I drop my head against his shoulder and nuzzle my nose into his warm neck. And we sit. Together. Tangled as one.

It's a long time later before David slides his fingers between my chin and his shoulder and my face turns to take in his.

'Are you okay?' he asks.

'Yeah. Kind of,' I say, pulling my floppy body away from his to sit independently. 'Sorry if I scared you.'

David shrugs. His familiarity with the situation pinches.

'It was an accident.' I nod, expressively. 'I … I … I tried to tidy up … but the glass was sharp… I didn't see it.'

'Okay. Okay.' David exhales like all the air in his body comes rushing out with those two simple words.

'David, it really was an accident. I didn't try to hurt myself on purpose. I promise.'

David's eyes meet mine. I love my husband's eyes. They're big and round, and they sparkle as bright as the sky on a summer's day. They don't sparkle now, and I realise they haven't in a long time. It's as if the weight of life and the stress of being married to me have dampened his bright spirit. He hides it well with kind words and kisses, but his eyes tell the truth. David is as broken as I am.

'Here, let me see,' David says softly.

I let him take my hand in his. He reaches overhead and grabs a clean tea towel from the draining board.

'I don't think there's any glass in here,' he says, gently manipulating my hand to catch the best light. 'But it's deep. Really deep. I think it might need stitches.'

'It's fine. I'm fine,' I lie.

I wince as David catches the edges of my gaping skin and gentle draws them back together with his shaking fingers. This isn't the first time David has pieced my wounded flesh back

241

into its rightful place, and the silence that hangs over us tells me David and I recall the same painful memories.

'There,' he says, wrapping the tea towel around my hand and applying a hint of pressure. 'I think we should go to the hospital and get this looked at.'

I shake my head. 'Honestly, it doesn't even hurt that much. Don't worry.'

I don't want to go the hospital. And I know he doesn't either. There was a time when I was there so often with various wounds that the doctors and nurses suspected I was an abused spouse. I still remember the way they looked at David. Like his existence made them sick.

'I'm sorry,' David says. 'I shouldn't have left the glass on the ground. I should have tidied up. But I was in a hurry.'

'It's okay,' I whisper. 'It was an accident. Definitely not your fault. And I really am okay. I promise.'

David tosses me a familiar look. The one that tells me he doesn't believe me. He doesn't believe I'm okay. Maybe he's right. Behind his composed façade is fear—David is constantly terrified. And for once, I understand he looks at me this way because he loves me. He's not afraid *of* me. He's afraid of losing me. He's petrified of feeling empty and lost without me. He's terrified of feeling exactly how I feel. Danny didn't just take his life when he jumped in front of that train. He took a piece of my heart. It's a piece I will never get back. It belongs with Danny. Wherever he is—that piece has always been his. I understand that now. There is a Danny-shaped hole in my heart where our conversations once sat. A cavity stings where our tea mornings and biscuit-eating afternoons belonged. And it hurts. It hurts so much more than any blade I've ever dragged

242

through my flesh. It hurts more than Amber sleeping with my husband or trying to pull my job and my life out from under me. And I realise if I can still wake up every morning, if the pain hasn't crushed the life out of me in my sleep, then I still cling to life. My life. This life. It belongs to me. Only me. Not even to David or Danny and certainly not Amber. It's mine, all mine, and it's up to me to make it the best life it can be. No one can fix me; I have to heal myself. And I want to.

'David, I have something I have to tell you.'

David swallows and slides a little closer to me until his thigh brushes against me. I guess he wants to touch me in some small way. Of all the things David could have said or done at this moment, his choice of subtle embrace is exactly what I needed. I wonder if he knows that. And I smile because I think he does.

I turn my head, close my eyes, and kiss his lips. He tastes of mint and warmth, and I don't want to ever draw away. But he makes the decision for me and pulls back.

'Thanks.' He smiles, like a shy schoolboy. 'What was that for?'

'Because I love you. I've always loved you.'

'Emma, I know. I love you too.'

'I want to remember what your mouth feels like on mine,' I say, struggling to hold back tears.

David's eyes narrow, and the familiar look of fear creeps in from the corners, hurting my heart.

'You want to remember?' he echoes. 'Are you planning not to kiss me anymore?'

'No,' I whimper. 'But I don't think you'll want to kiss me anymore once you know the truth.'

'Emma, I will always want to kiss you.'

David presses his lips onto mine for reassurance. 'Always,' he whispers from his open mouth into mine.

'Oh, David,' I break away, unable to hold back tears any longer. 'I've done something terrible. Something so terrible I don't know if you'll be able to forgive me. I don't expect you to, but I have to tell you. I can't keep this secret anymore. It's destroying me.'

David's body stiffens. He's petrified. I can read him. I wish I had told him the truth when we were just a pair of kids. It would have been easier then.

'David, I had an abortion,' I stutter; the words tumble from my lips like delicate drops of rain, and I instantly feel the dark clouds of guilt gather over my head just saying it.

'When?' David blinks.

'What?' I stiffen, oddly unprepared for having to answer the most obvious question.

'You heard me,' David says.

'It was a long time ago.'

'When, Emma?' David's lips move, but his teeth are pressed tightly together.

He's angry. I wasn't expecting anything less, but my stomach somersaults with apprehension nonetheless.

'It was just before graduation.' A dry cough rips against the back of my throat like a rusty nail. 'A month before my eighteenth birthday.'

David exhales slowly, and I wonder if he's counting backwards in his head. His eyes are glassy, and the lines in his forehead are deeper and more pronounced than usual, but if you didn't know him as well as I did, you could easily believe the news is slipping right off him as if his skin were made of wax.

'You took a trip to London just before your birthday,' David reminds me. 'You said you were going to check out universities.'

I open my mouth, but no sound comes out. I don't know what to say. I don't know any way to make this easier.

'I was so worried you were going to accept a course in England and move away.' He wilts.

'I'm sorry,' I say, my own redundant words disgusting me.

'Did you even check out universities while you were over there, or was it just a cover story?'

'I didn't visit any colleges,' I admit. 'I had to stay overnight in the clinic after the procedure so...'

'So you lied to me.'

'Yes.'

David's eyes swirl and finally find their way to land on mine. He shakes his head, but he doesn't speak. The low hum of the fridge is the only noise in the otherwise deathly silent kitchen.

'Please say something,' I beg, unable to take the stillness for a moment longer.

'I'm sorry,' he purrs.

'Sorry? God, don't be sorry. How is any of this your fault? I'm the one who should be sorry.' I search for a clue of how he's feeling in his eyes, and when I find his pupils are swollen and dark like the sea after a storm, my heart sinks.

I want him to be furious. I even want him to hate me. I don't want him to be upset or hurt. I don't want him to be broken. Broken like me.

'I'm sorry that I'm not the man I thought I was.' He sighs.

'What?' I shake my head.

'When I asked you to marry me, I wanted to spend the rest of my life making you happy. I never want you to feel afraid or scared. Especially not of me. I failed.'

'David, you do make me happy. Of course, you do.'

David drags his hands around his face, scrunching his skin and pulling it in different directions. 'Why didn't you tell me, Emma?'

'I didn't know how,' I admit. 'I was afraid.'

'Of me?'

'No. Just afraid. I thought you might want to break up. Or you might want the baby and I didn't. Not then. Not when I was only a kid myself.'

David's head bobs slowly up and down, but no other part of him moves. It's as if my words are reaching him, but I can't tell if they're bouncing off him or if they're really going in.

David reaches for my good hand, and I grab his so tightly I must be crushing his fingers, but he doesn't budge.

'Emma, I was an eighteen-year-old boy. I could barely decide what I wanted for lunch, never mind make a life-changing decision about whether my girlfriend should carry my kid. But you should have told me. It was my baby too. We should have figured it out together.'

'I know. I feel guilty about it every single day. Guilty for what I did. But even more guilty because I did it behind your back.' I allow my teary eyes to look at my husband.

'It was a life at the end of the day.' David sighs, and I wonder if he wants to cry. I do. 'One we created. But we were just babies ourselves.'

David twists on the spot until his whole body turns towards mine. 'Do you know my biggest regret?'

I shake my head.

'That I wasn't there for you. You must have been terrified, and I was probably out playing footie with the lads or something. I wish you had told me, Emma. But not for me. I wish you had told me for you. I wish I could have been there for you. Could have held your hand. Could have told you we would be okay because, no matter what, we would have been okay.'

'Are we okay now?' I drag my sleeve over my hand and use it to wipe my eyes.

'I've watched you torture yourself over the years, and it breaks my heart.' David pauses and glides his hand through his floppy blond hair. 'I don't think this is about me forgiving you, Emma. I think you need to forgive yourself.' David swallows a lump of air so large I actually see his throat swell trying to force it down. 'Can you?'

My grip on David's hand grows even tighter, and I nod.

'Then we'll be okay.' He smiles.

'I love you,' I say.

'I love you too.'

David untangles his fingers from mine and reaches around his back and slides something out of his jeans pocket. 'Do you remember this?'

I stare at the photograph in his hand. David's and my smiling faces are gazing up at me.

'That was a great day,' I say. 'I can't believe you asked me to marry you the day I graduated from college.'

'I would have asked you the day we finished school, but it took me four years of college to work up the courage.' David laughs. 'I still can't believe you said yes.'

'We're good together, aren't we?' I sniffle.

'Emma, I … Oh God, how do I say this …' David's grip on his hair is so tight it drags his skin taut across his forehead.

I press a single finger against his parted lips. 'Shh. It's okay. We're okay.'

David kisses my fingertip before pushing my hand away. 'Emma, it's Amber …' He can barely draw a breath.

'I know.' I frown. 'I know about the baby. She told me.'

'Oh, God. Oh, God.' David's shoulders round, and his whole upper body collapses.

'It's okay.' I slide my arm around his back and pull him close to me. 'I don't believe her.'

Chapter Thirty-One

DAVID

I lie in bed beside my wife and watch her sleep. I study every inch of her beautiful face. Her button nose and her eyes that flicker as she dreams. I want to check on her hand, but she has the duvet tucked tightly around her neck, and I'm afraid to move it in case I disturb her. It took hours to get her calm enough to close her eyes, even though I knew she was exhausted. She was so wound up.

We spent all evening talking. Well, Emma talked. I listened. She told me about Danny's estranged family and about her visit to his solicitor. I thought she'd be more excited about inheriting a share of an expensive property, but I could tell she was choking on tears as she told me. I tried to make her feel better. I suggested we put the money towards getting our own place. I said we should buy that cottage she had her heart set on. She was so excited about that house a few months ago, but she barely smiled at the idea now. No matter what I tried to say or however often I tried to change the subject, Emma always seemed to drag Amber's name into every second sentence. Emma is obsessed. She blames Amber for everything. I'm more worried about her now than I ever have been. And it's all my fault.

I'm tired. Weary. But every time I close my eyes, I see Amber's face. I reach for my phone from the bedside table and turn my back to Emma, so the light from the screen won't disturb her. I open my messages and stare at the most recent one. The black and white picture Amber sent me a couple of hours ago blurs before my eyes as I forget to blink. I've never seen an ultrasound before. I can't make anything out. I don't see more than a greyish-black square with some darker shadows here and there. There's a black oval in the middle, and I suspect that's the baby. I guess it's too early to tell. Amber hasn't told me how far along she is, but if my maths is correct, she's about eight weeks. I did some Google searching when Emma fell asleep, and it says a baby has a heartbeat by this gestation. *A heart. Actually beating.* I don't know how far along Emma was when she aborted our kid. I'm guessing she'd have been around about where Amber is now. And our baby would have had a heartbeat too.

I slide further away from Emma until I'm so close to the edge of the bed I almost fall out. I close my eyes and exhale until my lungs feel empty. For the first time in fourteen years, I allow myself to grieve. I've spent so long worried that Emma was losing her mind, I never realised I was hurting too. I grieve for my child. For the loss of a piece of me. I ache for a child who never stood a chance. I pine for the life we could have had. For the child who would be a teenager now. For the father I could have been. I didn't tell Emma I understand about the abortion because I don't think I could have looked her in the eyes and told her I forgive her. I don't.

Chapter Thirty-Two

AMBER

I hate mornings. I'm not one of those chirpy 'let's greet the bright light of day with a smile' types. And coffee sucks. Even when it's strong and thick like treacle, it still doesn't give me the buzz I need to face the day.

I fall out of bed, my legs heavy with the weight of the day ahead. I pause before I get dressed and stare at my thighs. The worst of the scars have faded now. There's no redness anymore. I run my hand over my bare skin. The dimpled flesh is soft, and some of the scars are small where I only jabbed a needle in once or twice. Other scars are not so subtle. The larger ones will never heal. The areas where the flesh was raw and gaping. The places where I'd jabbed the same spot countless times. One scar just above my knee is worse than all the others are. It's where the needle once snapped, and I had to dig it out with a kitchen knife. I was so high I didn't feel a thing. It was three days later before the infection was unbearable and I thought I'd lose my leg. They asked me in the hospital if I was an addict. As if the answer wasn't written all over my skin.

The scars on my flesh know I've been clean for five years. My skin is trying to heal as best it can. But the scars on my heart. No amount of time can help those.

I pull on my clothes that are waiting on the end of my bed. I picked out my outfit the night before; I didn't want to allow myself any time to change my mind. I dress the bed and open the curtains before I leave my bedroom. I stop in the doorway and take a look around, knowing this will be the last time I ever see this room.

Downstairs, I make some coffee, even stronger than usual. I savour the warmth of the cup between my hands as I stare out the french doors into the garden. 'I'm sorry, Will,' I allow myself to say. 'I really, really am sorry.'

Minutes later, I slam my empty cup against the kitchen table. I take my time in the downstairs bathroom. The mirror above the sink is tiny, and the overhead light hasn't worked in ages, but today, of all days, I need my makeup to be flawless. *Today, of all days—my last day.*

Half an hour later, I'm ready to leave the house wearing my best clothes and with a face full of makeup. I stop just before I step outside and open the drawer of the hall table. It sticks a bit, and I have to tug with my full weight to pry it open. There's a pile of crap in there. Random pieces of paper, an old phone book—stuff I've forgotten about. Stuff I haven't seen in five years. I rummage, quickly finding the photograph I'm after. I roll my eyes and smile at the same time as I take in my pale face resting on Will's shoulder. He looks equally as shit. We're both way too thin, and his t-shirt has a large, noticeable hole just below his left collarbone. His dark brown hair is spiky and unwashed, and he has that just-rolled-out-of-bed look. We sit tucked up on a filthy sofa. I think it may once have been a pastel colour, but I've only ever known it as a brownish-grey thing. Will's arm is draped behind my neck, and his hand is gripping my shoulder like he's holding on for dear life. Maybe he was.

I kiss the image of his face and slide the photo carefully into the zip pocket of my handbag.

'See you soon,' I whisper as I pull the front door closed behind me.

An hour later, I'm walking familiar streets. I stop outside a three-story redbrick building. It's shabbier than I remember. I definitely don't recall bars on the downstairs windows. A part of me itches to turn around and pretend I don't belong here. Pretend I never belonged here. But a larger part of me knows my heart has never left this place.

I cast my eyes up to the third floor and count five windows across. The curtains are drawn on my old apartment. The steps leading to the main doors of the block are as dull and cold as ever. Some new graffiti is scribbled across the depressing, grey concrete. I grab the wonky handrail as I climb the steps, two at a time.

I take a deep breath before I raise my arm and knock on the door. The pong from rubbish bins lining the street waiting for collection mixes with exhaust fumes from the traffic passing behind me. I wonder if it always smelt this repulsive. I don't remember. I don't remember much about this place. That's probably for the best. But I do remember the day Will died.

Mr Nowak opens the door as far as the latch and peers over his nose through the gap.

'Yes. Can I help you?' he says, his Polish accent as pronounced as ever.

'I'm Amber Hunter. We spoke on the phone.'

The latch chain rattles and he opens the door wide, revealing a long corridor behind him.

'Yes. Miss Hunter. Good to make meeting you.' He extends his hand.

His fingernails are long and dirty, and I grimace as I force myself to shake his hand.

'Come in. Follow me,' he says, stepping aside to allow me past.

The door slams behind us with a loud bang, and I twitch.

'You see apartment now. Yes?'

'Yes.' I swallow.

He doesn't remember me. I suspected as much, but I remember him. I remember how he'd pinch my arse when I would go upstairs to his apartment every Friday evening to pay the rent. Will and I paid weekly. I guess Mr Nowak didn't trust us to go a whole month and still have cash left at the end of it to pay for the roof over our head. More memories accost my brain with each step forward, and I'm desperate to turn around and run away.

We climb three flights of cold concrete stairs and turn right at the end of the corridor to stop outside a door that doesn't sit in the frame correctly. The hinges are rusted, and the paint is chipped and flaking off in large clumps in various places. A door on the opposite side of the corridor opens behind us, and I turn, out of curiosity, to see who comes out. A man in his early twenties appears. He's tall and clean cut. His clothes are respectable; slim-fitting jeans, tidy runners, and a black puffy coat. He carries a little girl on his hip. I guess she's about three, four at most. Her blond hair falls in curls in and around the hood of her bright red coat. She's smiling and giggling with the man I assume is her father. At first glance, they're the picture of domestic happiness, but I can see further. The familiar signs are there. The dark black shadows that sit under his eyes like half-moons. The purplish-blue bruises that outline his lips. His gaunt face, with cheekbones so pronounced there's scarcely a layer of skin covering them. My eyes drop to his hands that wrap around his adorable daughter's back. The marks are raw and new. They could easily be mistaken for cigarette burns, and maybe some of them are, but the majority are the telltale signs of a junkie shooting up.

'Welcome to the neighbourhood.' He smiles, the words rattling in his throat.

'Thank you,' I mumble.

I can't take my eyes off the little girl as he walks away. I wonder what will happen to her. What her future will be like, if she makes it that far. I shake my head. It's unbearable to think about. My heart pinches, and I know I made the right decision five years ago. I had to give my child a chance at a future. A future without me.

'Come. You see inside now, yes,' Mr Nowak commands as he opens the door to the apartment where I once lived.

I step into the open plan living area. I'm surprised to find it renovated since I was last here. A floral couch has replaced the slimy brown one I remember. It's obviously still second-hand but a definite improvement. The fabric is patchy in places, but at least no springs protrude through the cushions. The cream kitchen presses have been washed or maybe even repainted. The colourful splashes from spilt alcohol and the odd blood splatter once so pronounced on the kitchen tiles have been washed away. It's almost as if I was never here before.

'One bedroom, one bathroom,' Mr Nowak says. 'There.' He points.

My body trembles as I make my way towards the bedroom. The heels of my shoes make a weird tapping sound against the timber floor, and Mr Nowak eyes me with uncertainty.

'You clean?' he snaps.

'Excuse me?'

'You heard me.' His accent dilutes suddenly.

'Are you asking me if I take drugs?'

'Yes.' He nods.

'And if I do, do you really think I'd give you an honest answer?' I snort.

'Look, lady. You're wearing nice clothes, no doubt expensive. And you're polite. You don't belong here. So I gotta draw the conclusion you're either trying too hard to cover up your habit, or you're a cop or something. I got nothing to hide. I'm not doing anything illegal here.'

'Pretty good English for a guy who couldn't string two words together when I first got here,' I snap.

'Lady, what is your problem? If you're dealing, you can get out right now. I don't want trouble.'

'I'm not an addict, a dealer, or a cop.' I shake my head. 'I work in IT, actually.'

'Really?' He tilts his head to one side. 'Then what are you doing on this side of town?'

'I like the place,' I say. 'How much?'

'For you ...' He licks me with his eyes, stopping for way too long to stare at my chest. 'I say nine hundred a month.'

'That's bullshit. You said seven on the phone.'

'I changed my mind. Anyway, it looks like you can afford it. Do you want the place or not?'

'Let me see the bedroom first,' I say, confidently opening the correct door.

Mr Nowak follows me. He stands too close behind me, and I can feel the hiss of his warm breath reach the nape of my neck. I'd ask him to back off, but my memories have paralysed me. Everything about that day floods my senses as I stare into the room where Will and I once slept. And for a second, I think I'm going to lose control of my bladder.

The room is exactly as it was five years ago. The creamy brown carpet with an array of vomit and urine stains smells as bad as ever. Someone has attempted to scrub them out, but their efforts were futile. The same duvet covers the double bed where we slept the day Will died. My breathing is laboured, and I wait for Mr Nowak to notice I'm having some sort of meltdown. But he's too busy eyeing up my arse to notice anything else about me.

Finally, I force myself to look at the curtain pole. It's still warped in the middle where the weight of Will's lifeless body, dangling like a puppet on a string, dragged it down. I close my eyes and take a deep breath, transported to that day.

I had good news. News I couldn't wait to share with Will. I'd gotten a job. It was bag packing in the local supermarket. The money wasn't great, but it was enough to meet the rent and have some left over to put food on the table. I'd bought us some beers to celebrate. Will's favourites. I put them in the almost empty fridge, and I unpacked some groceries I'd picked up. Some nearly out-of-date stuff I got on the cheap, but it was good enough to eat, and I planned to make us a celebratory dinner. It took me a while to notice the apartment was eerily quiet. I knew Will was at home. I had the only set of keys with me, and I'd been gone for hours. He wouldn't leave with no way of letting himself back in.

I felt my heart sink with each step I took closer to the bedroom. The door was slightly ajar, and I guessed the bedroom window must have been open a fraction because the door rattled ever so slightly on its hinges. I began to call his name. Softly at first but by the time my hand gripped the door handle, I was screaming for him to answer me.

My knees had hit the carpet before I pushed the door back fully and my heavily pregnant belly slapped against my thighs, driving some acidy vomit into the back of my throat. I screamed. I remember because my throat was dry for days after. At the funeral, my voice was rusty, and I could barely get the words out to thank people for coming. Not that many people were there to thank at all.

When I open my eyes now, I can still see the urine soaked body of the man I loved dangling from the curtain rod. I can still see the bedsheets wrapped tightly around his neck, masquerading as a silk scarf. Cotton bedsheets … who would ever think they're a weapon capable of strangling the life out of a man?

Mr Nowak places his hand on my shoulder, and I yelp like a wounded animal.

'Sorry,' I apologise, pulling my eyes away from the window and turning to face the man who was once my landlord.

'So you taking the place or what?' he says. 'I've another viewing in half an hour if you're not interested.'

'Really?' I straighten. 'This place hasn't been rented in five years, yet you have two viewings in one day. What a coincidence.'

A whirlpool of anger gathers in Mr Nowak's grey eyes like a winter's storm. His rage stretches him by an inch, and he seems broader too. He's still not as tall as I am, but that's not unusual, even for a man. 'You're a fucking reporter, aren't you? Out. Get out. What the hell is wrong with you people? I knew I sniffed you out as a bullshitter. Girls like you don't belong here. Why are you dragging this story up after all these years? It's disgusting. A man can't die in peace these days without you monsters wanting to splash it all over the front page. Or even worse put photos on the internet. This world makes me sick. Sick, I tell you. Out. Out. Out.' Mr Novak waves his hand above his head, and his efforts to seem assertive or aggressive are almost comical.

I've already corrected his misconception about my occupation, so I'm not prepared to waste my breath further.

'Did you know William Burke took his last breath in this room?' I ask.

Mr Nowak scrunches his nose and rolls his shoulders. 'Yeah. Years ago. But the guy was a drug addict.'

'It wasn't an overdose,' I quip.

'But it was suicide.' Mr Nowak snorts.

'Suicide isn't a crime,' I snarl.

Mr Nowak shrugs, and his cold, indifference makes me want to push him out the window behind us.

'Will's life in this shithole just didn't seem worth living,' I mumble. 'Not even with a wife who loved him and a baby on the way.'

'Did you know William Burke?' Mr Nowak asks, and finally, I see a spark of recognition in his eyes.

'Yes.'

'Why are you really here?' he asks, squinting as he studies my face.

'I told you. I would like to rent this apartment.' I snort.

Mr Nowak shakes his head, and before he asks another stupid question, dancing around the truth I know he's already figured out, I cut across him. 'William Burke wasn't just some junkie who took his life here.' I point at the window as if Will's body still dangled there for us to see. 'He was my husband.'

'Jane?' Mr Novak blurts as if I've just slapped him roughly on the back with a crowbar. 'Jane Burke, is that really you? You look fantastic. I can't believe it.'

'Hello, Eddie.' I groan as I relax, and my natural, gritty inner-city accent makes its first appearance in five years. 'I missed you.' I grin.

'The years have been good to you,' he stutters, and I sense fear. 'What brings you back here?'

'Unfinished business.' I nod wide-eyed and breezy.

Eddie Nowak shrinks again, and I can tell the weight of his anxiety is crushing him. I catch him pull his mobile out of his back pocket. I really wish he hadn't done that.

'Who you going to call, Eddie?' I snarl.

'I wasn't going to call anyone.' He slurs his words as nervous saliva gets caught between his teeth and his bottom lip.

He disgusts me, and I want to slap the jabbering bastard across the face, but I wouldn't touch his vile skin with my bare hands.

'I need to use this apartment for a few days, Eddie,' I chortle. 'A week tops. So what do you say? For old time's sake, yeah?'

'I don't take on short-term lettings, Jane. You remember. I'd need you to sign a lease.'

My eyes narrow. 'Can't you make an exception?'

Eddie shakes his head.

'Come on. You can do a favour for an old friend.' Sarcasm and hate lace my words.

'Jane … I … I …'

'Oh Eddie, fuck this,' I growl, losing patience. 'I need this apartment, okay. And you're going to give it to me. Or would you rather I go upstairs and have some words with your wife. I'm sure she'd love to know all about the little junky girl you fucked on the rooftop.'

'I never touched you.' Eddie jerks away.

My eyes widen, and I roll my bottom lip between my thumb and fingers.

'It's dangerous up there. There's no railing and the wind would rip the arse off you in the winter.' Eddie darkens, his eyes darting to the ceiling. 'I never go up there.'

'I know that'—I shrug—'but your wife doesn't. I remember the way you used to look at me. Like your cock wanted a taste. And you haven't changed a bit. Your beady little eyes couldn't get enough of my tits when I came through the door twenty minutes ago. It wouldn't take much to convince your wife that you're a cheating little pervert.'

'Jane, please? I have kids.'

'I had a kid. But you didn't give a shit about that when you kicked me out with nowhere to go.'

'You couldn't pay the rent, Jane. I had no choice. If the other tenants found out I was going soft …'

'My husband had just killed himself. I was heavily pregnant, and you didn't even give me three whole weeks to get my head together. You're a vile bastard. Actually, maybe I should just go upstairs right now and have a quick word with Mrs Nowak anyway.'

'Jane. Please. Stop. Just give me a minute to think. I haven't seen you in five years. This is all a bit sudden, you know.'

'I'm not asking for a kidney, Eddie. Just a couple of nights here. It's the least you fucking owe me.'

'Why have you come back, Jane? Why now? I already told you I don't want trouble.'

'And I already told you I have some unfinished business I need to sort out.'

'Are you in trouble?' Eddie takes a step back and stuffs his shaking hands into his pockets. 'With the cops, I mean. Are they going to come looking for you?'

'The only person who's going to come looking for me is my sister. She's the only one who'll figure out where I am.'

Eddie's eyes are scrambling all over me. He's not ogling my body the way he was when I first walked through the door. Now, he's eyeing me like something he scraped off his shoe.

'Are you bringing your kid here too?' he slurs.

The corners of my lips twitch, and it takes concentration not to let how much I miss my son show on my face. 'No. It's just me.'

'Okay.' Eddie nods. 'Two nights. Three max. And then you have to go, Jane. For good this time.'

'Don't worry, Eddie. I'll definitely be gone for good this time.'

Chapter Thirty-Three

EMMA

It's early when I wake up. David is lying so far over the other side of the bed it took me a few seconds to realise he was actually there at all. He snores loudly, and I know he's in a deep sleep. I guess he stayed awake late last night, staring at that scan picture he thinks I didn't see.

I get dressed and creep down the stairs. David's a heavy sleeper, but I take a huge amount of care to tiptoe on each step nonetheless. I don't bother to make coffee before I leave, and I know I'll have a headache before I reach the end of the road. But I've no time for distraction this morning.

I wrap up warmly and pull the front door closed behind me. I flinch as it slams loudly, and I stand statue-like on the front step for a few seconds. The bedroom curtains don't twitch, and the house doesn't come to life. I sigh, relieved that David could sleep through a tornado.

A shower of early morning rain has turned the heavy snow into slippery sludge. My car needs new tyres, so I decide against driving. Walking will give me time to think. Time to prepare what I'm going to say.

A twenty-minute bus ride later, I'm standing at Kim's door. I tried calling her a couple of times from the bus, but she didn't answer. I know Kim adores clinging to the bed until the last possible moment, so I'm confident she's at home. I ring the doorbell and knock several times before I hear movement inside.

'Emma.' Kim gasps as she drags the door open. 'Is everything okay?'

'Um. No. Not really. I need your help.'

'Yeah. Sure. Okay.' Kim nods, her barely-there silky black nightdress doesn't offer much cover, and she shivers as the icy wind whips past me and into her warm house.

'Everything okay down there?' Andy's voice carries from the top of the stairs.

'Yeah. Everything's fine. Emma's here.' Kim twists away from the door to throw her voice. 'Go back to sleep.'

'He only just got here a few minutes ago,' Kim explains. 'He's on the night shift this week.' Kim's rosy cheeks and damp, matted hair tell me she and Andy have had a very busy few minutes.

'This is a bad time, isn't it?' I blush.

'It's okay. It's okay.' Kim shivers.

Andy comes into view at the top of the stairs. He's wearing white boxers and nothing else. Despite the freezing temperatures outside, my face is hot, and my back is sticky and sweating.

'Hi, Andy,' I say, waving my bandaged hand awkwardly as he approaches, and I can tell I instantly make him uncomfortable.

He tosses his eyebrows and politely waves back, taking position behind Kim.

Kim's eyes dropped to my bandage, and she shakes her head.

'It was an accident.' I defend myself automatically. 'Broken picture frame.'

'Right. Okay,' Kim says, and I know she doesn't believe me.

'I'm sorry. I can tell you're busy.' I clear my throat. Kim and Andy look at each other, and the level of awkwardness is off the scale. 'It's just, I need to find someone. And I know you can help me. It's really important. I wouldn't turn up like this if it wasn't serious."

'Oh, Emma.' Kim's eyes search Andy for support, but he doesn't say a word. 'It's freezing outside. Come in. Let's get some coffee.'

'Good idea,' Andy says. 'I'll get dressed and make myself scarce so you two can talk.'

Andy slides his arm around Kim's waist and pulls her close enough to kiss on the cheek.

'I'll call you later.' Kim smiles.

'Andy, wait,' I say. 'It's actually you I was hoping to talk to.'

Kim's eyes widen. 'Oh.'

'Yeah. Look, can we sit down or something? This is complicated,' I confess.

'Okay.' Andy smiles stiffly.

He must think I'm bonkers. And I hate that I'm sabotaging the early stages of Kim and Andy's relationship with my twisted drama.

'Let me just go upstairs and put something on.' Andy winces. 'We'll talk then.'

I follow Kim into the compact kitchen and pull out a high stool to sit on at the breakfast bar. Kim fills the kettle and takes a packet of half-open biscuits out of an overhead cupboard.

'Are you okay?' she says, placing the biscuits on the countertop and spinning them around, so the open end is facing me.

I nod and take a biscuit. 'Yeah. I think I am.'

'David called me yesterday.' Kim takes a biscuit too.

'And?' I say, taking a bite.

'And he told me about the baby. Oh God, Emma. I don't know what to say.'

I spit biscuit into my hand. 'Ugh, Kim.'

'Oh God, I didn't mean to upset you. I just wanted you to know that I know …'

I start to laugh, and Kim glares at me open-mouthed.

'They're stale,' I say, pointing at the biscuit. 'That's all. You haven't upset me. Don't worry.'

Kim bites into her biscuit and instantly spits it into the sink. 'Oh, Jesus, yuck.'

Kim laughs and passes me some tissue. 'Seriously, though. You have to be shaken after news like that. What are you going to do?'

I shrug. I scrape the soggy biscuit from my hand, roll it up in the tissue, and toss the mess into the bin beside me. I stand up and make my way around Kim to wash my hand in the sink.

'Emma, seriously. Look at me. I'm worried about you. This is a lot to take in. I can tell you're devastated.'

'I'm not,' I promise, turning around so Kim can see the honesty in my eyes. 'I don't believe her.'

'Oh, Emma.'

'Kim, trust me. I'm not in denial or anything. I know she's bullshitting.'

'How can you be sure?' Kim pulls out a high stool and sits down facing me.

I lean my back against the sink. 'She's trying to mess with my head. And so far, she's been doing a bloody good job. But this baby stuff is a step too far. What's the one thing you know I'm sensitive about?'

Kim shakes her head, and I can tell she has no idea what I'm talking about.

'Babies, Kim. Babies. I can't talk about them; I can't be around them. It's all just a big reminder of my past.'

'But Amber doesn't know that.'

'Actually,' I say wide-eyed, 'I'm pretty sure that she does. She seems to know bloody everything. And that's what I want to find out. How does she know so much about me? Why does she care?'

'Maybe David confides in her,' Kim suggests gently.

My eyes narrow. I hate the thought of David talking to Amber about anything personal. 'Well, he can't have told Amber about our baby – he only just found out himself.'

'You told him?' Kim balks.

I shrug her shock off.

'Oh, my God. Wow,' Kim gushes. 'What did he say?'

I scrunch my nose and shake my head. 'Can we not talk about this now? It was a long time ago. It happened a long time ago.'

Kim chews on the inside of her lip, and it pulls her chin into an unusual shape. 'Yeah, sure.' She nods. 'It *was* a long time ago. But you've never really gotten over it.'

'Kim, seriously. Please.' I roll my shoulders up and back. 'I don't want to go over all this again. That's not why I'm here.'

'Go over what again?' Andy says, striding into the kitchen.

He drapes a pink and white fluffy dressing gown over Kim's shoulders, and she slides her arms gratefully in.

'Nothing. Just girl talk,' Kim lies, nodding towards me.

'Have you two been so busy nattering you haven't even made the coffee yet?' Andy jokes, pottering about the tiny space gathering cups and sugar and milk. It's obvious he's comfortable and knows his way around Kim's kitchen.

'So,' Andy says, spooning some instant coffee into the cups. 'What did you want to talk to me about?'

I inhale sharply and shake my head. I dread the words that are about to come out of my mouth, but I have to say them.

'I need to find Jane Burke.'

Andy spills some boiling water on the countertop and jumps back. Kim rushes over with some tissues and checks that he's okay. They're a sweet couple. The more I get to know Andy, the more I like him.

'I know David asked you to look into all this stalker stuff,' I say, hoping to put him at ease.

'It wasn't anything official, Emma. There were no reports filed or anything like that. I really just pulled up a name. Just a small favour for David.'

'It's okay.' I smile. 'I'm not upset, and I don't think you were going behind my back or anything. I get it. David was worried, and you were helping. Thanks.'

Andy finishes making the coffees and passes them around.

'Thanks,' I say, glad to have something to wash the taste of rotten biscuit out of my mouth.

'Emma, what's going on?' Kim says, not touching her coffee. 'It's eight thirty on a Wednesday morning. You're not a morning person. And you never come over unannounced. I'm worried about you.'

'It's this Jane Burke stuff,' I admit, taking a huge slug of weak coffee. 'I need to find her.'

Andy shakes his head. 'We traced the broadband account, Emma. It's a pay-as-you-go plan. No address. It's a dead end. I'm sorry.'

'But you had an address you told David?'

'Just somewhere she lived years ago. Nothing helpful.'

'It's a start,' I say.

'Emma, this will fizzle. I'm sure of it. Nine times out of ten, this online nonsense turns out to be a disgruntled schoolmate holding a grudge. Or a bored teenager getting their kicks.'

'Maybe.' I shrug. 'But maybe not.'

'Emma, if you're really worried, come by the station later, and we can open a case. Would that make you feel better?'

'No. No. I don't want to waste police time. I'll look into it myself. Can you give me the address you found?'

'Are you going to go there?' Andy asks, his breezy nature suddenly being replaced with a strong, sterner self, and I can only imagine this is a peek at Andy, the policeman.

I shrug.

'Do you know Jane Burke?' Andy asks.

'No.' I shake my head. 'But I've seen her, I think. At the graveyard. And at Danny's funeral.'

'If you don't know her, how do you know you've seen her?' Kim asks, visibly confused.

'Because she's not Jane Burke. She's Amber Hunter.'

Kim gasps. 'Oh, Emma. That's crazy.'

'I know,' I agree. 'But you haven't seen the way Amber looks at me.'

'Emma, there's bound to be dirty looks,' Kim softens. 'Your husband has gotten her pregnant.'

Andy inhales sharply and does a poor job of hiding his shock at Kim's revelation. This was a bad idea. I shouldn't have come here. Neither of them believes me, I can tell.

'Identity theft is really serious, Emma,' Andy drones. 'You can't really go around accusing people of stuff like that. Even a bitch who slept with your husband.'

'I'm not accusing anyone of anything,' I snap. 'I'm just saying that Amber and Jane are the same person. One person. Two names. That's not a crime now, is it?'

'No,' Andy admits.

''Okay, how about we check out this address?' Kim suggests. 'Andy, will you take a look?'

Andy's eyes are narrow and black circles indented underneath emphasise his cheekbones. 'I have looked.' Andy's voice is deeper, and he's not making any effort to hide his wilting patience. 'As I said, there's nothing to go on. She used to live there. She doesn't anymore, and the landlord has no idea where she went. It's a dead fucking end.'

A bead of nervous sweat trickles down my back and comes to an uncomfortable stop on the band of my jeans. 'Andy, please? This woman is trying to ruin my life. I just want to know why.'

Kim's face droops, and I can see the sympathy in her eyes. Kim looked at me the same way when she visited me in the hospital after my first suicide attempt. She gave me the same look when I told her David had cheated. She doesn't even know she does it. I guess I bring that out in her.

'Okay. How about I check it out before work later? I'll speak to the landlord again. See if I can jog his memory,' Andy promises.

'Thank you,' I say on the verge of tears. 'I'll come with you, okay?'

Andy scrunches his nose, and his cheeks push up to meet his eyes as if my suggestion pains him. 'You want to physically go there?'

'Yes.'

'Emma, seriously. This is a wild goose chase. What are you hoping to find?'

'Honestly? I don't know. But Jane or Amber or whatever the hell her name is has it in for me. I want to know why. This isn't all just because she slept with my husband. I know that for sure. Please, Andy. I promise I'll never ask you another favour ever, ever again.'

Andy exhales forcefully and nods. 'Okay, Emma. If it'll make you feel better. We can go.'

'Thank you. Thank you so much.'

Kim straightens her back and pulls a face. 'Well, I'm coming too,' she snorts. 'Let's meet here at six o'clock. Andy, you're not at work until eight, right?'

'Yeah, eight, but I want to get in to the station by seven thirty. I've a load of paperwork that needs seeing to.'

'Okay. Seven thirty. Six should still leave us enough time. I mean how long are we going to be?'

'How about I meet you both there?' I suggest.

Andy eyes me curiously.

I twist my wrist and exaggerate my need to check my watch. 'I have to go. I need to get to work now, or I'll be late,' I lie. 'I have some stuff after school today, so I'll be tight on time, and I don't want to hold you up, Andy. Makes much more sense if I meet you there.'

Nervous lying is making me overheat, and I'm certain my red cheeks are a glowing, telltale sign of my bullshit. There's a noticeable pool of sweat gathering at the base of my spine. Andy must be used to reading liars all the time, and I wait for him to see through my lame excuse.

'Okay. Good idea,' Kim says. 'Let's meet there at six thirty instead?'

'Perfect.' I smile. 'Text me the address, okay?'

Andy pulls his phone out of his tracksuit pants and runs his finger around the screen. He doesn't look at me, and I wonder if I'm growing to be a thorn in his side. It certainly feels like it.

'Forty-seven Upper Mount Earls Street, Rialto,' he says.

'Upper Mount Earls Street,' I echo. 'Okay, got it. See you there later.'

'Emma, it's not a nice area. Don't do anything foolish, okay?' Andy warns, dryly.

I know for sure he's sniffed out my work excuse as a load of crap, and he knows I'm going straight there. I wait for him to stop me, but he excuses himself from the kitchen and drags his tired legs back into the hall. I cringe as he pounds up the stairs, taking his irritation out on each step. I know for sure he doesn't like me.

'Kim, I'm sorry.' I blush. 'I know it's a bit weird, me turning up like this this morning.'

Kim gathers the empty coffee cups and takes them to the sink. 'It's okay,' she hushes. 'But promise me, if we go to this place today and it's a dead end, then you'll let all this go? I know you hate Amber. I would too but don't let all this drive you crazy. Please, Emma. Promise me this is the last of this madness, okay?'

Kim has been my best friend since we were twelve years old. Sometimes, I think she knows me better than I know myself. And I know she loves me. As much as it's possible to love another human. But I also know she worries. I know her heart secretly races anytime David calls her because she doesn't know if he just wants to chat or if he's going to break some terrible news to her. I know she's afraid to tell me her honest opinion, sometimes, in case I fly off the handle and do something stupid. I know she worries that every time she says goodbye, she might be saying it for the last time.

I want nothing more right now than to suggest Kim puts the kettle on again for another cup of coffee. I want to sit beside my best friend and tell her everything I've figured out about Jane Burke. I want to hear my theory out loud, and I want to make Kim see I'm not crazy. I'm right. But I know all of that would be for my benefit. Not Kim's. If I shared the whirlwind of thoughts racing through my mind right now with Kim, she'd be more convinced than ever that I'm losing it. I can't do that to her.

'Okay, I'd better get going,' I insist.

Kim spins around and leans her back against the wet sink edge as if she needs the support to prop her up. 'I'll see you later, Emma. Won't I?'

I swallow. 'Absolutely. See you later.'

Kim jolts forward and wraps two soapy hands around my neck. 'Okay. Later then.'

Chapter Thirty-Four

DAVID

I sleepily roll over and stretch my arm out to wrap around my wife, but it falls against the empty, cold mattress where I expect Emma to be. I open my eyes, and my heart sinks to find the duvet thrown back on Emma's side. I desperately wanted to wake first. I wanted to make us breakfast in bed and spend a lazy morning tucked up together.

I made the decision not to go to work today at some stage during the night. I was ridiculously restless all night and woke often. I've a blistering headache now as a consequence. I sent an email to HR to say I wasn't feeling well, and I don't care if they believe me or not. I know Emma is more upset than she's letting on about Richard insisting she take a leave of absence from work. But secretly, I'm relieved. Maybe we can use her time off to get an appointment with Dr. Brady. He always has greater availability mid-week, and I'd like Emma to see him as soon as possible before she changes her mind. She's playing it way too cool about Amber's baby announcement. She scares me when she's like that, when she hides her real emotions. It's a recipe for disaster.

Dragging myself into the bathroom, I grab a quick shower and don't bother to shave. I throw on yesterday's clothes and make my way downstairs, calling Emma's name. Silence answers me back, and I'm instantly unnerved.

The house is like a living thing. It watches me and sympathetically shakes its head. I run my hand along the wall on my right side as I descend the stairs. The wallpaper is cold to the touch, and I swear I can feel the rise and fall of the bricks beneath my palm as it breaths nervously. The banisters on the other side seem to wrap around me like arms cradling my rounded shoulders as I struggle to propel myself forward, soothing me as I prepare to face whatever is waiting for me after the last step. I stop just before I reach the bottom and stand statue-like, swaying back and forth, afraid to take the next step. Maybe I could stay here forever, suspended in time on the second to last step of the stairs. Maybe if I don't take the next step, the future will never come. Everything is okay on this step. My world is still intact. But I know better than to believe that. Emma has already written her fate. And all I can do is discover if she's written our future with or without her in it.

My mind races, forcing me to blink too often, and my eyes are dry and stinging by the time I make it into the kitchen. It's empty. There isn't as much as a cup out of place. It's eerily still, and I clutch my chest as I scurry back into the hall. The frosted glass panels on each side of the front door offer me a blurry view of Emma's car parked in the front drive. *Maybe she's still here.* I begin to run; my bare feet are hot and stick to the floor tiles, torturing me. I can't move fast enough. I fiddle with the key in the back door, fling it open, and race to the garden. My heart is beating so fast I can hear the pound of my blood coursing behind my ears. The icy grass pinches the soles of my feet, but the cold is a welcome relief. I hurry towards the shed at the end of our walled garden. The door swings back and forth, thumping every so often against the wall. It's messy inside. The lawnmower and garden tools are strewn arbitrarily around the floor. *Emma's not here. Thank God.*

I step outside and secure the shed door behind me. The sudden wind chill rips through my shirt, slapping my chest. It's only then I realise I've been holding my breath. I breathe out and expel a loud, savage roar.

I don't know how long I spend in the garden. Long enough for my feet to go numb, my fingertips to ache, and my mind to clear somewhat. Back inside, the heat of the house takes a long time to work its way into my icy bones. I try calling Emma's mobile countless times, as I pace the whole house, but she doesn't pick up. I call her mother, but she quickly tells me she's on a cruise somewhere exotic, and unsurprisingly, she confesses she hasn't spoken to Emma in a while. Reluctantly, I bring Kim's name up onscreen, and I'm just about to hit the call button when the landline rings loudly, startling me.

'Hello,' I say.

'Hello,' a deep male voices replies. 'May I speak to Emma Lyons, please?'

'Emma's not here at the moment,' I explain, struggling to keep my voice steady. 'May I take a message?'

'Yes, thank you. My name is Bradly Mullins. I'm calling from Mullins and Company solicitors. Would you ask Emma to call me at her earliest convenience, please?'

'Oh. Bradly. Hi, I'm David, Emma's husband. Emma told me she met with you yesterday. Is this about Daniel Connolly's will?'

'Yes. Yes, it is. Apologies, David. I didn't know Emma is married.'

'Yeah. Just recently. We're married a few months now.'

'Oh. Newlyweds. Lovely.' Bradly's deep tone softens. 'Congratulations.'

'Thank you.' I smile. 'Um, I don't know when Emma will be home. Is there anything I can help you with in the meantime?'

'Eh …' Bradly pauses, most likely to decide if it's appropriate or legal to discuss this with Emma's spouse. 'Yes, actually. Would you let Emma know that we've had an offer on the house already?'

'Already?' I gasp.

'Yes. It's much sooner than we anticipated, but the buyer is beyond keen, making an offer without even viewing the premises. The auctioneer assures me it's a very generous offer. Based on other recently sold houses in the area, I agree. If Emma is happy, we'd like to close as soon as possible.'

'That's good news. I'm sure Emma will be pleased,' I say; my chest is tight as I worry if I'll get the chance to tell her.

'Oh,' Bradly blurts suddenly. 'Would you also let Emma know she's exempt from any death duties, so the full fifty percent, after the auctioneer's fees, is hers.'

'I'm sorry,' I interrupt, certain I've misunderstood something. 'Why exactly is Emma exempt?'

'Children don't pay tax when inheriting from a deceased parent.'

'Oh. Okay,' I stumble, shaking my head and almost dropping the receiver. 'I'll let Emma know as soon as she comes home. Thank you.'

'Thank you, David. A pleasure speaking with you. Goodbye.' Bradly Mullins rattles off the generic response and hangs up.

I stand with the receiver still in my hand staring into space. I wonder if there's been some huge mistake. Emma believes her dad died when she was a little girl. She's grieved for the absence of a father figure all her life. I sometimes wonder if that huge, missing part of her childhood affects her more deeply than she realises. I even suspect missing a male role model growing up contributed to her self-harming on some subconscious level. I shake my head. Bradly Mullins must be mistaken. Danny would have told Emma. He couldn't have spent years getting to know her and never confessed that he was her father. What man could not acknowledge their own child? I snort and catch my reflection in the mirror on the wall across from me. I can't be a man who abandons a baby. I can't be a bad father. But accepting responsibility for the life I've created will destroy my wife. *If it hasn't already.*

Chapter Thirty-Five

EMMA

I've never been over to this side of the city before. Its unsavoury reputation precedes it. I've heard all the rumours about drug lords and murderers living in every second house. But looking out the bus window, I find the streets quiet and inconspicuous. Neat, well-kept shops line the road, and the houses are small and tidy. It's a dull, grey morning, and the world outside the window is depressing but not scary.

Not many passengers are on the bus at this time. The scattered few look as unimpressed to be here as I am. It's almost ten a.m., but I suspect the man sitting across from me is still drunk from the night before. His warm breath reaches across the aisle and hits me like a tequila shot spilling in my face. His tattoos creep from his neck onto the lower parts of his jaw, and every time I catch his eye, he growls at me.

'Poor sod,' an elderly lady beside me says. 'Used to be a businessman, but he lost it all to drink and gambling. The wife left him after that. Can't say I blame her, really.'

'Oh, um.' I clear my throat, and my face glows.

The tattooed man lifts his head to stare in our direction, and I'm certain he heard her.

'That's very sad,' I say. Dropping my eyes to the ground, I hope she'll take the hint and not share any more gossip about the locals.

'Where are you headed?' she asks. 'You don't look like you're from around here.'

'I … I … I'm not,' I admit. 'I'm visiting a friend.'

'You're visiting a friend around these parts.' She snorts as if it's the most ridiculous thing she's ever head.

'Yes. I am.' I smile with my eyes narrow.

'What's the address? I'll help you find it.'

'I know where she lives,' I puff out. 'But thank you.'

'You've been here before?'

'Yes. Of course,' I lie.

'Really? Then why have I never seen you on this bus before?'

'I don't know,' I groan, my patience tested.

'I get this bus every day. Twice a day. Sometimes four if I forget my bits and pieces and have to take a second trip to the shops. I've never seen you before, ever. That's for sure.'

I shake my head. 'I usually drive.'

'But not today?'

I look out the window. It's started to snow again. Not as heavy as last night but enough to give the appearance that tiny pieces of the thick overhead clouds are breaking free and falling to the ground.

'The weather is too bad to drive today.' I smirk, satisfied with my believable argument.

'Too bad to drive.' She nods, following my gaze out the window to the cars whipping past. 'Too bad to drive.' She laughs with a throaty gargle.

'I'm not a good driver,' I explain. 'I haven't passed my test yet.'

'You're not a good liar either.' She laughs more.

I swallow a huge lump of frustrated air and will the bus to drive faster. I can't wait to get off.

'Don't get upset, love,' she softens. 'I'm only teasing. You must be wondering why I'm asking all these silly questions?'

I'm not wondering. I've already assumed she lives alone, and her daily bus ride is her lifeline. It's most likely her only opportunity to be around other people and to engage in a little light banter. I hope most people entertain her. She's condescending and irritating, but I doubt she means to be.

My mind is tired, and my palms are wet with nervous sweat. I don't want to talk to anyone about anything right now, but I find myself offering her the generic response I know she's hoping for. 'Yes, I suppose I am wondering.'

I expect to get her life story. Perhaps, her husband has recently passed. Or she has grown children who don't visit as often as they should.

'You remind me of someone,' she says gently.

'Really?' I smile, surprised.

'A girl.' Her eyes dance, and I see the blissful spark of a memory. 'She had eyes just like yours, and your smile curves up at the edges in the same way. She was my neighbour. A lovely young woman; pretty as a picture, she was. She visited me often, and we had tea sometimes. But she moved away a long time ago. One day, out of the blue, she just upped and left. She never came to say goodbye. I still wonder what happened to her. I miss her terribly.'

The bus turns down a narrow road with apartment blocks towering on both sides, blocking most of the natural light. I wonder how the bus will fit between the sea of cars parked ludicrously at leisure alongside and, sometimes, even on top of the footpath.

The elderly lady pulls on the back of the seat in front of us and uses it to propel herself out of her seat.

'This is my stop,' she explains. 'It was lovely to meet you.'

'You too,' I say genuinely.

I bend down and gather her bags from the floor. She smiles brightly and reaches for them, clasping my hand in hers on the exchange. Her warm, wrinkled fingers wrap around my palm, and she gives my hand a gentle shake.

'I really hope you find your friend,' she whispers with tears glistening in her eyes.

'Me too,' I reply poignantly, taking until now to realise we're talking about the same person. 'Me too.'

Chapter Thirty-Six

JANE

The apartment smells of piss. I walk around with my nostrils flared as I sniff deeply. It's not coming from the replacement couch or the laminate flooring that's been scrubbed so vigorously with antibacterial cleaner it's a shade lighter than I remember. It seems to be seeping from the walls, as if they have a memory of a time gone by, and they dare to spit a reminder at me now. It's rancid and makes my stomach heave. I take a large scented candle out of my bag and place it on the windowsill in the kitchen. It's never been used, and the stubborn wicks take a few seconds to accept the flame of the match I hold to it. But within minutes, the scent of pear and vanilla masks the urine. The scent is even stronger than I hoped, and I smile with deep satisfaction, suspecting it will hide the stench of a rotting body for a few days.

The smell of the candle doesn't reach the bedroom, and the whiff of damp hits my face like a wet cloth as soon as I step inside. I sit on the bed and stare out the window. The street below is coming to life. Delivery vans block the footpaths as they finish their morning run. Buses sweep past, their double-decker roofs reaching just below the bedroom window. I remember Will asking me once if I thought he could jump out the window and land on top of one of the buses as they pass. I laughed. He was high and giddy. I didn't take him seriously. Three days later, he was dead.

It's snowing. Just a light smattering, really. But enough to make the ground slippery. Parents take extra care as they hold their children's hands. One woman, in particular, catches my attention. Her long red coat is a vibrant contrast against the falling snow. It's not much more than a raincoat. It swings open at the front where it's missing buttons, and there's a noticeable hole in one of the underarm areas. She must be cold out there. She has a tight grip on a little boy's hand. He drags reluctantly behind her, purposely trying to step in as many slushy puddles as he can find. He's dressed for the weather. A bright blue, woolly hat with a bauble sits on top of his head; accessorised cosily with a matching scarf and gloves. His coat looks brand new. It's puffy and a little too big, making him appear broader than I'd say he really is. His schoolbag dangling off his back is almost as big as he is, and I can't stop smiling as I watch him. He's a happy child, I can tell. His mother's flimsy coat is a statement of their tight finances, and clearly, she spends every penny she does have on her beautiful little boy. But despite her own appearance, she's smiling, and I can see in her eyes just how much she adores her son. They must live locally. She's about my age, maybe a year or two younger, and her son is Marley's age. They could have been in school together. My son and hers. They could have been friends in another life. I would have liked that. I would have been happy.

I watched them until they turned the corner and disappeared out of view. I could stay sitting on the edge of the bed and stare out the window all day. It's like fine dining for the soul, and I'm enjoying a slice of my past.

My head is full of thoughts of Marley. How he smelt. His angelic face. How light and fragile his newborn body felt cradled in my arms. Marley was born on a beautiful summer's afternoon, three weeks and two days after his father died. And I loved him from the second I laid eyes on him. Marley was born six days early, but his weight was more like a six-week premature baby. He was a tiny three pounds five ounces, and his whole body wasn't much bigger than the palm of my hand. They barely gave me time to hold him. A midwife hovered beside me the whole time my son was in my arms. She was so close to me I could smell the garlic from her lunch off her hot breath.

I blinked, and when I opened my eyes again, two doctors were in the room. One sat at the end of my bed with his head between my legs as he stitched up my gaping skin. The other spoke only to the midwife. Doing as she was told, the midwife slid her arms between my chest and my son, and she took him from me.

Marley wasn't just my newborn son—he was a statistic. An addict's baby. He had a label. The doctor said it as if the words tasted of vomit. No one told me how long it would take him to detox; all they said was it wouldn't be pleasant.

It was half a day later when two women in poor-fitting black suits came to see me. My throat was raw and dry from screaming for my taken child. They didn't have to tell me they were from the Department for Children because I knew. They said they were there to protect Marley. Them. Two middle-aged bitches with bad hair and condescending faces. They decided Marley needed protection from me. His own mother. His own flesh and blood. Junkies don't make good parents, they decided. They were placing him in foster care, and there wasn't a damn thing I could do about it.

The dark black circles that hung under my eyes, my scrawny limbs with not enough fat to protect my bones, and the puncture wounds sprinkled across my skin like chocolate chips painted the picture of a shitty parent. Addict was tattooed into my soul. But where were those Child Services bitches when I was a kid? Who protected me? No one. My parents didn't wear their failings on their faces. There was nothing to see; well, not on the outside anyway. My tall, slim mother with her golden blond hair and ruby red nails was the elucidation of wholesome. No one saw the countless bottles of wine she hid in her wardrobe. No one saw the specks of glass I picked out of my hair when an empty bottle came crashing down over the back of my skull. My handsome father with broad shoulders and dark eyes was every inch the dapper gentleman. No one saw his disrespect for his wife and his inability to keep his dick away from stupid teenage girls happy to blow him off. No one ever saved me. I was alone. No one saw as I fell to my demise.

It wasn't always heroin. In the early days, it was just experimenting with some weed. My more extrovert friends even tried it. It was just a little smoking to make me feel better. But soon, that wasn't enough. I wanted to feel higher. Lighter. My friends slowly backed away. I was slipping, and they weren't going to slide with me. Some of them stuck around for as long as they could, trying to coax me back, but they all eventually gave up. Or I pushed them away. I don't really remember now. It was most likely the latter. Cocaine was too expensive, and I wasn't prepared to sleep with the dealers for my fix. I've never stooped that low. Heroin just made more sense. The guys I bought it off said it would be the best high I ever had, and they were right. They just didn't warn me that you could never come back down. Not ever. Not even if a baby, a baby you so desperately wanted, was growing inside you.

I left the hospital two days after Marley's birth with nothing more than the clothes on my back and an outpatient appointment for some clinic on the far side of the city to help me dry out; as if I was a fucking tea towel they could hang out on the washing line. I kept the appointment, but I didn't keep my baby.

I have another appointment today. An appointment for my new addiction—Emma. I hope the flowers I left on William's grave weren't too subtle a clue, and she'll figure it all out. I can barely contain my excitement. Now, I just have to wait for her to come.

Chapter Thirty-Seven

DAVID

Time is passing in painful slow motion. Emma's ignoring all my calls. Frustration sits in the pit of my stomach, and I feel physically ill. I pace the sitting room floor, sighing heavily. I've contemplated leaving the house to go look for her, but I'm worried she'll come back while I'm out. As usual, I'm afraid to leave her home alone, if she comes home at all.

I hold my breath as my phone vibrates in my pocket, but my heart sinks when I discover Kim's name instead of Emma's flashing on the screen.

'Hello,' I grunt.

'Hey. David. Hi,' Kim races.

'Is everything okay?' I ask.

My chest is so tight; it's hard to suck in air, and anything that does make it as far as my lungs burns.

'Where are you?' Kim asks. 'Are you at work?'

'No. I'm at home today. Why?'

'Is Emma there with you?'

'No.'

Fear and desperation collide inside me. I hate that Emma can do this to me. I hate that I'm so afraid of what she might be doing that I could actually wet my pants.

'Is she at work?' Kim's voice is a barely audible whisper.

'No. Not today.' My teeth chatter. 'Kim, what's wrong. What's going on? Has Emma contacted you today? She was

288

gone when I got up this morning, and I don't know where she is. She's not answering her phone.' I exhale sharply and admit defeat. 'I'm freaking out here.'

'Okay,' Kim rasps. 'Okay.'

I can't tell if she's trying to calm me down or trying to keep herself from losing it. Either way, she's failing on both counts.

'She was with me this morning,' Kim says.

'What? Why? Where?'

'Here. At my place. She's not gone long, David. Less than an hour.'

'Oh, Jesus Christ, Kim.' I surge. 'There's a lot she can do in an hour.'

'I know. I know.' Kim sighs. 'I saw her bandaged hand. Is she self-harming again?'

'She swears it was an accident,' I say, suddenly not so sure. 'Oh, God. I should call the police. I need to report her missing. I knew she was handling this baby news too well. Oh Christ, if she's hurt herself …'

'David, you know the cops can't do anything. Andy can't do anything. She's only been gone an hour.'

'How did she seem when she was with you?' I swallow, my thoughts scrambling.

'She seemed like Emma,' Kim says. 'She didn't seem like she was going to do anything stupid, but …'

'But you just don't know.' I finish Kim's sentence for her and fall silent.

'I think you should sit down,' Kim says. 'David, please. Sit.'

I don't want to sit. I want to find my wife. I want to tell her that I'm sorry for the mistakes I made. That I'm ashamed. But I *am* human. People make mistakes, and she can't keep torturing herself. Or me.

'Kim, what do you know?' I growl. 'Emma tells you everything. I know you think you're protecting her by keeping her secrets, but you're not. You never have been. Now, please, tell me what you know.'

'Are you sitting?' Kim slurs.

'Yes, I'm goddamn sitting.' I shake my head. 'Now, tell me.' I drill my feet into the floor, struggling to stay standing.

'Have you been on Facebook this morning?' Kim asks.

I omit a loud, throaty groan as if something has suddenly slapped me hard between my shoulders. 'No, Kim. I've a little more on my mind than checking Facebook, to be honest.'

'David, just listen, okay,' Kim sighs. 'Something has happened to Emma's Facebook page.'

'Is Emma online? Has she checked in somewhere? Does Facebook say where she is?' I race.

'David.' Kim whispers my name, and I know she's going to say something terrible with her next breath. 'Emma's Facebook page has been memorialised.'

'What?' My eyes narrow. 'What the hell does that mean?'

'It's appearing beside her profile picture. It says, *Remembering Emma Lyons*. It's creepy. Facebook is basically saying Emma is dead.'

I'm sorry I didn't take Kim's advice and sit when she asked me. I scramble to the couch now, before I collide with the floor. 'What the hell? Why would Facebook be saying that?'

'I don't know. It's very messed up.'

'Is it actually on Emma's profile?' I say, desperate for clarification. 'I mean it's not just a status update or a post by someone else? That weird troll messing around. I mean … have her account settings actually been changed to say she's dead?'

Kim clears her throat, and it resonates loudly in my ear. 'Her Facebook page is officially changed to a Remember Emma page. Someone has reported Emma as deceased to Facebook.'

'Christ.' I gasp, my hand slapping my mouth. 'That's sick. This troll crap is out of control.'

'Did Emma do this?' Kim's voice shakes, as the words drag from somewhere deep inside her, and the weight of worrying about Emma is etched in her tone. 'Is she trying to tell us something? Maybe she's finally hurt herself badly this time. Because of the baby. Oh God, David. I don't like the sound of this. I'm scared.'

'No,' I say sternly. 'Emma didn't do this. This is someone else. This is someone's idea of a twisted joke.'

'Or someone's prediction.' Kim gasps.

I shake my head and pound up the stairs; the friction of the carpet under my bare feet is hot and attempts to burn my toes.

'When Emma hurts herself …' I pant, trying to catch my breath as I round the top of the stairs and charge into my bedroom. '… she never thinks it through. It's an irrational action, something she does on the spur of the moment to take her mind off something else. Everything Emma does is reactive. It's never calculated or thought through. If it were, she wouldn't do it.' I bend down and slide my arm under the bed right up to my elbow.

'So what?' Kim quibbles. 'You're basically saying Emma just has a bad temper. I think there's a bit more to it than that.'

'Actually.' I smile as my hand smacks against my cold laptop, and I drag it out, open it, and switch it on. 'It really is as simple as that. Emma can't control it, of course, and the person she takes her frustration out on is herself. But that's exactly what it is. Frustration. An inability to cope when things stray outside the lines. When Emma gets like that, it's tunnel vision, and the only thing she can see is making the pain stop. There's no pause for thought. No time to weigh the consequences or even time to think about all the people besides herself who she is hurting. And certainly no time to fucking update Facebook.'

A slurping sound gargles somewhere in the back of Kim's throat, and I know she understands.

'Help me find her, Kim. Please, help me find her?'

'Stay there,' Kim says. 'Andy and I will come around. Try not to panic, okay. We'll be there soon.'

'Okay. Okay. Bye.'

I drop my phone onto the bed and switch my attention to my laptop. It's slow to come to life, and the internet is crawling. Finally, I manage to bring Emma's Facebook page up on the screen. My eyes round and widen as I stare at the offending words beneath Emma's profile picture.

Remembering Emma Lyons.

Kim's right. Emma's page has been memorialised. It's now an online shrine to her memory. My stomach heaves, and I belch, dragging acidic vomit up the back of my throat. It sprays past my lips, and I catch it in my hand before it hits my keyboard.

I wash my hands in the bathroom and stare in the mirror above the sink as I brush my teeth. My reflection meets me head-on. My hair sticks out at odd angles on one side from sleeping on it, and my beard is shaggy and overdue for a trim. I look the same as any morning on the outside. Maybe a little paler than usual, but that's it. My reflection doesn't see the pain on the inside. It doesn't reflect how my heart races furiously; so fast, I wonder if it will just give up soon out of pure exhaustion. It doesn't show that my lungs are weary and burning from breathing rapidly. Or that my mind is scrambled and unable to concentrate as hundreds of thoughts rip around inside my skull like a hurricane. My eyes are the only clue that something is wrong. They're glassy, and darting from side to side and fear resonates where the light hits them. My eyes speak volumes. They say I'm petrified that I'll lose my wife. And if I do, I'll most likely lose my mind.

The distinctive beep of my phone announcing a received message drags me out of the bathroom. My phone dances on the bed as message after message comes in. I can't believe the words on the screen. People are offering me condolences on my loss. *This can't be happening.*

Emma's Facebook page is filling up with expressions of sympathy. Picture collages of her past litter her page, accompanied by heartfelt grief and kind words.

Emma, you were beautiful inside and out.

I will miss you.

Rest in peace.

A college friend whom I haven't heard Emma mention in years writes. There's a string of messages before and after. I scroll down and read another.

Gone too soon.

You will be missed.

I assume the brief words are from one of the teachers at Emma's school. There's a photograph of Emma with her class attached.

Deeply saddened to hear the news of Emma's passing.

We haven't spoken in a long time.

I've been meaning to reach out and suggest we grab a coffee.

I can't believe it's too late.

Emma, I'm sorry.

I will never forget you.

I slam the screen down unable to read anymore. This is so messed up.

Chapter Thirty-Eight

EMMA

I've countless missed calls from David, and now, Kim's name is flashing on my phone screen. I guess they're in touch with each other. Talking about me. David has probably told Kim I've been forced to take leave from work. Kim will put two and two together and figure out I've gone to find Jane without her and Andy. She'll tell David where I've gone. *Dammit.* I know David and Kim worry about me—all the time—but today, of all days, I really don't want them checking up on me. This is my fight. And I'm going to be the one to end it. I ignore my phone and get off the bus.

The apartment block is smaller in reality than it appeared on Google Maps. It stretches several windows across, but it's only three stories tall. There are metal bars on all the ground-floor windows, and I imagine living inside must equate to life as an animal caged in the zoo. It's mid-morning, but the curtains are drawn on the majority of windows. The walls are badly in need of fresh paint. Overall, the building is a murky grey. The colour whites come out of the washing machine when a blue sock sneaks its way into the load. Patches of buttermilk peek through sporadically where the rain has washed the grubby neglect away to reveal the original colour of the walls. Graffiti decorates any part of the wall that's accessible from the ground, and bright spray paint even covers the steps leading to the main door. It's possibly the most depressing building I've ever seen. I can't imagine how anyone could be happy living here.

The main door swings open from the inside, and I race up the steps, without thinking, to squeeze inside before whoever's coming out closes the door again.

A woman about my age appears. She purposely avoids eye contact, but she keeps her hand on the door until I reach for it. It's heavier than I was expecting, and I have to push hard to stop it from forcing me out. Finally, I step inside and yelp when the door slams behind me with an aggressive bang. A long, dark corridor stretches out in front of me, and the only light is shining down the concrete stairs on one side. There's no flooring. The bare concrete painted a depressing grey, and in unison with the outside, it needs attention.

I've memorised Jane's address, but that doesn't help me now in my search for the correct apartment. Only some of the doors have numbers. I take a few steps forward and stop outside number nineteen. There aren't many more doors further down the corridor, and I suspect number forty-seven is on a higher floor. I begin to climb the stairs, one shaky step at a time. Every creak and crack of the old building paralyse me for a split second. I stop to catch my breath as I reach the first floor. I'm certain someone will notice me and realise I don't belong here. My heart flutters like the wings of a swallow trapped inside my chest. I am that bird. Caged and frightened but determined to survive. My life has not been my own since Jane Burke cast her net over me, and I need to understand why. I need answers so I can soar again. I need to fly free, and only Jane can let me go.

The third floor is the brightest. There are several roof windows and the natural light coming in makes up here seem far less depressing than the previous levels. There aren't as many doors on this floor, so I guess the apartments are larger.

The doors up here suffer from the same missing numbers as the previous floors. I quickly find number forty-six, but there's no forty-seven. Since the doors leading up to forty-four are all void of numbers I've no idea if forty-seven should be opposite or beside it. I decide to try beside it first.

I take a deep breath, raise my right hand, and knock firmly. The door creaks open within seconds, and a bare chested man in baggy tracksuit bottoms stands in the gap.

'Yeah?' he barks.

I clear my throat uncomfortably and force a gummy smile. 'Um, I'm looking for Jane Burke.'

'Who?' he grunts, his round belly shaking like jelly as it hangs low and over the edge of his pants.

'Jane.' I lean forward, thinking he didn't hear me. 'Um, Jane Burke.' I grimace, my eyebrows raised as if I'm in pain.

'I don't know her,' he snaps, slamming the door shut without warning.

I lunge backwards, almost losing my toes to the bang. I exhale sharply and take a couple of seconds to gather myself. I'm shaken and more on edge than ever, but I spin around and knock on the opposite door without allowing myself time to overthink it or to chicken out.

No one answers. I knock again. Still nothing. I press my ear against the peeling varnish and listen for signs of life inside. I hear a rhythmic tapping, and I guess it's footsteps against a timber floor on the other side. Instead of tapping my knuckles against the door again and knocking politely, I make a fist and turn my hand so the spongy part under my baby finger takes the impact as I pound on the door assertively.

The door swings open while I'm still pounding, and I jerk my arm back, red faced.

Chapter Thirty-Nine

EMMA

'Hello, Emma.'

'Hello, Amber,' I reply instinctively, recognising the face of David's boss staring back at me. 'Or should I call you Jane?'

'You can call me sis?' She grins.

Her white teeth sit straight between her cherry lips. She's wearing a floral apron with baby pink lace piping all around the edges. Her blond hair is clipped back off her face, and her makeup is subtle yet pristine. The shine off her black patent boots is impressive and catches the light. Her appearance is a stark contrast to her overweight, half-dressed male neighbour. She could easily be mistaken for a suburban housewife. She doesn't belong here. She doesn't fit in.

'Excuse me?' I snort.

'Nothing. Never mind. Call me whatever you like.'

'I want to call you by your real name. You're Jane Burke, aren't you?'

'Yes.' She nods as if I simply asked her if she would like a cup of tea.

She turns her back and walks away, leaving the door wide open. I have a clear view of the inside from the door arch. The door leads straight into an open-plan kitchen and living area. It's a decent size, and it seems to be better maintained than the rest of the building and the stairwell. Jane busies herself in the kitchen. I can smell cinnamon and dough, and it's obvious from the flour-strewn countertops that she has been baking.

'Are you coming in, or are you going to eat from the hall?'

'Eat?' I gasp, shaking my head.

'Yes. I thought we could share breakfast.'

'You were expecting me?' I deduce, suddenly feeling like coming here was a big mistake.

'Well. Yes. If not today, then tomorrow.' Jane slips on some oven glows that match her apron and bends down to attend to something in the oven. 'But I knew you'd come. Eventually. I was counting on it.'

'We need to talk,' I say, quivering as I pluck up the courage to cross the threshold.

'Sure,' Jane chirps. 'Close the door, won't you? There's a draft.'

I don't want to close the door. The prospect of sealing my escape route is terrifying. But I do as Jane asks.

'Do you like chocolate chip or cinnamon?' she says with her head leaning into the oven.

'Excuse me?'

'Muffins. I made muffins. Which would you rather? I'm having chocolate chip, but I've made both, so you choose.'

This is so fucked up, I think, staring at the tray of piping hot baked goods that she pulls out of the oven and spills onto a wire rack waiting on the countertop.

'The kettle is boiled,' Jane twitters. 'I'll have tea ready in a minute.'

I suck my lips between my teeth and search for words.

Jane glides her hand thorough mid-air and points at the kitchen table in front of me. 'Please. Have a seat.'

The table is dressed with cups and saucers, plates and highly polished knives and forks. There's two of everything. A setting for her, and the other for me, I guess. A vase of fresh ivory carnations takes pride of place in the centre of the table. I freeze as I recognise the simple bouquet. They're the same flowers Jane left on William Burke's grave. The flowers weren't a subtle clue, I realise. They were a trap. She wanted me to find them.

'Who is William Burke?' I ask, my eyes fixed on the back of Jane's head as she busies herself washing some raspberries and blackcurrants—no doubt to accompany the homemade muffins.

'Take a seat,' Jane reiterates, tossing her head over her shoulder towards the table.

Her voice is light like summer rain, but her jaw is square and reveals her distaste for my question.

'Who is he, Jane? Answer me.'

Jane slams the wire tray against the countertop. The loud bang startles me, and I squeak like a frightened mouse and jump back. My shoulders collide with the door behind me and slap noisy air out of my open mouth.

Jane twitches. She coughs just once and runs her hands over her apron, as if smoothing out the creases can smooth out her mounting temper.

'I'm sorry,' she says. 'I didn't mean to startle you. But I'd really like if you took a seat now.'

Jane begins to arrange the muffins in a basket, like a little girl who just wants to play tea parties and she's frustrated that her playmate doesn't want to join in the fun.

'Why won't you answer my question, Jane?' I say, my hand reaching around behind my back, patting the door as I try to find the handle. 'Do you even know the man buried in that grave? Are you really Jane Burke, or is that just another person you pretend to be?'

Jane's teeth snap shut. The crack of colliding enamel sends a shiver down my spine.

'I just want to have a nice breakfast. It's all I want,' Jane scowls. 'After everything you've done, it's the least you owe me.'

'What have I ever done to you?' I shake my head. 'I barely know you.'

I can't locate the door handle behind me, and when Jane opens a drawer to pull out a knife, I stop breathing. I know she notices because she looks directly at me as she slices the top off one of the muffins and does not attempt to hide her satisfied smirk.

'You need to reach higher,' Jane instructs, as she moves her attention from me to a china tea pot that she fills with loose tea leaves and adds boiling water. 'The door handle is just a few inches above your hand.'

I pull my arm out from behind my back and interlock my fingers as I tuck my hands tight against my chest where she can see them.

'You can leave anytime you want to, Emma. You're not my prisoner.' Jane laughs. 'You came here of your own free will, remember? I didn't even invite you.'

I don't know what to say. Everything Jane says is making sense, and there's no snarky undertone, but I can still tell she's not sincere. She's saying one thing when she means another. It's some sort of reverse psychology. She's making it seem like I'm the crazy one. She's always one step ahead, and it's mind boggling.

'Emma, sit.'

Jane uses the knife to cut an invisible wound through the air. She kicks a chair leg and sends the chair sliding back across the floor. When it steadies and comes to a stop, surprisingly without falling over, Jane points the tip of the knife at the tattered cushion resting on top.

'Sit,' she repeats, not bothering to separate her top and bottom teeth as she hisses.

I sit, terrified not to, and tuck myself into the table. Jane carries the goodies to the table on an old tray. The home baking looks delicious, and it smells even more appetising. But I can't take my eyes off the tray. It's grubby and worn out with more chips than the muffins. It doesn't fit her Domestic Goddess image. Jane can't miss the flowers in the centre of the table. They're pretty and a noticeable centrepiece, but she pushes the vase over with the edge of the tray, scattering the carnations messily and splashing water across the table to trickle onto the floor. Jane ignores the shambles and lays the tray down in the centre of the table.

'Have you decided?' she asks, looking me straight in the eye.

'Decided what?' I breathe; my eyes drift to the puddle in front of me.

'Which muffin do you want? Or, oh my gosh, where are my manners? Would you like two? One of each?'

'Um ...' I swallow, almost too careworn to push words past my lips. 'Chocolate chip, please?'

Jane smiles brightly as she places a steaming muffin on the waiting plate in front of me. 'We have the same taste.'

I don't tell her that if she had chosen cinnamon, I would have asked for cinnamon. I want whichever one she's having;

it's less likely to be laced with rat poison or something if she's eating it too.

'Tea?' Jane asks. The lid of the china teapot rattles as her hand wobbles, and I wonder if she's nervous.

'Yes. Please.'

'Oh good, you're a tea person. I wasn't sure, but I took a guess. You don't look like a coffee person.'

'I drink both,' I correct, dazed by the ordinary, almost boring conversation.

'Jam?' Jane asks.

I shake my head. 'No. Thank you.'

Jane giggles. 'We have a lot in common, Emma. I'm not a jam fan, either.'

'I like jam,' I protest, desperate to be different from her. 'I just don't want any today.'

Jane throws her hands above her head in mock surrender. 'Okay, no jam today.'

I watch Jane pull out her chair and sit with exaggerated grace. She takes a muffin out of the basket for herself and slams it onto her plate almost crushing it. I stiffen as she reaches for her knife and slices the muffin straight down the centre with undeniable aggression. The stainless steel blade clatters against the fine china plate. Jane glares at me and chortles loudly.

'Why are you doing this?' I say, unable to take anymore.

'I like to eat one half at a time.' She laughs.

'Jane, stop it. You know that's not what I mean. This is torture. Why me? Why have you targeted me?'

Jane picks up half the muffin and throws it across the room. It collides with the wall and crumbles upon impact. It falls to the ground in hundreds of crumbly pieces, leaving a dirty, brown stain behind.

'What makes you think this is about you? Christ, you're so conceited.' Jane rolls her eyes. 'Maybe, it's about me. Maybe, it's about what I want. Did you ever stop to think about that?'

'Jane. I don't know what's going on here. Or what your obsession with me is. But it has to stop. You have to stay away.'

'Is that a threat?' Jane stands up and towers over me.

I hop up and knock my chair over in the process. It smashes against the ground with a loud bang. Jane doesn't flinch.

'I'll go to the police,' I say. 'I'll tell them everything.'

Jane throws her head back, and a patronising laugh gargles in her throat. 'And what exactly would you tell them? That I slept with your husband, and it's driving you crazy? It's not illegal to have a one-night stand, Emma.'

I back away, but Jane follows. Her huge smile is forced and intimidating. *I never should have come here.*

'Maybe, David couldn't resist me. Maybe, he wanted me so badly he was prepared to throw everything away for one night in my bed.' The lines around Jane's eyes soften unexpectedly, and her tone is lighter and less tense. Suddenly, she looks less like she wants to slit my throat and more like she's in desperate need of a hug. 'Maybe, David didn't think of you at all. Maybe, he was purely selfish, and he never once considered how much his actions would hurt you. He told you he loved you. He promised he'd always be there for you, but he lied. He never stopped to think of how you'd have to pick the pieces once he was gone.'

'What?' I say, suddenly pulling myself up as straight as my back allows. 'What are you talking about? David hasn't gone anywhere. We're still together. You know that.'

Jane tosses her head and runs her hands through her hair. Her bun loosens and strands break free and stick to her clammy face. I can see tears glisten in her eyes, but they don't fall. It's a fleeting glimpse of pain, but she gathers herself before I see enough to understand.

'Jane. If this isn't about me, then what? Tell me. Help me to understand. What happened to you? Why are you so angry?'

'Don't.' Jane raises a hand, and I flinch as I prepare for her to hit me. 'Don't you dare pretend you care about me or my problems.'

'I don't care about you,' I say honestly, backing farther away. 'But you've made your problems my problems. You've barged into my life and made things a living hell for me. All I care about is making it stop.'

'There. Now, you're showing your true colours, Emma. You're selfish. Just like your mother.'

'You know my mother?' I gasp.

Jane grunts. 'No.'

'Jane, I don't understand. You're talking in riddles. I can't keep up.'

'I was a happy kid, Emma. I loved my mother and my father. And I thought they loved me. But my father only loved himself. You see, he was a scoundrel. A cheat. He had an affair. He got another woman pregnant. What kind of man does that?'

I stare at Jane through squinted eyes. Her ramblings seem to shave inches off her, and she doesn't appear as tall or as intimidating as moments before.

'David,' I whisper.

Saying my husband's name feels like a betrayal, but I know that's what Jane wants to hear and I want her to keep talking. I want to learn more. But she narrows her eyes, and I see a flash of temper. I've said the wrong thing.

'Men are all the same. Selfish. They will always abandon you. Every man I've ever loved has left me. You should thank me. I've done you a favour.'

'Jane, my husband isn't leaving me,' I interrupt. 'I keep trying to tell you that. No matter how hard you try, you can't drive us apart.'

Jane's lips twitch to one side, and her jaw cracks. I tread carefully, afraid to irk her too much.

'I've put David through hell over the years,' I confess truthfully. 'And he's always stuck by me. He was there for me at my lowest. He's still here now.'

'I know exactly what you've done. I know the type of person you are, Emma. You hurt yourself to ease your pain, but you never consider what that does to the people around you. You're a selfish bitch. Just. Like. Me.'

Jane's words sting. They hurt more than if she'd stabbed me with the knife she used to cut her muffin.

'You're right,' I say. 'I've done some terrible things. But I don't deserve this.'

'Maybe you don't,' Jane says. She walks back to the table and begins to tidy up. 'But I didn't deserve what happened to me.'

The door is just a couple of footsteps away. I can leave if I want to. Jane is giving me the green light. Her back is to me, and I suspect if I run now, she won't follow me. But something deep inside forces me to stay. I've seen something familiar in her eyes, in the way she hangs her head. I see me.

I follow her to the table, and I crouch on my hunkers as I pick up the battered carnations.

'Who is William Burke?' I ask for a second time since walking into this apartment. But for the first time, I suspect I already know the answer.

'My husband.' Jane swallows.

'What happened to him?' I ask, my heart aching as I ask the question that must be so hard for her to hear. 'Did he leave you? Is that who abandoned you?'

'He killed himself.' Jane nods, busying herself as she carries the cups and plates over to the sink.

'Why?' I whisper.

'Because he was selfish. I told you.'

I stand up and set the flowers down on a chair. Jane is leaning over the sink with her hands dipped into sudsy water. She submerges the crockery and clatters cups and plates together noisily. I approach her slowly, taking baby steps. I don't want to spook her.

I stand alongside her and wait in silence. Jane takes her temper out on the washing up. She works up a sweat as she splashes water all over both of us. She slams the plates and cups against the draining board. One plate snaps clean in half, and a cup loses a handle. Jane doesn't bat an eyelid. I don't move. I just let her work her frustration out, and for the first time since I stepped inside this apartment, I'm not afraid of Jane Burke. I feel sorry for her.

Minutes later, when we are both soaking wet and cold, Jane turns around, presses her back against the sink, and slides to the floor.

I sit beside her, cross-legged, in silence. Jane pants and puffs. Sighs and snorts and eventually begins to cry. I don't move. I understand it's years of anger and pain bubbling over. I wonder if Jane has ever admitted to another person that her husband took his own life. I doubt it. I wonder why she told me. I hope I find out.

Jane turns to face me. Her cheeks are red and blotchy from salty tears stinging her skin, and her eyes look too wide and round for their sockets. I've seen myself look exactly like that. In fact, her dishevelled face is uncannily similar to mine when I cry.

'Will thought I would be better off without him.' Jane heaves. 'He was so wrong.'

My breath catches in my throat. I've thought those same dark thoughts. On my worst days, when David really suffered because of me, I thought life would be better for him if I wasn't in it.

'But you're not better off,' I whisper.

Jane drags the bottom of her apron up to her face and wipes her eyes. 'William's death made everything worse. It's been five years. Sometimes, it feels like five minutes. Other times, it feels like five hundred years.'

'Jane. I'm sorry,' I say genuinely. 'It must be very hard. But you can't replace William with David. Even if David and I do split up. Even if you two get together, it won't be the same. David isn't the man you love.'

Jane scrambles to her feet and rummages around in her huge handbag sitting on the countertop next to the cooker.

'Here,' she says, returning and shoving something small into my hand.

'It's an ultrasound.' I sigh, fighting back tears. 'You really are pregnant.'

Jane taps a beautifully manicured nail against the greyish-black square in my shaking hand. 'I sent this photograph to David last night.'

'I know. I saw him looking at it on his phone when he thought I was asleep,' I admit, my heart heavy and aching as acceptance creeps in. 'But I thought it was an image you'd downloaded from the internet. I didn't think it was real.'

Jane is statue-like and glaring at me. I wish she'd say something. Anything. 'Is it really David's baby?' I ask, knowing if she says yes, I won't cope.

'Emma, you need to understand something,' Jane begins, and I physically place my hand over my heart, bracing myself for what she's about to say.

'My childhood was tough. I'm not using it as an excuse, just an explanation. My father cheated on my mother over and over when I was very young. Finally, he got another woman pregnant. My mother was strong enough to kick him out, but it broke her heart. She fell apart after that. She slipped into a deep depression and drank her troubles away. She died when I was nineteen. My father didn't come to the funeral. Maybe, he didn't even know she was gone. I was all alone.'

'Jane, I'm sorry,' I say genuinely. 'It can't have been easy to grow up with all that going on, but …'

310

'Shut up,' Jane barks, thumping her fist against the cupboard door behind us. The door rattles and shakes, and the cutlery on the shelf above jumps and clatters noisily. 'You came here for answers, didn't you?'

I nod.

'Well, fucking listen then.'

'Okay.' I swallow. 'Okay.'

'I didn't see my father for years,' Jane continues, the angry lines around her eyes softening as she calms down. 'He and my mother didn't stay in touch. He just disappeared. He wasn't there when I was growing up, and I really struggled by the time I hit my teenage years. Every child deserves a father, don't they?'

'David would never abandon his child, Jane. He's not that type of man,' I growl. Mixed emotion surges through my soul. David would be a fantastic father. Any child would be lucky to have him but not like this. 'You don't need to try to trap or blackmail him into being there for his kid with mind games.'

'Do you think that's what I'm doing?' Jane smirks. 'Do you think that's what this is?'

'I don't know what to think. To be honest.'

'This isn't about David, Emma. It never has been.'

'Than what, Jane? What the hell is it that you want?'

'I found my father again when I was in my early twenties,' Jane sharpens. 'He'd been right under my nose all those years, working at the local train station. Crazy, I know, right? I reached out to him, and we talked sometimes. Or at least, we tried to, but it was always strained. I couldn't forgive him for walking out on me. And he couldn't forgive me for turning to addiction just like my mother. He was ashamed of the woman I

311

had grown up to become. Can you believe that? He left me, and he had the nerve to expect me to be something better than a mess. He blamed William. Of course, he would. It was easier to blame my husband than blame himself.'

'Was it William's fault?' I whisper.

Jane's face sours. 'Is it David's fault you're a screw up?'

It takes a lot of strength to hold back and not slap her. But it takes even more strength to fight the feelings of disgust that bubble inside my stomach because I understand the point she's making. David was never to blame for my regrets, but I tortured him nonetheless.

I see some of myself in her, and it scares me. We have the same eyes. Hazel. And her lips are thin on top and full on the bottom, just like mine. David said she's around our age, but she looks so much older than we are, and I wonder if that's what years of drink and drugs do to you. Of course, there are differences too. I'm short, and she's unusually tall. Probably as tall as David is, and he's taller than most other men I know. But our most common ground is the regret and sadness that I see in her eyes. It resonates somewhere deep inside me. I wish I could scrape it out and throw it away so I could tell myself I'm nothing like her. But it's as much a part of me as my heart or lungs.

'I know what it's like to grow up without a father,' I say.

Jane eyes me sceptically.

'My dad died when I was six months old. I don't remember him.'

Jane snorts loudly. 'Is that what your mother told you?'

'Yes. Of course,' I dismiss. 'She doesn't talk about him much. I guess it's too hard. I don't even know where he's buried.'

'I do.' Jane gargles.

'Excuse me?'

'You heard me.' She snorts as her eyes glass over, and her head falls to one side like a puppet with a broken string.

'Jane, what exactly is going on here?' I ask, placing frustrated hands on my hips.

'I watched you, you know. Watched you all the time.'

'I know.' I stiffen. 'I screenshot all those messages. So even if you delete them now, I still have proof that you trolled me on the internet.'

Jane shakes her head, and the corners of her lips twitch. She's either about to cry or laugh, and she's so damn unpredictable, I can't tell which it will be.

'Seriously. That's what you're worried about?' she spits. 'A stupid internet troll? Can't you see the bigger picture?'

I shake my head. 'I don't understand anything that's going on here. I know you hate me; that's obvious. I thought it was because I was David's wife. I thought maybe you were jealous. But you say this isn't about him. Then what, Jane? What have I done to make you so angry? Tell me, please?'

'I tried so hard to break you, you know. I headhunted your husband to come work with me. I batted my eyelashes and flirted shamelessly for weeks. He never even noticed. His heart was so consumed with his new marriage and his broken fucking wife. You're all he ever cared about. Ironic really, isn't it. Because you're the one person who doesn't see how very much he worries about you. Maybe, I never had to break David.

313

Maybe, you would have done that all on your own. The online stalking was accidental. It was supposed to be just a photo; one photo to set up the affair with your husband. It was supposed to just be photographic evidence to plant the seeds of infidelity in your head. But it quickly became addictive. I began to think I could tip you over the edge. If you killed yourself, then I wouldn't have to get my hands dirty. It was a perfect plan. But you just wouldn't succumb to it. You just had to keep bloody fighting. You had to make things messy.'

Jane swirls past me and slams her back against the door with a loud slapping sound. Although she doesn't flinch, I know it must have hurt. Her eyes sit on me like an anvil, and her height seems more pronounced suddenly. My heart races so furiously that if it wasn't for the noise of the traffic on the road below us, I think I might actually hear it beat like a drum.

'O-okay,' I stutter, 'this is becoming ridiculous. I shouldn't have come here. I think I should leave now.'

Jane slides to the floor and sits cross-legged, but her back remains pressed firmly against the door.

'I want to leave now,' I insist, unable to keep the tremor out of my voice. 'Now. I want to go, Jane. Let me out.'

Jane tosses me a half smile, and her eyes narrow and glisten like glazed almonds. The hairs on the back of my neck stand to attention like obedient soldiers, and I realise the traitorous situation I've put myself in. I've always accepted human mortality. Whenever I lost consciousness because I hurt myself, I always embraced the darkness. The silence soothed and calmed me. And oftentimes, I was disappointed when I opened my eyes and discovered I was still here. But right now, I'm afraid. I'm terrified that Jane will see out what I never could. I genuinely believe Jane Burke is going to kill me.

'You said you want answers, Emma, but you don't want to stay and listen. Tut, tut. Didn't your mother ever teach you it's rude to interrupt your host?'

'Okay, Jane.' I swallow, my eyes shifting around desperate to find another exit, but we're three floors up, so I don't have many options. 'I'm listening.'

'Like I said, I watched you. I watched you all the time, and you never even knew I was there. I'm not talking about the internet crap; that was just for fun. I mean I really watched you. You and him and your fucking cups of tea and giggles at the station. He never offered me tea. Never.' Jane pauses and takes a deep, exaggerated breath. 'I like tea.'

Jane's face twists with hate, but her words are laced with a poignancy that is unmissable. Her heart is breaking; I can hear it.

'I watched you confide in him. Your smile so bright as you both chatted like you'd known each other all your life. And the way he looked at you …' Jane claws at her neck as if her skin is stitched on too tight. 'I mean you could see in his eyes how much he loved you. It makes me sick just to think about it.'

'Jane,' I rasp, taking a step back, not because I'm afraid of her, but so I can get some space to gather my thoughts. 'Are you talking about Danny? Danny Connelly from the train station? You are, aren't you?'

'He was so fucking proud of you. Never me. Always you. He forgave you for murdering your unborn child, but he couldn't forgive me for my addiction. An addiction he drove me to. It's not fair, Emma. He shouldn't have loved you more than he loved me.'

I drag my hands through my hair and tug a little. Jane's words are attempting to strangle me. It's as if I can't breath as I try to piece her ramblings together.

'Danny Connelly drove you to addiction,' I repeat the words tasting ludicrous in my mouth.

Jane plunges up and forward. She's towering over me before I have a chance to blink. 'Yes! The day he left my mother for yours.'

I shake my head, but the movement makes me dizzy, and for a second, I think I might black out. 'Too far, Jane. You've just gone way too far. Seriously? Do you really expect me to believe any of that nonsense?'

Jane points at the scan photo I'm still holding in my shaking hands. 'Look at the date, Emma.'

There are some letters and digits in the top left corner, but my eyes are tearing, and it's like trying to see out frosted windows. I close my eyes and dig the base of my palms into my sockets. Opening my eyes again, I check the date.

'This is six years old,' I heave.

'Yes.' Jane smiles, and I can tell the memory is dancing in her mind. 'It's my son. William's and my son.'

'You have a child?'

'Marley,' Jane says.

My hands open and the scan photo slips past my fingers and pirouettes to the floor like a leaf swaying in an autumn breeze.

'Marley,' I echo, the child's name shockingly familiar.

'Yes, Emma. Marley *was* my son. Danny's grandchild.'

'No.' I shake my head. 'I don't believe it.'

'Why not?'

'I … I …' I can't gather my thoughts. They race in my mind like horses on a track. 'You're Danny's daughter.' I point. 'It can't be. It just can't.'

'You know it's true, Emma,' Jane softens. 'You believe me. I can see it in your eyes.'

'Oh. My God. Oh, my God. That's why you were at his funeral. That's why you visited his grave. You weren't following me. You were just there too?'

'Sometimes.' Jane tosses her shoulders. 'But I followed you too. I wanted you to figure everything out on your own. I wanted you to go looking for answers, the way I did. But you're so fucking self-consumed that you couldn't see past yourself. It's always about you. How you feel. How you hurt. How your days have gone. Sometimes, I actually pity David. It can't be easy being married to damaged goods.'

'I did figure everything out,' I protest, pressing my fingertips against my closed eyes. 'I found you, didn't I?'

'You found me because I wanted you to, Emma.' Jane grins, smugly satisfied.

There's nothing to say back to that. She's right.

'Keep digging,' Jane suggests. 'You're getting close.'

'Getting close to what?' I spit. 'Enough with the mind games, Jane. Jesus. I don't want to play. I never have.'

'How many times have you said, *Danny's just like a father to me?*' Jane mimics. 'Didn't you ever stop to think about how comfortable that sounded? About how you loved to say it.'

My eyebrows narrow, dragging my forehead to meet my nose. 'It's an expression, Jane. Just a term of endearment.'

'Oh, come on, Emma. Even you're not that gullible.'

317

Jane's hazel eyes scorch into me, but I don't miss delicate tears glistening in the corners. She covers her inner turmoil with an icy exterior. She works hard to make sure it's so frosty and thick that it's almost impenetrable, but to me, it's paper thin, and I can see right through it. I know how it feels to be so conflicted. How it feels to have your head and your heart constantly at war with one another. Jane's hatred for me is matched by her genuine grief for Danny. It should be our common ground. We both loved the old man with all our hearts. But Jane can't get past her jealousy.

'Your father left your mother for another woman, you say?' I grunt, reluctantly processing.

Jane nods slowly.

'And that other woman … that other woman is my mother.'

Jane nods again, her eyes a little wider now.

'The woman he got pregnant?'

'Yes, Emma. Come on, spit it out.' Jane gallops.

'So that baby …' I pause, feeling ill. 'That baby …'

'Is you.'

My eyes roll, and I know for certain I'm going to throw up if it doesn't come out the other end. Or both.

'Hello, sister.' Jane grins so widely I can see all her teeth and part of her gums.

Chapter Forty

EMMA

On the rooftop, the wind whips around us like wild bears clawing at their lunch.

'Jane, this is crazy. It's freezing up here,' I protest.

The snow-speckled rooftop is slippery and dangerous. It spans two apartment widths across, and we walk slowly along the centre, but I'm not good with heights. My nerves are struggling to cope with being three stories up without any sort of railing or fencing around the perimeter. I'm surprised I agreed to come up here at all, but I couldn't think of any other reasonable way of leaving Jane's apartment or of calming her down. I hoped the fresh air might soothe her, but the surge of icy wind seems to have fuelled her madness even more.

Thick overhead clouds do their best to block out natural daylight, and it's dull and depressing up here. Jane links my arm and skips from one foot to the other like an excited child. She jerks her head towards me and growls with her eyes when I don't follow suit. Jane's mood sways like a metronome beating out a rhythm I somewhat recognise. One moment, she's venomous and aggressive like a bird of prey, and the next, she's bright and soaring like a beautiful swallow. Jane's behaviour is unpredictable and terrifying. It's hard to anticipate her next move when I know even Jane doesn't have control over what she will do next.

I understand the clinical definition of bipolar. I read all the goddamn pamphlets I could get my hands on when I first started showing signs of the disorder fourteen years ago. But seeing a manic meltdown play out in front of me like a dodgy B-list movie is terrifying. The scariest part is it's like looking in the mirror.

Doctor Brady diagnosed me with Bipolar Disorder when I was twenty-three, and the wounds I had carved into my chest were so deep, there was talk of needing a skin graft to repair them. He sat on the edge of my hospital bed and took my hand in his. He spoke calmly and softly as he broke his diagnosis to me. I snorted and blew a raspberry in his face. The illness has many triggers, and he told me it's genetic. It wasn't my fault, he promised. It's in my genes. I was made this way. I barely had the strength to breathe, but I raised my middle finger with pleasure and told Doctor Brady to go fuck himself because there was nobody crazy in my family. I guess I was wrong.

'Jane, we need to go back inside. You need to calm down.' I shiver. 'It's not safe for us to be up here, and the falling snow is getting heavier.'

'Oh, Emma, stop whining. Don't you remember what it's like to be a little kid when it snows?'

'Of course. But I'm not a little kid anymore, and it's cold and slippery up here.'

'I thought you were fearless.' Jane tosses an eyebrow.

'No. Just stupid sometimes,' I confess.

'C'mon, Emma.' Jane unlocks her arm from mine and reaches her open hand out to me. Let's pretend we're kids. Let's have an adventure.' Jane looks at me with heartbreak heavy eyes, pleading with me to take her hand.

I wonder if she's daydreamed about enjoying sisterly bonding all her life. I grew up with a younger sister, but it certainly wasn't a relationship to be envious of. Lucy and I have never been close. Lucy is spoilt and indulged, and my mother favours her shamelessly. I always thought I was the problem. I guess I understand my mother's struggles somewhat better now.

'C'mon. C'mon,' Jane bosses. 'Give me your fucking hand.'

I don't reach for her, and Jane can't hide her mounting frustration at my lack of cooperation. She tosses me a dirty look and twirls around on the spot. Her boots slip and slide effortlessly on the snowy ground. Jane's forced laughter is cumbersome and fills the air. She purposely slaps me with her hand as she spins by, like a sulking child. The child she never had a chance to be. In another life, I wonder if we could have been friends. Fear and hate are momentarily replaced with the sense of loss for something I never really had.

Jane's feet slip out from under her, and she lands flat on her back with an unmerciful wallop. She lies still with her eyes closed, and I hold my breath. Maybe, I could make it to the rooftop door before she picks herself up to chase me. I weigh the option in my head—I should go. I should run away right now and call someone. David. Kim. Anyone. Let them know where I am. Let them know I'm safe. But I find myself hurrying, as much as the icy rooftop will allow me, to check on her. I skid and slide and almost fall over too. I crouch beside the woman I've only known as my sister for less than an hour, and I check if she's okay.

Her breathing is heavy and laboured, and I can tell she's unconscious. I drop my face into my hands and allow myself to scream. Watching Jane spiral out of control, not knowing when or if she'll stop, is torture. I don't know how broken Jane's mind is, or if she'll stop at nothing to destroy me. Every bone

321

in my body is telling me to get the hell off the roof. I can call for help then. But my conscience won't let me leave her. *Jane isn't a monster*, I remind myself. She's ill. Surely, I should understand that better than anyone does. I can't leave her up here alone. She'll get hypothermia or something. I drag my phone out of my pocket and cry with frustration when I discover my battery is dead. Suddenly, I weigh so much. I'm like a broken ship sinking under the waves. Jane stirs, and I slide my arm behind her neck and raise her head a little. I saw in a movie once that you're not supposed to move someone who's had a bad fall in case they've broken their neck. I might make things worse, but she's struggling to breathe lying flat on her back, and I'm struggling just as much to think straight. The change of position seems to help, and Jane sighs and her breathing improves. She seems a lot better now, so I think she'll open her eyes soon, and when she does, I don't want her to see me. I lay her back down gently and skulk away slowly, my feet struggling to get a grip on the ever-tricking snow

I glance over my shoulder at the shabby door leading off the roof. The snow won't allow me to run, but I reckon I could powerwalk over to it in a matter of seconds. Before I have a chance to spin around and point my body in the right direction, Jane's hands suddenly collide with my chest, and she pushes with such force I'm the one on the flat of my back now. I scream as agony darts down my neck and out my shoulder. I yield to the pain as I drag myself to stand back up. My arm hangs loosely by my side. The rough rooftop surface has bitten my hand and re-opened the cut across my palm. I twist my arm around and gaze at my fistful of strawberries and cream as crimson blood soaks through the white bandage. I curl my fingers, attempting to protect the wound, and tuck my arm tight across my chest.

Jane rubs the back of her head, and when she takes her hand back down, I can see blood streaked across her fingers. She doesn't acknowledge it. Instead, she strips off her coat and lays it flat on the ground at her feet. She hops from one foot to the other like a child unable to contain their excitement on Christmas morning.

'It's a sled,' she says, bouncing.

Her eyes dance in their sockets as if she's high or drunk; a telltale sign that she's lost her mind completely.

'No,' I contradict sharply, backing away. 'It's a coat. Just. A. Coat. Jane. We're not kids. We're not about to play together in the snow. You can't rewrite the past. You just can't.'

Jane lunges towards me and grabs a clump of my hair as she drags me back towards her waiting coat. My feet scramble to keep up, and I skid repeatedly.

'I want to go sledding,' Jane bellows. 'Sit down.'

I squint and glance behind me at the door that has blown open to reveal the stairwell leading back onto the sanctuary of the third floor. I'd never make it down before Jane caught me. I lower myself carefully onto her coat and resign myself to riding her manic episode out.

Jane bends down, grabs the edges of her coat, and drags it and me across the ground. I'm heavier than she must have anticipated, and she groans fiercely as she tugs. The snow covering underneath me is not thick enough for the coat to glide smoothly. My bottom and thighs scrape along the rough, stony felt roof, but Jane doesn't give up.

I scream loudly as she swings me dangerously close to the edge, more than once.

'Jane, stop, please,' I plead, attempting to stand up, but she presses my shoulder. I yelp, realising it's possibly dislocated, and I quickly sit back down.

'I'm scared,' I finally admit.

Jane lets go of her coat and reaches an open hand out to me. I grab on with my good hand, and she pulls me to my feet.

'See,' she says, smiling wryly. 'Now, wasn't that fun?'

I look back at the coat. It's frayed and has jagged holes in various places. I have corresponding tears in my jeans. My thighs burn where the roof surface has shaved my skin raw.

I try to shake my hand free from Jane's, but she has a grip so tight her nails are digging into my flesh. She's much stronger than I am, and my efforts to free myself amuse her. Jane takes a couple of steps backwards, her eyes locked on mine. I dig my heels into the ground, but my efforts are futile as I slide with her regardless. The wind roars in the alleyway between this building and the next, scaling the bricks to reach the rooftop with temper. Huge, angry gusts blow my hair across my face almost blinding me.

'Do you ever think about what it's like?' Jane asks, her back mere meters from the edge.

'What what is like?'

'Dying. Do you think it's peaceful?'

'I don't know. I don't think about it,' I lie.

'Let's find out. You and me, together, right now.'

'Jane. Stop it. You're scaring me.'

'C,mon, Emma. Let's fly.'

'No,' I bellow, trying desperately to free my hand from hers. 'I don't want to die.'

'Yes, you do.' Jane grins. 'Danny told me about all your suicide attempts, and how he was so proud of you for overcoming your demons, blah, blah, fucking blah.'

'Did you push Danny?' I ask, my heart aching as I cling onto his name on my lips.

Tears trickle down Jane's cheeks, and she squeezes my hand even tighter. Jane's melancholy eyes blink. She's wearing the pain of loss and guilt openly in the scrunched up lines of her forehead and in her lips that are subtly parted and turned down ever so slightly at the edges.

'It was an accident.' She trembles. 'I didn't mean to. He fell.'

I shake my head. 'No,' I growl. 'Danny was careful. He knew that platform like the back of his hand. He would never put himself in danger. He would never intentionally get too close to the edge. I know you pushed him.'

'He wanted to go. He left a letter.'

'No.' I swallow. 'You did. You wrote it, didn't you? You wrote it knowing I would read it and then all your ramblings would make sense. You killed our father.'

Jane jerks her arm back, dragging me forward. I scream loudly as I lunge terrifyingly close to the edge. For a split second, I think this is it. Today is the day I will die, and based on my history, everyone will think I jumped. Jane Burke will take my life, and no one will know. Just like she took Danny's.

'Emma. Emma. Stop. Wait. Don't do this.' David's voice carries across the rooftop and wraps around me like a warm blanket.

I turn my head towards his familiar sound and begin to sob loudly as I see my husband making his way across the roof with baby steps. He has one hand raised with his palm open and pressed against an invisible wall, like a policeman directing traffic.

'Stop,' he repeats. 'Please. Stop.'

Jane laughs. 'See. Even your husband thinks you're going to jump. And he thinks you're going to drag me with you, you crazy bitch.'

I shake my head, knowing Jane is right. David probably believes I'm the villain in this scene. And it's all my fault. I've given him every reason to doubt me over the years.

David creeps forward slowly; taking care not to spook us. He must be terrified, I imagine, but he's hiding it well.

'Stay there,' Jane bellows. 'Don't come any closer.'

David freezes instantly. His eyes search for mine, and we gaze at each other, saying more than words ever could. And I realise he knows everything. We're one soul. Two bodies. He understands. *Thank God.*

A truck grunts in the laneway below us. I guess it's struggling to battle its way back onto the main road against the artic conditions. It chugs and grumbles and the noise of the wheels spinning on the ice carries softly to the rooftop. The driver shouldn't have come down the laneway. It's narrow and a challenge to manoeuvre for a vehicle that size even on a bright summer's day. Snow and ice make handling the heavy machine almost impossible. But the truck roars more. I hear voices and shouting as people come to help. They heave and push as the engine bellows, working in unison to free the truck. Within seconds, I hear the truck drive away. I don't miss the metaphor, and I look at the sky as if I will see Danny's face smiling back at me telling me he sent the message. The truck driver made a mistake. His load was too heavy for the narrow laneway. He couldn't have made it back out alone. But he didn't have to. People came to help. There's always help. You just have to accept it. *I just have to accept it.*

'Amber, look at me,' David says sternly, and I feel Jane's grip loosening as she offers David her attention. 'Please don't hurt my wife. I'm begging you.'

Jane snorts and a little sticky saliva flies through the air. 'She was my sister before she was your wife.'

'I know. I know.' David nods. 'But she doesn't belong to either of us.'

'I have nothing,' Jane retches. 'Nothing. No one.'

'Jane,' I say, waiting for her head to turn back towards me. 'We can find Marley.'

Jane's narrow, comma-shaped eyes glisten, and her shoulders shake as she cries loudly for the child she gave up.

'We can search foster and adoption records,' I suggest. 'Stuff like that is easy to trace on the internet. David and I can help you.'

'Amber,' David whispers. 'We have a friend. A cop. He has connections. He can help us. We can all look for Marley together. But you need to step away from the edge and come inside.'

'I would have been a good mother.' Jane shakes. 'We could have been happy. But Will killed himself. He said he loved me, but how could he if he killed himself? And I had nothing. Nothing. I didn't even have somewhere to live.'

Jane's grip on my hand relaxes as she talks, and I concentrate on gently wriggling away from her. I'm desperate for David to keep her talking. Keep her distracted.

'I loved my baby so much I couldn't keep him. But you.' Jane's eyes burn into me like hot coals. 'You loved yourself so much you didn't even give your baby a chance. You think I'm a monster. But you're the real villain.'

I have no words. There's nothing to say. David stands still and silent also. And I wonder if his heart is as heavy as mine is with the thoughts of the child we never knew.

'I gave my son away because I wanted him to have a better life than I could ever offer him,' Jane says. 'You see, I loved him. I loved him as he grew inside me. And the day he was born, I thought my heart would explode. He was so like his father. He was beautiful.'

'Jane … I …' I begin.

'Shut up and listen,' Jane instructs.

I close my mouth and nod.

'I signed the adoption papers when he was four days old. Four days. Just four days. He was so tiny and new. They said I did the right thing. They said it was a brave decision as if I deserved a goddamn medal or something. They gave him to a family in Kansas. I never saw him again.'

'They were right,' David says. 'You did do the right thing.'

'Really?' Jane darkens, and panic bubbles inside me. I don't know what she wants to hear. How can we talk her down if we don't know what to say?

'Marley is dead,' Jane cries, the cold air sticking her dry lips to her teeth. 'He died three months before his fourth birthday.

It was a farming accident. So no, David, it wasn't the right thing to fucking do.'

'I'm very sorry,' David breathes. 'No one should ever lose a child.'

'But I did.' Heavy sobs shake Jane's body. 'I thought giving him up would give the best chance at a happy life. But he died. He died because I didn't keep him. He died. My baby died.'

'I can't imagine how hard that must be for you,' David continues.

Jane's grip once again strengthens and crushes my fingers she still holds. 'Yes, you can. You lost a child too. Didn't you? That bitch ...' Jane's eyes flick from David to me. 'She stole your child from you. You must hate her.'

David shakes his head slowly. 'I don't hate my wife.'

'I do,' Jane says, taking a huge step backwards.

We're so close to the edge that vertigo threatens to drag me over the brink if Jane doesn't.

'I hate you,' Jane insists. 'I was a good kid. My father should have loved me. But he didn't. He loved you. I tried everything to earn his love. Everything. But you were always there in the background having your fucking cups of tea. I was an addict, and it made him sick. But you are a murderer. Our father loved the wrong child. He should have loved me.'

'Jane, I didn't steal Danny from you. I never even knew he had kids. He was lonely, and I liked spending time with him. That's all.'

'When I told my father I was pregnant, he looked at me with disgust. I was high, as always, and he was ashamed of the woman I had grown up to become. He didn't think I could get myself clean. He didn't believe in me. Danny was the reason I put Marley up for adoption. I didn't want to screw up my son the way my parents had screwed me up. I wanted to be better than they were. It was all his fault.'

'Did you tell Danny about Marely's accident?' I swallow.

'Yes,' Jane says. 'He needed to know. He needed to know that he killed my boy.'

'Jane, Danny didn't kill anyone. And I don't believe he killed himself,' I whisper.

'I got clean. I did it. But it was too late. Too late for Marley.' Jane foams at the mouth. 'I spent the last year searching for him. Hours and hours on the internet. Endless phone calls. I thought I was getting close but all the time I was getting close to a grave. My baby's grave. I went straight to the train station. I wanted my father to hold me. To wrap his arms around me and tell me it would all be okay. I wanted him to look at me the way he so often looked at you. But he didn't. He just walked away.'

'He felt responsible,' I say, my heart sinking into the pit of my stomach.

'He shouldn't have turned his back on me,' Jane barks. 'My son died because of him.'

'Your son died because of an accident, Jane. An accident. It was no one's fault. Not Danny's and not yours.'

David edges forward. He's inches from me. I could reach out and touch him if I tried. Jane doesn't seem to notice. She too fired up on hate and jealousy to see past me.

'I got clean.' Jane sours. 'I haven't touched alcohol or drugs in five years. I could have kept my son. I could have given him a good life, but no one believed in me. I didn't even believe in myself. And now, I have no one.'

'Did you push Danny?' I cry.

'He shouldn't have turned his back on me. Not again.'

'Did you push him?' My voice is so loud and rough, the words charge like cavalry out of my mouth.

'I didn't know a train was coming.' Jane trembles. 'I swear.'

'You did. Oh, my God, you did.'

'He shouldn't have turned his back on me,' Jane repeats like a broken record. 'He shouldn't have done it.'

My body shakes uncontrollably, but it's not because of my icy, snow-speckled clothes. I hate her. I really, truly despise the woman who took Danny from this world. Ill or not, I can't forgive her for that.

'We may have the same blood running through our veins, but I am nothing like you, Jane. Nothing. You can go to hell.'

Jane's lips twitch, and her smile oozes a terrifying malice. Before I have time to think about what I'm doing, I spit in her face.

'With pleasure,' Jane snarls, 'but I'm taking you with me.'

I dig my heels into the ground, and my eyes seek out David. He's nodding, and I know he's got me. He has to have me.

'People die as they lived,' David exhales. 'Funny people die with their last joke lingering in the air. Strong people die fighting for that last breath. Sad people die with regret lacing their last moments. We all die with a tattoo of our life on our soul. Don't let your tattoo be hate, Jane. Don't be so consumed by a life you could have lived that you destroy any chance of changing the one you are living.'

'Oh, that's good.' Jane laughs loudly. 'Did you read that on a bumper sticker?'

'Yeah, something like that.' David swallows. 'Jane, look at me. This isn't the end. Not here. Not like this.'

But Jane doesn't look at David. She looks at me.

'I see so much of me in you, Emma. My eyes. My feisty spirit. My father.' Jane's fingers are sweaty and hot. Her temper is driving fire through her body. Despite her best efforts, she's struggling to keep a firm grip on me.

Jane tosses her head towards the sky and allows some snowflakes to fall onto her nose. I manage to wriggle my clammy fingers free while she's distracted. Within a split second, Jane's eyes are back on me, and she's reaching for a grip of my clothes. But all she catches are fistfuls of air. David's arm is firmly around my waist tucking my back against his chest. I can fell his hot breath against the top of my head, and his panicked heart is beating so fiercely I think it might jump out of his chest and into mine.

Jane's feet seesaw on the edge of the rooftop. She throws her arms out to her side and helicopters her hands around and around, struggling to keep her balance. Her eyes are wide and terrified, and for a fleeting moment, I see the girl whose life betrayed her. I see the girl who lost a child. The girl who should be my sister. And I reach for her. My fingers brush the cotton of her apron, and if I clasp my hand now, I'll just about catch hold of her. But with my next breath, I find myself bending my elbow and pulling my arm away. David's grip around my waist tightens, and despite how much he trembles, I know he has me. I know he won't let go. Jane looks at me head-on and takes a huge, deep breath. I can see her chest swell. Her eyes never move off mine, and neither of us dares to blink. She exhales slowly and sharply, her hot breath dancing across the cold air like a cloud. And then, she's gone.

The rooftop suddenly grows to enormity. The howling wind pauses as if to offer its respects. And for a moment, the world doesn't spin. At some point, David must have pulled me away from the edge. Because when the world begins to move again, we're sitting tangled together in the centre of the icy rooftop.

Commotion chimes in the alleyway below. Screams and hollers ring in my ears. Footsteps race to help. People don't understand. The carnage scares them. Within minutes, sirens loop in the distance, growing closer all the time. Hurrying as if it's not too late. Racing to help Jane now, the way no one came to help her when she was alive. Tears trickle down my cheeks. I will never forget the look in her eyes just before she left this world.

Chapter Forty-One

EMMA

'You came to find me,' I cry, turning my face into David's chest as we sit in the back of an ambulance.

The rear doors are wide open, but the wind doesn't seem brave enough to creep in here.

'I will always come, Emma.' David strokes my hair. 'Always.'

'Is that okay?' a paramedic asks as she adjusts the IV line running into my arm. 'We're getting some fluids into you. You should feel better soon.'

'I'm fine, really.'

She looks at David and smiles softly, telling him she doesn't believe me. But David believes me. I can feel it.

Someone has wrapped a blanket around my shoulders. I don't know if it was a paramedic or a random passer-by on the street trying to help. Everything is a blur. I've no recollection of leaving the rooftop or of walking onto the street. My injured left shoulder is strapped and steadied in a sling that ties around the back of my neck. And the cuts and scrapes on my legs have been cleaned up a little, probably with something antibacterial.

'We're going to move soon, Emma,' the young, friendly paramedic says. 'Will you be okay if we close the doors now or do you need a little longer?'

David must catch my blank explanation. 'You were in shock, Emma. You kept pushing the oxygen mask away, but you needed air. That's why they've left the doors open for so long.'

I cast my eyes around outside, taking in as much of the street as I can. A police car sits a couple of hundred meters away, and two policemen with notepads are speaking to some people stopped on the street corner. A second ambulance is parked outside a humble fruit and veg shop. The lights are switched off, and all the doors are closed. The ambulance sleeps, just waiting to carry Jane's body away. Tape cordons off that portion of the street, stretching from one side to the other as if it wraps around an invisible box. I can't see clearly, but I imagine nothing more than a white sheet hides Jane's lifeless body from the curious spectators lurking for a glimpse of the girl who jumped. I'm sure some of the people waiting are witnesses, the ones who wear the most solemn expressions. The ones who saw too much and will never be able to wipe their memory clean. The rest are simply nosy busybodies. They'll go about their lives in an hour or two. They'll read the story in the paper and get their thrills from telling a neighbour or friend that there were at the scene when it happened. Few will think about Jane again in a day or a week. I will never forget.

A guy in uniform from the local coffee shop carries a round tray dotted with paper cups with steam coming out the top. People nod and smile and take a complimentary hot beverage gratefully, but no one speaks. Even the most nosy and curious people don't chance words.

'I'm not the only one in shock,' I say, pointing towards the world outside the safety of the back of the ambulance. 'The people who saw her fall must be shaken.'

'Yeah, I think everyone is pretty freaked out.' David sighs. 'It'll make the news, they reckon,' David explains. 'We should probably be prepared for that.'

'They reckon? Who's they?'

'The police. They say to expect journalists knocking on our door in the coming days. They'll be after the story. I suppose it's not every day a body falls out of the sky on the streets of Dublin.'

'Yeah. I guess not.'

'Maybe we should go away? We could stay in a hotel down the country. Just until all this blows over.' David wilts. 'There'll be a new story in a few days.'

'Someone else will have killed themselves by then, eh?' I sour.

'No. God no, Emma. That's not what I meant. I just … Look, I'm worried about you. I want to protect you. I'm doing the best that I can here.'

I lift my head and press my lips against David's open mouth. 'Just stay beside me. Then I'll be okay. We don't need to run away.'

'But the journalists?'

'They just want a story, David. Not blood. I can handle a few questions.'

'Actually,' the paramedic pipes in. 'If you're able for it, the police would like a word. You can do it now, or they'll come to the hospital later. Whichever you're most comfortable with.'

'Later,' I say, taking one last, long look at the street. 'Can we go now, please?'

'Sure.' The paramedic smiles. 'I'll let the police know which hospital we'll be in.'

I watch as she walks into the distance and taps one of the many policemen scattered about on the shoulder.

'Are Kim and Andy here?' I ask, relieved to finally be alone with my husband.

David shakes his head. 'They're on the way. I called them.'

'Did they tell you where I'd be?'

'I think they were going to, but I just couldn't wait. As soon as I knew where you were, I had to come.'

'How did you figure it out?'

'You left me clue without even knowing it.' David smiles. 'You left my laptop logged into my emails. As soon as I knew you read the address that Andy found, I knew you'd go searching. I just wasn't too sure what you'd find.'

'Me neither,' I admit. 'I should have told you. I'm sorry if I freaked you out.'

'But you're okay now. You're safe. That's all that matters.'

David kisses my free hand, and the tears twinkling in his eyes pinch my heart.

'Here …' David unbuttons his coat and reaches inside to fish out an envelope. It's small, white, and my name is stretched across the front in handwritten, capital letters. 'It's from Amber. I mean Jane. The police will probably want to see it, but I thought you'd like to read it first.'

'Where did you get this?' I say, my fingers fanning the white paper, and I recognise the writing. It's David's writing. Not Jane's.

'Amber left it for you. Well, sort of.'

'Really?' I say. 'I didn't see any letter.'

'Well, it's for you. It has your name on it.' David trembles as he points at the envelope, awkwardly.

'What does it say?'

'There's only one way to find out,' David whispers.

I poke my finger into the tiny gap on one side under the flap and tear the envelope open, taking care not to damage the note inside. My hands tremble, and my chest tightens as I pull out a piece of white printer paper. It's folded in half and typed in easy to read, large black font. A little ink is smudged around the edges where the paper was forced into the envelope before the ink had time to dry.

Confused and disturbed by the words I'm reading, I drop the paper. It falls onto my knees, the letters blurring and no longer forming words as I stare down at it.

'What is this?' I say; my eyes switch to my husband's face in search of clues.

'They're messages that people have left for you on Facebook. I printed them off …' David begins.

'No,' I cut him off, pointing at the paper. 'These aren't normal messages. These are condolences. Some of these say RIP, for fuck's sake. I don't understand. Why would you show me this? What even is it?'

'Emma, I have no doubt Jane intended to push you off the rooftop today. Or if not, she certainly wanted to drag you with her.'

'Yes. I know.' I exhale. 'But she didn't. I'm still alive. I'm still here. Why are people posting messages saying they'll miss me? Do people think I'm dead?'

'Yes.' David sighs. 'Yes, people do. Your Facebook page says you passed away.'

'What?' I flinch. 'That's fucked up.'

David nods. 'Yeah. It is. I'm sorry I didn't take you seriously when you told me about all this internet troll stuff. I had no idea how twisted Amber really was. It's so messed up; I can't really get my head around it.'

'David, why are you showing me this?' I shake my head.

'Because this is what the world would look life if you weren't in it. Read on, Emma. These messages are heart breaking. People would be distraught without you. There are almost a hundred messages. A hundred people whose lives would instantly be worse if you were gone. I've never been able to get you to understand that before, but maybe you will understand now.'

I drop my eyes onto the paper and read more, my gut twisting and my heart breaking with each word.

'What does the next message say,' David asks when I shake my head and sniffle back tears.

I reach for his hand, and his fingers instinctively slip between mine. I pull my eyes away from the blurry words and stare at the worried face of the man I love. 'It says I'm going to be okay.'

Chapter Forty-Two

DAVID

I wake before Emma every morning. It's become a ritual, but I usually pretend to be sleeping when she finally stirs. I don't want her to know the nights are long and I'm restless, and when I do finally drift off, nightmares poison my sleep.

The hospital phoned yesterday, and Emma took the call. I watched on as she nodded and listened, running a single finger under her eyes every so often to catch a stray tear. Before Emma hung up, before her eyes found mine, and before she opened her mouth to say a word, I knew what she was going to tell me. The look on her face said it all. The results of the autopsy were back. The hospital confirmed the news that Emma and I were desperate never to hear. Jane was pregnant when she died.

The hospital also explained that, as Jane's only living relative, Jane's body would be released to Emma—if she was happy to receive it. I voiced my objection and disgust, but Emma ignored me. She busied herself making tea, and she found a packet of biscuits in the cupboard. We sat, drank, and ate. We didn't talk. I watched Emma's hands shake as she raised the teacup to her lips and sipped on the too-hot-for-comfort beverage, and as if I could see straight into Emma's head, I knew exactly what she was thinking. She was thinking of Danny. She was thinking of how much she wished things could be different.

Emma reacted how I imagine many people would when told their deceased, estranged sister was coming to them. She poured some mid-morning wine and made a few phone calls. Within a couple of hours, the local funeral director and the priest were both on their way to our home. A home Jane had never stepped foot inside. I looked on, unable to partake in the charade. Jane almost destroyed my wife, and now, we're supposed to butter up a few sandwiches and have a wake. Have a send-off for a woman who nearly split us up. If Jane had her way, I'd be saying goodbye to Emma.

I watched Jane or Amber or whatever the hell her name was fall to her death right in front of me. I watched her tumble off the roof like discarded rubbish. Dragging my child that grew inside her with her. Sometimes, at night when I'm lying in bed staring at the ceiling, Emma asks me if I'm okay. And I lie and say I am. Sometimes, I ask her the same question, and she lies too.

By the time the morning of Jane's funeral rolls around, Emma's and my relationship has deteriorated to mere snippets of conversation as we pass each other in the hall. Today, I'm even more exhausted than usual. I pull on a suit and tie. It's dark navy—so close to black I doubt anyone will notice the subtle difference. The crisp, white shirt and charcoal tie I pair it with darkens it even more. It's taken me four attempts to get the knot in my tie to stick, and even now, it's uneven and doesn't sit right. But there's no point in trying again as my hands are shaking too badly to get it right. I stare at my reflection in the mirror, and a stranger looks back at me. He's wearing my face and a suit that I've worn to work often, but he's not me. I don't want him to be me. I don't want to be a man with a sad heart and dull eyes.

Emma has been in the bathroom for a long time, so I breathe a sigh of relief when I hear the key rattle in the lock. Emma appears and looks beyond elegant, but I can tell she's on edge. She's wearing a figure-hugging black dress that stops just below her knees. Her legs are slim and defined. She's thinner than ever, and it's unnerving, but I'm far more worried about the state of her head today.

'We need to be in the church by ten thirty,' she mumbles as she collects some pearls out of her jewellery box on her dresser. 'The coffin is closed.' Emma coughs and clears her throat. 'So there won't be many people coming up to offer their respects.'

I had no doubt the coffin would be anything other than closed. *It's a funeral, not a horror show.* And for the first time, I realise I'm bitter. I'm angry that life can be so easily extinguished. One moment, you're standing on a rooftop, and a change of footing later, you're gone from this world. Life is so fragile. Why does nobody ever notice?

'Okay. We should leave soon. I'll drive, yeah?' I suggest even though my head is foggier than if I'd been drinking the morning away.

Emma eagerly agrees, and moments later, we leave our home and get ready to say goodbye to a woman who has changed our lives forever.

We park close to the church gates, and despite the artic conditions, it's a relief to get out of the car because I'm desperate for fresh air. The last time I walked this footpath was at Danny's funeral. I certainly didn't think I'd be walking this same path again so soon.

I'm not religious. I don't attend church, and I never pray. But today, I find myself wondering if there is a God, and if there is, I want to thank him for sparing my wife and plead with him to help her get through this in a way I'm not sure if she can.

The church is empty, but it comes as no surprise. There's a harpist perched ready to play in one of the side aisles, and she catches my eye and smiles, unsure. Emma and I take a seat in the first pew. The priest told us that was where we should sit, being family. I wanted to scream, but I smiled and held my wife's hand as we spoke about readings and prayers as if this was all normal.

I take one more look around the silent church, drop my head, close my eyes, and will the next hour to be over. Within minutes, the pews behind us begin to fill. Soon, people are in the aisles, and someone behind us mumbles that there isn't any more standing room inside. Mourners are spilling out the doors into the church grounds.

'What's going on?' I whisper into Emma's ear.

'Everyone is here to say goodbye.'

'All these people can't possibly know Jane,' I say. 'There must be a couple of hundred people here.'

Emma looks up at me and smiles. I haven't seen her smile so brightly in years. I see a spark of the teenage Emma who I feel in love with, and for a split second, I believe that girl is still in there.

'They don't all know Jane personally. But they know *a Jane* of their own. They know someone who left this world too soon. Or they've been suicidal themselves. They're here to say goodbye to Jane and to make a stand against suicide,' Emma explains softly

'How do they know? How did they know to come today?' I shake my head.

'I answered the journalists' emails.' Emma's smile grows even wider, and for a second, I forget to breath as I remember how beautiful she looks when she's happy. 'I gave them copies of the letter.'

'What letter?' I ask. 'Did Jane leave a suicide note? I didn't see it.'

'No. The letter isn't from Jane. It's for her. The national papers printed it. Most of the smaller presses did too. Jane is trending on Twitter. Can you believe it?' Emma says. 'Hashtag be strong for Jane. It has a nice ring to it, doesn't it?'

I pull out my phone, and despite being in a church, I search for the hashtag. The hits are endless but taking pride of place is a link to a letter printed three days ago in the Irish Press.

Dear Jane,

You died on a winter's day when snow was scattered on the ground. You were thirty-three years old. You were my sister. And you took your own life.

I wonder how you felt when you got up that morning and you knew you would never face another day. How did you feel knowing you would never again wrap up in a warm coat with a hat, scarf, and gloves and walk through crunchy snow under your boots? Did you stop to think what you were giving up by giving up? How did you feel knowing you would never see another sunrise or gaze up at another starry night sky? Never feel blissful summer sun kiss your skin until you are golden brown. Never swim in the sea, never see another movie, never eat until you think your belly might explode. Never. Live. Another. Day.

I read somewhere once that more than seven billion people are on this planet. Yet it is possible for someone to feel completely alone. I understand. I bet many of the seven billion people understand what loneliness feels like. I am sorry that you will forever more be a statistic. I am sorry that you won't be a name, just a number. A number among the other hundreds of people who take their own lives around the world. Every. Single. Day. I am sorry that you will never grow old. But mostly, I am sorry for you. I am sorry for the pain inside your head, and I'm sorry that the only way you knew how to make it stop was to make your heart stop beating too.

And I am so, so sorry that you won't be the last.

With love,

Emma

'Emma, you amaze me.' I smile, sliding my phone back into my inside jacket pocket. 'I don't think I could ever forgive Amber the way you have.'

Emma breaks away from me, and her eyes meet mine with intensity so fierce I swear I can feel the heat radiating from her pupils. 'I don't forgive her. I think I understand her, on some crazy level—which scares me a little. But I didn't deserve her venom. I never asked to be born. I never asked for Danny's love. But she also never asked to be abandoned and rejected. I hate Amber Hunter, the crazy bitch who tried to ruin my life, but I feel sorry for Jane Burke, the girl who lost her whole world. And. Her. Mind.'

I reach across Emma's knee to find her hand resting on top. My fingers slip between hers effortlessly, and I squeeze gently.

345

'I don't forgive her,' Emma reiterates, turning her head away from me to look straight ahead. 'But I finally forgive myself.'

For the first time since I was a little boy, I allow myself to cry. My body quivers and shakes as tears stream like salty raindrops down my cheeks. Maybe I'm crying for Amber and for the colleague I thought was a friend. Maybe I'm crying because no one should die because life makes him or her unhappy. Or maybe I'm crying because, for the first time in longer than I can remember, my wife wraps her arms around me and cradles me close to her and tells me she looks forward to growing old together. And I believe her.

Chapter Forty-Three

Six weeks later

EMMA

The waiting room for Dr Brady's office has a unique smell. It's always been that way; a cocktail of mentholated spirits and something acidic like lemon juice. Sitting here now, with my legs crossed and my arms folded, I feel a little like a scared kid again. It's painfully silent. Only one other patient is waiting, and she's not a talker. David hasn't arrived yet. I texted him to confirm the appointment time twice yesterday and once this morning, but he didn't reply. I can't help but worry he's not coming. Things have been hectic for him with his huge promotion in work, taking over Jane's role and overseeing the merger of the Dublin and Boston office. Maybe he hasn't had time to check his phone. Or maybe his mother has been in his ear, telling him to stay away from me. My mother has certainly been offering me the same advice. She can't seem to get past David's mistake, and she's pleaded with me not to stay married to a man like my father.

We've spoken about Danny a lot. The things my mother loved about him, and the things she didn't. It's been good. It's certainly brought my mother and me closer now that there are no more secrets. The years of lies still built a wall between us, but I hope that one day we'll both climb it.

It's easier with David. The wall isn't quite so high, and we're both determined to knock it down. I've decided that today is the day. David had been staying with his mother since

Jane's funeral. I suggested it, and he obliged, reluctantly. We're supposed to be taking it slow. We have two date nights a week. They usually end with kisses and me asking him to come home, but he doesn't think I'm ready. Maybe he's right. But I miss him. I miss who I am when I'm with him. Days are long, and I have a lot of time to think. Richard apologised and invited me back to work, but I've taken some sick leave, and he's agreed it's for the best.

The secretary calls the other girl ahead of me, and the silence of the large white waiting room is even more engulfing than before. I look up to find David standing over me. His tie is slack, the top button of his shirt is open, and I can smell the coffee from the takeaway cups he holds in each hand. He looks casual and more comfortable than I've seen him in a long time. His enthusiasm is contagious, and I find myself grinning up at him.

We sit side by side for a long time. Sometimes, we talk. Sometimes, we don't. Sometimes, we just drink our coffee in silence, but all the time, I'm smiling.

Sometime later, when the secretary calls us, it takes me a moment to recognise my name. But David reaches for my hand as we stand up, and we walk with our fingers knitted together.

'It's good to see you, Emma,' Dr Brady says as soon as I walk through the door.

'You too,' I say genuinely.

'Please, have a seat,' Dr Brady offers as he gestures towards two leather arm chairs waiting in front of his desk and closes the door behind us.

David and I separate and take our individual positions. Dr Brady scurries around to his side of the desk and sits with his arms folded against the highly polished pine.

'I'm so glad you're here, Emma,' he begins. 'And, David, I'm really pleased you're joining us.'

I smile.

'So, Emma, how have you been?' Dr Brady continues. 'Let's talk about how you've been feeling.'

'Okay.' I nod, ready.

'I'm so very sorry for the loss of your father and sister. I read about it in the papers. It must have been a terrible time for you. Would you like to talk about how that made you feel?'

'Actually'—I scrunch my nose—'I'd like to talk about something I did fourteen years ago and how it's been making me feel every day since.'

David spins in his chair, and I see teeth. I haven't seen his toothy grin since we were seventeen.

'I'd like to get some help now,' I say.

The End

Message from Janelle

On the 26th of February 2016, I received a phone call from one of my sisters that would change me irreversibly. She called to tell me that our beautiful, funny, intelligent nineteen-year-old niece had taken her own life.

Laura was an amazing person. She wasn't just my sister's child, she was my best friend, and I loved her more than words could ever say. At first, I was angry, I admit. I was bitter that she left me. *How could she do it, did she not love me as much as I loved her and I'd never take myself away from her?* But I wasn't suffering from depression. I wasn't so low that I couldn't see any light at the end. I wasn't in Laura's shoes.

Laura is gone six months now, and people say time heals but it isn't getting any easier to be without her. I think about her all the time. I talk to her in my head, and I cry – a lot. Sometimes I sit and flick through her old Facebook posts and savour the memories. And every day I wish that I could spend one more day with her.

Laura didn't mean to break her mother's heart. She didn't mean to devastate her family. She didn't mean to hurt us so bad that missing her is a physical pain.

Laura never meant to hurt anyone. Not even herself. She just wanted her pain to stop. Laura succeeded in ending her pain when she took her own life, but what she didn't know was that pain lives on without her. It's etched into the hearts of everyone who loved her because life without her is pain for us. Every. Single. Day.

Suicide is never the answer. NEVER.

If you have been affected by the themes in this book, if you are Laura or you know and love a Laura then please seek help. Dark days don't have to be the end. I would give anything to take Laura's hand and walk together again until it's bright, but I can't. But it's not too late for others. There can still be light…

http://www.samaritans.org/

http://www.pieta.ie/

http://www.mind.org.uk/

Acknowledgements

I always thought my first book would be the hardest. I was so wrong. Honestly, it never gets easier. I was completely blown away by the reception to No Kiss Goodbye. And while that makes releasing See Me Not very exciting, it always makes me incredibly nervous. I truly hope this second novel lives up to expectation. Do let me know what you think, good or bad; it's always a pleasure to hear from readers.

As usual the list of people to thank is endless. My wonderful writing besties, who are always honest with me and tell me when my first draft is shit, but encourage me not to drink my liver into oblivion and just get on with writing the next draft. Natalie and Caroline, you are fantastic writers and I'm so grateful for your help, encouragement and friendship.

The Book Club on Facebook – well, now, this thank you is a biggie. Tracy Fenton (founder) runs a tight ship and The Book Club is an absolute credit to her. Twelve months ago the members of The Book Club changed my life. They took a chance on some girl who stuck a book on the internet with a pretty cover. I have no doubt the success of No Kiss Goodbye is down to the wonderful reviewers and kind support of this group and I will remain forever grateful.

This year has been very difficult on a personal level. I lost my father and seven weeks later I lost my niece. They both encouraged me to pursue my writing dreams and I hope they're looking down on me now, and I hope I make them proud. Always missed. Never forgotten.

My family. I have an awesome husband who doesn't ask for divorce when I jump out of bed at 4am and flick on the bedroom light and start scribbling on random pieces of paper because a plot point has just popped into my head. And my kids. They rock. I know all mothers think their own kids are the best, but mine really are, seriously, they are! You believe I'm not bias, right?

Finally, you. Thank you for reading. It never ceases to amaze me that people actually want to spend time reading my stories. I really appreciate you.

Janelle

x

About the Author

Janelle Harris is the alter ego of USA Today bestselling romance author Brooke Harris. Janelle lives just outside Dublin, Ireland with her young family. She often dreams about living in a warmer climate, but secretly she loves the green fields and heritage of home.

Janelle loves to travel, and even her fear of flying can't keep her grounded for long. She enjoys taking her characters on adventures to cities she has visited.

Where to find Janelle/Brooke...

Twitter @brookeharris_
Or email brooke harris writes at gmail dot com

20000034R00207

Printed in Great Britain
by Amazon